More Praise for *Deep as the Sky, Red as the Sea*

Named a Most Anticipated Novel by:
The Washington Post ★ Tor.com ★ Goodreads ★ LitHub ★
Debutiful ★ Chicago Review of Books ★ The Rumpus

"This is richly researched historical fiction with lush mythology and all the excitement and intrigue of action and suspense." —Tiphanie Yanique, author of *Land of Love and Drowning* and *Monster in the Middle*

"*Deep as the Sky* will captivate readers regardless of what genre or style they like. This is beautifully written with a sharp eye for pace. It feels cinematic." —Debutiful, Most Anticipated Debut Books of 2023

"A gripping, powerful portrait of a woman on the high seas who is as ferocious as she is human, determined to survive. Brimming with adventure and intrigue, passion and prophecy, fierce battles and moving moments of grace, this novel captures us on a pirate ship and does not let go until long after we've turned the radiant final page." —Carolina De Robertis, award-winning author of *Cantoras*

"Rita Chang Eppig is such a daring, thrilling writer. *Deep as the Sky, Red as the Sea* sets a whole new bar for words like *swashbuckling*, recasting their assumptions while giving us all the big moments: seafaring battles, swords and family intrigue, tales of love and revenge. It's all here. And in Shek Yeung, Chang-Eppig has given us a heroine for the ages. This is the start of a big career." —John Freeman, author of *How to Read a Novelist*

"Historical fiction fans craving high-seas adventures will want to request this look at Shek Yeung, China's legendary pirate queen, and her fight to command the South China Seas." —Bookish in NetGalley's 32 Highly Anticipated Books Hitting Shelves in 2023

"I loved this book. With prose as rich and elegant as it is fierce, *Deep as the Sky, Red as the Sea*, paints a complex portrait of one of history's most powerful women, Shek Yeung, while considering the roles that gender, motherhood, and fate play for us all. Gorgeous, vivid . . . Rita Chang-Eppig has made something truly special." —Erika Swyler, bestselling author of *The Book of Speculation* and *Light from Other Stars*

"It's refreshing to see not only a mixed-gender crew but also a woman with a complicated relationship to motherhood, her intended place in the world, and her ambitions. *Deep as the Sky, Red as the Sea* is a non-stop adventure with danger at every turn, and Shek Yeung is forced to make decisions to ensure her survival. But she remains ruthless throughout, and her adventures will make you want to take up the sword and learn to sail." —Tor.com, 30 SFF Titles to Look Forward to in 2023

"So absorbing that I kept neglecting my real life so I could keep reading. I'd have followed this novel's courageous, complicated pirate heroine anywhere. A dazzling feat of storytelling." —Clare Beams, author of *The Illness Lesson*

"*Deep as the Sky, Red as the Sea* is a riveting, heart-pounding exploration of ambition, grit, and what it takes to survive in a world on the brink—all seen through the eyes of the fiery, magnetic Shek Yeung. Rita Chang-Eppig has delivered a singular heroine and a truly unforgettable tale." —Kirstin Chen, *New York Times* bestselling author of *Counterfeit*

"A pirate queen's adventures in the South China Sea, based on the life of an actual early-nineteenth-century icon—I'm sold a hundred times over on this debut." —Julia Fine, author of *The Upstairs House*, in Chicago Review of Books' 17 Most Anticipated Books of 2023

"A powerful, gripping and vivid portrayal of one of history's most fascinating women, and the knife edge she had to walk to survive." —Samantha Shannon, *New York Times* bestselling author of *The Priory of the Orange Tree* and *A Day of Fallen Night*

"Kaleidoscopic . . . In this historical fiction novel about adventure and bravery, we meet an instantly classic heroine." —Our Culture, Most Anticipated Books of 2023

"Epic yet intimate . . . Rita Chang-Eppig charts the journey of a brilliant and brave heroine who fights for the survival of her fleet—and her family's—against a fascinating historical backdrop. A stunning debut." —Vanessa Hua, bestselling author of *Forbidden City*

"Suspenseful . . . Y'all had me at the words 'pirate queen.'" —R.O. Kwon in Electric Literature's 62 Books by Women of Color to Read in 2023

"A stunning novel filled with adventure, intrigue, and stirring contemplations of what it means to endure in a world of scarcity and violence. Chang-Eppig combines the scope and lyricism of Gabriel García Márquez with the propulsive storytelling of Susanna Clarke. This is an epic novel with the intimacy of a portrait, a literary adventure not to be missed." —Seth Fried, author of *The Municipalists*

"This heart-pounding high-seas adventure is also the moving story of a girl with no options who finds a way to survive, and the costs and consequences of that survival. Shek Yeung—a pirate queen, a mother, a ruthless killer and a loyal friend—is an unforgettable heroine whose journey will keep readers hooked from beginning to end." —Anna North, *New York Times* bestselling author of *Outlawed*

DEEP AS THE SKY, RED AS THE SEA

DEEP AS THE SKY, RED AS THE SEA

A Novel

RITA CHANG-EPPIG

BLOOMSBURY PUBLISHING
NEW YORK · LONDON · OXFORD · NEW DELHI · SYDNEY

BLOOMSBURY PUBLISHING
Bloomsbury Publishing Inc.
1385 Broadway, New York, NY 10018, USA

BLOOMSBURY, BLOOMSBURY PUBLISHING, and the Diana logo are trademarks
of Bloomsbury Publishing Plc

First published in the United States 2023

LIBRARY OF CONGRESS CATALOGING-IN-PUBLICATION DATA IS AVAILABLE

ISBN: HB: 978-1-63973-037-7; eBook: 978-1-63973-038-4

2 4 6 8 10 9 7 5 3 1

Typeset by Westchester Publishing Services
Printed and bound in the U.S.A.

To find out more about our authors and books visit www.bloomsbury.com and
sign up for our newsletters.

Bloomsbury books may be purchased for business or promotional use. For information
on bulk purchases please contact Macmillan Corporate and Premium Sales Department
at specialmarkets@macmillan.com.

*To my maternal grandparents, who fled war on a leaky boat,
and to my grandmother in particular, who filled her pockets with
hard-boiled eggs so that she and the child inside her would not starve*

Deep as the Sky, Red as the Sea

PART I

The King Is Dead

I

The moment Shek Yeung saw the enemy's cutlass carve through her husband, she learned two important things about herself: First, she loved Cheng Yat more than she'd ever thought she would be able to love the man who had, without much consideration of her wishes, stolen her away to the sea. Second, she would not mourn him.

Their fleet had passed the tenth lunar month here raiding off the coast of Vietnam, sails and spirits both a bit tattered after the most recent typhoon season. Merchant ships were passing through the area on their way to the Chinese emperor, each laden with silver like a noble's bride under her headdress. The emperor needed all this silver because he had spent the past few years suppressing rebellions all over the country. The imperial treasury was empty. Nevertheless, he'd recently launched an expensive campaign to end piracy in the Pearl River Delta. Not that the new laws had made any real impression in the minds of people like Shek Yeung and her crew, who lived and died by the sea's vagaries. They were starving long before the milksop emperor succeeded the throne, and they would be starving still had Cheng Yat not gathered them like limp reeds and bundled them together to make them stormworthy crafts. So yes, she loved him. She loved him because she feared death.

Slashing her way to his side, crouching instinctively at the occasional boom of cannon fire, she shouted for Cheung Po to come to her aid. The boy spun around at her voice, narrowly sidestepping a dagger to the gut as he did so. No, not *boy* anymore. She just still thought of him as one, even though he was already twenty-five and would soon inherit Cheng Yat's fortune. His habitual smirk slackened at the sight of Cheng Yat sprawled on the deck with a dark sash of blood across his torso. He loved the man, too, in his own way.

It had all gone very wrong, very quickly. They'd boarded the Portuguese merchant ship in the night. If the ship had been full of silver for the emperor, they would have been looking at a windfall. Even if they'd found only sugar and sappanwood, they would have still done well for themselves. A few of her men could have made enough to feed their families for the entire year, could have returned to their homes farther inland until the next famine came along, which it always did.

But the Portuguese had come prepared for war. The ship was awash with Portuguese navy sailors, all trained to stand against the pirate ships that fogged the harbors of the South China Sea, all awake despite it being the dead of night, as if forewarned. Perhaps they'd been sent directly by their government to secure the trade route, or perhaps they worked as soldiers of fortune in their spare time. Europe almost certainly had its own share of famines. Last she'd heard a madman named Napoleon had gotten himself elected as the first emperor of France and was warring against seven nations at once. Where there was war, there was hunger.

The foreigner who had injured Cheng Yat, fighting through what appeared to be a dislocated left shoulder, cleaved apart yet another one of her men with his good arm and turned his attention on her. His size alone made him formidable, and if he'd felled the commander of the feared Red Banner Fleet, then his fighting ability was likely first-rate. Shek Yeung stood to gain nothing from a one-on-one fight. As far as she was concerned, honor was scarcely different from stupidity.

He lunged at her. She reached behind her back, pulled out the flint-lock pistol she kept there for emergencies, and whispered a prayer to Ma-Zou that the black powder had not gotten wet in the chaos.

A loud crack, and then the smell of charcoal and sulfur filled her mouth like a piece of burnt, rotted fish. The foreigner fell backward into the taffrail. Unsure whether she had dealt a final blow or simply grazed skin, she strode over to the man and kicked him into the sea. She hadn't gotten to where she was in life by not being thorough.

The numbers were on their side. Piracy was, more often than not, a matter of convincing the target of the futility of fighting back. The fleet probably would have triumphed had they continued the battle—except the merchant ship caught fire. A member of her crew might have set the fire deliberately, or someone might have knocked over a lamp. "Retreat!" she yelled. Smoke grew thorns inside her lungs, reemerging from her mouth as gray roses. To Cheung Po she said, "Help me get him back to the ship."

Somehow they managed it, helped in part by the fact that the Portuguese became preoccupied with putting out the fire. When she ordered Binh to set a course for Hainan, Cheng Yat tugged on her sleeve. "Canton," he said.

"That's ridiculous," she said, "You'll never make it to the physicians in Canton."

"I won't make it either way."

If their relationship had been anything other than what it was, she might have tried to convince him he would live through this as he'd lived through so many other injuries in their six years together. But she was his wife, captive, chief strategist, and equal partner. Her days of muttering empty reassurances into the ears of powerful men as they lay in her arms were behind her. "I'll see to it that your family gets word," she said.

He squeezed her hand weakly.

Having finished helping the rest of the crew off the merchant ship, Cheung Po rejoined the two of them. He knelt, cupping Cheng Yat's face with one hand. Sometimes she forgot that the boy had been with Cheng Yat since before she joined the fleet. How exactly Cheung Po felt about the man who'd pressed him into service as his ship- and bedmate, she never bothered to ask. It hardly mattered. Typhoons and cannonballs cared nothing for the complicated little folded cranes of feeling that beat their wings in the heart. What mattered was that Cheung Po fought with ferocity and loyalty. What mattered was that he'd never tried to use his own intimacy with Cheng Yat to wrest power away from her.

"The alliance will fail if there's a rough power transition," Cheng Yat said. "You must do everything you can to ensure success. Without the alliance, we have no hope against the emperor's forces."

By morning, he was dead. Shek Yeung and Cheung Po kept vigil at his bedside, neither speaking to nor making eye contact with each other. Cheung Po had his foot over his knee and was fidgeting with the dagger hidden inside his boot, making it difficult for Shek Yeung to pay attention to much else. One by one, the ship's officers came to pay their respects: Binh, the helmsman; Old Wong, the navigator, his arthritic fingers clutching at his route map as if it were a holy book; and Ahmad, the boatswain, who traveled from Malacca years ago and just never went back. Last came Yan-Yan, the purser, tears downpouring from her storm-cloud-colored eyes. It made sense that the girl would take the loss hard. Being young, Yan-Yan hadn't yet lost many people close to her, didn't know intimately the contours of grief. Shek Yeung gently pulled her up from the bedside where she sat wailing and guided her out of the cabin. The other deck crew lined the hallway outside the cabin, heads bowed. Some of them, especially those whom Cheng Yat had press-ganged, might have been there only to make sure he was dead.

The passage back to Canton was swift in spite of the westerly headwind. The first two days, she and Cheung Po barely spoke. Both of them, she suspected, were preoccupied by what the commander's death meant for their own futures. Shek Yeung herself had maintained control over half of the fleet by Cheng Yat's decree, and while he'd been alive, no one had dared question her authority. Cheung Po, on the other hand, was Cheng Yat's "adopted son" and thus legal heir. Such a pretense had been necessary to ensure that the fleet would go to a man Cheng Yat trusted upon his death. And though Cheung Po hadn't exhibited any particular affinity for power grabs while Cheng Yat had been alive, it was hard to know where he stood now. Would he balk at her insistence on holding on to her half? Would this turn bloody?

A leery sun bided its time behind clouds, giving the afternoon an unsettled feel. Waves flexed and stretched, muscling the ship along. In the distance, manta rays breached and valiantly winged through the air but inevitably plummeted back into gray depths. Those in the sea's thrall, the sea never released.

As a child, she'd gazed out at the waves and seen only freedom. As an adult, she knew nothing was so simple. For every measure of freedom the sea gave, it took one away. In the eyes of the law, she was a criminal now and forever. It didn't matter that Cheng Yat had coerced her into joining. Eventually, she'd accepted this ship as her new home. The O Yam, named after the red dragon of the South China Sea, was the largest and most stalwart junk in the fleet. With its three majestic masts and vermilion lugsails, the O Yam had witnessed the births of her two children and the deaths of two more, one while still in the womb, the other upon arrival, blue as though it would bleed the ocean if cut. She and Cheng Yat had returned that child to the waves, where it clearly belonged.

If Cheung Po took issue with her position, if they clashed and he won, the kindest outcome would be exile. What then? Back to those dank little "flower boats," back to those drunken men with heavy hands that they raised at the slightest displeasure? The thought of having to leave behind her life at sea confused her almost as much as it frightened her.

"You promised me a life," she said to Ma-Zou. The sea did not respond.

At dusk, Yan-Yan came to her cabin. Her face was dry now, but the tear tracks were still visible. Shek Yeung had brought Yan-Yan on board three years ago after catching the girl cheating at a pai gow game in a gambling den in Macau. Yan Yan had been the only woman in the entire establishment—besides Shek Yeung—who was not serving or accompanying the men, so naturally she stood out. Shek Yeung had watched, intrigued, delighted even, as Yan-Yan won game after game, all the while coyly fending off the men demanding her attention. Shek Yeung couldn't help but be reminded of her younger self, the one who had earned the respect of all the fishermen with her talent and grit. That this tiny girl had talent (and no small amount of nerve) was clear, but talent went only so far in the underworld. It would have been only a matter of time before one of these men decided he was sick of losing to a woman or of being denied her affection. The outcome would have been terrible, and terribly familiar to Shek Yeung.

Instead of turning her in to the pit boss, Shek Yeung pulled her aside after a game. "Girl, you're good with numbers?"

"We understand each other," Yan-Yan said, her expression haughty. It was the haughtiness of youth but also of genuine skill. Shek Yeung herself had worn this expression once, before the flower boats.

"Then *we* can understand each other," Shek Yeung said.

Yan-Yan had run away from home after being married off to a rich man with "exotic appetites," who'd developed an obsession with her because of her gray eyes. To support herself, she'd started patronizing pai gow parlors, relying on her skills to increase her funds, namely, the taels of silver she'd stolen from the rich man and the wedding jewelry she'd pawned. But what she possessed in number sense, she lacked in knowledge of the underworld. Only sheer luck and some semblance of self-restraint (she cashed out immediately after small wins) had prevented an early death.

In the years since joining the fleet, Yan-Yan had become indispensable not only because of her duties, which she indeed performed well, but also because of her chattiness. She chatted with people when they were feeling sad, when they were feeling excited, when they maybe wished she weren't chatting so much. Even still there was something comforting about the chatter for Shek Yeung, who'd lived the first half of her life surrounded by the gossip and unsolicited advice of other women. A few months ago, Yan-Yan had turned most of her attention toward one of the newer crew members, a tall, wiry woman from northern China at least five years older than Shek Yeung herself. From afar, the two looked more like mother and toddler than potential lovers. Shek Yeung often heard the two talking late into the night in their characteristic pidgin of Cantonese and the northern dialect.

She gestured Yan-Yan into the cabin. The girl slunk down to the floor by her feet, swishing her own legs to one side and partly behind the hips like a cat's tail. She rested her pointy chin on the back of her hand, which she rested on Shek Yeung's knee. "Big Sis, me and some of the others were talking, and we were wondering if—" Yan-Yan began.

"I don't know," Shek Yeung said, cutting her off.

"But do you think he'll try?" Yan-Yan asked.

She had a right to be concerned. If Cheung Po won, he would be foolish to not kill the deck crew most allied with Shek Yeung. That definitely meant Yan-Yan. Ahmad, whom Shek Yeung had also person-ally recruited, would perhaps be in danger. Binh was probably safe, having provided supplies to the fleet long before Shek Yeung herself joined—Cheng Yat had welcomed him aboard when the Tay Son rebels in Vietnam finally met with defeat. Old Wong was . . . Old Wong. Nobody knew these waters better than he did.

Shek Yeung sighed. "It wouldn't be rational. Any infighting would weaken him enough to make him a target for the commanders of the other fleets, even if he managed to win. But greed compels men to do strange things."

"I don't know what I'd do if I had to run away again," Yan-Yan said, looking downcast. "Did you know my father used my fiancé's bride price to try to get my other suitors to pay more? I might as well have been a sow he was auctioning off."

She patted the girl's head. "I'd see to it you're safe," she said, though she really was in no place to promise anything. But Yan-Yan seemed so worried. The girl's greatest fear, short of death, was probably having to return home to be the fourth wife (or whatever) of her betrothed.

Sometimes Shek Yeung wondered what would have happened had her own parents survived. They hadn't been wealthy either, so perhaps she'd have met with a similar fate. A kind husband would have meant silken fetters; a cruel one, well, who knew? She might have ended up escaping to the sea anyway. Women's life stories were written by their men, messily, elegantly, or in the case of violent men, tersely. Now that Cheng Yat was dead, Shek Yeung finally had a turn at dictating the course of things. She might have been born thirty-one years ago, but her story was only now hers.

After the girl left, Shek Yeung pulled a stool up to Cheng Yat's body and sat, as if they were about to have a conversation. They used to do this all the time in the early days of their marriage, though usually he was the one who sought her out. "I want your opinion on something," he would say, and she would brim like a wedding toast, so joyful, thankful, that here was this man who valued her for her thoughts.

Except now she didn't know what to say. So much for her thoughts.

Dead, Cheng Yat looked more like a congenial uncle than the man who had decimated the previous emperor's legions and driven the current emperor close to financial ruin. His thick, peaked brows and the upturned lines by the corners of his eyes gave the appearance of perpetual amusement. The only thing that gave him away was the knife scar on his left cheek.

She rolled up his sleeves to count the scars. There were a lot more now than there had been when they met seven years ago. This one had come from a pirate from a rival fleet five years ago, before the alliance. The man might have succeeded in killing Cheng Yat if Shek Yeung hadn't run him through from the back. This one had come from a skilled naval officer three years ago, shortly after the alliance and also the birth of her second child. In her weakened state, she hadn't been able to defend herself. But Cheng Yat had stepped in in time. He'd always done everything in his power to keep her alive, though of course they wouldn't have even been fighting the naval officer if he hadn't insisted on raiding the imperial ship before Shek Yeung had fully recovered.

This last one had come from Shek Yeung herself only months ago. They had been in the thick of battle, and she'd mistaken him for an enemy. For some time afterward, rumors abounded that she'd wounded him deliberately. She never contradicted the rumors. She knew she wouldn't be able to convince anyone if she couldn't even fully convince herself.

She, too, was a mess of scars, some dealt by enemies, some by Cheng Yat. No wonder she had no words. This man had both saved and destroyed her life.

For a moment she thought she might cry, but she did not.

2

Five days passed before the craggy coastline of Canton appeared, a splotch of ink gradually seeping through the scroll-paper mist. All around her, sailors were celebrating, their sandy voices washing over to her cabin belowdecks. Many of them had originally hailed from and would be returning to this area when they'd made enough money. These seasonal crew members made up the bulk of the crew: they fished and peddled during times of abundance, turning to piracy after tax collection or devastating typhoon seasons. Only a few, like her, Cheung Po, and the deck officers, spent most of the year doing this. For better or worse, they were a different breed. Their skin stretched thicker over their bones, calloused by the sea winds. Their hands were steadier, muscles firmed by a thousand swings of the cutlass.

As they neared, she saw through the porthole the heads that the emperor's men had mounted on spikes at the edge of town in warning to the weaker of her kind. The large fleets they couldn't touch, and even if they could, few wanted to. Shek Yeung kept many officials in her pocket. These days much of Yan-Yan's work was figuring out who needed to be paid when.

Shek Yeung regarded her husband's body as though it were a trusty old ox that had plowed its last row. "Well then," she said to him.

Together with Cheung Po and two others, she carried Cheng Yat to his aunt's home for preparation. The procession was to take place in three days and would undoubtedly be a spectacle. Generations of pirating had left the Cheng family quite wealthy. It didn't seem entirely right to her that Cheng Yat should be interred—he belonged to the sea as much as his stillborn daughter—but that was the Cheng family tradition.

One of the servants opened the gate for Shek Yeung and indicated that she should wait in the entry hall. Given the early hour, most of Cheng Yat's relatives had only just awoken for the day and needed time to change out of their sleep garb before receiving her. Even at a time like this, they apparently felt it unseemly to appear before an outsider without first robing themselves in silk damask and piling their hair high with coral combs and pins. (And Shek Yeung would always be an outsider to them, daughter-in-law or not.) She would almost certainly be underdressed next to them, even in the relatively formal clothing she currently wore: the black Manchu-style men's tunic with tapered sleeves and long slits over a pair of pants. She preferred to wear Manchu-style clothes when possible because they were well suited for horse riding and archery, which meant that they were well suited for fighting, and one never knew when one might get called upon to fight.

Shek Yeung was fine with waiting. It gave her time to gawk at the ridiculous anteroom, as wide as maybe five regular rooms and held up by tall columns. Carved crossbeams painted green, ruby, and cobalt at the joints gave the impression of exotic birds atop trees. Then there were the doors of the main gate, emblazoned with ruddy, bearded door gods to protect the ill-gotten gains inside. One wielded an ax, the other a crescent-bladed spear, the kind usually reserved for ceremonial purposes, though Shek Yeung had once watched an imperial guard swing one around, the point goring one after another of her men, the crescents slicing open throats and limbs.

Shek Yeung had visited the Cheng estate for the first time six years ago. She had just turned twenty-five, had just been bought by Cheng Yat from the flower boats where, for nine years, she'd lain interred in the rocky soil of her captivity. It was the first time she'd ever set foot inside a rich family's home. She'd felt so afraid to touch things, afraid to even sit on the rosewood furniture on the chance that she might dirty it. After the fear came the anger. How dare they live so luxuriously when so many people like her were so poor! Even still, her anger toward the Cheng family gradually abated. After all, they had acquired their wealth by stealing from people even wealthier than they.

Finally, Cheng Yat's relatives emerged from the interior of the house. They were wet-eyed—it seemed the servant had already informed them of Cheng Yat's death. His mother and many aunts and sisters greeted the body with a loud collective squawk. They flocked over it, their colorful wide sleeves flapping, filigree fingernail-guards clawing. None greeted Shek Yeung.

Later, they all sat down in the main hall to discuss funeral proceedings. Shek Yeung's two sons hid behind their wet nurse, eyeing Shek Yeung warily. Ying-Shek, who felt more comfortable around her simply for having known her longer, eventually emerged from hiding and sat on her lap. She stroked his back falteringly, her cold hand a disembodied thing haunting the stone path of his spine. A little after that, Hung-Shek followed his older brother's lead and approached, except he stopped at arm's length and just stood there, picking sullenly at a loose thread from the lion embroidered on his robe. The last time she'd seen him was a year ago, for his third birthday. He probably didn't even remember her.

She'd become pregnant with Ying-Shek shortly after marrying Cheng Yat. For months she couldn't even tell between the morning sickness and the seasickness, and no one on the ship knew how to comfort her. In quieter moments, she considered just pitching herself into the sea. By the time Hung-Shek came along two years later, she felt better prepared to be a mother. But Cheng Yat was at that point in the midst of his campaign to create an alliance of pirates to counter imperial forces, and she, as his chief strategist, could hardly abandon her duties, not when failure meant the lives of ten thousand men and women. "Any mush-brained woman can nurse," he'd said to her. "I need you here with me, negotiating with the commanders of the other fleets."

Bored by the funeral planning, Ying-Shek hopped off her lap and ran out of the room. His brother stumbled after him.

Cheng Yat's relatives were bickering over the exact order in which people would march. Shek Yeung took a deep breath. "Perhaps we should consider letting some of the ship's company join," she said.

One of the aunts gasped. Another looked as if Shek Yeung had suggested setting everyone on fire. The grandmother, in her quiet, steely voice, said, "Is that what you think?"

"They are among Cheng Yat's oldest friends, after all."

"And that is what matters, is it not? Length of friendship? Come to think of it, there is a street cat that wanders in these parts that Cheng Yat has been feeding since he was a young man. Perhaps we should ask the cat to march."

Finally, the discussion ended. As they departed the Cheng estate, she told Cheung Po, "We need to talk."

"After," he replied, setting off for the center of town, no doubt to seek one of the many gambling parlors or brothels there.

She grabbed his forearm. "Now that we're on shore, it'll be a matter of days before all of the other fleets catch wind of the news. The continuation of the alliance was Cheng Yat's final request. Surely you'd want to respect that."

"Will *you* respect it?" he asked. She didn't answer. He smiled inscrutably, slipped out of her grip, and continued on his way.

She should have guessed he would try to delay the conversation until after the funeral. Cheung Po was exceedingly, surprisingly superstitious. To him, discussing matters of succession before Cheng Yat was even in the ground was an affront to the gods. But villains waited for no god, and in the end, villains most of the fleet commanders were. She had no delusions about them, alliance or not. In fact she wouldn't be surprised if they thought the same of her.

The biggest threat to the alliance was the leader of the Black Banner Fleet. Despite commanding only two hundred compared with the Red Banner Fleet's three hundred-plus ships, he wielded significant influence over the leaders of the Green and White Banner Fleets. If the Black Banner Fleet left the alliance, so would the Green and White. Losing the White Banner Fleet's paltry fifty ships would not be catastrophic. Losing the Green Banner Fleet's one hundred-something ships would pose a greater problem. The Blue Banner Fleet, with its hundred and fifty ships, would likely stay, but two fleets made for a sorry alliance.

Part of what kept the uneasy peace among the fleets was that each had claimed its own little corner of the Chinese coastline: the Red and Black Banner Fleets in the south near the Pearl River Delta, the Blue Banner Fleet in the waters around the island of Taiwan, and the White and Green Banner Fleets in the north near the Yangtze River Delta. The apportioning of territory kept each fleet well fed, which wasn't to say that none of the leaders wished to expand. In particular, Kwok Po-Tai, leader of the Black Banner Fleet, had on occasion hinted at his dissatisfaction at having to share space with the Red Banner Fleet. He wanted an unbroken span of sea from Canton in the east to Vietnam in the west.

For all she knew, Kwok Po-Tai had tipped off the Portuguese and that was why they'd been so well prepared. A weakened Red Banner Fleet would work in his favor.

There wasn't much she could do, until Cheung Po was ready to talk, except visit her old friend Wo-Yuet. When she was sure Cheung Po had gone too far to double back and follow her, she headed in the other direction.

Wo-Yuet's home sat on the outskirts of town, a sam-hop-yuen much like the kind found throughout Fujian, where Wo-Yuet had grown up: a main building with two perpendicular wings, one to the left and one to the right, all facing a center courtyard. The only deviation from the Fujianese style was the wall around the property, built to deter the bandits in this area. Shek Yeung had bought the modest structure with money she'd made in the fleet, after buying Wo-Yuet's freedom from the flower boats. Her friend had been growing more and more despondent about the line of work in which they'd found themselves. Once, in the dense hours of the night, after most of the customers had either fallen asleep or left, Wo-Yuet had confided in Shek Yeung that she'd prepared a vial of centipede poison for herself to drink one day. She didn't know when that day would come, Wo-Yuet said, but she would know when she knew.

Wo-Yuet came to the gate in a simple gray tunic and skirt. Her complexion had a touch of the sallow that Shek Yeung did not like, but aside from that, she looked dignified as ever, all soft-eyed and fine-boned, a sharp contrast to Shek Yeung with her wide cheeks and strong jaw. Madame Ko used to say that Wo-Yuet was the songbird to Shek Yeung's cat. Where Wo-Yuet was pale and delicate with a small round mouth, the kind of beauty plain at a glance, Shek Yeung was dark and feral with thick hair and deep-set eyes, the kind of beauty one learned to appreciate only after realizing how useful the possessor of said beauty could be.

"Cheng Yat is dead," Shek Yeung said in lieu of a greeting.

Wo-Yuet showed her in. The paint on the vermilion columns was peeling, the stone tiles in the sam-hop-yuen's courtyard stained gray-brown from kumquats that had fallen from the tree and smashed open. Wo-Yuet seated her in the main hall and left to make some tea. Here the air was stale and faintly sour, though there was also a sharp herbal smell underneath it all like a splinter under a nail. Dust formed a skin over the dark lacquered tables and stools, thickening into scabs in harder-to-reach areas like the shrine to Ma-Zou. Shek Yeung wriggled a finger through the dust. When she realized she had drawn waves, she added a little boat heaving atop it.

"How long?" Wo-Yuet asked, setting down the teapot and cups.

"A few days," Shek Yeung said. "Killed in battle."

"Some people will think you did it."

"I don't care."

"Of course you don't. What now?"

"That depends on Cheung Po. I don't fully trust him, but if I rally my supporters too early, that might tip him over to the side of hostility. It would be best for everyone if this didn't become a full-blown conflict."

Wo-Yuet exhaled shakily. "But you're saying it could."

Shek Yeung shrugged. "Life and conflict go hand in hand. I'm no stranger to either."

"They don't have to!" Wo-Yuet looked a little embarrassed by her own outburst, but she continued. "What if you walked away? What if you just turned over the entire fleet to Cheung Po, in exchange for your safety and the safety of your supporters, and maybe a comfortable retirement sum? Cheng Yat was the reason you joined the fleet and the reason you couldn't leave. Now he's dead. So what's keeping you there?"

Between preparing for the funeral and wondering about Cheung Po's intentions, the idea of leaving the fleet genuinely hadn't occurred to Shek Yeung. Her friend was right, of course. Cheung Po would have to be an idiot (and he wasn't, not by a long shot) to risk a bloody conflict and possible defeat when he could just give her a guarantee of safety and some spending money. What was keeping her there?

Let's say Cheung Po agreed to her request. That would preserve her from ever having to return to the flower boats. She could buy a piece of land close to this one she'd bought Wo-Yuet, build a sam-hop-yuen like her friend's on it. There would be kumquats in the fall and longan in the summer. Her sons would remain with their father's side of the family, naturally, but perhaps, with more frequent interactions, they would cease to be so wary of her.

But her children didn't need her. The fleet did. It was under threat from the emperor, from the commanders of the other fleets in the alliance, and from the Europeans, especially the Portuguese, who'd somehow prepared for this most recent attack. She had a responsibility to her crew, who had children of their own to feed and clothe. What good could she possibly do if she stayed behind in Canton? She didn't cook or weave. She no more knew how to care for children than for wild dogs. How would she pass her days except in idleness, her thoughts her only company aside from Wo-Yuet.

"I'm sick," Wo-Yuet said.

This startled Shek Yeung from her thoughts. "What?"

"It's probably nothing," Wo-Yuet said. But now that the words had been spoken, Shek Yeung began to make sense of all that she'd observed. "Just dampness in the lungs. I'm taking herbs for it. They help."

Shek Yeung took her friend's hand.

"Madame Ko had dampness in the lungs, and she lived until she was sixty," Wo-Yuet added.

"Do you want me to leave the fleet?" Shek Yeung asked, not sure she actually wanted to hear the answer. If Wo-Yuet demanded her retirement, Shek Yeung would find it difficult to say no. And if she stayed with her friend, she knew she would always feel a little resentful for having been denied a real choice.

Wo-Yuet sighed. "I don't want you to do anything you weren't already going to do anyway. I've known you for a long time."

Since before I was even myself, Shek Yeung wanted to say, remembering those first months on the flower boats, the bruising on the hips and thighs, the heady jasmine and sandalwood perfume that nevertheless failed to cover the sour, briny smell of the men. Wo-Yuet had let her climb into her bed whenever Shek Yeung couldn't sleep.

"I'll burn some incense for you at the temple," she said.

"Burn incense for yourself," Wo-Yuet said.

Shek Yeung thanked her for the tea and rose. "I'll think on what you said."

Partings between the two of them were never more than a nod or a clasping of hands. The words for "goodbye," more accurately "see you again," sounded too much like a challenge against Heaven, and no mortal who challenged Heaven won. One could only try to decipher the will of Heaven and then to abide by it, devote oneself to it even, to let oneself be borne on it as on the winds and the waves.

And here she was accusing Cheung Po of being superstitious.

The local temple to Ma-Zou sat on top of a hill some eleven lei from Wo-Yuet's house. It was busy as usual. Most of the folks around here were water people, "poor misfits" (so styled by the government) who had no place in the social hierarchy of scholar, farmer, artisan, and merchant. The altars were heaped high with fresh flowers: rhododendrons; lascivious lilies with their stamens thrusting out; many-petaled chrysanthemums; wide-mouthed gladioli stacked atop long stems like heads on spikes. Off to one side, Ma-Zou's sandalwood palanquin sat, covered with red silk and topped with a small golden lion sculpture. On festival days the priests placed the Ma-Zou statue inside and carried her around town, led by a standard bearer waving his banner to ward off evil spirits and accompanied by all manners of dancers and musicians. Smoke dark as night issued forth from the large incense brazier at the center of the courtyard, the bright camphor scent of the joss sticks like a crescent moon glinting in the black.

First Shek Yeung stopped by the temple shop to buy a handful of joss sticks. After some consideration, she also bought a paper talisman for good fortune that depicted Ma-Zou sitting on her throne with celestial maidens on both sides and a talisman for good health that was just several characters written in complicated calligraphy. She could give these to Wo-Yuet the next time she saw her.

Lighting the incense sticks, she approached each shrine at the temple in the designated order. At the shrine of the Jade Emperor, the Heavenly Grandfather from whom all gods descended, she bowed and left one stick. She repeated the process at the shrines of the Goddess of Mercy, the God of Wealth, and the patron god of the city.

There were many gods in Heaven, one for whatever a person lacked (after all, wasn't lack the foundation of being human?). There were gods for ensuring happy marriages, gods for winning wars, gods for passing the civil service examination. To Shek Yeung, though, only one god truly mattered.

She approached Ma-Zou's shrine at the center of the temple. The goddess had many names: Granny Mazu, Heavenly Consort, the Jade Girl of Miracles. The goddess also had many faces: crone, maiden, empress, concubine. This version of the goddess, carved from violet jade, was a noblewoman with cone-shaped lotus shoes, which indicated bound feet. She wore a golden robe decorated with blue gemstones, yellow tassels, and mother-of-pearl buttons, and clutched a scepter of what also appeared to be jade. Word had it that pirates had gifted the statue to this temple. And where had they gotten the statue? From another temple, where else?

"Benevolent Lady," Shek Yeung whispered, "I have come to seek your guidance. Wo-Yuet says I should leave while I have the option, but I have made this fleet what it is. For these men and women I have given up two sons. Cheung Po is clever but unsteady, too easily swayed by his heart. I know I would make a worthy commander. But I also know that fortune favors no one forever.

"Please, Ma-Zou. Tell me what Heaven wills of me." She closed her eyes and waited. And waited.

Shek Yeung opened her eyes. The statue of Ma-Zou regarded her knowingly, her gentle red smile a little painted boat.

Sighing, Shek Yeung tripped down the hill. At the bottom, she decided to take one of the back roads to the Cheng estate, just in case Cheung Po was also on his way to the temple. She didn't want to see him until she'd made a decision.

It was there on that dusty back road that Heaven responded to Shek Yeung for the second time in her life.

3

Girl, why do you seem so troubled?"

"I don't know how to make this decision, Ma-Zou. Should I stay or leave? Would the fleet be all right without me? Would I be all right without it?"

"You have many questions."

"How could I not? This has to do with my future."

"This is true, but you are forgetting something."

"What's that?"

"The past and the future are but points on a circle. What will be, always was. To look to your future, we must first look to your past."

"What does my past have to do with my future?"

"Silly girl, is it not clear? Let me ask you a question, then. What are the junk's greatest strength and greatest weakness?"

"The greatest strength is the hull. It's made up of small, sealed compartments so that if one part of the hull gets damaged, water floods only that compartment."

"That's right. Junks can keep sailing even if damaged, even if parts of them have been utterly broken. The seawater is compartmentalized so that the rest of the ship can function. What about the junk's greatest weakness?"

"I still don't understand, Ma-Zou."

"The junk is not very good at going upwind. It produces less drive than the Westerners' rig. When the junk is running downwind, though, its speed is unparalleled. Unlike the Westerners' rig, there are no shrouds to get in the way. With a junk rig, you simply need to let out the sails, and the winds will do their work.

"You can certainly sail a junk upwind, but the journey might be beset with trouble. So if you have any desire for what awaits downwind, then go as far and fast as you can in a junk, until the wind will take you no farther. Ask yourself, girl: in which direction has the wind been blowing all this time?"

"But what if there are things upwind that I also want? If I choose to sail downwind toward one shore, will the winds ever change and carry me back toward the other?"

Silence.

"Ma-Zou. Ma-Zou?"

. . .

What a strange girl, the aunties in the village said of Shek Yeung when she was a child. Lovely but strange. Her father and older brother did the best they could, but a girl couldn't learn to become a woman by watching men. It was really too bad about the mother—so young.

Clear days found Shek Yeung down by the sea, playing by herself. She had a little bamboo toy boat that her brother had carved for her. She would place it on the water and, with a flick of the wrist, skim it along the surface until it reached her other hand.

Her father and brother were fishermen, though they couldn't afford their own ship. Instead, they worked on a two-masted junk ship for a merchant from Canton who'd never even bothered to board the vessel himself. This was just fine by them. The last thing seasoned fishermen needed while navigating dangerous waters was a queasy rich boy barking ill-considered orders at them.

When Shek Yeung grew bored of the toy boat, she set other items on the water surface to see if they would sink or float. Sometimes she used whatever she found lying around: a bit of broken pottery, a baby's shoe, a pouty-lipped seashell. And sometimes she stole away from her house with special objects, her mother's heirloom bracelet with shiny amber glass beads, for example. Shek Yeung had fully intended to return it to its hiding place after the experiment, but then she slipped. The cord snapped, and the beads floated away like water lanterns for the dead. That had earned her twenty lashes of the cane from her father.

"Ma-Zou, Ma-Zou," she would say whenever an item was lost to the sea. "I brought a gift for you." And though Ma-Zou never responded, Shek Yeung always felt certain the goddess had heard.

The aunties tried to discipline her the best they could, but she was a slippery one—that was the word they used, *slippery,* like the eels they loved to cook so much. She'd been eight or nine years old the first time they'd made her help in the kitchen. They ordered her to clamp down on the eel's neck and tail so they could do their work with the knife. As the knife opened the head lengthwise, the animal thrashed under her hands, its neck expanding and contracting, its gills fluttering against her skin like the eyelashes of someone about to cry. She ran off to throw up into a bush.

She eventually got used to helping out in the kitchen, though she never developed much of a talent or taste for cooking, so the aunties banished her to take care of the younger neighborhood children. This task she found dull. The ones who had learned to talk already wouldn't stop talking, despite never saying anything terribly interesting, and the ones who hadn't learned yet mostly slept. Once, relegated to babysitting indoors on a beautiful morning, watching a swaddled newborn snore away, she'd started kicking at one of the legs of the chair on which the baby was resting, trying to jostle him awake. Suddenly that leg gave out, and the baby half-rolled, half-flopped to the ground. She ran off so that she would be nowhere near the scene when one of the aunties came along to find a broken chair and a screeching, possibly broken baby.

The aunties didn't know what to do with her after that. Sometimes they used her as a go-between for the different households, and sometimes they made her clean the musty, rancid shit in the chicken coop, which she did with one hand pinching her nose. But none of those things took up the entire day. This was great as far as she was concerned because it left her more time to swim, to nap, and to scavenge for treasures in the sand.

The summer of her fifteenth year, she joined her father and brother on the ship. "The sea is no place for people who shrink from hardship," the old captain said by way of a welcome, watching her dubiously, the beginnings of a cataract silvering over his left eye. Shek Yeung didn't feel worried. She learned quickly. She was strong for a girl and fast, faster than even some of the boys in the village. The captain could have done worse than inviting her aboard.

The workings of the small two-masted junk were simple enough to master. From her brother she learned to rig the sail, from her father the art of twisting rope. She listened to the old men tell their stories of the sea and competed with the young men over any and everything: who could climb the mast the fastest, spit the farthest (the loser had to wash the deck afterward), steal the most from the captain's stash of sunflower seeds without his noticing. When the catch was bad, they hungered together. When the catch was good, they tossed everything they wouldn't be able to sell into a large cracked pot that was being held together by the crew's collective force of will and then fought over the cooked fish heads. Shek Yeung was particularly skilled at removing every trace of flesh from the head, saving her favorite part, the eyes, for last. Those she liked to pop into her mouth one by one, tongue and teeth working past the salty, fatty outer layer to find the satisfyingly crunchy center.

For a while the craft sailed with just her family and a few other men, until another woman joined the crew. How her brother goggled at Yu Lan, who had hair so long and full she might have been a willow tree in a past life. Eventually he won Yu Lan over, though not before Yu Lan pulled her aside to ask the important questions. ("Does he drink too much? Does he hit? Do his feet smell?") The young couple started discussing marriage. Typhoon season was a good time, they decided. They would be landbound by then anyway.

The night the pirates came, Shek Yeung had just put away the captain's book of sea routes, which he allowed her to read when he wasn't using it. In the couple of months since she'd started studying it, she'd memorized almost half of the rhymes. *If lightning appears in the west, then tomorrow will be clear. If lightning appears in the north, then rain is surely near.* Rumor had it that the captain planned to retire soon. Not that Shek Yeung harbored any hopes of succeeding him, but her father had a good chance, and she wanted to stay on to help him. It filled her with pride, the idea that she and her family might take over this ship, even if they needed to operate it under the banner of its merchant owner. To have a ship was to have the world.

The pirates killed the cabin boy who'd been assigned as lookout. Eleven men and women against a fleet of armed criminals—Shek Yeung and her family never had a prayer.

"Give us what we want and you can all go home," one of the pirates said, dragging the tip of his broadsword along the deck. Dark spots made a nautical chart of his bald head.

"We don't have money on board," the old captain said. "What do you think we are? Merchants?"

"That's too bad," the pirate said. "My men went through a lot of effort, you know. They expect to be paid. We have no choice but to take your ship and your crew."

At this Yu Lan began to sob. It wasn't until the pirate spoke again that Shek Yeung understood why.

"Your men are now my men," he said, "your ship my ship. These two girls here will fetch a good price at the flower boats."

"We're good workers," Shek Yeung shouted. "I'm good with ropes, and she's a good cook."

"I don't allow women in my fleet. They cause too much trouble around my men." He glanced between her and Yu Lan. "But I'm feeling generous today.

"You," he said, crooking a finger at Shek Yeung's brother, who stood from his place next to Yu Lan. His legs were trembling. "I'm guessing that one there is your girl, the way she's clutching at your shirt. What about this one? What's her relationship to you?"

"She's my sister," her brother said.

"Good, good," the pirate said. "Tell you what. I'll let one of them go free. You pick which one."

Her brother froze. "You want me to—"

"Yes."

Shek Yeung met her brother's eyes. He seemed to be trying to communicate through them. She couldn't tell if he was promising to keep her safe or asking her to forgive him.

"We don't have all day," the pirate said. And then before her brother could respond, the pirate added, "Oh, never mind," and slit his throat.

Behind her, Shek Yeung heard her father scream.

She tried to get to her brother, but another pirate held her in place. Blood from the neck, Shek Yeung noted offhandedly, flowed unexpectedly dark.

"He was taking too long," the pirate with the broadsword said. "Don't you know the emperor has been sending his dogs out to sea to hunt us?" He sighed peevishly, raising his eyebrows at Shek Yeung, as if to ask, *Well, what else would you have had me do?*

She couldn't have said for certain what happened afterward. Her memories of that night, on the rare occasions she cast her mind back to it, had a vaporous quality that made it hard to discern what had actually transpired versus what she had dreamed in the many nightmares since. All she knew for sure was that they locked her and Yu Lan in the captain's cabin. The pirate leader came to her a couple of times, or maybe it was two different men. The second time, he didn't even have to pin her hands. Each time she recited to herself the rhymes from the book of sea routes. *Clouds that curve mean a path that swerves.*

Eventually she fell asleep. Sometime later she awoke in the dark to Yu Lan's voice. "We must jump," Yu Lan said.

"What?" Shek Yeung said.

"When we get a chance. I'm a strong swimmer. You are, too."

"We're at least half a day out."

"There will be no escape once we're on the flower boats."

"We'll die."

No answer.

"Yu Lan?"

"Then we die."

Except Shek Yeung didn't feel particularly ready to die. For one, her father was still alive. For another, she wasn't clear on what happened after death. Some of the aunties in the village told stories about spirits that, instead of passing on, lingered like rumors. Usually these spirits had died horribly (and what was more horrible than death by drowning?), and when they encountered a living person, they wailed about how they'd met their ends. Sometimes they sought to bring harm to the living out of rage or jealousy.

Even if she passed on, what then? The dead needed money and food just like everyone else. Who would make offerings to her besides her father, assuming he survived this?

They stiffened at the sound of steps coming toward them again. "Please, we can do this," Yu Lan said.

"I won't jump," Shek Yeung said, "but I'll help you if that's what you really want."

The door opened to reveal one of the younger pirates, maybe younger than Shek Yeung herself, if his pimples were anything to go by. He was carrying cups of water. She wondered if he'd been pressed into piracy like the men of this fishing junk soon would be.

"I know where my captain keeps his silver hidden onboard," she said to the boy. "I'll show you where it is."

The boy looked skeptical. "He said he didn't have any money."

"Of course he said that. He was hoping he'd find a chance to escape with it."

"I'll get in trouble if I let you out of this cabin."

"You'll get in bigger trouble if my captain ends up escaping with the silver."

"Why are you telling me?" he asked.

"I don't want to get sold," she said. "If you help me sneak off once we're on land, you can keep all of it. If you insist on telling your captain, then maybe he'll let me exchange the money for my freedom."

The boy thought for a long time before he finally nodded.

He hauled Shek Yeung up and pushed her toward the door. She could hear Yu Lan creeping behind them. At a particularly loud creak, the boy turned around, but it was too late. Yu Lan swung a wooden board at his head. Shek Yeung caught him before he fell and lowered him to the deck soundlessly.

They'd almost made it to the stern when a pirate spotted them. Shek Yeung launched herself at the man, wrapping her arms around his legs and squeezing his knees together, a trick she learned fighting with her brother. He went down, not so soundlessly. If the other pirates had been asleep, they weren't anymore.

"Run," she told Yu Lan, who sprinted toward the edge.

Meanwhile, the man on whom Shek Yeung was currently sprawled had regained his senses and was struggling to peel her off. When that proved more difficult than anticipated, he began to pummel her with fists and elbows. Shek Yeung gritted her teeth, trying to buy the other girl more time.

Clambering over the railing, Yu Lan dove into the water.

The man might have beaten Shek Yeung to death had the pirate captain's voice not rung out. "A dead girl fetches me no profit," he said. Squatting next to her prostrate body, he murmured to her, "It's too bad about your friend. But you, you're a survivor. That's good. That'll serve you well in the years to come." And then he backhanded her so hard that she passed out.

When she awoke again, the junk was no longer moving. The sounds of people shuffling overhead and thumping cargo around suggested that they had docked. Wherever she was, she'd arrived at her new home.

4

In one of the stories about Ma-Zou, she lived, in spite of expectations. The Lam household was awhirl that morning. Madame Lam had awoken with contractions, but nevertheless she'd risen and, cradling her belly like an overfull washbasin, shuffled into the kitchen to prepare fresh man-tau for her husband and four sons so they would have enough food for a long day's fishing. Only after the dough balls had finished steaming over the deep stove pit did she return to bed and call for help from her mother- and sister-in-law.

All three women had experienced and witnessed enough childbirths to know that, for reasons only Heaven could comprehend, some babies were born to die. Madame Lam herself had already lost several upon birth, and her sister-in-law had lost her twin in the time it took for the umbilical cord wrapped around the two children to be severed. So when Ma-Zou arrived, eyes shut, deathly silent, the women assumed the worst. It wasn't until Madame Lam picked up the girl and clutched her to her breast to say goodbye that she felt breath on her skin. Bending her ear to the bony little cockleshell of a chest, she heard there the deafening sound of waves.

As a child, Ma-Zou never cried and hardly ever spoke. The people in the village called her the Silent Girl, somewhat in jest but mostly in praise—a girl like her would undoubtedly grow up to be a virtuous woman because what was a virtuous woman if not quiet, squelching her own pain so as to better hear the needs of the men in her life? But what the villagers mistook for modesty was in fact an extraordinary capacity for observing and learning: by age eight, she had mastered the works of the Master, and by eleven, the sutras. Still, her family members and neighbors planned for her an ordinary woman's life, never expecting what Heaven had in mind.

5

How did any girl learn to become a woman? By observing the
women around them—the aunties were correct in that regard.
But by observing the women around them, girls also learned what they
didn't wish to become. The aunties never mentioned this because, naturally, they thought themselves paragons of womanhood.

The "flower boats" neither sold flowers nor functioned as boats.
Roped together so that one could easily cross from one vessel to another,
these waterlogged sampans were more like oyster beds, each tiny boat
a pried-open shell presenting its pearls. If a tall man took a very wide
stance while standing on the sampan, his feet would touch both the port
and starboard sides. If he stretched his arms overhead, he would be able
to touch the covering, which was sewn together from discarded sails.
When it rained, water dripped from the seams into chipped crockery,
the ones deemed too unpretty for customer use. Sometimes Shek Yeung
had to wake up multiple times over the course of sleep to toss the water
overboard. Once she slept too deeply and awoke to a listing sampan.
After she and a few of the other girls finally got the boat dried out, she
received twenty strikes of the cane. She never made the mistake of deep
sleep again.

Some of the girls decorated their sampans with veils and fresh blooms,
but there was only so much one could do to beautify these rotting vessels
reeking of brine and unwashed skin, of the buckets in the corner that
collected human waste, and of semen-stained bedclothes that never

seemed to lose that faintly metallic scent no matter how well one washed them. The truth was none of the customers cared how the boats looked or smelled—the decoration was for the girls themselves, something to make them temporarily believe they had control over their own lives.

At the sale, Madame Ko had gently tipped Shek Yeung's bruised face up to the light. "Pretty, this little one," the woman said. And though the muscles of her face were burning, the skin stretched tight from all the swelling underneath, Shek Yeung wished she looked uglier. Maybe then Madame Ko would put her to work in the kitchen or something.

Needless to say, Shek Yeung never saw her father again. The pirates had taken him away before she'd even awoken from the blow to the head.

After a healing period of a few days, she began taking customers. Madame Ko didn't give Shek Yeung any of the quick-tempered men— those she saved for the girls who'd worked there longer, who knew the tricks to pacifying them, one of which involved slipping a little bit of powdered jujube into the tea. Shek Yeung supposed she should be grateful for this reprieve from Madame Ko. Still, there were days she hardly slept (nights were reserved for customers), too preoccupied by thoughts of her father and Yu Lan, hoping the former was still alive, wondering if she maybe should have joined the latter when she had the chance.

She considered escape a lot, but this hope, too, died when a girl who'd escaped was dragged—actually dragged, as evidenced by her blood-streaked skin pitted with bits of stone and broken glass—back to the flower boats. Then, even though the girl had begged for Madame Ko's forgiveness, the old woman had ordered her beaten until her face was unrecognizable and her left elbow bent at an impossible angle. This had terrified Shek Yeung if for no other reason than its aberrance. When Madame Ko wanted to punish a girl, she usually caned the soles of the feet. The girls were, after all, merchandise. So Shek Yeung quietly buried this hope, scared to speak it even to herself.

The irony was that Shek Yeung's quality of life on the flower boats was technically slightly better than her life on the fishing boat had been. She no longer lived in constant danger from storms and pirates, and she hardly ever went hungry—the customers usually allowed her and the other girls to partake of the food they'd ordered for themselves, and whatever they didn't finish they left behind. Yet she could no longer summon her old appetite. When morning came, she eyed the plates of cold food with aversion: the strips of poached chicken with ginger sauce brushed over their slimy skin; the century eggs with their corpulent-smelling yolk, transformed gray-brown by the clay and salt in which they'd been preserved; and the lightly sweet lotus seed buns, pale except for the single red dot on top like a pricked finger. In her first month on the flower boats, she lost a terrifying amount of weight, even as the customers pinched and poked at her breasts and hips, urging her to eat a little more.

Shek Yeung met Wo-Yuet a little after that when the older girl came under Madame Ko's ownership through some kind of exchange. Though Wo-Yuet had worked on flower boats for years, she was not like the others. She'd none of the honeyed venom of many of the veterans, that way they had of smiling sweetly even as they plotted someone's demise. (One of them, perhaps feeling threatened by Shek Yeung's growing popularity among customers, had dusted her clothes with some kind of itching powder that left her clawed up and unable to work. Madame Ko blamed Shek Yeung for being "careless" with her hygiene and punished her with a foot caning.)

Wo-Yuet asked for her story, and Shek Yeung told it.

"If my father can stay alive," Shek Yeung said, "he'll find me. He'll figure out a way to buy my freedom."

But instead of reassuring her, Wo-Yuet grabbed her shoulders and turned her to face one of the flower boats a ways down. Through the rather sizable holes in the veils drooping from the tarp, Shek Yeung could make out three women slumped in their cots.

"What do you see?" Wo-Yuet asked.

"What do you mean?"

"What do you see?"

"I don't know what you want me to say."

"My cot looks out onto that boat directly, so I've had no choice but to pay attention to what goes on there since I arrived. And you know what goes on? Nothing. Absolutely nothing. At night the girls take customers and smoke opium with them. In the mornings they smoke some more and then sleep the entire day. How do you think they got that way?"

Of course Shek Yeung had noticed them during her time on the flower boats, these women whose minds and bodies were hollow like open graves, though she didn't know any of them well. They never really tried to converse with her or, for that matter, anyone else. For some reason, she'd assumed they had always been "that way."

Wo-Yuet turned her back around and said, "Look, you need to stop having these silly fantasies about being rescued because fantasies lead short lives in places like this, and once they die, you'll try to resurrect them through opium. Be smart, watch and listen closely, and learn when to use the things you see and hear to your advantage. All you have left now is you."

And if Shek Yeung hadn't taken that piece of advice to heart then, she would have a few months later, when one of the girls was strangled to death by a customer. Madame Ko didn't even turn the man in to the authorities, just banned him from her shop. At dawn they gathered around the girl, whom Shek Yeung hadn't known very well, and dressed her in a white robe. They burned some spirit money, the little slips of silver paper shriveling to nothing. Her body was carted away.

After the girl's funeral, Shek Yeung stayed out on the deck. All the others had gone to sleep. In the distance, the gray waves had a wispy quality, as if the ghosts of all those who had died at sea were struggling to rise from it. The wind howled. The aunties had talked about all different types of ghosts: hungry ghosts, who'd died from famine; sodden ghosts, who'd died from drowning; and burning ghosts, who'd died from crimes of passion. But they'd never mentioned the ghosts of girls who'd worked on flower boats, who'd died from other people's indifference. Even in death they had no stories.

If she jumped into the water and simply swam out until she no longer had the strength to swim back, no one would mourn her. And perhaps that would still be a kinder option than to spend the rest of her days on this boat that was never leaving the dock.

Shek Yeung edged up to the bow. "Ma-Zou," she said, "I don't know why you've turned your back on me and my family. We always made offerings to you, even when we had little money for food. If you have any mercy, then please grant me this one last request. Let this be as painless as possible."

She was about to swing her legs over the side when she heard the voice: "Girl, is your life worth so little to you?"

Shek Yeung whipped her head around but could not find the source of the sound. That was when she realized the water had stopped rippling. The wind was silent, like a child who'd wailed for so long that he'd tired himself out and fallen asleep.

"Why should I grant you a merciful death?" the voice asked. "Do you think I owe it to you because your family made offerings to me? Do I owe mercy to everyone who has ever made an offering to me?"

"So I should endure this, then?" Shek Yeung cried.

"You are alive."

"What I have here can't be called life," Shek Yeung said. When no response came, she added, "I don't think you owe me anything. I'm only asking for your help the way a beggar asks a rich man for a scrap of food. Give it or not, but I'm ending this today. And if it must be painful, then so be it."

"Then you are fortunate," the voice said, "that I am of a charitable nature. Stay alive, and you will have life once more. This I promise."

"How do I stay alive in a place like this? Among people like this?"

A pause, and then: "However you can."

The wind started up again. Shek Yeung fell back into herself, a sensation not unlike what she sometimes experienced on the brink of sleep. Near the red horizon, the waves roiled as if being heated by an immense fire. No one, it seemed, had overheard her conversation.

Nodding at the water, she went back inside.

· · ·

She couldn't have articulated what kept her going those first years on the flower boats. Finding a friend in Wo-Yuet certainly helped. Like an older sister or a mother, Wo-Yuet shielded her from the worst of the clients, kept her from wandering down the paths of malevolence or self-dissolution as so many of the other girls had done. But more than that was this inexpressible sense of purpose—Ma-Zou had spoken to her, breathed between them a secret. No matter what happened now, Shek Yeung knew the goddess favored her, cared for her even. Whenever she felt the call of death, she repeated to herself stories about Ma-Zou. In some of the stories, Ma-Zou was a shaman, in others, a warrior. In all of them Shek Yeung saw the versions of herself she might one day become.

And so instead of wilting, she sprawled herself over flower boat life, hooked into it the way vines hooked into and crept up a wall until it was all but covered, until the wall's very face seemed incomplete without them. Much of importance transpired in such places, she quickly learned. Merchants whispered the contents and worth of their cargo in the delirium of opium. Soldiers complained about the difficulty of new training regimens and the remoteness of future battlegrounds. With sweet words and warm hands, one could coax information out of all but the most guarded of the men. Information could be sold or bartered. Information built empires and decimated armies.

They called her Heung-Koo, fragrant maiden. Shek Yeung didn't care for the name—any maiden would smell good if she spent hours a day censing her robes and rubbing honeysuckle oil into her skin—but nevertheless she came when they asked for her, lilting her words, pursing her lips in that way that men interpreted as coquettish. Many became repeat customers. One or two even offered to buy her freedom in exchange for her hand. They might have been serious or just muttering nonsense in the afterglow, but Shek Yeung always declined. *Why not*, they demanded to know. *Why wouldn't you want a house, nice clothes, fat sons?* To this she had a prepared reply: *Madame Ko and this place would not function without me.* But really she said no because she knew the alternative was simply another flower boat, one that was on land and serviced a single customer. Ma-Zou had promised her a life, and somehow Shek Yeung knew this wasn't it.

One evening during her twenty-fourth year, she emerged from her quarters to find that the other girls were aflutter over a customer who was rumored to arrive soon. A few were sitting on the floor in a circle, each braiding or otherwise styling the hair of the one in front.

"You have so much hair!" one girl said to another. "I wish mine looked like yours."

"Well, I wish I had your skin!" the other girl replied. "You're going to catch his attention for sure."

"No, you are!"

"You are!"

It seemed to Shek Yeung that each girl gripped the hair of the girl in front a little tighter.

Wo-Yuet was in a corner by herself, working on her embroidery. She looked up for just long enough to roll her eyes at Shek Yeung. They shared a smile.

Many newer, younger girls had been brought onto the flower boats since her own arrival. Many of the older girls had died from illness or violence or complications that inevitably arose when the medicine they drank for pregnancies worked a little too well at ending life. How strange it was that Shek Yeung was now the one they looked to for advice.

"Big Sis," Siu Fa, one of the youngest, said to Shek Yeung, "settle an argument for us. Do men like faces that are more or less powdered? Jung-Jung says less, but why would any man want to see a craggy face?"

"I do not have a craggy face!" Jung-Jung shouted.

"Did I say you did?"

"Men like faces that are powdered a medium amount," Shek Yeung said because she didn't want to upset either girl but also because she didn't have the patience to continue with this conversation.

She went to stand by Wo-Yuet. "So what's all this about?"

"It's the captain of a large fleet," Wo-Yuet said without looking up from her embroidery. "Supposed to be very wealthy."

"Ah," Shek Yeung said.

"Will you be trying to win him over?"

"It's not like there's that much we can do about it. Men like the looks they like."

"True enough."

He arrived a few hours later, accompanied by four of his crew, all armed with cutlasses. He himself also had a pistol tucked under his sash. Big Brother Cheng, his men called him. At rough glance he appeared to be in his mid-thirties. "Tonight's on me," he announced, laughing the deep, easy laugh of someone much more corpulent despite having only a hint of a paunch. He wasn't bad to look at so long as one didn't look too carefully, the way a sail up close might show all the places where it had been patched and darned but from afar was like the fin of a magnificent fish.

Shek Yeung had put on her finest tunic and styled her hair with a little more care than usual, rouging her lips only down the middle to give the appearance of a smaller mouth, but she harbored no delusions about the outcome. She'd never been the prettiest of the girls, and these days she certainly wasn't the youngest. Cheng and his men sat. Siu Fa and Jung-Jung immediately sidled up next to them bearing liquor. Jung-Jung had powdered her face more than usual, Siu Fa less.

Things progressed as they typically did. The men grew louder as they grew more inebriated. What started out as chitchat about recent exploits turned into a heated debate about the projected price of pepper. Occasionally, Shek Yeung approached the group to top off their drinks, but for the most part she ceded the stage to the younger girls—that was, until she overheard one of the men advising Cheng to sell off all their pepper now while the price was high.

"It'll keep climbing," Shek Yeung said, pouring the liquor.

They turned to her. "What?" said the man in favor of selling.

"Old Lai is on his deathbed and his son has a large gambling debt. Without the pepper brought in by his trade network, the price is going to climb."

The man gaped at her as if he'd heard a monkey talk. Then his expression soured. "And what experience do you have of commerce, girl? Don't you know it's 'Men above, women below'? Save your energy for opening your legs and leave the thinking to men." He turned to Cheng. "Womenfolk."

Cheng just stared at Shek Yeung.

Shek Yeung retreated to her quarters. If she turned her focus to other customers now, she could still earn some money for the night. Rouging her lips again and loosening her elaborately pinned hair a little to stave off an oncoming headache, she readied herself to go back out but was interrupted by Wo-Yuet. "Come now," she said.

"What is it?"

"Foolishness," Wo-Yuet replied, already running off.

It turned out that Siu Fa and Jung-Jung had gotten into a fight, but not the kind of fight men liked to cheer on. Jung-Jung had pulled the knife from one of the men and was brandishing it at Siu Fa. "You always do this!" she was saying.

Despite their weapons and superior size, the men had backed away from the girls. Shek Yeung noticed Siu Fa's handkerchief in Cheng's hand, remembered that Jung-Jung had been the one sitting on Cheng's lap, and put the story together.

"Big Sis," Siu Fa said, somehow managing to look both scared and smug, "she's gone mad. All I did was talk to Big Brother Cheng alone for a moment."

"Shut up," Shek Yeung said to Siu Fa. To Jung-Jung she said, as softly as she could, "All right, what happened?"

"He was about to leave with me!" Jung-Jung said. "I spent hours. . . . She always does this!"

"It doesn't feel fair to you."

"Yeah, she thinks that just because she's more popular, she can get away with whatever she wants. I'm not gonna let her anymore. She should have left town with her lowlife family."

"A lot of people in your shoes would be angry, too."

"Anyone would be. She calls my skin craggy, tells me I'm getting fat. Like she's so nice to look at herself. But do I say that to her? She doesn't treat me with respect even though I've been here two years longer."

"I get it, you just want her to respect you."

Jung-Jung nodded, lips quivering.

"So what do you think we should do to get Siu Fa to respect you?"

"I don't know."

"Well, we're all here, so let's work together to figure this out," Shek Yeung said. She glared at Siu Fa. If the girl said the wrong thing next, Shek Yeung was going to kill her herself. "Siu Fa, what do you think?"

"I'll be nicer to her," the young girl muttered.

"All right, that's a start," Shek Yeung said.

"But it's not like she's nice to me all the time either!" Siu Fa said, having apparently forgotten that Jung-Jung was holding a knife. "She says my breasts are so small that only men who are into boys would choose me."

"You weren't supposed to hear that!" Jung-Jung said.

"Oh, so it's better to say things behind other people's backs?"

"Either way," Shek Yeung interrupted, "you both now have a choice. Jung-Jung, you can let Siu Fa apologize to you, or you can stab her and get beheaded. Siu Fa, you can apologize—and be sincere about it, or I promise you it won't work—or you can let her stab you. Both of you can win today, or both of you can lose."

Siu Fa pouted so extravagantly, she might have succeeded in balancing drinks on her lips. Then with genuine contrition, she said to Jung-Jung, "I'm sorry for always making fun of you and stealing your customers."

But Jung-Jung didn't put down the knife.

"You don't believe her?" Shek Yeung asked.

The girl began to cry. "I'm in so much trouble. Madame Ko is going to punish me."

Shek Yeung sighed. "Probably. But mostly she'll be glad that she didn't lose her two most popular girls. I'll talk to her. The punishment won't be too rough, I promise." She held out her hand. Jung-Jung gave her the weapon.

Shek Yeung sent the two girls back to their respective quarters for the night. She turned to the men to offer them complimentary services for their next visit, but Cheng spoke before she could. "What's your name?" he asked, taking back the knife. "I'm called Cheng Yat."

"Heung-Koo," she said.

"Your real name."

She paused. "Shek Yeung."

"All right, then," he said.

He chose her as his companion for the night. It seemed to her he was trying to be gentle, as if the evening's turmoil had pushed her close to breaking, as if she hadn't spent the past six years of her life ossifying herself. Sometimes she felt that she was nothing but carapace, that there remained nothing of the girl who'd shipped out with her father and brother, all daydreams and heart-blood. She found his considerateness naïve, but nevertheless she appreciated it, an appreciation she immediately pocketed away to keep it from doing any harm.

After, as they lay there, he asked, "The thing you said about Old Lai—how do you know this?"

"Word gets around."

"Still, that's some good thinking. You're sure about his shipping network?"

"His son favors one of the girls here."

"The same son with the gambling debts?"

"And prostitution debts. I've seen his tab."

Cheng Yat laughed.

He left before dawn. Shek Yeung felt relieved but also a little disappointed because she hadn't enjoyed the company of a man this much in a long time. She didn't expect him to come back.

Except he did. And again. And again.

· · ·

She was in the middle of washing her hair one day when she figured out Cheng Yat's true vocation. Rinsing soy and osmanthus powder out of the strands, she considered the things he'd mentioned over his various visits: his base off the coast of Vietnam; his friendship with the infamous Tay Son brothers there; the fact that he'd come from a wealthy family, though no one ever talked about the origins of that wealth. The realization sat sour in her stomach.

Throughout her years on the flower boats, she'd made it a point to never directly ask her customers about their line of work. Such an arrangement was best for everyone involved. The ones who wanted to share this information did so. The ones who didn't, didn't, or they made vague references to working at sea. By decree of the emperor, all pirates were to be executed.

For her part, not knowing made it easier. In any case, many pirates were not pirates by choice (not that the emperor cared about this distinction). Her father, if he were still alive, was a pirate now.

The next time Cheng Yat visited, she feigned monthly troubles and convinced him to choose one of the other girls. The time after that, she made sure she was already occupied with a customer. Unfortunately, Cheng Yat did not lose interest.

"Now, now," Madame Ko said, "why don't you have a look at Mei here. She's from the western parts of the country, you know. A very exotic beauty."

"I'm not leaving until I see Shek Yeung," Cheng Yat said. "And I'd advise against you trying to make me leave."

When she showed him to her quarters, he plopped down onto the cot. She hovered by the gangway, ready to run if need be. Her gaze kept darting to his cutlass. "You've been avoiding me," he said.

"I haven't. Why would I?"

"You tell me."

"I'm sorry we've missed each other." She lowered herself onto the cot, smiling, hoping to distract him from his anger. She unfastened the closures on the side of her robe.

He put out a hand. "Let's talk," he said.

Cheng Yat asked about her family. She answered, omitting the details: mother dead of illness, brother dead of violence, father's whereabouts unknown. Cheng Yat asked about her plans.

"What do you mean?" she asked, genuinely baffled by a customer's intentions for once.

"Well, I was planning to ask you eventually anyway, but you've forced my hand with your recent unavailability. How would you like to join me on my ship?"

A life as a pirate. The promise of that kind of freedom warred with the understanding of what that kind of a life entailed. Would she be able to kill someone in cold blood? Do nothing as the men raped captive women? Though sometimes she wondered if she and Yu Lan would have met with their fates if that pirate's crew had included women.

"Your talents are wasted here," Cheng Yat said. "You know this."

"Madame Ko needs me," she said.

"That old fox will be fine without you. Give me a better excuse."

She couldn't.

He sighed and said, "I thought I might have said too much the last time I was here when I mentioned the Tay Son brothers. A silly woman would have missed it. But we'd been having such a good conversation, and I couldn't stop myself."

"So you *are*—"

"I am, but don't let that deter you from considering my offer."

"I can't," she said.

"No? I think you're mistaken about what life in my fleet is like," he said. "You probably haven't spent much time on the water."

Shek Yeung chose not to correct him.

"Maybe you're imagining chaos, or savagery. That's not the case. Men need to be governed, or they become animals. But the governing need not fall to the officials. Rather, it *should* not, because officials are often corrupt and blind to citizens' needs. Think about their response to the most recent famine. They grew fat while everyone else starved. Then when the poor got caught trying to steal food and money for their families, they executed them. The only proper response to tyranny is insurrection.

"I bring order to the men and women of my fleet. I set rules they follow under threat of death. No captives are killed unless they try to rebel. Plunder is distributed fairly instead of being hoarded by officers. There are no fewer laws in my fleet than in the emperor's court. In fact there may be more."

Cheng Yat leaned back. His cutlass swayed, the gold cloisonné on the hilt flicking the candlelight at her like a rich man flicking a coin at a beggar.

He gave her until the end of the month to decide.

She sought out Wo-Yuet's counsel. "Would you do it?" she asked her friend.

"I don't think you have much of a choice," Wo–Yuet said. "Men like him are not used to hearing no."

"He said he would be fine with whatever I decided."

"You know his true vocation now. You have a sense of where his base is. Your decision, Little Sister, is between life and death."

That day she dreamed of a massive junk, painted black from bow to stern. It was night, but the water was aflame with lanterns for the dead. There were so many people on board she could hardly keep count, some laughing and drinking, some dead and cocooned in funeral linens. Among the passengers, she glimpsed two musicians who were playing a sad melody on the silk-stringed yeung-kam and on the yee-wu with its pungent, rosined bow. She wanted to cry, but her eyes were drought-dry. Finally, the song came to an end.

The boat began to move.

PART II

Long Live the Queen

6

At the funeral, Cheng Yat's aunts and sisters clutched one another's arms, dabbing their faces with lace handkerchiefs plundered from European ships. His mother wailed, crumpling to the ground and pulling at her hair as if to extirpate her grief from her body. Having come from a family of pirates, the older woman had already lost her husband, her other son, and no small number of relatives and friends to the sea. One would think she would have seen this day coming and prepared for it.

The only people who didn't cry were Shek Yeung and her sons. Shek Yeung couldn't fathom the luxury of grief. True, she'd grieved years ago after being separated from her brother and father, but that grief had been mist-thin, easily burned through by the sun of her fear. There simply hadn't been time for all-consuming sadness on the flower boats. In the evenings there had been customer after customer, and in the mornings, the long cleanup. When the girls finally got to lie down, sleep possessed their bodies like vengeful ghosts.

As for Shek Yeung and Cheng Yat's sons, they were too young to understand this spectacle that was happening on account of a man they hardly knew.

Cheng Yat's funeral procession wended through the center of town. At the fore plodded the priest, ringing his little copper bell. Behind him, musicians huffed into their so-nap and banged their pat together to scare away spirits. Shek Yeung, her sons, and Cheung Po followed on foot. Then came a team of sixteen men who conveyed the casket on their shoulders by means of long bamboo poles. The casket had been intended for one of Cheng Yat's uncles before Cheng Yat jumped the line. It'd been carved out of a single piece of hardwood and then painted with a red phoenix, a black tortoise, a blue dragon, and a white tiger surrounding a giant pearl. The scowls of the Four Guardians gave the impression that they were warring over the pearl instead of protecting it. The palanquins bearing the older female family members and others unable to endure the march brought up the rear. Crowds gathered for the sight, the young exclaiming at the musicians, the old eyeing the procession warily because everyone around here knew the provenance of the Cheng family fortune was questionable, even if they didn't know for certain why.

All anyone could do in this world was try to stay alive and pray that, when the time came, Heaven would overlook whatever crimes one had committed to survive. Forgiveness wasn't inconceivable, Shek Yeung often told herself, not even for murderers and thieves. The reasons mattered. Murder to protect one's own differed from murder out of jealousy or spite. Theft from the rich hardly offended moral sensibility in the same way as theft from the poor.

At length they arrived at the burial site. The servants lowered Cheng Yat's body slowly. From the palanquins, robed in loose white burlap, Cheng Yat's mother and sisters fluttered like moths. Shek Yeung trailed behind them as they meandered to the gravesite, squinting in the afternoon glare to take stock of their surroundings in case enemies were nearby. A small distance away, Cheung Po appeared to be doing the same.

He caught her eye and nodded. She nodded back. All clear.

What would become of this fleet, now that Cheng Yat was gone? She had been his equal in strategy. Cheung Po had been Cheng Yat's equal in combat and thus possessed the respect of all the men. Both of them were essential to the survival of its twenty thousand crew members, but did the boy understand this?

Ma-Zou's message to her three days ago had all but confirmed her instinct. The wind was still blowing in the direction of the alliance. Until it changed, she would continue the work she and Cheng Yat had started. It was too early to furl the sails.

Keeping the junk running smoothly and at full speed was a different matter. Shek Yeung's claim over the fleet vanished the moment Cheng Yat died. By law, everything was Cheung Po's now. She would need to marry the boy to retain control over her half, but she doubted that he wanted to marry her. He had a penchant for pretty girls on flower boats and for luxurious accoutrements that she found wasteful. He would likely see marriage as getting in the way of those things. She'd have to convince him that marriage was in his best interest, a business decision that wouldn't get in the way of whatever he wanted to do to whomever. At the same time, she would apply pressure to the ship's officers because Cheung Po couldn't damn well sail the ship by himself.

Clump by clump, the servants shoveled dirt onto Cheng Yat. Dust prickled Shek Yeung's eyes, causing them to water. On an impulse, she knelt and laid his golden cutlass atop his casket. "Thank you," she said.

"He should've been buried at sea," Cheung Po said. He'd somehow made it to her side without her noticing.

"His mother wanted him buried next to his family."

"*We're* his family."

His vehemence surprised her a little. "In a manner of speaking. But I've no desire to quarrel with them about this. Do you?"

"I don't fight unnecessary battles," he said.

She wanted to ask him what he meant, but Cheng Yat's relatives were already climbing back into the palanquins. No doubt they wanted to get as far away as possible before sunset. According to the aunties from her village, demons swarmed fresh graves at night to eat corpses' hearts.

Shek Yeung once asked them if anything good ever happened to the spirits of the dead—the stories made it seem as if everyone became a ghost or a demon. Did spirits ever just travel the world? Did they reincarnate, as some people claimed? "What happens after death is not for us to know," they'd answered.

That evening, Shek Yeung stopped Cheung Po as he was leaving for the gambling dens. "I spoke to Ahmad before the procession. His sources down at the docks say the Black Banner Fleet will arrive tomorrow," she said. "What we tell Kwok Po-Tai will determine whether the alliance succeeds or fails."

She led him into her bedroom and poured him a cup of expensive rice wine. Cheung Po eyed it.

Shek Yeung grabbed the cup and drank it herself. This seemed to satisfy him because he poured himself another. "I'm not afraid of Kwok Po-Tai," he said.

"It's not about being afraid. In sheer manpower, we outnumber him. But if his fleet leaves the alliance, so do the others."

"That snake is not dumb enough to leave the alliance, not with all the new decrees from the emperor."

"Can you bet on that? Can you bet the lives of our people on that?"

Cheung Po looked annoyed. This was not how she'd planned for the conversation to go. If Kwok Po-Tai didn't scare Cheung Po, then she would have to find someone else who did. Cheng Yat always said that nothing brought enemies together better than a common threat, and since the failed raid on the Portuguese, she'd had a vague suspicion. "Haven't you been wondering how the Portuguese knew we were coming?"

His eye twitched, which meant that he had. Nevertheless, he said, "Maybe fortune was on their side. The Europeans have known to expect us for a while now. They prepared."

"But to have prepared to such an extent? I can't be the only one wondering if they'd received word beforehand. If they had, then there is a spy among us, or at least a loose-lipped fool. Word of an uneasy alliance between the two of us or between us and the Black Banner Fleet would immediately reach the Europeans and the emperor. We must not betray any dissent. We must act as a single fist until we've discovered the identity of the spy." Forcing a smile, she laid her hand atop his. "What do you hope for yourself? What do you see for your future?"

He shrugged. "Money. Women."

"You want to keep this going."

"Can't complain about my life right now."

"I'm glad," she said, lightly squeezing his fingers. "If we handle this transition properly, you can continue to have all those things and more."

"You're the one saying that Kwok Po-Tai will be a problem."

"Maybe," she said. "If the transition makes us unstable, he'll make a play for our resources. We need to make him understand that we would be as effective a pair as Cheng Yat and I were, and that when it comes to my half of the fleet, there won't even be a transition."

Cheung Po considered this. "All right."

"All right?" Now this conversation was going suspiciously well.

"When we meet with Kwok Po-Tai in a few days, we'll tell him that we're taking over operations for the Red Banner Fleet. You and I were Cheng Yat's most trusted advisers. He knows all this."

"We'll tell him that I'll maintain control over my half of the fleet," she repeated.

Cheung Po looked confused. "Of course you will. What are you talking about?"

A laugh escaped her in her relief. "Never mind, ignore me. When would you like to hold the wedding?"

"The what?"

"The wedding."

"Why do we need a wedding? I promise I won't touch your half of the fleet. You know my word is good."

It was true, Cheung Po was generally a principled man. But Shek Yeung had been in this world too long to gamble her life and the lives of her crew on promises. "Fortune is rarely predictable or kind," she said. "Say something happened to you."

"You saying I'm going to die?"

"Or you changed your mind."

"I won't."

She smiled in a way that she hoped was reassuring. "Look, if you're concerned that I'll try to interfere with your personal affairs, don't be. The marriage would be in name only."

"And what's to stop you from killing me the instant we're married? I have no heir. The entire fleet would go to you."

Apparently, he'd already thought through the potential consequences of each option. She knew that he was clever, but even she got fooled sometimes by his presentation, which made people underestimate him. At the moment, he was slouched in his seat in his purple silk robe, one foot propped on the table. Per the rules of the Manchu court, Cheung Po shaved the front half of his head and kept the rest of his long hair in a braid, but he certainly didn't keep his hair neat. Straggly strands were always poking out from his braid, falling in front of his face, and clumped together with bits of dirt and dried blood. Whether the blood was his own or others', he probably couldn't tell you.

"I wouldn't try to kill you," she said.

He sniffed at his wine and took a sip. "I'll think about it." He rose and swept out of the room in his ridiculous robe.

Cheung Po didn't end up going out that night, perhaps out of fear that she would have him followed and killed. Shek Yeung lay in bed, deliberating what they should say to the Black Banner Fleet's captain when they inevitably encountered one another. If she and Cheung Po didn't appear wholly aligned in their interests, the battle was already lost.

Kwok Po-Tai was dangerous—she knew this as surely as she knew the paths of the stars. The man had been Cheng Yat's protégé until Cheung Po came along and supplanted him, at which point he left and founded the Black Banner Fleet. Convincing him to join the alliance had been infuriatingly difficult. Had he not maintained a fundamental respect for Cheng Yat, he would not have acceded.

Hair loose, still in her nightclothes, Shek Yeung marched into Cheung Po's room. "Make my older son your heir," she said.

In the dim light of her lantern, he looked much younger than someone in his mid-twenties. In recent years his face had grown wider and sharper, as was common for men his age, and his chin had developed a small cleft. Right now, though, he looked much as he had when they first met, smooth-skinned and round-cheeked. "What?" he said.

"If you die, and your death is in any way suspicious, have Ying-Shek succeed you. I would never kill him, and I certainly can't marry him. It would prevent me from taking power again."

Cheung Po scoffed. "He's what, five? Someone would have to run things until he came of age. No doubt it would conveniently turn out to be you."

"You can specify who you want to take command in the interim. I trust you to make a sound decision on behalf of the fleet."

"And what if I don't want the fleet to go back to the Cheng family?"

She resisted the urge to bash his head in with the lantern. But she had a negotiation tool at her disposal that Cheng Yat never had. "Then I'll bear you a son. And as soon as that child is born, you can have all rights transferred to him. Agreed?"

Cheung Po looked her up and down. "No time like the present," he taunted.

She climbed onto his bed and straddled him. Calloused hands slid under her nightshirt and up her waist. He smelled like he'd recently washed, just a hint of sourness under the starchy, earthy smell of the expensive ash-and-lard detergent the Cheng family imported from Peking. "The wedding will be tomorrow, in full view of our crew," she said. "Afterward we request a parley with Kwok Po-Tai, if he hasn't requested one already. We tell him *exactly* what we discussed earlier."

It was nothing new, sex between the two of them. Cheng Yat had made no secret of his relations with other men. But Cheng Yat had favored Cheung Po in particular, and after she arrived on board, Cheng Yat occasionally involved her in their activities, making her watch or participate or perform with Cheung Po as if they were trained monkeys. What was new this time was the forthrightness, no feigned hesitation or desire, just the transaction. It was easier like this.

So she was surprised when he pulled her close afterward and immediately fell asleep, despite all his supposed apprehension about her trying to kill him, and she was even more surprised to find him still sleeping when she awoke a short time later. She slipped out from under the blanket and padded back to her room, rehearsing the speech to Kwok Po-Tai as she went.

7

The wedding took place as they'd agreed the following evening, on the deck of the ship. Though many of the seasonal crew had already returned to their homes farther inland, the officers and the regulars attended. Enough for there to be no doubt about her position moving forward, which was all she needed.

A lifetime ago, when Yu Lan and her brother had been planning their wedding, Yu Lan had asked for Shek Yeung's opinions: What should they serve at the feast? Who should perform the hair-combing ceremony? Would they be able to afford musicians? Shek Yeung hadn't known the answers to any of those questions, and once after a bad night's sleep, she'd snapped at the other girl to never talk to her again.

"But don't you ever see yourself getting married?" Yu Lan had asked her.

"I'm married to the sea," she'd said, maybe a little dramatically.

"Come on."

"I am! I'm going to keep working on this ship when my father takes over for the captain. And then, when he retires, I'm going to take over."

"Shouldn't your brother take over?"

"My brother can't navigate his way out of his own butt. I don't get what you see in him."

On the flower boats, the other girls (usually the new ones) sometimes prattled about which men might propose to them and rescue them from the life. They imagined gold bangles and fat pigs roasted to a delicate crisp, a giant canopy bed embellished with carvings of phoenixes and dragons. Whenever they talked like this, she and Wo-Yuet shared a glance. It took only a few moon cycles to learn: the poor men could hardly afford the weddings of which they dreamed, and the rich men already had wives at home.

Her wedding to Cheng Yat had also been a practical affair—they'd planned to set sail for Vietnam the next day to intercept an English ship that had docked there. At the insistence of Cheng Yat's family, she wore a red modesty veil (as if Cheng Yat didn't know full well what she looked like) that left her sweaty and dizzy under the sun.

She could barely see or hear through the veil, modest as she was. During the ceremony, she was steered around the ship and turned to face one thing after another. Somebody set off a few firecrackers. A crew member blew (badly) into a so-nap. But at one point Cheng Yat gripped both of her hands and leaned in so that she could hear. "Those other men didn't know your true worth, but I'm no fool," he said. "As long as you do what I tell you, you will have everything you ever wanted and more."

How was she supposed to respond to that? How was she supposed to feel? She dug her fingernails into her palms and said, "Yes."

Now Ahmad was the one playing the horn. There were no firecrackers, but Yan-Yan was waving joss sticks about wildly as if shooing away flies. The girl looked pleased, convinced, no doubt, that this new union meant safety for her and the others Shek Yeung had brought on board. Shek Yeung herself wasn't so sure. People questioned wives' deaths a lot less than they questioned husbands'.

Cheung Po was wearing one of his best robes, this one gold, bordered with the same red hue as that of their fleet's banner. On his chest, a dragon clenched between its teeth the pearl of the sun. Shek Yeung was wearing her favorite piece of armor, a lamellar breastplate stitched together from a thousand little metal squares. *Like fish scales,* she'd thought the first time she'd seen this kind of armor on an imperial guard passing through her village. Then, *like a fish on dry land,* because these guards lived in Peking, far away from the water. One of the first things she did after joining the fleet was to procure for herself a suit of armor like this. It felt like rectification, returning fish to the sea, bringing order to an orderless world.

After the ceremony, Shek Yeung gathered her crew. "You may be expecting a trite speech from Cheung Po or myself about this happy occasion," she began, "but we will not waste your time. What we will do is make you a promise.

"We have led difficult lives, all of us. We are here because we have been starved, or robbed, or sold. We are here because fate has made it impossible for us to be anywhere else. But we are also here because we are strong, because we have refused to die hungry and silent, as the pigs in Peking would have us do.

"Every one of us has suffered under Manchu rule. They rode into China on their filthy war beasts, told us what crops to grow, how to dress, whom to worship. Yet they do not lift a finger to help us when our crops fail. Nor do they allow us to stop growing their silk so we can grow more rice. They expect us to kneel, but we will defend ourselves. If they kill one of us, then we will kill ten of them. If they try to starve us, then we will gorge ourselves on their food.

"To defy power, one must possess power. Our power lies in our unity. Big Brother Cheng understood this best. His family has been defending southern China against the Manchus for almost two hundred years. We do not raid villages that swear fealty to us. They are our people. We do not kill fisherfolk who cannot afford to pay their own ransom. And although Big Brother Cheng is gone, his legacy remains. Here and now, Cheung Po and I pledge our lives not to each other but to this legacy, to all of you. Your hunger is our hunger, your triumph our triumph. We rise or fall together."

There was quiet for a moment, and then Yan-Yan shouted, "Hear! Hear!" The cheering started. From somewhere in the crowd came a flash of light and a single loud pop. It seemed someone had found a fire-cracker after all. Yan-Yan, spooked by the sound, yelped loudly and then immediately started laughing, which made Shek Yeung laugh, and soon everyone on board was in fits, thumping one another on the back or, in Yan-Yan's case, tirelessly bobbing up and down as if powered by the waves.

8

In one of the stories about Ma-Zou, she turned disadvantage to advantage.

Wind-Flow Ears was a demon with ears wide as oars that could hear for many lei from any direction. Green-skinned and short-tempered, he carried a heavy ax to cut down humans who displeased him either by not paying him tribute or by accidentally waking him from sleep. His friend, Thousand-Lei Eyes, had eyes like burning coals that could see for, you guessed it, a thousand lei. Red-skinned, with an even shorter temper than Wind-Flow Ears, Thousand-Lei Eyes carried a crescent blade to slice open humans who displeased him by not providing him enough food or simply by being a "sorry sight."

One evening the two demons were down by the sea when a storm arose, swirling up fog so thick that even Thousand-Lei Eyes could barely see and whipping sand about with so much force that even their tough demon hides were pained. Suddenly, on a cliff in the distance, a light sparked. A beautiful young woman stood in a red dress that tumbled and coiled like the waves. She held aloft a lantern to guide ships home. It seemed to the two demons as they strained closer to the woman, entranced, that where the hem of her garment touched the ground, the pebbles began to shine. They opened their hands to catch the pebbles being flung off by the wind and saw that they were pearls, white and yellow and pink and blue-black, as if someone had taken a thousand dawn skies and rolled each into a tiny orb.

Each demon decided that he would marry her. They proposed to her, but Ma-Zou refused, for her heart contained only love for humanity. Humiliated and angry, the demons threatened to destroy village after village until she married one of them.

In response, Ma-Zou issued a challenge: she would marry the one who defeated her in combat. First, she fought Thousand-Lei Eyes. She chose a night on which neither the moon nor the stars shone so that his eyes would not present an advantage. He charged at her, crescent blades slicing every which way, but she subdued him.

Next she fought Wind-Flow Ears. She chose an echoing valley so that his ears would not present an advantage. He charged at her, ax swinging with enough force to fell a tree in one blow, but she subdued him.

The demons were so awed by Ma-Zou's powers that they swore fealty to her. In exchange for their promise to never harm another human again, she forgave them their crimes and appointed them her guardians, thus proving that even the worst of individuals could be redeemed, the bitterest of enemies made friends.

9

The wedding celebration continued late into the night. Shek Yeung, not so young as the rest of her crew, gave up a little before dawn and headed to bed. She noticed Cheung Po flapping around like a drunken bat in his wide-sleeved robe and decided to put him to bed, too. On their way to the stairs, they passed by Yan-Yan, who was sitting on the deck playing pai gow with Binh and a few of the others. As usual, the girl was taking the men for all they were worth. Shek Yeung leaned in so the girl could hear her. "Be nice," she said.

"I'm always nice," Yan-Yan said, then thwacked Shek Yeung on the shin hard enough that it actually stung.

"And all of you!" Shek Yeung said to the men. "You should know better than to play against her. Don't you ever learn?"

The men merely laughed and waved goodnight. Once belowdecks, Shek Yeung said to Cheung Po, "We should decide on the rules and then present any changes to the crew."

"Rules?" he slurred.

She eased him onto the bed she and Cheng Yat had shared, flinching a little at the vinegary smell of the wine, then perched at the edge of the desk on the other side of the cabin. All of the maps and ledgers were exactly as Cheng Yat had left them; some of his clothes still crouched in a heap next to the desk. The lone lantern shadowed the room more than it illuminated it. Was it Cheung Po or Cheng Yat lying on the bed? In the end, would there be much of a difference?

"If you want to establish new rules," she said, "we need to tell the crew while this transition is underway. They're pliable right now."

In the years since meeting Cheng Yat, she'd come around completely to his philosophy: men were animals who needed governing. Together they'd enforced Cheng Yat's long-standing rule of not killing hostages, and then after a few months on board, she'd added a few of her own. First, crew members were not to rape the female hostages. Second, female hostages were to be released if they couldn't be ransomed. Cheng Yat had been convinced the ship's company wouldn't abide by the new rules, but he also, thank Ma-Zou, never argued with her decision.

And Cheng Yat had been right, to a point: At first, the crew didn't listen. Some of the men scoffed at the "delicate new empress" as if she couldn't hear them. So one day she dragged a man who'd just raped a hostage onto the deck, ordered his head held down on a block, and beheaded him herself. He probably screamed loud enough to alert passing ships, but she hardly registered the sound over the blood in her ears. She felt more than she heard the crack of the spine.

"He is not the only one here guilty of this crime," she said after, wiping her cutlass on the sleeve of her tunic. "I will forgive any previous transgressions, and believe me, I know which of you have transgressed. But be assured, there will not be a second warning."

The men who'd previously scoffed at her quickly fell in line, grateful for having been spared. That was also the first time she'd, of her own volition, killed someone outside battle, and it surprised her that she didn't feel as bad about it as she ought.

Cheung Po sat up to remove his boots. "What's wrong with the rules you and Big Brother Cheng set up?"

"Nothing. But you can set rules too, if you wish."

"If nothing's wrong, then why are we talking about this?" Off came the robe. He was taking her offer to bear him a son very seriously.

"You have no interest in discussing this at all?"

"You've done all right commanding this fleet," Cheung Po said, a little begrudgingly. "Like I said, I don't fight unnecessary battles."

Maybe this partnership wouldn't be as fraught with difficulties as she'd feared. From the beginning, Cheung Po had treated her with basic respect. It had been nice to have someone on board who responded to all of her orders with eye contact and a simple acknowledgment. Everything in her life had taught her that she shouldn't expect more.

Once early on, Cheung Po had found her alone in Cheng Yat's cabin just staring at a spot on the wall, muttering Ma-Zou stories to herself. Without saying anything, he'd sat with her until she was finished.

How life with the fleet had changed the two of them! Cheung Po himself had been pressed into piracy when he was only fifteen. His tribe, whom the government called "sea nomads" with no small amount of derision, fished for a living, which made them easy targets for pirates. Sometimes she found herself wondering what he'd been like as a child; an oddball like her, maybe; a scamp, breaking vases and then running away; or a crybaby, clinging to his mother.

As for herself, she was happier now than she'd been on the flower boats, except for all the times she was sad about the inevitability of her own defeat. She was more mistrustful than on the flower boats, too, but wasn't mistrust the price one paid for power? She was meaner, or perhaps she simply knew better where she drew her lines.

If they had a son, what would become of the child? Cheung Po would probably want the child raised on the ship. Such was the way of his people, but more than that, if he truly intended the child to take over at some point, he would insist on training him early. Cheung Po never said anything outright, but he disapproved of the way the Cheng family was raising Ying-Shek and Hung-Shek. She could tell by the way he side-eyed their refined clothes (not that he didn't wear those clothes himself, but he probably believed he'd earned the right to do so) and by his sigh every time Hung-Shek fell and started to cry. She could sense his frustration because she'd felt that same frustration whenever a girl new to the flower boats had burst into tears. *Pity me,* the tears said. Shek Yeung always wanted to reply, *Heaven pities no one. If you must cry, then cry for everyone in the world. In the end the only thing a person can be promised in life is suffering.*

· · ·

The parley with Kwok Po-Tai occurred two days later, in a tavern both parties had agreed upon. Shek Yeung and Cheung Po checked their weapons at the door after inspecting the premises. The tavern owner brought them free drinks, but Shek Yeung declined hers, wanting to stay fully alert. Cheung Po drank hers instead.

Kwok Po-Tai arrived late. "The new Mrs. Cheung," he said upon entering the tavern. "My condolences and my congratulations. Forgive me my tardiness—important matters, you understand. My fleet recently subdued a rather sizable township on the eastern shore. We have established a wonderfully lucrative partnership with them, but they keep us quite busy. You are fortunate to not have to manage such a large township."

"The honorable Mr. Kwok, it is so delightful to see you again," she said, pulling out a chair that was at right angles to both her and Cheung Po. She had insisted on arriving early so she could control the seating arrangement. This one made the meeting seem less a confrontation than a discussion. It also allowed her and Cheung Po to keep each other's face and hands in view so they could communicate nonverbally.

Kwok Po-Tai stared at the chair for a moment but sat without quibbling. "Indeed. You look young as ever, lambent like the vernal sun."

"Oh, you flatter me. You yourself seem to be in radiant health."

They continued like this. Kwok Po-Tai, she'd learned a while back, required a soft touch. At first blush, he appeared no different from any other pirate: stout, with deeply tanned and lined skin and salt-coarsened hair he'd wrestled into a braid. Unlike Cheung Po, he chose his clothes for function rather than for aesthetics. The material was sturdy, and he'd added various loops and pockets to hide weapons. Only those closest to him knew about the man's massive floating library of history and poetry books. Word had it he composed poetry, too, for whomever he was courting.

"Mr. Kwok," Cheung Po said, looking annoyed at being left out.

Kwok Po-Tai nodded.

Shek Yeung used this gap in the conversation to launch into the speech she'd prepared. "As you undoubtedly already know," she said to Kwok Po-Tai, "we lost Cheng Yat recently in a battle with the Portuguese."

"Foreign bastards," Kwok Po-Tai said. He poured himself a drink, swigged it, slammed the cup back down onto the table, then signaled the barmaid for more. The poor young woman, in the middle of carrying several full plates to another table, stopped, thought hard about it, and set the plates down nearby so that she could fetch Kwok Po-Tai his wine first. The table awaiting their food protested meekly but knew better than to raise trouble.

"He fought hard," Shek Yeung said, "but in the end he was bested by one of theirs. His final wish was for the continuation of the alliance, which I think you would agree has served us all very well. With the information network among the fleets and our coming to one another's aid against governmental incursion, we have not only held on to our territory but also expanded. Villages that had previously been hostile to us have begun providing our crews with resources in exchange for protection."

"Yes, my men have developed quite a fondness for said villages and their hospitality."

"That's good to hear. You also know that Cheung Po and I are thoroughly familiar with the workings of our fleet, both of us having served under Cheng Yat for a long time. We are united in our commitment to fulfilling his last wish, so we are meeting with the commander of each fleet to affirm this. We are starting with you, naturally, because of the amount of respect all the other captains have for you and for your powerful fleet."

Kwok Po-Tai laughed and banged on the table. "Do you know, Choy Hin of the Blue Banner Fleet is always asking me for advice? He was begging so much of my time that I finally just directed him to Master Sun's *Art of War*. 'Nothing I've taught you can't be found in the book,' I told him. Yet he continued to implore me. I am starting to suspect that agile little monkey can't read!" He laughed again, but then his cheer faded. "There is, though, the issue of the cave where Cheng Yat stowed all his loot."

"Absolutely not, the Southern Cave is ours," Cheung Po said. Shek Yeung's glare did nothing to stop his outburst—so much for sight lines. "What do you even need it for? We deal in goods from Siam far more than you do. We need it for tactical retreats from both the Siamese and the imperial navy."

"How is it yours?" Kwok Po-Tai said angrily. "Cheng Yat showed me the location of the cave just as he showed it to you. You have no more claim to it than I."

"Did Cheng Yat leave his fleet to you or to me?"

Shek Yeung had expected this demand from Kwok Po-Tai and had been prepared to steer his attention toward another cave, one that would still be beneficial to him but that the Red Banner Fleet needed far less. The reaction from Cheung Po had all but dashed her plans. Now that Kwok Po-Tai saw how much Cheung Po wanted it, like a competitive sibling, he was not going to back down. She regretted having tried to secure Cheung Po's cooperation with sex—he might not have absorbed what she'd said with his mind on something else.

"Wait," she said.

"You best keep your cur under control," Kwok Po-Tai said to her.

"Who're you calling a cur?" Cheung Po growled.

By now, the men on both sides were aware that the negotiation had soured. They rushed to Cheung Po's and Kwok Po-Tai's sides, unarmed but nevertheless ready to fight. So eager to prove their manhood, these boys, so assured of their own invincibility. A single punch could kill, if the punch landed just right. Just because no one was armed didn't mean that no one would die.

What would Cheng Yat have done? "People waste too much time trying to convince others of lies," he once said, "when all they have to do is interpret the truth in a way that benefits them. Swindlers know this well. If my purse is empty, I cannot convince you that it is full. You have eyes. But if I show you my empty purse while dressed in my finest clothes and say that I was robbed, then not only are you likely to believe I am a rich man, you may even 'loan' me some money in hopes that I will repay you with interest."

"Wait," she said more loudly. When it became clear that no one was listening, she picked up the wine jug by the handle and smashed it against the table. This proved effective. "Maybe," she said to Kwok Po-Tai, "Cheng Yat left the Red Banner Fleet to Cheung Po because he believed that you had the ability to start your own fleet. Have you considered that?"

Kwok Po-Tai didn't answer.

She continued, "When he was alive, Cheng Yat frequently spoke of your resourcefulness. Think about it—to whom would you leave the family business that practically runs itself? The son who needs his hand held, or the son who would succeed no matter the circumstances?"

She was, of course, lying. Cheng Yat had definitely favored Cheung Po, and Cheung Po knew it. She dug her fingernails into the boy's thigh, willing him to stay quiet.

Kwok Po-Tai lowered his fists. "There is still the issue of the cave."

"There is," she said. "And I believe we can arrive at a compromise. There is a cave farther east, already stocked with supplies, with many spots where one can hide ships. It's true that it's not as close to certain trade routes as the Southern Cave, but what it lacks in convenience, it makes up for in secludedness, which, given the emperor's recent edict regarding piracy . . ." She paused here, as if doubting her own decision to offer up this cave.

Kwok Po-Tai nodded slowly. "My men could use something closer to the Pearl River Delta."

"Exactly."

They drank on it, exchanging more overblown compliments. Across the table, Cheung Po fumed. She might have attributed his outburst to the alcohol he'd accepted from the tavern owner earlier, except she'd more than once seen him put away an entire jug of liquor and then go into battle (and, as suggested by his continued existence, win).

After the parley, upon their return to the Cheng estate, she shouted at Cheung Po, "What were you doing?" She shut the door to Cheung Po's room so that others couldn't hear—one gossipy servant was all it took for the world to learn just how tenuous her partnership with the boy was. She leaned back against the door, feeling exhausted. Cheung Po struggled free of his many-buttoned riding jacket with an annoyed grunt and flung the thing into a corner.

"Kwok Po-Tai is a liar. You know very well that Choy Hin is as good a commander as any of us. He's saved my life twice. And he can read just fine."

"So you let your friendship with Choy Hin take precedence over an agreement that would determine the future of our fleet?"

"He's your friend, too. And you just sat praising each other like two dogs sniffing each other's asses. 'Honorable Mr. Kwok'! 'Lambent as the spring'! How do you stand it?"

"It's called negotiation!"

Cheung Po flopped down onto a velvet-upholstered chair that Cheng Yat's father had stolen from the Dutch. This room, which the Cheng family kept for guests, had stayed largely the same since she married Cheng Yat six years ago. It was meant to show dominance. European goods occupied every nook and cranny: plump pillows, settees wide enough for an entire family, and daybeds on which a knotted-up noblewoman could do her best impression of an undone sash. From what she'd seen, Europeans valued their comfort greatly, valued it so much they believed in a kingdom of everlasting happiness and bounty after death. Over the years she'd encountered a couple of their missionaries. She didn't understand how anyone could espouse something so ridiculous. Nothing in the world was everlasting: not kingdoms, not peace, not happiness.

"You know you're not working on the flower boats anymore, right?" Cheung Po said.

She stared at him, confused.

"I'm just saying. You don't have to be all . . ." He mimed something, wrists limp and hands flapping, which she guessed represented a prostitute wheedling a customer.

"You think the strategies of surviving as a leader are different from the strategies of surviving as a prostitute?" she said.

"No," he said. "Yes. Look, I know this is what you're good at. Convincing people, talking. I don't like talking."

"Most of our job is talking. That's why Cheng Yat brought me on board."

He looked uncomfortable. "I know. I just didn't like seeing it." He stood and stomped toward her. She moved aside, wary, but he was just letting himself out of the room.

After he was gone, she returned to her own room and barred the door, just in case Cheung Po's anger got the better of him in the night.

. . .

66

As expected, the meeting with Li of the Green Banner Fleet a few days later went smoothly. The man had a good head on his shoulders. For some reason, though, Ba of the White Banner Fleet missed their parley. Was it an act of defiance? "Ba is an idiot," Cheung Po said. "You know what he's like. Can't count on him for anything."

Cheung Po insisted on arranging the meeting with Choy Hin. They had spent years in the waters between Canton and Taiwan, raiding sugar boats together. Of all the commanders, Choy Hin was probably Shek Yeung's favorite. Small but sinewy, slow to anger but quick to laughter, he was as dependable as the North Star, appearing exactly when and where he said he would. He'd turned to piracy during a famine. His only real weakness was his fondness for opium, a fondness he and his wife stoked in each other.

This meeting took place aboard Choy Hin's junk. The number of people there who were compatriots of both men made it as close to neutral ground as one could find on a ship belonging to another fleet. Choy Hin's wife, whom crew members called Matron but whom Shek Yeung knew as Lam Yuk-Yiu, ordered a cabin boy to bring out some rambutan from Malacca. The cabin boy then positioned himself behind her and began massaging her back. Shek Yeung slit the hairy peels of the rambutan open with her cutlass and squeezed the fruits directly into her mouth. They tasted wantonly sweet except for the bitter seeds inside, which she spat overboard one by one.

"Too bad what happened to Cheng Yat," Choy Hin said, "but you two will take good care of the fleet."

"He was a good man," Lam Yuk-Yiu said. "Taught Choy Hin here a few things about being a good husband." She snapped her fingers. Another cabin boy came out. This one knelt down and started massaging her feet.

Choy Hin chuckled. "I wanted to keep her happy. Buying her was the best thing I ever did."

Lam Yuk-Yiu rolled her eyes but smiled.

As far as Shek Yeung was concerned, Lam Yuk-Yiu was a bit of a puzzle, one of the few people she couldn't fully comprehend and therefore couldn't predict. She didn't mistrust the other woman, necessarily—like her husband, Lam Yuk-Yiu had proven to be a worthwhile ally during battles, perching herself in the crow's nest of the ship with an English musket, with which she was quite the markswoman. She struggled as fiercely for her own life in battle as she seemed to struggle to end it with opium. On more than one occasion she'd used so much that her cabin boys barely managed to revive her. Sometimes Shek Yeung wondered what Lam Yuk-Yiu's ambivalence about living meant for the future of the Blue Banner Fleet.

Her first husband had sold her to pay back debts. Her second husband had beaten her, a lot, and then sold her when he grew tired of her. Choy Hin was her third. After she joined his fleet, she took over many responsibilities. These days she was, for some reason, trying to assemble a vessel crewed only by women. Shek Yeung asked her why once. She replied a little cryptically, "Maybe men and women weren't meant to coexist." Having lived all her life surrounded by men, Shek Yeung wasn't against the idea so much as confused by it. What kind of a woman did a girl growing up without men become?

Choy Hin offered her and Cheung Po some opium, which Shek Yeung declined for both of them.

"On to business, then," Choy Hin said. "There is a shipment of European pistols nearing us soon. A Dutch ship. This information is coming from one of my wife's English sources, who's been very reliable so far."

"The English don't want the Dutch to establish a stronghold in this region any more than we do," Lam Yuk-Yiu explained. "They've been more than happy to provide information."

"And you think we should try to take it," Cheung Po said.

"It would give us an advantage over the emperor's forces," Choy Hin said.

"Do we really need it, though?" Cheung Po asked. "Firearms are much harder to resell than other goods. People want sugar, pepper, herbs. That weakling in Peking hasn't done any of the things he's threatened."

Lam Yuk-Yiu shook her head. "That may soon change. A bureaucrat told me that the emperor has hired an expert."

"Expert?"

"In suppressing piracy. Pak Ling. Up until recently he was helping to suppress the northern rebellions. They are calling him the Emperor's Sword."

Cheung Po snorted. "Then we have nothing to fear! The emperor spent all his money fighting those rebels."

"Yes, but how many of those rebels are still alive?" Lam Yuk-Yiu said.

The rebels were not the only ones who'd died. Because the rebellion had been largely helmed by common folk, the government had run into trouble telling the rebels apart from ordinary villagers. In response, the army slaughtered villagers to ensure that no rebels escaped. At this point, very few of the rebels remained, and it was just a matter of cutting off their supply lines and waiting them out. It was an effective strategy, Shek Yeung had to admit, but cruel, even by her own standards. A huddle of peasants could do little in the face of an army, a huddle that the Manchus had sworn to protect under the Mandate of Heaven no less. Regardless of whether the villagers had rebelled, no government should ever treat its own people as it would an invading force.

"What's even more concerning," Lam Yuk-Yiu added, "is that the White Banner Fleet missed its meetup with our fleet last month. Our sources up north say some kind of large naval battle happened there recently that resulted in heavy losses on one side."

Shek Yeung felt the hairs on the back of her neck stand. Cheung Po sat up in his chair. Had the White Banner Fleet fought the navy and lost? Or had it perished while attempting to plunder European ships that had been warned about the attack? Dying certainly would've gotten in the way of Ba appearing at the parley.

But surely they would've heard if the White Banner Fleet had sunk.

"Ba is an idiot," Cheung Po said again, though he didn't sound so certain this time. "He probably just forgot."

"He hasn't responded to any of our subsequent messages."

"Maybe he's ill?"

Lam Yuk-Yiu shrugged in a way that suggested that Ba was more likely dead than ill and that maybe Cheung Po was the idiot.

"We'll send a few ships up north," Shek Yeung said. "See if the rumors are true."

Lam Yuk-Yiu nodded. The four of them sat quietly. None of them wanted to come across as alarmist, but all of them were probably worrying about the fate of the White Banner Fleet.

Choy Hin broke the silence. "So what do you think? Between your fleet and mine, we should have no trouble taking that cargo."

Shek Yeung and Cheung Po exchanged a glance. "We'll have an answer for you by tomorrow," she said. They thanked the other couple and left for their own ship.

Unsurprisingly, Cheung Po wanted to go. He often recounted his adventures with Choy Hin fondly, and though he might not have been particularly concerned about the government's new "expert," he understood the benefit of increased firepower. "The more we have," he said, "the less likely Kwok Po-Tai will try to grab territory from us. Isn't that what you want? Since you're so concerned about him? And what if Choy Hin invited Kwok Po-Tai after we turned him down?"

In battle, Cheng Yat always relied on their superior numbers more than the weapons they possessed. Flintstocks failed to ignite and could be taken by force. One man with even the most dependable of guns had no hope against ten steadfast unarmed men (as long as a few of them were disposable). "Overarming ourselves might be interpreted as hostility," she said. "We may be better off focusing on strengthening the loyalty of our crew."

"The hostility is already there. The question is, do you want to be more or less armed than the enemy when the fighting starts?"

It was hard to argue with his logic. The fact was, nobody ever voluntarily disarmed. Nobody voluntarily gave up power. Over time the Europeans' weapons had only grown more numerous and powerful. Had the sailors on that Portuguese ship not been so heavily armed, Cheng Yat might still be alive. And if she and Cheung Po didn't go, then nothing would stop Choy Hin from turning to Kwok Po-Tai for support. She disliked the idea of such weapons falling into Kwok Po-Tai's hands.

As for this government expert, she didn't quite know what to think. First, they didn't know for certain that Ba was dead. As Cheung Po said, the man was an idiot who'd arrived at his position more through sheer brutality than through any kind of cunning. He was no less likely to be sleeping off his alcohol somewhere than dead by the expert's hands. Second, the emperor had sent men after her before, and each time she'd triumphed, through battle or through assassin's poison. The iron of these men's resolve had liquefied the instant they realized just how deeply they'd underestimated her. These days the Qing court was a carp pond of tame, overfed sycophants, each waiting with his mouth open for the emperor's favors. Every now and then one of them took it upon himself to solve the problem of piracy in the South China Sea, believing it would invite the emperor's largesse. Shek Yeung had dispatched them all swiftly and smilingly.

It was true, though, that the northern rebellions had ended poorly for the rebels. Accounts differed, but the common thread seemed to be that peasants, angered by the unfair tax policies of the Qing court, had fallen in with a religious sect called the White Lotus that promised salvation in exchange for cooperation. The soldiers killed so many peasants that the army came to be known as the Red Lotus. The government arrested the peasants who weren't killed, regardless of whether they were actually affiliated with the sect, and it wouldn't release them until they could pay the fines, which of course they couldn't.

Cheng Yat had often boasted that he treated the crew he'd abducted better than the Qing treated the people they'd conquered. This had been true, to the best of her knowledge. He'd kept everyone fed. He hadn't killed indiscriminately, even if she didn't always agree with his reasons for wanting someone dead. If she needed to press-gang men at times—and she did—then the least she could do was to continue treating them as Cheng Yat had.

She discussed with Yan-Yan the costs and benefits of sailing with the Blue Banner Fleet for a while. The girl seemed intrigued by the idea. At first she wouldn't tell Shek Yeung why, but after a lot of cajoling and the tiniest bit of bribing, she revealed that she wanted to go sightseeing in Taiwan with the northern woman. Leave it to Yan-Yan to think of an important, dangerous mission as a vacation.

The next day Cheung Po left Choy Hin a note in their usual tree hollow saying that the Red Banner Fleet would lend him fifty of their ships, including the O Yam. Before setting sail, Shek Yeung paid another visit to Wo-Yuet's home. In her arms she cradled paper bundle upon paper bundle of qi-fortifying herbs she'd bartered from Lam Yuk-Yiu for a few chests of sugar and pepper. Lam Yuk-Yiu had assumed that Shek Yeung was already pregnant with Cheung Po's child.

"I see you two wasted no time getting started," she'd said, winking.

The main gate of the sam-hop-yuen stood open. As she stepped in, a harried-looking man dressed in gray scholar's robes emerged from the interior. His overall presentation was neat, hair pulled tightly back, mustache stiff and straight like pine needles. But his thick-lidded eyes gave the impression of someone who hadn't slept in days.

"Who are you? What do you want?" he snapped at her.

"I'm here to see Wo-Yuet," she said.

"Go, go," he said, waving his hand impatiently. "She's not fit for visitors."

"She'll see me."

He sighed loudly and popped his head inside. A moment later he signaled for her to enter. "Don't get too close," he said. "The heat pathogens are deep within her body."

Wo-Yuet was struggling to get out of bed. Shek Yeung hurried to her side and gently laid her back down. "Your physician is gruff," Shek Yeung commented.

"I didn't hire him for his pleasantness," Wo-Yuet said.

"You didn't hire him for his looks, either," Shek Yeung said, and the two of them burst into laughter. She inspected her friend's complexion. She'd seen this gray color before in many of her crew members, just before they . . .

"He said the heat runs deep," Shek Yeung said.

"He says lots of things."

"You hired him for the things he says."

"Don't be difficult," Wo-Yuet said, rolling her eyes. "So what did you decide?"

Having spent the previous evening debating whether to accompany Choy Hin on his journey, Shek Yeung was taken aback, wondering how her friend could have possibly heard about the meeting with the Blue Banner Fleet already. It wasn't until a long moment passed that she realized Wo-Yuet was asking about her decision to stay with the Red Banner Fleet. So much had transpired since the vision from Ma-Zou days ago. She opted against telling Wo-Yuet about it. She wasn't sure the other woman would understand. If anything, she could imagine Wo-Yuet chiding her, saying, *Did Ma-Zou encourage you to stay or do you just want to believe that? I've known you a long time. You listen to the signs you want and disregard the ones you don't.*

"Cheung Po and I are married," she said.

Wo-Yuet inhaled sharply, which triggered a coughing fit. Shek Yeung pounded her back even as the other woman tried to shake her off. After the coughing subsided, Wo-Yuet said, "May I ask why?"

"Why I married him?"

"Why you didn't walk away."

"It wasn't time."

"When will it be time?" Wo-Yuet asked. "No, don't tell me, let me guess. You'll know when Heaven tells you?"

Shek Yeung poked at a spot of dried blood on the blanket.

"Heaven lies," Wo-Yuet said. "Convincingly. All the time."

"It wouldn't lie about this. The signs—"

"We cannot know Heaven's will," Wo-Yuet said, "because Heaven doesn't even know it. That I've suspected for a long time. You must be careful, Little Sister, chasing after power like this. There was a time when all you wanted was to be free. You wanted to buy your freedom, then buy a small junk and set out on your own."

"I am free," Shek Yeung said.

"Are you?"

"Having power allows me to be free. If my brother and father had had power, they would still be alive."

"Perhaps," Wo-Yuet said. "You know, I've been reading the sutras. As best as I can, at least. You know how those things are written."

"You never believed this stuff before."

"I never disbelieved it either. What do you think happens after death?"

Shek Yeung eyed her friend warily. "Why? What are you planning to do?"

"The ones I've been reading, they talk about the Pure Land. It's a beautiful, peaceful place where people can work toward enlightenment. Only in enlightenment is there true freedom. This world we live in, it makes it almost impossible for anyone except maybe monks to focus on spiritual matters. There is too much lack, too much suffering. So we do whatever we can to make up for what we lack, whether it's to lie or to steal or to cling to power. The Pure Land makes all this unnecessary. To go, all you have to do is chant the name of the Buddha, O-lei-to-fat, with total faith." Wo-Yuet recounted a few of the stories she'd read.

When she finished, Shek Yeung said, "Sounds to me like another god who wants offerings."

"He doesn't punish or give rewards. He just wants everyone to be free."

Shek Yeung considered this. "I don't believe any god is so selfless, but I'm glad you do."

They chatted about Shek Yeung's upcoming journey with Choy Hin and Lam Yuk-Yiu's plans for a women-only vessel. At the end of the visit, Shek Yeung reached out to clasp hands as they usually did, but this time Wo-Yuet pulled her into a hug.

"What are you doing?" Shek Yeung said, suddenly deeply alarmed.

"I'm wishing you luck on your journey," Wo-Yuet said.

"No, you're not."

"You. Are. So. Difficult." Wo-Yuet punctuated each word with a light smack on the back of Shek Yeung's head. "Tell me. How did I put up with you for all those years?"

. . .

They set out two days later, fifty vessels strong to the seventy Choy Hin had brought along. In the distance they could see Choy Hin's junk, its blue sails puffed like the chests of tropical birds. Cheung Po was in particularly good spirits, reunited with his good friend. Striding the deck, he joked with the crew, challenged them to arm-wrestling matches, and bellowed the songs of his people.

Likewise, Yan-Yan seemed excited to be visiting a new place, having never ventured far from China before. She came to Shek Yeung with a brush and a ledger and demanded to know what she should buy in Taiwan. Shek Yeung recommended the local beadwork and then, remembering the girl's predilection for spending, recommended she save her money instead.

"Or"—Yan-Yan waggled her eyebrows—"you could buy the bead-work for me."

"Isn't that the northern woman's job?"

"She doesn't make as much as you do."

Shek Yeung huffed. "I pay you almost what I make myself."

"Therefore it's fine for me to spend some of it!" Yan-Yan said triumphantly.

The plan was to head northeast, hugging the shoreline before darting across the strait to Taiwan, where they would reportedly find the Dutch ship. Despite losing the territory to the Chinese long ago, some Dutchmen, finding the island far less regulated by the Manchu court than Canton was, had continued the trade of wool and lead for sugarcane. According to Lam Yuk-Yiu, the English, unsettled by the possibility of the Dutch retaking such a strategically and commercially viable piece of land, had begun making incursions there as well. A few of them were "privateers," which Shek Yeung learned meant government-sanctioned pirates (what a society those English must have had!).

One privateer she had met in passing, a portly middle-aged man with a chin that looked like it had lost a battle with the rest of the face and retreated into the neck, came from a well-to-do family but had no claim to the fortune because he was the second-born. In his youth he'd served on other privateer vessels, working his way up the ranks until he came into command of his own brig. The way these Englishmen saw it, the more of the Dutch that the pirates killed for them, the better.

Because of this shared antipathy of the Dutch, Choy Hin's fleet, as a general rule, didn't attack English ships. Lam Yuk-Yiu's partnership with the English was too profitable for both parties to risk damaging.

And how had Lam Yuk-Yiu developed such a close relationship with the English in the first place? Rumors abounded, none of which the woman ever confirmed or denied. There might have been an English lover, a bastard child who conveniently disappeared. A history of bad blood with the Dutch might have led Lam Yuk-Yiu to seek out the English for collaboration. The elders of Taiwan told of an attack on their ancestors by Dutch soldiers, who chased the locals into a cave, blocked up the entrance, and then filled the cave with sulfur smoke. After many days, they unblocked the entrance to find the corpses of three hundred people inside. Surviving villagers were sold off.

"There is no true difference between pirates and soldiers," Cheng Yat once told Shek Yeung. "They get their power from different places, but in the end, power is power."

Shek Yeung had been thinking a lot about Cheng Yat's words, and Wo-Yuet's. Was power a resource to be amassed in preparation for conflict, the way people amassed food in preparation for famine? Or was it the cause of conflict, creating a need for itself like the opium that Lam Yuk-Yiu smoked? Would her father and brother still be alive, or would they have been murdered anyway by those who wanted their power?

Just then, off in the distance, the quality of the light changed. Mist obscured the coast of Canton. The sky dimmed and the clouds became banded, as though Ma-Zou had combed her fingers through her hair, but no one else seemed to notice, not even Binh and Old Wong, who had a preternatural sense about these things. Shek Yeung was about to bring the change to Binh's attention when a red light shot from the sea.

Up it rose, a bright beam that seemed to bring with it the fragrance of agarwood: warm and sweet yet sharp, like a baby's first teeth grazing the breast. Up it rose into the clouds, squeezing between two of the bands as if through a crack between doors.

In that moment Shek Yeung knew, without really knowing, that Wo-Yuet was gone. She felt a sensation in her chest and throat, a breathlessness. It was like burning; it was unbearable. She wanted to weep the fire out of her eyes, to scream it out her mouth. And yet she also felt oddly empty, as if someone had left a window inside her open and the wind had blown away all the things she'd guarded there, leaving in their place only a chill.

This miserable world never deserved her friend. Wo-Yuet herself had apparently realized this near the end when she began praying to the Buddha about that realm free from hunger and violence.

"O-lei-to-fat," Shek Yeung chanted for her friend. She hoped Wo-Yuet would find her way to wherever it was she wanted to go.

10

The Portuguese named the island Formosa, their word for "beautiful," and Shek Yeung could hardly disagree. Taiwan appeared before her now after half a month at sea, its deep blue waters paling into turquoise closer to land, as if the waves were frightened by the reptilian spine of green that stretched the length of the island. A low fog herded across the mountains, licking at treetops as it went.

To think the emperor called this place "an insignificant ball of mud" and made no attempt to profit from it. How insignificant could it be, given the number of European powers that had fought over this island? In their efforts to take control of the spice trade in the region, the Dutch had successfully held it, or at least parts of it, for a while, to the consternation of the Spanish and Portuguese. Unlike the emperor, the European monarchs were always seeking to expand, by art or by violence. The emperor wanted China to stay the same forever, a realm onto itself like the Eight Immortals' home on Mount Fung-Loi.

"How much time do you think the Qing have left?" Cheng Yat had asked Shek Yeung once. The two of them had been on the main deck, gazing up at a night sky pricked by a thousand silver needles.

"What do you mean?"

"Everything ends," he said. "Before the Manchus, there were the Han, and before them, the Mongols. Who will seize power after the current dynasty falls?"

"Probably just another emperor. Someone always finds a way to put himself on that throne."

"You think? I think we're near the end. Look at these foreigners preparing. Look at how much faster their ships have become."

"What does it matter? It's not like the emperor cares for us any more than the Europeans would."

Cheng Yat drew her close and rubbed her arms vigorously. She didn't actually feel cold, and she disliked the sensation, but she didn't feel comfortable telling him. "I think the way the emperor doesn't care for us is different from the way Europeans don't care for us," he said.

"What?" She pulled back from him so she could study his expression. When he didn't protest, she pulled back a little more.

"Never mind, I just wanted to know your thoughts. The strangest notions preoccupy me sometimes. But you're right, it doesn't matter at all." Without saying another word, Cheng Yat had retired to their cabin, leaving her to wonder why he'd brought up the topic.

Taiwan was close enough now that the Blue Banner ships were dropping anchor, the crews rowing to shore. Shek Yeung could hardly wait to be back on land—a fortnight at sea was long even for someone who loved the sea as much as she did. A few of the smaller junks that needed repair were being hauled onto the sand. The plan was to rest for a few days before setting out again to intercept the Dutch. Lam Yuk-Yiu had a loyal base of supporters here because her family was from the area. These supporters provided her fleet with resources. In exchange, Lam Yuk-Yiu and Choy Hin protected them from the Europeans.

"What's the count?" she asked Ahmad when they reached land.

The boatswain scratched the scar on his shoulder, which had been pierced by the tip of a spear months back. When the wound began seeping, they'd all thought he was good as dead. He'd even dictated a letter to Cheng Yat and made him promise to deliver it to his family in Malacca. Now Cheng Yat was dead and Ahmad was alive and well. "Eleven need their bottoms cleaned and oiled," Ahmad said. "Five need significant repairs. We might not be able to salvage them before the Dutch come, if at all."

"The merchant ship will most likely have an armed convoy. We'll need all the ships we have." She thought about this. She knew what Cheng Yat would do here, and uncomfortable as it made her, it was the most practical decision. "Patch them up, not too well, just well enough so they'll run. Cheung Po and I will handle the rest."

A couple of years ago, the Blue Banner Fleet had claimed an old Dutch fort in this area. According to Lam Yuk-Yiu, the Dutch had built it after a rebellion by five thousand local peasants armed with farming implements. They killed four thousand with their muskets and condemned the remaining thousand to forced labor, labor that helped transform this tiny island into a trading hub for rice, deerskin, and sugarcane. Parts of the fort had already fallen down, but it served the Blue Banner Fleet's purposes, which were less about defense than about storage. Stacked from Batavian bricks mortared together with a mixture of sand, sugar, rice, and oystershell ash, it guarded the couple's cache of weapons and loot.

Lam Yuk-Yiu led Shek Yeung and Cheung Po across the dust-choked plaza where the Dutch had once hanged locals. They passed through the outer fort, its walls crumbling from banyan overgrowth, the foreign brick no match for the native species that had rooted itself deeply into the cracks to slowly grow in size and power. Along the walls, rusted European cannons still sat on their carriages with their noses turned up. Lam Yuk-Yiu then led them through the three layers of wall protecting the inner fort, which had contained the governor's and the holy men's quarters. Shek Yeung recognized the cross on the wall and wondered why Lam Yuk-Yiu hadn't melted down the golden ornament already—in fact, the room with the ornament was unexpectedly tidy, as though recently cleaned, with a foreign book lying open on a table.

Lam Yuk-Yiu slept in the luxurious Western-style bedroom that had belonged to the governor's wife. Or rather, once-luxurious. The smell of decaying fabric wriggled into Shek Yeung's nostrils, warm and faintly sour. She was struck by how dark the space was, dark even when compared with the bowels of a ship. After her eyes adjusted, she noticed the heavy curtains. Glowworms of bluish light crept from behind tattered folds.

Lam Yuk-Yiu drew aside the curtains. Because of the location of the room, the open curtains only slightly brightened their surroundings. Now Shek Yeung could see the massive four-poster bed at the center, crimson tapestries seeping from the canopy as if the wood were severely wounded. Dried white wax blistered a blackened, multipronged candle-holder. Above the pillows hung a painting that depicted a man wearing a sharp-looking headband and bleeding from the head. Shek Yeung thought it a weird subject for bedroom decor.

Somehow the room succeeded in being both somnolent and completely unconducive to rest. Lam Yuk-Yiu invited them to sit in elaborately carved chairs while she draped herself across the bed. "Isn't this wonderful?" she said. "The bed was already here, of course, but my boys brought those chairs you're sitting on from the other parts of the building. Europeans. They're good for some things."

"They're also good for information," Choy Hin said.

"Yes," Lam Yuk-Yiu said. "This will be tricky, but doable. The problem we must solve is the convoy."

From under the bed, she pulled out a nautical chart. "The Dutch will be coming near here after departing from here," she said, finger tracing the route. "The flagship will have a convoy. We won't know the strengths and weaknesses until we see them for ourselves, so we'll need to send out some smaller ships ahead of time."

"We have a few we can spare," Cheung Po said.

"We do, too," Lam Yuk-Yiu said. "No more than five or six, though, or they'll be suspicious."

"Why not disguise ourselves as the navy?" Shek Yeung asked. "That has worked well for us in the past. It requires fewer ships, and they'll be less likely to hassle us to avoid diplomatic trouble."

"They've grown wise to that. Now they look for the emperor's seal on the sails, and even then . . ." Lam Yuk-Yiu smiled sweetly at her husband. "We're too good at what we do. They're scared now, prepared. One of these days we'll be our own downfall."

"If our scouts confirm that the flagship can be seized," Cheung Po said, "then what?"

"I've been thinking about that, actually," Shek Yeung said. She told them about the junks that she'd ordered Ahmad to partially repair.

"You want to sacrifice those junks and the people on them?" Cheung Po said. "You don't even like to throw away rotten food because you think it's wasteful."

True, she disliked waste. There were only two kinds of people: those who did not have enough and those who had too much. The latter, lacking in morals, threw away things the former would have hoarded as treasure. She always swore to herself she wouldn't take her possessions for granted even if she came to have too much. But then she'd met Cheng Yat, who'd made a different case, namely, that what appeared to be waste was often in fact investment. Even discarding an old pair of boots could be an investment if wearing a new pair increased the odds of a business agreement. He'd been so good at twisting her thoughts around. Sometimes, by the end of an argument, she could barely remember why she'd started arguing.

"Sometimes one must lose to gain," she said, quoting Cheng Yat. "Those junks have very little time left anyway. It would cost us more to repair them than to burn them. As for the people, a skeleton crew will be enough. We can use the men who are already ill, who have not been doing their work properly, or who have been suspected of inciting mutiny. If they survive, well, then they survive by Heaven's will. They can even leave the fleet if they want. We can't force them to stay when Heaven clearly favors them."

Lam Yuk-Yiu nodded. "Clever."

From where he was sitting, Choy Hin leaned close to Cheung Po and slipped an arm around his waist. Instead of pulling away, Cheung Po bent his head so that it was almost touching the other man's. "I'm so glad you decided to join us. This'll be like old times," Choy Hin said in a way that had the feel of a whisper but wasn't quiet enough to be, the kind of talk lovers might share lying in bed. The exact nature of Cheung Po's past with Choy Hin became clear to her. No wonder he'd gotten so mad when Kwok Po-Tai insulted Choy Hin.

Preparations began immediately. Against the sides of the ships, the agile crew members attached fishing nets and ox hides. The dexterous ones carved bamboo receptacles and pikes or bound hay stalks together. The strong ones sharpened swords, cleaned cannons. Old Wong and Binh discussed routes and steering. Yan-Yan and Ahmad took stock of their supplies to make sure there would be enough for the battle.

The reconnaissance ships went out, disguised as traders. Lam Yuk-Yiu ordered the company to maneuver close but not too close to the Dutch. They returned with good news: the flagship could be taken, if everything went according to plan. If not, then they would strategize on the spot as they had done a hundred times before.

After some debate, Cheung Po and Shek Yeung decided that she should be the one to inform those chosen to crew the damaged junks. There was no point in trying to deceive them regarding their chances of staying alive. Some of these men she knew personally. She and Cheng Yat had conscripted them when they couldn't pay their own ransom.

By and large, conscripts successfully adapted to life in the fleet, particularly if they'd been seafarers beforehand. In some ways, they were safer in the fleet than out of it—the alliance protected them from other pirates, and the generally larger and better-cared-for ships meant easier passage across turbulent waters—to the extent that a few of them even brought their families on board. But some struggled with the violence required of them. Battles didn't occur as often as an outsider might have guessed—most targets surrendered upon realizing that they were outnumbered—but when they did, every crew member was expected to fight. Those who were skilled with blades engaged in close combat. Those who weren't maneuvered the cannons or launched thunderbolt balls or fire hawks. There was no place for clean hands in their world.

Shek Yeung neither enjoyed killing nor felt a compunction against it. Cheng Yat had explained it like this: Man killed animals for food. How was it so different for man to kill man, who often behaved more savagely than animals, for the sake of food? If only one bag of rice were left for two men, one a good husband and father, the other a rapist, did the family man not have a right to kill the rapist? ("Now replace the rapist with a Qing official who subjugates us, or a traitor who allies himself with that official.") She certainly didn't feel a compunction against killing in defense of oneself or one's family. In fact she'd spent many years on the flower boats wishing that she'd slit the throat of the pirate who murdered her brother and raped her.

Of course she understood things were rarely so simple. A Qing official could subjugate legions but be kind to his own family. Occasionally she'd killed someone and then, in the moment of death, saw in his face the face of her brother or father, not even their features necessarily but just something in the expression like her father's solemnity or her brother's unrepentant mischievousness. And she'd wanted to cry, but the tears never came.

As for unprovoked killing, that she had to learn to do. Her first time had been at Cheng Yat's command. One day, about a month after she'd joined the fleet, he called her onto the deck. A man knelt crying, surrounded by men she knew to be very loyal to Cheng Yat. One of them proffered his cutlass with both palms up to Cheng Yat, who accepted it with equal courtesy but then immediately tossed it to Shek Yeung. "Cut off his head," he said.

"What did he do?" Shek Yeung asked.

"I know what he did."

"What if I refuse?"

He smiled. "Then both you and I will know what you did."

The afternoon after the meeting with Choy Hin and Lam Yuk-Yiu, Shek Yeung gathered the crew for the damaged junks, watched their faces pale as she explained their duties. One of the men, unable to control himself, jumped to his feet. "You scoundrels!" he yelled. "It wasn't enough that you took me against my will but now you'll have me die for your crimes? I won't do it!" He hurled himself at her.

She drew her cutlass and deftly sliced his stomach open. Then she signaled for someone to drag him out of sight. He'd been on the brink of mutiny for months anyway, and just now he'd charged her with the intent to kill. Surely.

There was no other choice. Cheng Yat would have agreed. Junks didn't sail themselves, and these men, the ones who were already ill notwithstanding, posed a risk to herself and every other crew member.

The ones who were mutinous were dangerous for obvious reasons, but even the shirkers were dangerous in their own way because they could not be counted on to support their comrades in battle.

"No doubt you are frightened and angry, but I encourage all of you to think clearly," she said to the others. "As I have just demonstrated, the punishment for insubordination is death. What I'm asking of you is difficult but not impossible. So fight harder than you've ever fought in your life, and if Heaven wills it, you might survive to begin anew elsewhere, a free man."

She dismissed all of them except Old Tam, who had joined around the same time as she and had performed admirably on all his tasks until he developed a terrible heat disease a few months ago. A good man, with a slow-witted brother who depended on him. "I am unhappy to require this of you," she said, patting him on the shoulder, "but no one who has developed your symptoms has lived. You know this."

He laughed bitterly. "Better quickly than slowly, I suppose."

"I will be sure to send some rice to your brother. Your fighting skills are no longer what they were, so it's best that you help aim and reload the ship's guns. Do you think you can still maneuver a twelve? Or should I give you a nine?"

"I can."

"A twelve, then." She leaned closer. "These junks will be equipped with their usual boats. When it becomes clear that the fight is lost, and it almost certainly will be lost, you may wish to remember what I just told you."

They clasped hands. "May Ma-Zou smile upon you," she said.

After sunset, they weighed anchor and stood toward the Dutch, advancing northwest. Shek Yeung paced the deck, aspersing her crew with garlic water for spiritual protection. Around their heads they wound the black fabric they wore in battle. The evening breeze and sea spray masked their faces as though with tears.

The Dutch ships were large and laden with cannons, which increased their defensive power but decreased their speed. At some point, European black powder had become superior to Chinese powder, and the Europeans knew this, often relying on cannonades to subdue attackers.

One of their men-of-war had up to twice as many large guns as one of Shek Yeung's.

Generally speaking, compared with European ships, junks were less powerful, which was not necessarily to say that they were at a disadvantage. Junks were versatile and thus had been adapted for many purposes over the centuries. There were massive war junks made from Ceylon ironwood—a tree known for its sturdiness—and small, scull-powered junks used primarily for reconnaissance. There were "sand" junks with flat bottoms and shallow drafts for sailing on rivers and running aground, "good fortune" junks with single pointed keels for speed, and "wave opener" junks with sharp bows that cleaved rough waters apart. Then there were the junks built with high railings to prevent others from boarding, and the junks built with no railings to facilitate boarding of others. The Red Banner Fleet had a number of each, and when they all sailed together, it was an unforgettable sight, as if all the manifold creatures of the sea were rising from the depths to rage against Heaven. The red sails set the sky aflame, turned day to dusk.

Shek Yeung's ship was a little bit like her, or so she liked to think: primarily wind-powered but scullable (adaptable), with a semiflat bottom (fast but not so fast as to be unstable) and railings of medium height (operating from a defensive stance unless provoked or driven to necessity by an enemy).

Taking advantage of the fog, the sacrificial junks crept closer to the Dutch, pretending to be traders anchoring for the night.

The Dutch didn't react. Shek Yeung exhaled in relief.

Instead of dropping anchor, the junks quickly slipped between the flagship and the convoy. At Shek Yeung's signal, the Red and Blue Banner Fleets opened fire at the convoy from a distance of about three lei.

The cannonade accomplished very little except to distract, but this was expected. "Reload and fire!" Ahmad ordered the people manning the large guns, which slipped and slid in their makeshift rope carriages. The gunners did their best, but they could go only so fast with the equipment they had.

Now that they had the Dutch's attention, two things happened simultaneously. First, the sacrificial junks engaged the Dutch in combat.

Their crew lobbed over thunderbolt balls, black-powder-covered bamboo receptacles that exploded to spray the iron scraps inside. The balls set fire to the sails. Some of the Dutch sailors rushed to the fires, the others to the guns. They volleyed cannonballs back. She heard wood crunching. The Dutch attempted to board, but this was largely prevented by the ox hides the crew had installed. Still, the cannonballs were doing their jobs well enough. The hulls of the junks began to take on water.

The other thing that happened was that the remaining junks in the fleet converged upon the flagship and began drawing it away from the convoy. The flagship was also well armed, but with the convoy preoccupied with the sacrificial junks, Shek Yeung and her crew had numbers on their side. They hurled fire hawk pikes that spread their hay wings to release thick smoke and stones that bit like hungry ticks.

Disoriented, the people on the flagship barely noticed the additional junks rapidly standing toward them, hardly had time to react when the pirates began to board. And so all 150 men and women on Shek Yeung's junk, plus the thousands of others with the Red and Blue Banner Fleets, entered the fray.

11

She'd learned to fight from Cheung Po seven years ago, shortly after she joined. Cheng Yat would have seen to it himself, but he was too busy commanding the fleet. At the time Cheung Po had been no more than eighteen, impatient and with little sense of strategy. Yet he was already one of the strongest fighters. He'd encouraged her to learn the spear. It was, after all, more practical than the cutlass: the motions were more intuitive, and it doubled as a staff. But Shek Yeung had insisted on the cutlass. It seemed a smarter option given the close quarters on some ships. More importantly, the cutlass was Ma-Zou's weapon.

She must have cut herself at least twenty times in training. The first few times Cheung Po had shown concern, but then he grew exasperated and would yell while dressing her wounds, "Why are you so bad at this? Learn the spear! There's only one sharp part, and you just have to keep it pointed away from you. You know that if you die, Big Brother Cheng is going to kill me, right?"

After several months, she developed enough proficiency that Cheng Yat bequeathed her the cutlass his cousin had wielded. A beautiful weapon it was, too, with an oxhorn grip, a silver-studded handguard, and a curved blade tapering down to a tip fine enough to pin a fly between its wings. Several months after that, she acquired from the Blue Banner Fleet her small flintlock pistol, a piece from England with gold inlay on the grip in the shape of a rose. Sometimes she wondered if she should learn to fight with anything else, just in case. After all, there were as many different types of weapons in use among her crew as there were nations from which the crew hailed. Most of them fought with the single-edged cutlass or the double-edged straight sword, but a careful look also revealed axes, repeating crossbows that fired up to three arrows at once, and maces (or as some of her men called them, "hard whips"). Then there were the tiger-head hook swords, which were used in pairs by only the most accomplished fighters, with so many edges and points that one might as well put out one's own eye for efficiency's sake rather than try to use it in battle without proper training.

As her eyesight and speed deteriorated with age, Cheung Po had asked her if she wanted to learn to fight with a more forgiving weapon. Each time she'd pushed the question aside—she was far too busy managing the fleet. But at times like these, with nerves running high before a battle, she wanted to kick herself for not having listened to him.

After a signal from Cheung Po, the Red and Blue Banner Fleets thronged the Dutch ship. These days Cheung Po fought with two short Malayan swords, which he kept lashed under one arm—the exaggerated curve of the blade, reminiscent of a humpback, greatly increased slashing power. He sprinted toward a musketeer and then quickly dropped into a roll to avoid the musket fire. In the instant it took for him to get back on his feet, he had both swords unsheathed. One he swung from above at the man's head, and when that blow was parried by the gun barrel, he swung the other from below, taking the man out at the knees. Meanwhile Choy Hin and Lam Yuk-Yiu appeared over the starboard side. Lam Yuk-Yiu immediately scaled the mainmast to the crow's nest, rifle slung over her shoulders.

There wasn't much of a fight. A few of the Dutch chose bravery, a problem for which Lam Yuk-Yiu had an efficient solution, but the rest, seeing that they were outnumbered and that the convoy was occupied far away with other junks, surrendered. Choy Hin took command of the vessel, and crew and cargo secured, he bore up and headed back down the coast.

Shek Yeung and Cheung Po returned to their junk, ready to follow. By now, the sacrificial junks were undoubtedly at the bottom of the sea and the convoy hunting the O Yam. It would be foolish for the two of them to wait around for survivors.

About halfway back to the fort, they spotted a few junks in the distance.

"Whose are those?" she asked Ahmad. He scaled the mainmast, and when he came back down, he answered, "The emperor's. Maybe war junks, the way they're riding low in the water."

"Too few for war, though," she said.

Cheung Po, who had been abnormally quiet, said, "They're probably just doing reconnaissance or practicing maneuvers. I've seen this before."

"Threat?" Shek Yeung asked Cheung Po.

"Not too high. If we've sighted them, then they've definitely sighted us. The fact that they're not engaging means they probably won't."

"Good." She wanted to return to the island as soon as possible to repair and restock. If the imperial ships intended to feign blindness to see another day, then she would, too.

She left to help wounded crew members belowdecks. Halfway down the stairs, she felt the junk turn. She looked out a porthole. They were standing straight toward the war junks.

"What is happening?" she shouted, tripping up the steps. There, at the helm next to Binh, stood Cheung Po. Seeing her, Binh immediately said, "He told me to approach."

Cheung Po's body was taut with unspent energy. He'd expected a bigger fight against the Dutch but didn't get it, and now he was risking their lives for a second chance. She fisted his collar; he shook her off easily. "We don't have enough round shots left," she said.

"We do," he said. "I checked."

"No, we don't. And Choy Hin's ships are already too far ahead of us to help."

"We still have almost all our ships. More than enough."

"Have you gone mad? Those are war junks."

"*One* war junk. Plus a few other vessels. If we can't subdue them with our forty-five, we don't deserve to fly Cheng Yat's red banner."

"If we go down, there'll be no banner left to fly."

Seeing their approach, the imperial ships opened fire. Unlike them, the navy possessed large-caliber guns and good carriages. Most of the round shots missed, Chinese black powder still being what it was, but a couple punched through their hull and the hulls of the junks next to them. The O Yam shook.

"Keep going," Cheung Po ordered Binh. "Junks were designed to take a few hits. We just need to board."

"Turn around," she ordered Binh. "They're weighed down by their guns. We might be able to outrun them if we leave now."

Binh looked completely at a loss, his knuckles pale from gripping the wheel. A small crowd had gathered around the three of them, drawn by the sound of argument. Shek Yeung realized that if she and Cheung Po kept arguing, everyone would soon learn about their infighting.

"Ready the cannons and fire hawks!" she shouted. Off to her right, a few of their smaller junks were sinking, the men and women on them abandoning ship and rowing over to the other vessels in the fleet.

At last, they came within boarding distance. They climbed over, and Cheung Po got his fight.

He rushed into the melee, both swords unsheathed. Shek Yeung followed, swinging her cutlass. The emperor's men retaliated ferociously, slashing and skewering. If a soldier's weapon broke or became lost to the sea, he picked up the weapon of a fallen compatriot and continued to fight. A thin dagger stung her forearm, and she saw the injury before she felt it, the bubble of blood expanding and then bursting. She pulled off her headcovering and wound it around her arm.

Unlike the Europeans, who could surrender and who had people willing to pay their ransom, these men knew that the punishment for refusing to fight was death. They struggled the way desperate men struggle, the way Shek Yeung and her crew did. Death wrought its spell two by two, with each man taking the life of his adversary before quickly having his own life taken in turn.

Only about a third of the imperial sailors remained before the captain finally surrendered. He emerged from one of the cabins, a rotund man with pale, unspotted skin, his armored vest still perfectly clean and orderly. He didn't look like he was accustomed to life at sea, yet here he was in this position of power. The only explanation was that he had come from a family of some influence and been appointed captain as a favor from the emperor. "I am Qiu Liang-Gong," he said to Cheung Po in the northern dialect. "Let the rest of my men live."

"What if I don't?" Cheung Po said.

"You've already won," Qiu Liang-Gong said. "You gain nothing from killing them."

"I gain a reputation as the fiercest pirate in China."

"What about ransom?"

"The emperor doesn't pay ransom. Everyone knows this," Shek Yeung said.

"I can persuade him," he said to Cheung Po.

"You're wasting our time," Shek Yeung said.

"These are the emperor's newest ships," he said to Cheung Po, "and his best men. He will accept your terms."

"He says he can persuade the emperor to pay," Cheung Po said to Shek Yeung, laughing. "And funny, he doesn't appear to be able to see you because he keeps talking only to me!"

Shek Yeung huffed. "You now have a choice," she announced to the captives. "Join us and live, or die. So long as you do what we tell you, you will have food to eat and plunder to keep. You may even see your families again."

She strode back up to Qiu Liang-Gong, grabbed his chin, and pulled his face down to hers so there was no question to whom he was speaking. "As for you, rich man," she said, "you we can ransom."

Most of the sailors defected. Those who refused to swear allegiance to the red banner were thrown overboard. Placing the war junk in Ahmad's charge, Shek Yeung returned to the O Yam and ordered Binh to set a course to the fort.

As Shek Yeung sat in her cabin, cleaning her wound, Cheung Po entered. She ignored him.

He squatted next to the pail of water and reached for the piece of cloth on her lap. She slapped his hand away.

"You looked like you needed help," he said.

"I don't."

He stayed squatting, elbows braced against the insides of his knees, head propped up by the heels of his palms, just looking at her. She tried to knot the bandage with one hand but dropped an end and had to start over.

"You sure you don't need help? I can jump in," he said.

"No one asked you to. But then, you like doing things that no one asked for."

"We won."

She threw the bloody bandage in his face. "We were unprepared. We almost ran out of round shots."

"But we didn't," he said, looming over her now. She pushed away the sudden fear she felt, even though Cheung Po had never hit her. "Because I counted beforehand. I know you think I'm still a stupid kid, but I spent years learning strategy from Cheng Yat, too. I knew we could win the battle, and we needed those ships to replace the ones you sacrificed today."

"Are you forgetting about the ones *you* lost picking a fight with the navy?"

"We lost a couple of old boats and gained a war junk. With proper gun carriages and everything. Cheng Yat would have made the same decision."

"He would never have—"

"I was his second-in-command before you joined. He always trusted me to make decisions for the fleet. You act like I don't even know how to wipe my own ass."

"Just because he sometimes left you in charge doesn't mean that you can't make mistakes. And why do you keep bringing Cheng Yat up? What does he have to do with anything? I'm saying you showed bad judgment—you, today. Not just today. The other day at the parley with Kwok Po-Tai, too. All this impulsivity is weird, even for you."

"It has everything to do with Cheng Yat," Cheung Po said. He was pacing the cabin now.

"How?"

"It just does. He left the fleet to me. He chose me over all the other boys he took, over even someone as slippery and two-faced as Kwok

Po-Tai. Do you know how many of them died immediately in battle because they couldn't hold their own in a fight? Or got executed by Cheng Yat because they wouldn't do the things he required? I'm commander now because I deserve it. I did everything he told me to, even when I didn't want to, even when it hurt . . ."

"He wouldn't have left you the fleet if he didn't trust you," she agreed, feeling like she was missing something, or like there was something more she was supposed to say. "I know that."

She left the cabin in search of clean bandages, but also so that she wouldn't have to be alone with him. She was finding herself doing this more and more. She often felt discomfited by him, by his slightly too persistent gaze. After they were finished apportioning the loot with the Blue Banner Fleet, she planned to take half the ships and return to Canton alone. Cheung Po could stay behind and renew his friendship with Choy Hin. The fleet was used to operating in separate squadrons. It would be a good opportunity for the two of them to see how they functioned together, apart.

12

In one of the stories about Ma-Zou, she was ruthless and unforgiving. In the 256th year of the Ming dynasty, a young couple gave birth to a boy. The boy's father, Cheng Chi-Lung, was a powerful pirate descended from a pirating family with whom you are already familiar. His mother, Tagawa Matsu, was descended from the goddess herself. The couple was gathering shells on a beach when suddenly the clouds blackened and swirled. Cold rain pricked them until they felt as porous as sponges, as though they might float if set upon the sea. The waves and winds grew so strong that they washed a whale ashore. Seeing this massive, dying beast, the young mother swooned onto the sand. And so Koxinga, Lord of the Imperial Name, was born, though he wouldn't go by that title until he had won many battles and named himself thus with the kind of bravado indigenous to so many young men.

Koxinga was in his twenties when Peking fell to the Qing. The Manchus defeated his father and besieged the town in which his mother was living. Instead of surrendering, the proud woman killed herself by running a blade through her own neck. Full of rage and grief, Koxinga called on Ma-Zou to wreak vengeance on the Qing. He went on to kill many of them, and though the Qing eventually prevailed, Koxinga and his men were able to escape across the strait to Taiwan.

In Taiwan, on a day very much like the one on which he was born, Koxinga received a vision at the seaside: a red light appeared under the waves, shining brighter and brighter until the sea in its entirety seemed to burn red. From it arose a beautiful woman. Her beauty was not the kind that men sought to possess or, failing that, to defile. Rather, it was a majestic beauty that made them realize their own smallness and wretchedness, as storms at sea did to the commanders of even the largest and sturdiest vessels. Koxinga knew immediately that she was his maternal ancestor, a fragment of whose glory lay within himself.

The goddess spoke. Her voice was like an outflowing tide combing through pebbly sand. She ordered Koxinga to drive the redheaded barbarians from the island so that he might ready his forces there and, in time, retake China.

Koxinga banded together Ming loyalists, native Taiwanese, and two companies of formerly enslaved African men who had learned the use of muskets. They laid siege to the Dutch fort and captured it despite being outgunned. The men they decapitated, stacking the heads like round shots. The women and children they sold. They believed their unlikely success meant that the goddess was on their side, that she would forgive all they had done and would do in the interest of retribution against the Qing. What they could not foresee was that, in only a few decades, the Qing would make landfall on Taiwan and secure a decisive victory. Men who survived the battle reported seeing a woman fighting on the Qing's side, each swing of her cutlass as powerful as a squall. She'd been wearing red armor, or perhaps it had been ordinary armor covered in blood.

For the sea is fickle, and Ma-Zou owed no mortal her loyalty, not even if they were descended from her.

13

They moved the hostages to the part of the fort that had been used to imprison locals. Though many years had passed since the Europeans last used it, the cell still reeked of excrement and something metallic, probably blood, judging by the hook and pulley in the corner. The stone walls looked like misaligned, rotted teeth, mold stuck in the cracks like bits of food. Into this room they crammed the Dutch officers—Lam Yuk-Yiu had decided to lighten the load by tossing the rest of the company overboard—and Qiu Liang-Gong. The hostages received some dirty water and gritty rice that they would have to split up among themselves for the next few days. Meanwhile messengers were being sent out with ransom demands: ten thousand for the Europeans, twelve thousand for Qiu Liang-Gong.

"Why are you asking so much for just one man?" Lam Yuk-Yiu asked Shek Yeung.

"He made me angry," Shek Yeung said. "Let's just say I don't particularly care if the emperor pays the ransom."

The only nonofficer Lam Yuk-Yiu had kept alive was a youngish man. (Was he twenty? Thirty? Shek Yeung never could tell with Europeans.) For her collection, Shek Yeung assumed. Red-haired and freckled, he was now in the care of her head cabin boy, whom Lam Yuk-Yiu had kidnapped from Ceylon.

Shek Yeung supposed she could see the appeal, if she concentrated: there was a delicate symmetry to the foreigner's features that reminded her of a paper cutting. Or maybe he wasn't actually attractive and Lam Yuk-Yiu just wanted him for novelty's sake. Life on the flower boats had made Shek Yeung leery of novelty. She could control the customers she understood.

Thinking over her conversation with Lam Yuk-Yiu, Shek Yeung went down to the dungeon. She beckoned Qiu Liang-Gong to approach the iron bars. The man looked tired and ill but still carried himself haughtily, unwilling to show weakness to either his captors or to the Europeans in the cell with him. This made her like him slightly more.

"I'll be demanding twelve thousand," she said to him, wanting to see his reaction. "Are you still confident in your relationship with the emperor?"

He didn't respond, but she could read the doubt in his eyes. "I thought not," she said.

But when she turned to walk away, he asked, "How did you come to this life?"

"How did you?"

"My father served the Qianlong Emperor. I wanted to continue his work."

"How sad for you," she said. "A caged bird doesn't know the breadth of the sky."

"You think you know the breadth of the sky just because you serve no master? Your master is your arrogance, and one day he will abandon you."

Shek Yeung laughed. "You think you can go without food until the messenger returns from negotiations?"

"It hardly matters at this point, does it?" he said. He smoothed his tunic; he was the kind of man who insisted on his own dignity even as he rotted in a dungeon. "I say this for your own benefit because you are a woman, and no woman ends up in a life of crime without having been compelled in some way—it is not in your nature. The emperor has only grown more committed to eradicating piracy in recent years. He wishes to restore China to its former glory, and eventually he will succeed."

She felt surprised by her own sudden fury, given that what he'd said had been more or less true, at least in her case. That he presumed to know her nature, to know the nature of all women, was the true insult. How dare he assume she could have only ended up here by being a man's puppet? No wonder he'd refused to acknowledge her after the battle. As far as he was concerned, Cheung Po was the true commander of the fleet, and she his hapless whore.

So she turned her scorn on the emperor he loved. "And how will he succeed? By hiding in his palace? By ignoring the needs of his people? Or will he succeed by keeping a screen between China and the rest of the world, because if his people don't know what's going on elsewhere, then they'll be less likely to revolt?"

"He is on the throne by the Mandate of Heaven," Qiu Liang-Gong said.

"Heaven lies all the time," Shek Yeung said. When she realized she had quoted Wo-Yuet, she added, "In any case, emperors have lost the Mandate before. Who's to say it won't happen to yours?"

He didn't answer. She smirked and walked away.

Sitting in the plaza later, watching her crew bustle about repairing the damage from recent battles, Shek Yeung wondered if women in fact turned to lives of crime only out of desperation. Were they, as Qiu Liang-Gong suggested, gentler by nature? Did the presence of a womb mean that they were fated to swoon at the sight of blood, as if blood weren't the very vehicle that women used to convey life, the red-inked seal they stamped upon the foreheads of their children to send them into the world?

But then how would one explain Yan-Yan's enthusiasm when she was asked to join the fleet, or the fact that, the first time Shek Yeung killed a man in battle, she'd felt neither guilt nor sorrow but a kind of heat in her face that quickly descended into her limbs, along with the sense that she could keep doing this, that she had the right to keep doing this. (It was how power felt, she came to understand.) How, as a child, she'd once watched, rapt, as a cat knocked a terrified mouse about before tearing into it with fangs and claws. Maybe there was an essential violence in women, too, this thing that pricked at them from the inside like a needle a seamstress had forgotten to remove from a beautiful embroidered robe.

"You were meant for this," Cheng Yat had said after her first battle. By Ma-Zou, how she'd preened.

She saw Cheung Po approaching from a distance. Before she could sneak away, he called her name.

"Twelve thousand?" he said, throwing his hands in the air. "Choy Hin told me."

"He says he's close to the emperor," Shek Yeung said.

"You just want him to die," Cheung Po said.

"What do you care? Have you taken a liking to him?"

"I care about getting money!"

Shek Yeung sighed. She did want Qiu Liang-Gong to die for the way he'd slighted her. He'd treated her as invisible, just as the customers of the flower boats had. It was by no means an offense that merited death, she knew this, but she couldn't stop feeling so wrathful. "Fine, how much?"

"Six thousand," he said.

"We'll see what Peking says. If they show interest in negotiating instead of outright turning us down, then we negotiate, with six thousand as our base."

He nodded. Seeing him relax, she decided to broach the topic of splitting the fleet. "It might be a good idea for you to take half the ships and operate around here for a while after we've gotten our ransom. The Europeans have been very active in this area. Choy Hin will enjoy having you close again. You can find some time to just be alone with each other. I can go back to Canton, manage things there."

The ensuing silence pushed her to add, "Only for as long as you want," which she immediately regretted. She was undermining herself.

Finally, Cheung Po spoke up. "Cheng Yat died not even two months ago. Is it a good idea for us to be apart when many of our men are still feeling uneasy about the transition?

He had a good point, but she barreled ahead anyway. "Their morale is strong, and whatever doubts they have about our leadership will be put to rest when they receive their share of the ransom and the weapons. It'll be fine."

"I'll think about it," he said.

Fortunately, he didn't come to her bed that night—she was too busy doubting her own decisions. She'd known full well she shouldn't place feelings above profit by ransoming Qiu Liang-Gong for that much money. Nevertheless, she'd succumbed to spite. As for the decision to split up the fleet so soon after a major transition, she still couldn't tell if she was taking a smart risk.

Cheng Yat had been a good leader, which was not to say he never made bad decisions, or selfish ones. He'd cut Kwok Po-Tai loose because of his own infatuation with Cheung Po instead of, as Shek Yeung would have done, giving the man a squadron of ships to keep him close and therefore under control. Yet he never seemed to question himself. Everyone around him had told him since he was a child that the sea was his birthright, that he would be a good leader because of the Cheng blood. Though in his defense, he'd been aware of the flaw in that line of reasoning. After all, he'd left the fleet to Cheung Po, not to his own sons.

She lay back onto the overstuffed bed in her room in the fort, her back protesting each lump. She was now almost the age Cheng Yat had been when they'd met. There were days after battles when her limbs felt like ribbons loosely tied to the rest of her. Injuries took at least twice as long to heal as in the past. Perhaps she should have listened to Wo-Yuet and left the fleet to Cheung Po, who still had the vigor of someone in his twenties, but she just didn't fully trust him to lead. The incident with the war junks had only confirmed her worries.

Sleep did not come. She decided to take a stroll and found herself down by the docks. A handful of people on the O Yam were still awake, including Yan-Yan (speaking of youthful vigor), who was keeping the northern woman company during guard duty. She pulled the girl aside and told her about her desire to temporarily split up the fleet. "How would it affect us financially?" she asked. "You know the numbers much better than I do."

Yan-Yan fished some papers out of a trunk, flipped around until she found what she was looking for, and spread them out in front of Shek Yeung. "It balances out," she said. "If Big Brother Cheung stays here, he'll have access to goods we don't typically get back home, but he'll also have to share the profit with his friend."

"So you think it's a good idea."

"I don't think it's a *bad* idea." Yan-Yan looked a little uncomfortable. "You seem to want him out of the way."

"Look, Cheng Yat and I trusted each other to function independently. Before he died we often split the fleet, as you know. Cheung Po is different. I don't know how to explain this, but he wants to do everything together. Or rather it's more like he wants me there so I can see him do things."

Now the girl looked almost amused. "And you're telling me you really don't know why he's like this?"

Well, she had an inkling. She'd wondered if Cheung Po might have feelings for her beyond physical attraction but pushed the thought aside. She knew how to traffic in lust. Genuine feelings made people unpredictable, sometimes downright unreasonable. Even Cheng Yat's feelings for her had arisen from a place of strategy—he'd treated her as his co-commander first and as his lover second.

"How are you liking Taiwan?" Shek Yeung asked, eager to change the topic.

Yan-Yan chewed her lip. "I like it fine. It's different. Dawa likes it more than I do."

"If it's different for you, it's definitely different for her. It's all horses and grass where her people come from."

"She talks about leaving the fleet sometimes. I don't know if she wants to go back home or move somewhere like here. She doesn't like Canton, though." Yan-Yan paused. "Ah, but don't worry, I'm never leaving! You would never make it without me! You would just, you would just . . ." She pressed the back of her hand to her forehead and pretended like she was about to faint.

"I did all right before you joined!" Shek Yeung said, trying not to laugh. But Yan-Yan just continued with her noblewoman impression until Shek Yeung's chest hurt from the effort of holding her laughter in.

They chatted until Shek Yeung was yawning uncontrollably. She thanked Yan-Yan and returned to the fort, but before she could fall asleep she recalled the earliest part of their conversation. In an instant her lethargy was gone. If Cheung Po indeed had feelings, then it was best if they separated for the time being. It would give her time to devise a plan for dealing with him and him time to cool his heart.

. . .

The next morning Shek Yeung was awoken by one of Lam Yuk-Yiu's boys timidly knocking on her door.

"The Matron requests your help," he said.

Shek Yeung found Lam Yuk-Yiu in the dungeon, shouting in what sounded like English at one of the Dutchmen, who dangled from the hook in the ceiling. He had bleeding welts on his bare back. Lam Yuk-Yiu's whip was tucked into her sash and trailed on the ground behind her like a line of thought she'd lost interest in. The Dutch officer's eyes and cheeks were so swollen he had the appearance of a split, overripe fruit. Shek Yeung remembered the girl who'd been physically dragged back to the flower boats. Torture was the primitive's tool, even Cheng Yat had agreed. One got better information through manipulation.

"Help me," Lam Yuk-Yiu said. "This bastard is being very stingy with information."

The other prisoners kept their faces turned away. A couple had tears rolling down their cheeks.

Shek Yeung pulled Lam Yuk-Yiu aside. "This won't work," she said.

"It will as soon as you and I think of something more painful than the whip," Lam Yuk-Yiu said. "Too bad I can't use a sword. The Dutch are very insistent that we return their people to them in one piece."

"A sword isn't the answer either. You're doing this in front of all his men."

"To encourage them to speak, or the same will happen to them."

"Men look to one another for courage in situations like this. They're strengthening one another's resolve."

"What do you recommend?"

Shek Yeung thought about it. "Put him in a nicer room, alone. Keep him restrained but not too restrained, just enough that he can't escape. Let me speak with him. And let me use one of your boys, someone who can speak English or Dutch. Dress the boy up first. And also prepare a basin of water for me with a rag."

A short while later, Lam Yuk-Yiu's head cabin boy, who introduced himself as Buddhika, showed up at Shek Yeung's room to guide her to the Dutch prisoner. He was wearing a sumptuous blue robe, the fabric just a little too snug across his muscled shoulders, the high shiny collar emphasizing his cheekbones.

"You speak English? Dutch?" Shek Yeung asked.

"I speak Sinhala, Tamil, Dutch, Cantonese, Hokkien, and a little bit of Portuguese," the boy said proudly.

"How do you know so many languages?"

"My family spoke Sinhala, but some of my friends spoke Tamil. The Portuguese controlled my island before the Dutch took over. Cantonese and Hokkien I learned from the Matron and the other boys. Actually, I forgot to mention, the Matron has taught me some English, too."

"Impressive," Shek Yeung said. It hadn't occurred to her that Lam Yuk-Yiu used her boys for nonsexual purposes. In her own fleet, finding an interpreter was a haphazard process. Usually she just hollered at the top of her lungs whether anyone spoke such-and-such.

Buddhika led her to one of the interior rooms, where the Dutch prisoner sat chained to a heavy table. Shek Yeung picked up the basin of water that had been left for her and pulled up a chair.

He shrank at the sight of her. "Tell him I won't hurt him," she said to Buddhika.

Buddhika rattled off something. The Dutch man glared at her.

She soaked the rag in the basin and lifted it to his face. Very gently, she dabbed at it, wiping away the crusted blood. He flinched but stayed still when he realized she wasn't going to be rough.

"I'm sorry this happened," she said to him. Buddhika immediately translated the sentence. "Lam Yuk-Yiu's ancestors were savaged by your people. She doesn't think clearly when it comes to the Dutch."

The man muttered something. Buddhika said, "How is what happened hundreds of years ago any fault of mine?"

"It's not. But all of us pay for others' crimes all the time. Did you know, I wanted none of this life? My father was a simple fisherman. Then we were captured by pirates, and, well," she said, sighing deeply, "I can't return to my old life now even if I wanted. Can't raise a family like I always hoped. The emperor would have me beheaded, even though I didn't choose any of this."

"There are many women in the fleet," the Dutch man said via Buddhika.

"And most of us are not here by choice. As you know, women are kinder by nature," she said, parroting Qiu Liang-Gong.

The Dutchman nodded.

"Do you have any children?" she asked him. He didn't answer.

"That's all right," she said, "you don't have to tell me. But if you do, I'm sure they want to see you again. It would be terrible if, in Lam Yuk-Yiu's anger, she . . ."

She ordered Buddhika to bring the Dutch man some food and then left him to his meal.

Back outside, Lam Yuk-Yiu said, "I ask you to get information out of him and you put food into him?"

"The information will come," Shek Yeung said.

"How?"

"Mercy, even if it's mercy from abuses that you yourself devised, invites gratitude," Shek Yeung said. "Give me time."

Shek Yeung visited the Dutchman, Willem, regularly over the next few days, always with a basin of water or a bowl of broth. Buddhika translated so invisibly that she came to blot him out of her awareness entirely and look only at Willem when he was speaking, keeping one of her hands on his chained forearm, as if absorbing his thoughts through his skin. This allowed her to observe him more closely and learn his tells: roving eyes and a thinner voice when he was lying, a squared jaw when she'd guessed something close to the truth. Aside from her and Buddhika, Willem saw no one else. Shek Yeung had insisted on this.

"Are you sleeping with him?" Cheung Po asked her one day.

"What?"

"Don't forget, you promised me a son."

She walked away. He didn't chase after her.

She understood why Cheung Po, and probably everyone else, believed she was sleeping with Willem. Men, along with some women, liked to talk about the immense power women wielded through sex, but if that were actually true, then the world wouldn't look the way it did. The flower boat girls who'd rested their faith in this supposed power had all met sad ends.

In reality, she and Willem just talked—about the current state of affairs in Europe, his company's plans for Asia, and the things he missed most about home. After a while, he also opened up about his family. (He did, indeed, have two daughters.) Through their conversation Shek Yeung learned several things. First, the Europeans, tired of having trade restricted only to the port of Canton, wished to craft a new agreement with the emperor, who was on his best days unimpressed and on his worst downright hostile to the idea. Second, the Europeans were growing increasingly vexed by the outflow of silver from their coffers: China, being relatively self-sufficient in terms of goods and raw materials, didn't accept anything aside from money in exchange for its silk and tea.

"What will your people do if the emperor says no?" Shek Yeung asked.

"There is something your people need," Willem said. His gaze flickered over to the pipe tucked into Buddhika's belt. "I hear the English are having a plan." Very unexpectedly, he laughed. "That terror of a woman you work with thinks my people are the ones to worry about."

"He's full of lies," Lam Yuk-Yiu said when Shek Yeung relayed his words. "I have no love for the English, but they've kept their word in all of our dealings so far. My fleet is as well armed as it is because of them. What I want from this bastard is his country's plans for this region."

But Willem continued to deny a Dutch agenda. They'd given up, he claimed. "This island no longer interests us. I trade in Asia for many years, and this is my first time on Formosa. I make much more from the spices and cash crops on the East Indies. My family is happy. Why would I change?"

"Why were you transporting all those guns, then?" Shek Yeung asked.

"We were going to Dejima," Willem said. "I don't know what you heard, but we were."

Shek Yeung believed him. Not only because she'd spent the past half-month learning his tells but also because something about Lam

Yuk-Yiu's story, or rather, the story the English had told Lam Yuk-Yiu, didn't make sense. The Dutch lost Taiwan more than a hundred years ago. Why would they try to retake it now after all this time?

If the Dutch had in fact given up on Taiwan, then the English were providing erroneous information to Lam Yuk-Yiu—intentionally, if Shek Yeung had to bet, but to what end? Feeling annoyed, she walked down to the shore. Once there, she took off her shoes and wandered around on the pebbly sand, feeling the points dig into her feet. The pain refreshed her attention.

The best-case scenario was that the English simply wanted to weaken their Dutch rivals without getting their own hands too dirty. The worst-case scenario was that they wanted to direct the attention of the pirate fleets onto someone else while they executed their own scheme, which, as Willem seemed to suggest, had something to do with opium and the current trade imbalance between China and Europe.

"Do you trust Lam Yuk-Yiu?" she asked Cheung Po later when they were alone.

"I trust Choy Hin with my life," he said.

"That's not what I asked. Do you trust Lam Yuk-Yiu? Or rather, do you trust her judgment? I'm starting to think she's being fooled by the English. She's so convinced that they share her hatred of the Dutch that she takes everything they say as truth. If I were them, I would use her to further my own plans."

"Let's say you're right," he said. "How does that affect our fleet?"

"I suppose it doesn't, for now. But we need to be careful with any future alliances with them. Lam Yuk-Yiu's sources are not as trustworthy as she believes."

"Do you still want me to stay in the area and work with Choy Hin given this?"

"Well, there's still time to decide," she said.

In the end, Shek Yeung wasn't worried enough about Lam Yuk-Yiu's judgment to remove herself and her fleet from the current situation, at least not until she had gotten her share of the ransom. Choy Hin and Lam Yuk-Yiu had set up a decent stronghold here in Taiwan. Though several parts of the fort were crumbling, it was relatively safe from attackers. Nearby villagers actively supported their endeavors, supplying food, fishing nets, and occasionally, wives. It helped that Lam Yuk-Yiu was one of their own. But more important, the alliance ensured that, so long as a village cooperated with one of the fleets, it was safe from *all* fleets. That was another reason why Cheng Yat's dying wish had been the continuation of the alliance. Before, villages that had been immensely valuable to one fleet often ended up being destroyed by another. In chaos, no one won.

The next day Shek Yeung awoke with an impulse to visit the village. She enlisted Buddhika, who knew the area well and spoke the local dialect. Dressed in plain clothes, weapons hidden, they skittered down the pebbly hill toward shore, lashed by the occasional cord of wind. The humid air clung to her like a large sweaty hand. The purple-tinged morning clouds were powdered-over bruises.

The village consisted of no more than fifty buildings, each with red roof ridges shaped like waves. The walls had a spotty, irregular appearance—coral stones, Buddhika explained, gathered at low tide and then stacked atop one another. The locals had moved here from the nearby archipelago generations ago, bringing with them their construction techniques.

The building materials were a little different, as was the style of the homes, but still Shek Yeung couldn't help but be reminded of the village in which she'd spent her childhood. All around them, people bartered goods, washed their clothes, cooked with their windows and doors flung open to let out the oil and steam. Shek Yeung's eyes and mouth watered at the hot bursts of basil and garlic.

Even after she gained her freedom from the flower boats, she never went back to her home village. It wasn't that Cheng Yat had forbidden it. There just didn't seem to be a point. What was left for her there except ghosts? Besides, when she admitted it to herself, she didn't think she could face the aunties, those of them who were still alive. The way they would look at her when they realized how many people she'd killed and abducted. Maybe they would mutter about how she'd soiled her family name, how she should have died instead of her mother or brother or father. Or maybe they would fail to recognize her altogether, even after she introduced herself: *You are not one of us. You can never be one of us again.*

At the center of town, a temple cocked its extravagant red comb of a roof. They entered, wandering past painted clay figurines enacting the expulsion of the Dutch from the island. A stele just past the entrance of the temple recounted the town's beginnings. In this story about Ma-Zou, she'd appeared on this island to lead the early settlers to where they should build their new homes, and on the exact spot where she'd disappeared, they'd erected this temple. Shek Yeung hadn't heard this story before. She wondered if Ma-Zou had foreseen that the Europeans would seize this area only a few years later.

The statue of Ma-Zou had been carved from a single piece of wood and looked like it weighed at least fifty gan. The locals had thrown a fishing net across her shoulders as though it were a shawl. The offerings in front of her were almost exclusively seafood instead of the usual smattering of fruits and desserts.

She and Buddhika burned some incense to Ma-Zou. "How do you feel about Lam Yuk-Yiu?" she asked him.

"The Matron?"

"You've been with her for many years now, right? Don't worry, I won't tell her what you tell me."

He chewed his lip, clearly unsure whether he should trust her. She didn't blame him. "She keeps us safe, me and the other boys," he said. "Even when the fleet ran into hard times, we always had food to eat."

"Do you miss your family? Ceylon?"

"It was a long time ago," he said.

After the temple, they went to the marketplace. Shek Yeung bit into a guava so ripe it dissolved in her mouth like seafoam. Buddhika, who'd received some spending money, bought a rattan hat for himself and haggled over a couple of abalone necklaces for Lam Yuk-Yiu. Shek Yeung bought a small beadwork pouch for Yan-Yan. The village seemed to be doing well in spite of all the food it regularly supplied to the Blue Banner Fleet. This made Shek Yeung feel a little better. Cheng Yat had explained to her that such arrangements were mutually beneficial: the villagers were buying safety with food and money, and whatever the pirates did couldn't be worse than what the Europeans would do if the village ever fell back under their control. A part of her always doubted him. Still, every month, she charged Yan-Yan with adding up the tributes from these villages and Ahmad with dispatching men to threaten those villages that came up short.

Another reason she never went back home after winning her freedom was this: What if she'd returned to find only ruins? She'd on more than a few occasions heard Cheng Yat ordering the crew to burn down villages resisting their control. She'd wanted to ask him if such an action was really necessary—couldn't they seize the villagers' supplies and be done with it?—but she'd been too afraid. What if someone had burned her village the same way?

She and Buddhika introduced themselves as traders when asked. No point in endangering themselves if they happened to meet some villagers displeased with the arrangement, not when all she had on her person was a short dagger and a finicky pistol. It was not a bad place to live, she concluded as the two of them walked around. If she settled here, the emperor would never find her. She would be able to start over. Build a spotted house, sell fish at the market, eat guavas every day.

Something small and soft collided with the side of her leg. Shek Yeung looked down—a girl, no more than four or five years old, was sitting in the dirt. Water trailed from her eyes, snot from her nose. Her shriek was like midday sun directly in the face after a night of heavy drinking.

"Ah, I'm sorry," Shek Yeung said to the girl.

The girl, impossibly, shrieked louder.

People were starting to look. "She ran into me," Shek Yeung explained to everyone.

"I wonder where the mother is," Buddhika said.

"You saw," Shek Yeung said, wanting his corroboration. "She ran into me."

He nodded absently, eyes still scanning the marketplace for the child's mother.

"Let me help you up," Shek Yeung said, holding a hand out to the girl, who didn't even look at it. She could feel her patience fraying. "Are you done crying?" she said. "Get up."

"Let's just leave," Buddhika whispered.

"No, she's being unreasonable." Shek Yeung squatted so she could look the child in the face. "Are you planning to cry forever? Or are you just crying because you hope someone will comfort you? What will you do if no one comes?"

A shadow fell over Shek Yeung. A tall woman, probably the mother, bent over and picked up the child. She and Shek Yeung locked eyes, and Shek Yeung saw there a combination of disbelief, anger, and fear. Suddenly Shek Yeung understood.

They all knew exactly who she was. They'd simply been playing along with the story she and Buddhika had been spouting. Although the villagers supported Lam Yuk-Yiu and Choy Hin and received protection in turn, that didn't mean they weren't deathly afraid of them. When someone wielded that much power over someone else, fear would always be a barrier between them, no matter how well the one in power treated the other. However much spending money Lam Yuk-Yiu gave Buddhika, Buddhika would always, first and foremost, fear her. Shek Yeung had felt the same toward Cheng Yat. Even after he'd given her command of half of the fleet, even after she'd helped him secure the cooperation of the other fleets, those dregs of fear still got stirred up whenever she made a mistake or contradicted his opinion. When he died, she'd felt sadness, yes, but also relief.

Maybe that explained some of Cheung Po's recent behavior as well. Since the attack on the Qing war junk, she'd been mulling over his words about how Cheng Yat had chosen him. *So what if he made you do things? He made all of us do things,* she'd wanted to say. But she'd already been in her mid-twenties when she met Cheng Yat. Cheung Po had been, at most, fifteen. She'd been taken from a joyless life on the flower boats, whereas Cheung Po had been taken from his family and community. What it must have been like to be so young and so far from home, watching all the other boys his age die one by one, and then, after doing enough terrible things and having enough terrible things done to him, to be told that he would become heir to a fleet whose power paralleled that of the navy. Oh, how Cheng Yat had both favored and tortured the people he'd deemed special enough to "mentor," her included. Sometimes she didn't know if she was supposed to feel grateful or resentful.

And then Cheng Yat had gone and died. Maybe Cheung Po was trying to prove to her and the rest of the fleet that he was indeed as special as Cheng Yat had believed, special enough to deserve outliving the other boys, or maybe he was just trying to prove to himself that all his suffering had been necessary in preparing him to lead. If he could subdue fleet commanders that had posed a problem for Cheng Yat, if he could capture war junks that Cheng Yat would have struggled to capture, then maybe Cheng Yat had indeed been a genius of foresight and not just another tyrant who destroyed lives for no other reason than that he could.

She would feel pity for Cheung Po, except she sometimes suspected she was doing the same herself.

. . .

The junks Shek Yeung had sent up north for reconnaissance finally returned—with bad news. They hadn't found Ba and the White Banner Fleet. Nor had they found any bodies or wrecks. Was the fleet truly gone, or was it simply in hiding from Pak Ling? If everyone had died, why would Pak Ling have gone through the trouble of destroying all the evidence? According to the captain of one of the reconnaissance ships, the area had experienced a lot of storms recently. That might explain the fleet's disappearance.

Shek Yeung shared this information with the other three commanders. "We may have to accept that Pak Ling is a bigger threat than we believed," she said.

"But he hasn't proven to be a threat to any of us yet," Cheung Po said. "All right, maybe, *maybe*, he defeated Ba. We don't have proof of that either. But being a threat to a tiny fleet with a commander who's drunk all the time is different from being a threat to us."

"Has he made any incursions into your territory?" Shek Yeung asked Choy Hin.

Choy Hin looked conflicted. "No, but we've been seeing more imperial junks right outside our territory. We thought they were doing training exercises. That war junk you two captured was probably one of them." He turned to Lam Yuk-Yiu. "What do you think?"

"I don't like this Pak Ling," Lam Yuk-Yiu said, "but I also don't think he's an immediate threat. Peking has never taken much of an interest in this island. Sure, they came here to kill the Ming loyalists, but that was because the loyalists were a threat to the Qing. Why would the emperor all of a sudden care about us? We shouldn't get distracted. The ransom is happening soon. We need to focus on getting as much money from those Dutch savages as we can."

As they drew closer to the ransom date, Lam Yuk-Yiu had become even more obsessed with the Dutch. She talked about them during meals, during meetings, during friendly games of pai gow, as if she were daring Shek Yeung to question her judgment. But Shek Yeung didn't voice any disagreement. It was true Pak Ling wasn't yet worth their concern—unless, of course, he'd had something to do with the failed raid that had cost Cheng Yat his life.

Shek Yeung brought up the possibility of a spy with Cheung Po again. "I haven't noticed anything suspicious," he said. "Have you?"

She hadn't. "I've been thinking about it," he continued. "I'm not saying the Portuguese didn't get a warning, but it was probably accidental. You remember what happened five, six days before the attack? A few of our men got really drunk and caused a scene at the tavern?"

She had no memory of this, but she wasn't too surprised. She didn't spend nearly as much time socializing with the men as Cheung Po did. But she understood what he meant. Drunk men were talkative men. Years on the flower boats had taught her that.

If Pak Ling had intensified his efforts, the best thing would be for her and Cheung Po to stay in Taiwan for the time being. It didn't matter that she wanted some distance from Cheung Po—the combined power of the Blue and Red Banner Fleets meant relative safety. After they received the ransom amounts, the fleet would be in a better position to deal with Pak Ling's schemes, whether or not they included a spy.

· · ·

"I need to speak with you," Shek Yeung said to Buddhika a few days after the meeting about Pak Ling. In the meantime she'd come to the conclusion that she needed more information. Cheng Yat wouldn't have circumvented the commanders of an ally fleet for information, but he hadn't known Lam Yuk-Yiu well. Shek Yeung found Buddhika in a different wing of the fort and dragged him all the way back to her room so they could talk in peace.

"How often do you accompany your Matron when she is conducting business with the English?" she asked.

"Sometimes," Buddhika said cautiously. "Why?"

Shek Yeung had been hoping for an answer along those lines. After all, he was Lam Yuk-Yiu's favorite. It also didn't hurt that he spoke a little English. And whatever meetings he didn't attend, he likely heard about from Lam Yuk-Yiu herself.

"I'm concerned about your safety," Shek Yeung said.

She had grown quite fond of him over their time together, she explained. Begun to think of him as a younger brother, maybe even a son. "But in truth I'm also concerned about your Matron," she said. "I fear the English are deceiving her."

"How so?"

"You've been in the room with me every time I've talked to Willem," she said. "Do *you* think he's lying?"

He broke her gaze. "Right," she said. "If Willem's not lying, and the English do have a hidden agenda, then you, your Matron, and possibly the whole fleet are in danger. However you feel about your Matron, I know you don't want harm to come to yourself and to all the other boys.

"There is a problem, Buddhika," she continued, tilting his chin gently until he met her gaze again. "And you're the only one who can solve it."

"I can't—"

"I would never ask you to do anything to betray your fleet. Remember, I want to help. But for me to help, I need more information."

"Let's say there is a problem—" he began.

She put up a hand to stop him. "Not much would need to happen at all. It would just be a matter of passing information along. Your fleet docks at Maynila quite often, isn't that right? When do you think you'll find yourself there next?"

"Three months?"

She swore inwardly. She would have preferred to receive this information sooner—who knew how much damage Lam Yuk-Yiu might inflict, how many alliance secrets she might cede to the English in the meantime—but there was simply no better way to communicate with Buddhika. Carrier birds worked only if the message's intended recipient was at a set location, and Shek Yeung's fleet couldn't risk staying in one place for too long. The remaining methods, like drop spots and middlemen, all required her physical presence.

Still, late information was better than no information. "I happen to know a great inn in Maynila that serves the best *pancit*," she said. "The proprietor is a lovely older gentleman who speaks almost as many languages as you do and is a very good listener. Once our fleets are done here and start traveling again, you should try the noodles there."

Buddhika nodded. She patted the back of his hand. For now, there was nothing to do but wait.

. . .

By the time the messengers returned with news from the Europeans and the emperor, winter was coming to an end. The emperor had made a counteroffer. The Europeans had outright agreed to the named price. Rumors of pirates' brutal treatment of captives had spread far and wide, some of them started by the pirates themselves to incite fear. No doubt the Europeans were imagining their brethren being flayed, disemboweled, and cannibalized.

Even Shek Yeung didn't know whether certain stories were true. So much depended on the fleet, the squadron, the ship, the season, the amount of liquor everyone had had to drink. Could she ever cannibalize another person? Sure, if she was hungry enough.

They agreed to the emperor's counteroffer, two thousand more than the amount they'd thought they would get, and scheduled Qiu Liang-Gong's exchange for the day before the Dutchmen's. All four commanders had agreed that Lam Yuk-Yiu and Choy Hin would not take part in Qiu Liang-Gong's exchange. The Blue Banner Fleet had not aided in the capture of the war junk, thus they had no claim to the ransom. If the handoff went smoothly, the entire negotiated amount would go to the Red Banner Fleet. If it didn't, then Shek Yeung and Cheung Po would have to fend for themselves.

Shek Yeung hadn't set eyes on Qiu Liang-Gong since that time she visited the dungeon. As her men dragged Qiu Liang-Gong out, guilt briefly breached the surface of her mind, like a drowning man's face in water, before she shoved it back down. Qiu Liang-Gong's wrists were so thin they might as well not have been manacled—a vigorous wiggle and he would have been free. Skin hung like wind-rippled sails off the battens of his ribs. It wasn't how she would normally treat a captive, but it wasn't any worse than how the Qing would've treated her.

"Be thankful," she said to him. "Your emperor has agreed to pay."

When they'd arrived at the agreed-upon location in the strait, Shek Yeung sent a man, himself a captive and therefore inconsequential to the fleet, on a small boat toward the imperial navy. The navy, which had been warned to stay at least ten lei away, would wait for the man to fire a gun. Then they would load the ransom onto the boat. Once Shek Yeung had verified the amount, Qiu Liang-Gong would be sent back to the navy.

The small boat returned with the money. Yan-Yan popped out from her cabin to count the sum. At her nod, Shek Yeung's men heaped Qiu Liang-Gong onto it like a pile of rags. He would probably recover from the ordeal in time, though people occasionally died from less. Who knew what Heaven had planned for him? If his ship hadn't happened to be in that particular area at that particular time, or if Cheung Po had gotten the fight he'd wanted from the Dutch, Qiu Liang-Gong would still be in command of his ship.

"For all our sakes, may our paths never cross again," Shek Yeung said to him. It was the kindest thing she could think to say.

Qiu Liang-Gong pushed himself up onto his elbows and said to Cheung Po, "This is not over. I will see to it that you regret your actions against the emperor."

Shek Yeung rolled her eyes. The boatman rowed Qiu Liang-Gong away.

That night Lam Yuk-Yiu called a meeting in her room. Shek Yeung noticed a few European trinkets that had not been there last time—taken from the Dutch prisoners, most likely. Among them were a few more of those European cross ornaments, some big enough to be hung on walls, others small enough to be hidden away on the person. Lam Yuk-Yiu was again sprawled across her bed, Choy Hin next to her. Shek Yeung and Cheung Po sat on chairs. Instead of reviewing the logistics of the next exchange, Lam Yuk-Yiu announced her intent to increase the ransom demand to fifteen thousand. "The Dutch pigs have money, and they'll pay anything to get their men back. I say let them."

"I don't like a change this big, this close to the date," Shek Yeung said. "The messenger has already been sent out with the instructional letter. Any exchange with foreigners is already complicated enough. We don't know how they think, where they draw the line."

"Don't worry," Choy Hin assured her. "Lam Yuk-Yiu and I have raised the price at the final moment before." He turned to Cheung Po. "Actually, haven't we done this before, too? Near the Matsu islands? Sorry, my friend, if that wasn't you. My memory's getting worse and worse."

"That was me. We were fighting the Portuguese. You saved my life that day."

Choy Hin laughed. "Yeah, that's right! I'd never met anyone so eager to fight! I remember thinking, 'Ma-Zou help this boy.' I didn't think you were going to make it past your twentieth year if you kept on like that, but look at you now."

Shek Yeung sighed inwardly. With all three of them in agreement, there was no way she was going to convince them to settle for the lesser amount. If Cheng Yat were here, he would have found a wedge.

But then Cheung Po spoke up. "What that experience taught me is that the Europeans are unpredictable. I narrowly escaped death. This time I might not be so lucky. I vote that we take the ten thousand. Better to live so we can take ten thousand more another day."

Shek Yeung turned to him, surprised. Cheung Po continued, "These Dutchmen are officers, not nobles. No lineage depends on their continued existence. And there are probably many men waiting to take their place, who wouldn't mind if something happened to them if it meant an opportunity for promotion. I think this is the most we can expect out of these captives."

"Well, maybe . . ." Choy Hin said.

Undeterred, Lam Yuk-Yiu said, "They didn't even try to negotiate the price. These pigs are important to them. We just don't know why. Somehow we failed to get the information." She cut her eyes at Shek Yeung.

"Not everyone responds to the cane," Shek Yeung said, trying to hide her anger. "Flexibility has gotten our fleet more things than stubbornness ever did."

"*Flexible* is another word for *spineless*," Lam Yuk-Yiu said.

"Yuk-Yiu," Choy Hin warned.

"How about this," Cheung Po said. "What if we give you a larger portion of the ransom to help cover the amount you'd be missing out on?" He darted Shek Yeung a quick look to make sure she agreed. She nodded.

"Well, I can't complain about that," Choy Hin said.

They drank on it. "That was good thinking," Shek Yeung said to Cheung Po later in his quarters. He replied, simply, "I did what was best for the fleet."

"It must have been hard, disagreeing with your friend."

"It was what was best for his fleet, too. Now drop it."

"I was certain you'd side with the two of them."

"Why? Because you think I'm irresponsible?"

"I didn't say that."

"You have before. Again, I don't fight unnecessary battles. Or maybe I'm saying that wrong. What I mean is I don't fight battles I can't win, or battles where I would lose too much. The battle with Qiu Liang-Gong, we won, and we didn't lose much. This one with the Dutch, it's hard to say."

"I get it."

"You asked me a few months ago what I saw for my own future. Something like that. Well, I see myself alive. That is the only real thing I've seen for myself since Cheng Yat took me from my village."

His voice was bitter. For some reason, she'd never fully appreciated the similarities between them. Maybe it was because, by the time of her marriage to Cheng Yat, Cheung Po was already a skilled fighter and officer. She never met the boy torn from his family, raped by a man twice his age and size. But he was probably the only other person she knew capable of fully understanding her. She didn't like it, the idea of anyone understanding her this well, not her fear of failing all the people who depended on her, not her knowledge that if forced to choose she would sacrifice almost all of those same people before she sacrificed herself. But she didn't dislike it all that much either.

"You're alive," she said. "He's not."

"I know."

"You've already won." The same could be said for her, she realized. Some part of her always assumed that Cheng Yat would kill her the instant she made an unforgiveable mistake.

"I know."

She sat down next to him, laid his head on her lap. His fingers crept behind the flaps of her tunic and dipped under her waistband. She felt a bright twinge of arousal in her belly, a zither string plucked by jade-tipped fingers.

"Stay tonight," he murmured into her thigh.

"Tomorrow's an important day."

"Please," he said.

So she did.

14

The afternoon before the exchange with the Dutch, Shek Yeung paid a final visit to Willem. Buddhika didn't accompany her because Lam Yuk-Yiu had called him away for services that clearly were not his to perform. Shek Yeung hoped Lam Yuk-Yiu hadn't grown suspicious of the boy's time with her. Finding a new informant in the Blue Banner Fleet would be a headache.

Willem was in much better shape now compared with his time in the dungeon. At first glance one wouldn't guess he'd been captured at all. Yes, he'd lost some weight, but nothing worse than what people experienced during periods of food shortage. The bruises and cuts on his face had healed—whether the ones on his body also had, she didn't know. She placed a basin of water on the table in front of him and gestured to her own face to indicate that he should clean up before returning to his people.

He splashed some water on himself. "*Donk-yeh,*" he said. Shek Yeung nodded.

An open book lay face down on the chair next to him. It looked like the one Shek Yeung had glimpsed in the room with the golden cross, except the lettering on the spine had mostly worn away and the leather cover was scratched up. She had no idea where he'd gotten it.

She pointed at it and made a gesture of confusion. He pointed at the ceiling. He might have been trying to tell her that the book was about his god, or that it had come from somewhere upstairs.

She produced the amulet of Ma-Zou that she kept inside her tunic. Carved from rosewood, it was a gift from the priest of the temple that Cheung Po had built in Ma-Wan. He sired temples the way that other men sired children—at the moment, he was erecting another farther east. For a while, the fleet had even traveled with a floating temple, a boat that served no purpose except as a shrine to Ma-Zou so that he could maintain his worship while at sea. There had been an oracle whom Cheung Po abducted, whose one and only job was to read Ma-Zou's signs. As far as captives went, the man had an easy life—that was, until the boat capsized during the most recent typhoon season. Maybe he hadn't been very good at reading signs after all.

Come to think of it, she didn't know that the priest had given the amulet to her specifically. That was just what Cheung Po had muttered when he plunked it down in front of her the night she saved a squadron of their ships by countermanding one of his orders. It was more likely that the priest had given it to Cheung Po, who'd then passed it on.

She showed Willem the amulet and then pointed at the sky as he had. "Ah," he said.

He took the amulet from her, tracing his fingers over the figure. He said something that sounded like "dah-mm." When she indicated that she didn't understand, he made a hoop with his arms in front of his stomach.

"Oh!" she said. "Yes, a woman."

"Ma-li-ah," he said. She didn't understand this either, but when she pressed for more information, he just waved a hand in a "forget it" sort of way.

The whole interaction was proving fairly useless without Buddhika. She took the amulet from Willem, smiled tightly, and turned to leave. She was already at the door when he called out to her.

She turned back. "What is it?"

"De-en-gos," he said.

Those words she recognized. Buddhika had translated them for her enough times.

"What about the English?" she asked.

Willem looked pained, fluttering his hand in front of his mouth as if he were choking on all the things he couldn't say. Shek Yeung empathized. As someone who made her way in the world by being good at talking, she found the communication barrier between the two of them deeply vexing, especially now as he was about to give up potentially valuable information on the English.

He dropped his hand and glanced around in search of something. She gestured for him to wait and ran out of the room, returning with a brush and an inkstone with some ink already on it. Placing those in front of him, she indicated that he should draw on the book by his side.

Willem appeared hesitant to do this, but he relented when he saw that Shek Yeung had no intention of running back out again. Sighing, he opened to a blank page and dipped the brush in the ink. He wielded the brush clumsily, pressing down so hard that the fibers separated into two sections, swirling it in too much ink when he redipped and thus leaving a huge blotch in the middle of the page. But when he moved his hand, she was able to recognize the general shape of an opium pipe.

She mimed the action of smoking. He nodded.

He flipped to another page and drew again. A map this time, except for the life of her, she couldn't tell what country he was drawing, the orientation and scale being very different from what she was used to seeing. Finally, he made a tiny dot in the middle of a blank area. "Formosa," he said, pointing to the dot.

Everything became clear then: the large land mass to the west, the cluster of islands to the south.

"Yah," she said, proud of herself for remembering how to say yes.

Willem looked pleased. He flipped his brush around and tapped the uninked end on the jut of land to the southwest of China. "Ben-ga-luh," he said.

"Right," she said. She'd heard Europeans use that name before. There were a couple of people in her fleet who hailed from that general region. They prayed to a cross-legged, bare-chested goddess with a playful smile, as if she alone knew the punchline to the universe's grand joke.

Now Willem drew a series of arrows pointing from that region to China. He tapped the brush on the opium pipe and then again on the map.

He was obviously referring to the smuggling of opium from one place to the other, but everyone, or at least everyone in her line of work, knew about that already. Surely he didn't believe he was revealing a big secret.

"Yah," she said, motioning to him to explain. But he just drew another arrow and repeated, "De-en-gos."

She sighed. Willem seemed to be trying to tell her that the English were involved somehow, though she could have guessed that by herself. What she couldn't figure out was how the English plan for smuggling opium into China might affect her fleet except maybe to change the general market price of the drug.

It soon became clear they weren't going to get any further. Still, she appreciated his efforts. She silently prayed to Ma-Zou that the exchange would go well. If the Dutch failed to pay or attempted any kind of subterfuge, then Willem was as good as dead. Lam Yuk-Yiu would see to it herself.

. . .

A few hours before dawn, the Red and Blue Banner Fleets pushed out to sea, Shek Yeung and Cheung Po on their flagship, Lam Yuk-Yiu and Choy Hin on theirs. Shek Yeung had ordered the captains of the more dilapidated junks to stay behind at the fort. If for some reason the Dutch decided to pursue, those ships would have trouble escaping even with the ten-lei gap specified by the instructional letter, which Willem had written and Buddhika had read to the best of his ability to prevent deceit.

The fog was already quite thick and would only get thicker. This was good. They had chosen this hour for the exchange knowing that the conditions would help cover their tracks if they needed to escape. Together, the ships surged like an undertow beneath the waves of fog. Beside her, Cheung Po was pacing.

"You think something will go wrong," she said.

"Lam Yuk-Yiu wasn't happy with the decision, even though we agreed to give them a larger cut."

"She cares more about making the Dutch lose money than about making money. At least Choy Hin agreed with us. He'll keep her in check."

Cheung Po shrugged.

This alarmed her. "What?" she demanded.

"Choy Hin has changed," Cheung Po said. "I still trust him. Or maybe it's more that I trust his word. He used to be one of the shrewdest men I knew, but now . . ."

"The opium?"

"Or just time. He's older than me by at least twenty years. How many of us live past forty-five?"

Shek Yeung chuckled bitterly. "How many of the people on land live past fifty? Is there really much of a difference in the end?"

They reached their destination. In the distance, a signal went up: the Dutch, announcing their presence. A small boat darted out from between two of Choy Hin's larger ships like a viper from between boulders and glided toward the Dutch.

The boatman fired into the air to announce his presence. Shek Yeung raised the spyglass to her eye. Soon a Dutch boat appeared. The Dutch sailor heaved a large sack into the other boat, which promptly returned to the Blue Banner Fleet.

Choy Hin counted the ransom. Even without the spyglass, Shek Yeung could see his satisfied expression. The pirate who had retrieved the payment loaded the hostages onto the small boat, and together they set back out. Shek Yeung let out a breath she hadn't realized she was holding.

The boat was about three lei from the Dutch fleet when a cannon rang out. The round shot barely missed the boat, plummeting into the water right in front of the hull on the starboard side and sending up a giant spray. Shek Yeung turned her glass toward the direction of the shot. A junk had emerged from the fog and was firing continuously at the boat. Most of the shots fell short, though one grazed the stern, ripping off a fair-sized chunk. For the first time in her life, Shek Yeung found herself thankful for the inferiority of Chinese black powder.

"Whose goddamn ship is that?" Shek Yeung shouted at her crew members. "Somebody find out." To Cheung Po she said, "Is it one of ours?"

"No," he said, looking puzzled.

Believing that they were being ambushed, the Dutch fleet began to withdraw. Shek Yeung wondered if they needed to retreat themselves. Betrayals were not unheard of, even with the alliance in place. She and Cheng Yat had needed to make a spectacle of punishing rogue pirates with beheadings. Perhaps one of the other fleets had heard about the ransom amount and decided to make a grab for it, but who would be stupid enough to try to take on two well-armed fleets? Not the current leaders of the White and Green Banner Fleets, certainly. And as far as she knew, Kwok Po-Tai was still back in Canton.

Over on Choy Hin's ship, the crew simply stood there watching. Shek Yeung made a gut decision. "Return fire!" she ordered her men.

At their fire, the lone junk ceased its attack. The boatman ferrying the hostages shook off his paralysis and stood rapidly toward the Dutch fleet. Finally, they reached the Dutch, who pulled their men and, surprisingly, the boatman on board. They set off, eager to get as far away from the pirates as possible.

"Approach cautiously," Shek Yeung told Binh. Out of the corner of her eye, she saw Choy Hin's ship turn toward the junk that had opened fire. Both vessels arrived at around the same time.

They boarded. The crew of the lone junk surrendered immediately. "Mercy!" the helmsman cried. "We didn't know it was you!"

"You didn't recognize us by our banners?" Shek Yeung said angrily. "You must either be lying or blind."

"We didn't notice you through the fog! All we saw was this boat by itself—we thought we could make some easy money. Please, you must believe us!"

"Visibility is very low right now." Shek Yeung jumped at Lam Yuk-Yiu's voice. She hadn't noticed the other woman board.

"You believe them?" she asked Lam Yuk-Yiu.

"We chose this time and this spot for a reason," Lam Yuk-Yiu said. "We can't blame them for us doing our jobs well, right?" She fixed her gaze on the helmsman.

"No, M—" the helmsman began to say. Lam Yuk-Yiu cut him off by putting up a hand. "In any case," she said, "it's done. We got our money. The hostages have returned to their people. It's what you wanted."

But Shek Yeung wasn't so easily appeased. "Who's your commander?" she asked the helmsman.

"Commander?"

"To what fleet do you swear allegiance?"

The man shook his head frantically. "We're just fishermen," he said. "We've had a bad couple of months and only recently turned to piracy. We don't belong to any fleet."

It seemed like a bald-faced lie, but there was little she could do to prove otherwise. "Take them back to the base," Shek Yeung told her crew. "We'll figure everything out later."

"It's all right, leave them to me," Lam Yuk-Yiu said. "I'll think of a fitting punishment for them."

Shek Yeung reluctantly turned the captives over. Lam Yuk-Yiu smiled coldly at her.

Back on their ship, Shek Yeung pulled Cheung Po into her cabin so they could talk in private. "You heard him, right?" she said. "He'd been about to say 'Matron.'"

Cheung Po let out a long sigh. "Maybe. A lot of words begin with that sound."

"She put those men up to this and then told them to deny their allegiance so that it wouldn't be traced back to her."

"Maybe," Cheung Po repeated. He winced, as if already regretting what he was about to ask. "Are you going to confront her?"

She didn't answer.

"Remember the alliance," he said, tapping the side of her wrist.

She glared at him. "As if I can forget. As if you, of all people, have the right to remind me."

Because no one had believed it could work when Cheng Yat had proposed the idea. Honor among thieves? Kwok Po-Tai had laughed outright. Except she'd wanted to believe it. Most of them were not thieves, she'd argued, not by choice anyway, but rafts set adrift on the rough waters of fate, men and women who would have been happy living peacefully had Heaven been more benevolent to them. She'd wanted to believe in the alliance so much that she'd handed Hung-Shek to a wet nurse and walked away without looking back, and now he didn't even know her name.

She slept fitfully, half-expecting Lam Yuk-Yiu to send an assassin in the night. By the time she awoke, it was already midday. The four commanders gathered to divide up the ransom. As promised, they gave Choy Hin and Lam Yuk-Yiu a larger cut. Choy Hin looked thoroughly pleased.

"It's been great working with you again, my friend," he said to Cheung Po. "Why don't you stay longer? More and more Europeans pass by this little island every day."

"It's time to regroup with the rest of our people," Cheung Po said. "The transition is still new to them."

Choy Hin nodded. "Putting the fleet first. You've become a good leader."

"All because of your guidance," Cheung Po said. The two men saluted each other in a comically formal way, a closed right hand under an open left, as if they were a couple of Shaolin masters. But then Choy Hin thumped Cheung Po on the back, and both laughed.

Shek Yeung sat down near Lam Yuk-Yiu, who was observing the two men, smiling in a self-satisfied way. "I'm curious, what did you end up doing with the crew from last night?"

The woman glanced out the sides of her eyes at Shek Yeung and turned her gaze back toward the men. "I delivered them to my boatswain. He'll take care of everything."

"A public beheading is a good way to teach others the consequences of going up against us," Shek Yeung said.

"They couldn't see us," Lam Yuk-Yiu said. "They'll receive some lashes and an offer to join my fleet. If they refuse, then I'll behead them."

"Are you sure they weren't already a part of your fleet?"

Lam Yuk-Yiu's expression didn't change. "What are you saying?"

"It was just a thought I had. Your fleet is so dominant in this region. Someone would have to be exceedingly brave or stupid to engage in piracy without your blessing."

"Then I guess you met some exceedingly brave or stupid people last night." Lam Yuk-Yiu paused. She was still smiling that infuriating smile. "But let's pretend they'd acted under my orders. I can't imagine the deaths of some foreigners and my one crew member would have affected you negatively. Unless, of course, your loyalties have changed."

"My loyalties lie with the alliance," Shek Yeung said, trying but failing to keep the edge out of her voice, "which makes a lot of its money from foreigners, who will stop paying ransoms if they believe that their people are going to get killed anyway."

Lam Yuk-Yiu finally turned to face Shek Yeung, hands folded neatly on her lap. "Which is why those men weren't a part of my fleet but just fishermen acting independently. My loyalties lie with the alliance, too."

"I'm glad to hear that," Shek Yeung said, standing. "Time to leave," she said to Cheung Po. He bade his friend farewell one last time and, slinging an arm across her shoulders, walked out with her.

. . .

They pushed out and, bearing up into the wind, set a course for Canton. Behind them, the blue-green shoreline of Taiwan faded away like an old contusion, like pain itself, which was always duller in memory than it had been in life. It was a lucky amnesia that allowed one to live unfettered by the past, to *choose* to do what one needed to do. Giving birth to Ying-Shek had been so painful that, afterward, Shek Yeung swore to never give birth again. When the Cheng family pushed for another child, though, she convinced herself that Ying-Shek's birth hadn't been all that bad. But Lam Yuk-Yiu lived surrounded by her ancestral pain, on that island the Europeans had found so beautiful they'd desecrated it. Unable to put distance between herself and the pain, she couldn't forget and thus couldn't move on.

Shek Yeung shook her head, remembering Ying-Shek's birth. Sometimes she could swear that experience had happened to a different person. She leaned back against the taffrail to admire the moon, which smiled lopsidedly, as if it knew a secret she didn't. And that was the moment she realized what she'd missed while preoccupied with all the business on Taiwan.

PART III

Deep as the Sky

15

Ying-Shek had arrived a half-month earlier than expected, impatient to lay claim to the dominion of all of his forefathers. Shek Yeung had planned for the ship to dock in Canton soon so she could settle into the Cheng estate, where the midwife and the bevy of aunties, all of whom had children of their own, awaited to help her through the birth—where Shek Yeung would be safe from rival fleets, as this was in the days before the alliance. But Heaven laughs at the certainty of mortals, so her contractions started while they were still a whole day away from shore, amid a thunderstorm.

At some point during the fourth or fifth set of contractions, Shek Yeung experienced a sudden clarity. She saw all the branching paths leading up to the present moment, saw how she had chosen all the wrong branches along the way. There was that older boy from her village who'd wanted to marry her, but she never could look past his dull wit and sharp back hump. There was the decision to work on the same boat as her father and brother instead of, as the aunties had exhorted, selling fish in the marketplace. ("Or better yet just marry Hou-Hou, he's a good boy who'll take care of you, who cares if he's not very clever or handsome?") Then of course there was the decision to join Cheng Yat's fleet. Maybe she should have tried harder to talk her way out of it—she was good at talking, after all. She might have coaxed Cheng Yat into a compromise, one that would not have resulted in her being here, now, about to give birth on a violently lurching ship to a child she wasn't sure she wanted.

Maybe this was Heaven's punishment for her, a woman who'd dared to want more than the fate that Heaven usually allotted women.

"Where is Cheng Yat!" she yelled at Yan-Yan, who was crying panicked tears because she'd never witnessed a childbirth prior to this. Freezing seawater sloshed from a pail onto Shek Yeung's blanket, which was already soaked through with sweat and birthing fluids. The fabric tangled around her, slimy and sturdy, like kelp dragging her to the seafloor. This was it, wasn't it? She was going to die by drowning after all. Ma-Zou had at last lost her patience, and Shek Yeung was going to drown as she should have all those years ago.

One of the men popped his head through the cabin door. "Big Brother Cheng is coming! His ship is having trouble getting closer in this storm."

Fung Wan, one of the newer recruits, angrily waved him away, telling him to give the womenfolk some goddamned privacy.

The "womenfolk" in question consisted of Shek Yeung, Yan-Yan, and Fung Wan, who had a daughter of her own and therefore had at least a sense of what needed to happen going forward.

"You need to breathe," Fung Wan said, but Shek Yeung wasn't doing very well at this very basic task. She tried again, dragging the air into her lungs, feeling it claw her insides on its way down like a recalcitrant cat.

She pushed. Yan-Yan gripped her hand as tightly as Shek Yeung was probably gripping hers back. Suddenly the girl cried, "I see it! I see it!" And then she said, "Oh."

"What?" Shek Yeung said.

"Stop pushing," Fung Wan said. "The baby's feet are coming out first. We need to turn it."

"Turn it?!"

"I saw a midwife do this once," Fung Wan said. She splayed her hands on Shek Yeung's belly and pushed on it at an angle, as if kneading dough. This she repeated a second time, and then a fourth and a tenth. Finally, she said, "I think it's too late. The baby's going to have to come out feet first."

"Can it do that?" Yan-Yan asked.

"Maybe if we tried a different position," Fung Wan said. She and Yan-Yan helped Shek Yeung shift onto her hands and knees.

Ma-Zou, Ma-Zou, Shek Yeung prayed. *I'm sorry for everything I've ever done. I promise I'll make better decisions from now on, just don't let it end this way.*

"The legs are out," Fung Wan said. "You're almost there."

Fung Wan and Yan-Yan shouted the name of each newly visible body part with an enthusiasm Shek Yeung would have found comical had she not been in so much pain. At last, she felt the child shrug free of her as if she were a coat that he no longer needed. She collapsed onto her elbows; the side of her face scraped against wood. Hands turned her so that she was once more lying on her back.

Fung Wan placed the baby in her arms. A boy, just as both the fortune-teller and the midwife had predicted. She gazed at his vaguely pointy head, his wrinkled brow, and his tiny, folded limbs, and over-come by a feeling of love (or was it revulsion?), she picked up the knife at her bedside, unsheathed it, and cut herself free of him.

Cheng Yat arrived later that night. He found her and Yan-Yan in her cabin. Fung Wan had retired to the crew quarters, and Yan-Yan had fallen asleep by Shek Yeung's feet, spilled out in all directions. Cheng Yat nudged the girl awake, and she too returned to her quarters. Behind Cheng Yat, Cheung Po flickered like a flame, jumping and bending, trying to catch a glimpse of her and the baby without stepping in front of the other man.

"My son," Cheng Yat said proudly.

Shek Yeung handed him the baby. Cheng Yat shook the baby's toes and fingers. When he poked at his nose, the child awoke and began to wail.

"A strong cry," he said. "Definitely a good sign. A nice broad fore-head, too. We'll have to take him to the fortune-teller, of course, but no doubt he'll say the same thing." He patted her shoulder. "We'll reach Canton soon enough. My relatives will take over from there. You just focus on regaining your strength so we can set out again as soon as possible."

She would be lying if she pretended she didn't feel relieved. Cheng Yat had wanted a son, as all men did, whereas she had wanted something to bind the two of them together. Not that bearing his son guaranteed her safety, but it was better than relying on her appearance and wits to keep him from throwing her overboard the instant he grew tired of her.

She'd thought only as far as bringing the child into the world. Of course she was relieved to hear that he didn't expect her to actually raise it.

They docked in Canton the following day. She disembarked more carefully than she usually did, clutching the baby close to her chest like a shield. At the Cheng estate, the women circled her and the child tightly, smelling overwhelmingly of the crushed jasmine and agarwood that dangled from their persons in jeweled filigree pouches. Finally, a wet nurse came to take the child away. Then a servant guided her to the room where she would spend the next month recuperating.

The Cheng women were emphatic that Shek Yeung abide by the tradition of sitting out the month. That meant no going outside, no bathing, and no partaking of cold foods or drinks for the entire period. It also meant bundling up in layers and layers of clothing despite the warm weather. Shek Yeung couldn't decide if she liked the tradition. A few days in, she was already feeling restless. The one time she wandered near a door, an auntie scolded her so viciously she all but scampered back to her room, apologizing the whole way. (Imagine her, the woman who co-commanded the largest and most fearsome fleet in the South China Sea, being cowed by a wobbly old lady!) At the same time, there was ease in this kind of a life. Every few hours, servants delivered to her pungent, nourishing broths of green papaya and fish head (both eyes present and accounted for); fist-size tangles of noodles prepared with blood cake and pig's kidney, the tang of the blood setting off the creaminess of the kidney; and to top everything off, ginger and jujube tea, the sweet fruit boiled for so long that she could make the petals of flesh blossom in her mouth by just wriggling her tongue into the center. She needed only to sniffle before someone dashed into her room to ask if she required anything, and she abused this power a little more than she knew she ought. Shek Yeung began to see why so many of the Cheng women had chosen their silk-collared lives of leisure despite the other opportunities the family business afforded them.

The fortune-teller the family hired, a man with a scraggly gray beard, hailed from Peking and was supposedly known far and wide for his accurate predictions. Cheng Yat's father had consulted him before several important battles and then gone on to win every single one. What about the one he eventually lost, the one that cost him his life? Well, this fortune-teller hadn't been available then. If he had, then Cheng Yat's father surely would have lived, or at least that was the consensus among the family members.

He called himself Master Tian, but there was no way that was his real name. His real surname might have been something similar, perhaps the word for "paddy," changed to the word for "sky" so that people would have to, in effect, call him Skymaster, which admittedly sounded a lot more impressive than Paddymaster. Shek Yeung sat with the baby in her lap; Cheng Yat stood by her side. The Skymaster leaned very close. The baby started to cry, possibly reacting to the fortune-teller's sour breath.

"This child has a smooth, broad forehead, which means he will have a life filled with good fortune. His long earlobes tell me his good fortune will continue into his old age."

Cheng Yat gave her a look that said *See?* She rolled her eyes. He laughed.

"Now, look at these cheeks," the Skymaster continued. "You see how nice and plump they are? He will go on to have many children of his own, including sons." He turned to Cheng Yat. "Your bloodline is secure, no question about it."

Cheng Yat seemed pleased to hear this. For her part, Shek Yeung was beginning to wonder about the Skymaster's credibility. It wasn't that she didn't believe in fortune-telling, but she'd spent enough time crooning what men wanted to hear to know when she was in the presence of someone with a resonant vocation.

"See this birthmark? The dark color is inauspicious, and its location near the heart suggests he will have heart problems when he is old. He will have to be watchful."

Everyone has heart problems, Shek Yeung thought, *if they're lucky enough to grow old.*

"But here, ah, this is very good. This mole on the right shoulder means he will be very brave, a consummate warrior. Whatever challenges come his way, he will surely triumph over them."

The Skymaster made a few more predictions, but Shek Yeung stopped paying attention. Only as the Skymaster readied to leave did she speak again. "Thank you for your time and wisdom," she said. "We simply could not have guessed any of this."

Cheng Yat showed the man out. A little later he returned and sat next to her. "Master Tian is a true sage," he said.

"Mm-hmm."

"I was thinking about our son's name. Given that he's destined to be brave, shouldn't his name reflect that? What do you think about Ying?"

"That's fine."

"He should have another name, though. Cheng Ying . . . Cheng Ying what? What do you think?"

"Whatever. We can ask your mother if you want."

He stared at her. For a moment she worried she'd responded too flippantly. But then Cheng Yat grinned.

"Ying-Shek," he said. "Cheng Ying-Shek. So he can have a little bit of my name and a little bit of yours."

The sentiment was so touching she didn't know how to respond. At times like these she wondered why she ever doubted his feelings for her. Maybe he intended to keep her. Maybe he valued her for exactly who she was. She allowed herself, very briefly—like a child who'd trapped a firefly between her hands—to peek at a potential future: the two of them, retired but still healthy, surrounded by children and grandchildren. There would be servants to massage her back and oily broths hot enough to scald the tongue.

But that was ridiculous. He was going to die in battle, and then she was (or vice versa). And then no one would be left to check if their son indeed grew up to be a brave warrior or have heart problems. That was how the reputations of people like the Skymaster stayed intact.

All she said was this: "Cheng Ying-Shek. I like that very much."

. . .

Yan-Yan came to visit about a month after Ying-Shek was born. She gaped at the luxurious surroundings, running her hands over the brocade wall hangings and lacquered rosewood cabinets. Squatting, she knocked around a few of the porcelain figurines on display, rearranging them so that the two female figurines appeared to be talking to each other and the male figurine was facing the wall. Then for some reason, she picked one of the figurines up and sniffed it.

"Big Sis," she said, wrinkling her nose and putting the figurine down, "you sure you can't convince them to let you stay after the month is up? It's *nice* here."

"You could have had nice things too if you'd stayed with your husband," Shek Yeung said.

"That's different," Yan-Yan said. "Can I see the baby?"

Shek Yeung called for the wet nurse, who bowed upon entering the room, the baby in a sling around her shoulders. The child was so thickly swaddled, Shek Yeung might have mistaken him for a bedroll if she'd just found him lying somewhere. Might even have tried to sit on him.

Yan-Yan squealed and bounced toward the wet nurse. "Ah, he's already so big," she said. "I want one."

"Ahmad likes you," Shek Yeung said.

"Not interested."

"Binh?"

"Ew."

"You know there's only one way to get a baby, right?"

"I'll just steal yours," Yan-Yan said, smiling with all her teeth.

Shek Yeung sighed. In the months since Yan-Yan joined, Shek Yeung had grown quite fond of the girl, even more so now that the girl had helped her through the birth of Ying-Shek. But in so many ways Yan-Yan was still a child, the younger sister Shek Yeung always wanted but never got.

"Sometimes," she said, searching for the words, "we have to do what we don't want to get what we want. When I was your age, I couldn't accept that everything comes with a price. Do you understand what I'm saying?"

Yan-Yan went back to making faces at the baby, pretending not to hear.

One day, Shek Yeung thought, *Heaven is going to punish the girl for her optimism.* The gods did not suffer happy mortals because happy mortals didn't need gods. Whatever happened to Yan-Yan, it was going to be unexpected and devastating. The thought made her sad. She liked Yan-Yan.

The wet nurse left. Yan-Yan sat down next to Shek Yeung. "So you're coming back soon? Big Brother Cheung has been driving everyone mad. I think he's lonely without you and Big Brother Cheng."

"I doubt that."

"It's true! He's always making us do training exercises. I hate the spear."

"You knew you were going to have to fight when you joined."

"But I'm no good at it! Besides, you recruited me to manage money."

"There would be no money to manage if we were all dead. But I'll talk to Cheung Po when I return. There are other important skills you could be mastering besides the spear."

Yan-Yan beamed.

Shek Yeung knew she shouldn't be coddling the girl, but it was also true that a well-run fleet needed much more than fighters. She liked having someone on board untainted by war, whose instinct was not violence. Someone who felt completely safe. Someone to remind Shek Yeung of whom she might have been. In any case, she struggled to imagine a situation in which Yan-Yan would ever have to be on the front line. By the time an enemy had killed the fleet's best fighters, the rest of the fleet would definitely be ready to surrender. And if the enemy didn't believe in mercy, well, then, what good was little Yan-Yan and her spear going to do?

When the baby started crying, Shek Yeung called for the wet nurse, who didn't come. She and Yan-Yan took turns rocking him, but that just seemed to offend him because he screamed louder. *Such a Cheng male,* Shek Yeung thought, *wanting what he wanted and unwilling to settle for anything else.* Someday she would have to tell him how his father had refused to leave the brothel until she'd agreed to marry him.

"Do you mind getting her?" she asked Yan-Yan when the screaming grew intolerable. Yan-Yan left the room, only to return a moment later alone. The wet nurse had stepped out to shop.

"He probably just needs to be changed or fed," Yan-Yan said.

They unswaddled him, but he was dry. They tried to feed him, but he wouldn't latch. Shek Yeung felt she might lose her mind if the noise continued. She'd grown accustomed to working through, even sleeping through, noise while on the flower boats, but something about the baby screaming was deeply unsettling. It quickened her heart rate and her breathing, made her feel as though she were entering battle when all she was doing was sitting there in front of the least dangerous creature she'd ever encountered in her life. The crabs she liked to catch for food at least had pincers—this child didn't even have teeth. Then again, young children struck fear into their parents not because of anything they could do but because of everything they couldn't.

Eventually Ying-Shek tired himself out and fell asleep. Shek Yeung slumped against her and Cheng Yat's wedding bed, which they'd used for all of one night before returning to work despite superstitions about keeping it occupied for the first month after the wedding. A covered, four-walled structure made of camphor with one side cut out for entry and exit, it was sturdier than some of the homes she'd been in, not to mention more expensive. The wall panels and eaves bore carvings of joyous couples. Was she happy with Cheng Yat? She wasn't sure what happiness looked like.

"You know, I don't think I've seen you so out of your depths before," Yan-Yan said. "Didn't you ever have to take care of younger siblings? Neighborhood children?"

Shek Yeung shook her head. "I was the youngest. And the aunties didn't trust me with the other children."

"Why not?"

"Probably because my mother died right after I was born. They didn't think I had a good example. My father was at sea most of the time. If anyone raised me, it was my brother, and he stopped as soon as he was old enough to join my father." Shek Yeung smiled a little sadly. "He was still my brother more than anything else, though. He liked to drop hermit crabs down my clothes. Once I awoke from a nap to find that he'd drawn all over my legs with ink."

She'd always thought she would learn to take care of her own eventual children by babysitting her brother's. When Yu Lan came along, she'd figured the time was near, the way the other girl and her brother kept pawing each other. She'd felt excited about the prospect of nieces and nephews but also disappointed because it would have meant staying behind on land more. (And then she'd felt guilty about feeling disappointed—a good woman was supposed to look forward to that kind of domesticity.)

"I think you're thinking too hard about this," Yan-Yan said. "Babies are like dogs. He was just reacting to your nervousness."

"Says the one without a baby," Shek Yeung said, a little irritably.

"I have plenty of experience with babies," Yan-Yan protested, "and even more with dogs. You'd get the hang of it quickly if you just spent more time with him, but it's almost like you don't want to. I don't get it. If he were mine, the wet nurse would have to pay me to take him off my hands."

"How much would I have to pay you to stop talking?"

What Shek Yeung didn't know how to explain to Yan-Yan was that some part of her feared spending more time with the child. She feared that, if she softened, she would never be able to harden again, much in the way that waterlogged wood never returned to its original shape. What use would she be to anyone then?

After Yan-Yan left, Shek Yeung returned to her packing. She needed to decide what to leave here and what to bring back to the fleet. Some of the presents from Cheng Yat's family and friends, little material comforts like vests for cold nights, would be useful on board. Other presents she couldn't even regift: delicate painted bowls; loud, dangling necklaces that just as easily became garrotes; horse-hoof shoes with wooden heels so tall one couldn't walk three steps in them without falling down. After all, the kind of people who normally used such items were not the kind of people who regularly surrounded her.

She glanced over at Ying-Shek. Sleeping, the child's face looked startlingly like Cheng Yat's: the fleshy nose, the large ears protruding like oars, the self-satisfied expression. She could see nothing of herself in him.

She didn't pick him up out of fear of waking him, though she did sit down next to him. "Hello," she said, feeling stupid as soon as she'd said it.

"We'll be leaving soon, me and your father. We have a lot of work to do. There is a lot of conflict among the different fleets. The emperor's men are hunting us. We can't just stay here like this.

"Your grandma and aunties will take good care of you. Ah-gu, too—I forget her name. Your nurse. It doesn't matter. The important thing is that you'll be fine. You'll have everything a child could want. Other children will be hungry, or cold, or hurt, but you won't. You'll have what I didn't."

She rubbed at what she thought was a spot of dirt on his face, but it turned out to be just a faint birthmark. She didn't even know where his birthmarks were. "Maybe one day you'll be angry at us for leaving you. Maybe you'll be more angry at me than at your father because you'll be surrounded by women, but none of them will be your mother. That's fine. I'm fine with being a bad mother because I'm a good co-commander. I can help your father bring stability to the fleets and stockpile money before we die, and then you'll be able to grow up with power and wealth. Love can't give you those things. Love only gives you something to lose."

She patted his swaddled form and got up to leave. She didn't know how to be a mother, but at least she could let him sleep.

16

Shek Yeung stared at the newly waxing moon rising over the mountains of Taiwan and counted in her head: fifty days now. She'd been so concerned about the ransom process that she'd forgotten to keep track. It could be an aberration brought on by fatigue or . . . the other thing. There would be no telling until more time had passed.

She lifted the hem of her tunic. Even in this light she could see the stretch marks from her previous pregnancies, as if the creatures inside her had tried to claw their way free. She could hardly blame them. She slept very little and worked a lot. During meals, she gulped down her food out of some vague fear of it getting taken away from her. Her children would have probably preferred a noblewoman with bound feet who'd sat around all day, someone who practiced calligraphy or embroidery.

At least she was on her way home—she didn't want to imagine dealing with a pregnancy in Taiwan, all the while safeguarding against Lam Yuk-Yiu's machinations. In Canton there were respectable physicians and safe dwellings, taverns that served rich, nourishing fare. If the bleeding had not yet started by the time they arrived, she would call on the midwife who'd aided most of the Cheng women through their births.

A few years ago such concerns would have barely crossed her mind. Now, in her thirty-second year, she saw this pregnancy for what it was: a risk. But this had been the agreement with Cheung Po.

"Why do you need all this power?" Wo-Yuet had asked her. "So that others don't have power over me," Shek Yeung had answered, or something to that effect. And she stood by her statement, she probably always would. The better question was, at what point did it become more dangerous to pursue power than to let it go? Freedom in death was no freedom at all.

She found Ahmad in his cabin. The man was kneeling atop the small rug he kept with him, performing one of the many prayers he performed daily. She waited for him to finish.

"How many women do we have right now?" she asked.

He looked puzzled. "In the whole fleet?"

"Your best guess is fine."

"Two thousand? Three? There might be more now. Our numbers went up during the recent famine, and I hear that some of the men from the other squadrons have taken wives."

"You wouldn't happen to know if any of them have midwifery experience."

He shook his head. Cautiously, he asked, "Is someone—"

"Just wondering," she said, shooting him a look that prevented further questions. Obviously, the plan was to be on land for the birth, but experience had taught her to be prepared for all possibilities.

She returned to her own cabin, feeling rather silly when she caught herself tiptoeing past Cheung Po's, as if he'd be able to tell by simply looking at her. She doubted he noticed any of her physical changes short of gaping wounds. As a general rule, she believed that men actually paid little attention to a woman's appearance beyond a vague sense of whether they found her attractive enough to bed. All the little details that the girls on the flower boats had knotted themselves into decorative hangings over—a flower plaited into the hair here, a swipe of vermilion lacquer there—were just them torturing themselves. Once a man found you attractive enough to bed, all his energies turned toward that end. And once a man found you not attractive enough, well.

If she were indeed pregnant, then Cheung Po would find out soon enough. Still she felt compelled to keep the matter secret, at least until she knew for certain, or until she decided how to wield the information.

The world was full of people who'd triumphed because they'd clung to their secrets and people who'd succumbed because they'd loosed their secrets too easily or too early.

From the bottom of her trunk, she fished out an almanac, dragging her fingertip down the narrow, red-printed columns to keep track of her position. It was currently the third lunar month; typhoon season would not start for a few more months. Her stomach soured at the realization that the child would be arriving *not* during typhoon season but after. She'd be giving birth at thirty-three years, near the end of pirating season, when all the temporary crew would be trying to squeeze in as much pillaging as possible before returning to their families for the winter.

"You always come at the worst time," she muttered to her own belly, though she knew she wasn't being fair. It wasn't this child's fault that his two brothers had elbowed and kneed their ways into the world at inconvenient moments.

Precautions would have to be set in place—not just for if she had to give birth at sea again, but also for the chain of command, battles, and unforeseen catastrophes. Given that this was his child, she could probably trust Cheung Po not to sabotage her while she was vulnerable. The other squadron leaders, though unlikely to mutiny (she'd handpicked most of them, after all), might nevertheless get ideas, the kind a child gets when none of the aunties are looking, like taking money from the communal coffer or neglecting to report new loot to avoid splitting it. As for people like Lam Yuk-Yiu and Kwok Po-Tai, it was best to, somehow, keep the whole pregnancy secret from them.

"Why do you need all this power?" Wo-Yuet had asked her. *So that I can have complete control,* she should have answered. Because the moment a powerful woman loosened her grip on the reins, even a little, someone immediately tried to wrest those reins from her. This "someone" was usually a man who believed she should never have had them in the first place.

Shek Yeung spent the night counting days and making plans, tracing her fingers up and down the almanac until they were ink-stained, the red pillars of text propping up her heavy eyelids. Even after she fell asleep, some part of her kept counting, backward and forward, in ever-widening circles and vanishing arcs like half-formed rainbows, so that when she awoke in the morning she felt certain she'd counted down not only to the birth of this child but also to her own death.

17

I n one of the stories about Ma-Zou, she was born.

The bodhisattva Kwun-Yam, who is sometimes male, sometimes female, and sometimes neither (for nothingness has no gender), had cast off their human passions. Yet they would not allow themself release from the cycle of death and rebirth because, having fully awoken, they now heard the cries of all living beings. It was a terrible sound, mournful as a lone chime ringing in a forgotten temple and violent as a mighty tree being splintered apart by lightning, loud enough to reach the tops of the tallest mountains and the bottoms of the deepest seas, so that there was no place one could hide from it.

Kwun-Yam could not comprehend, could not accept, all this suffering. They vowed to remain in this world until they had freed all beings. Thus they reentered the cycle and became reborn as the daughter of a poor fisherman by the name of Lam.

Once, as a young girl, Ma-Zou accompanied her mother on a trip into town, where she encountered a statue of Kwun-Yam. She stopped walking and would not move no matter how much her mother yelled or tugged at her. The peddlers and laborers passing by saw a child gazing in devotion, some might say in possession, at the statue, a frail-looking child whose oddly clean feet remained rooted in the dirt despite her mother's full-bodied jostling. As for the passersby who were really paying attention, they also saw the porcelain lotus in the statue's hand beat heart-red before quickly fading back to white.

Who knew what had gone through young Ma-Zou's mind when she recognized her earlier self? In that moment, Ma-Zou remembered her past and perhaps glimpsed into her future, a future neither particularly cruel nor kind, in which she would lose her brother to the sea and be betrothed to a man she didn't want to marry, in which she would, at the age of twenty-eight, climb a mountain utterly alone (after all, the fate of any extraordinary individual is ultimately to be alone) and ascend into Heaven, leaving her work among humankind incomplete because there is no way to complete the work of humankind.

Had Ma-Zou felt scared? Or had she simply felt overwhelmed by the impossible task before her? Was it fair for any child, any person, to be burdened this way, even if the person had chosen the burden themself?

18

They arrived in Canton six days later, a little after dawn. By now Shek Yeung was fairly certain she was pregnant, having awoken ill the past two mornings (then again, nausea was hardly unusual for anyone who lived at sea and slurped down whatever the waves spat up), not to mention bone-tired. She sneaked away from Cheung Po so she could visit the midwife who'd aided her through Hung-Shek's birth, telling him she needed to handle some business regarding a piece of personal property, which wasn't altogether false. After a few detours to elude potential pursuers, she arrived at the midwife's place in the center of town.

Tse Po-Po circled her twice, measured her pulse, squinted at the coating on her tongue, and let out a long sigh.

"So am I . . ." Shek Yeung said.

"I'll help," Tse Po-Po said. "But I have to say, your chances aren't great."

The old woman plunked a teapot onto her dining table and poured a cup of a "warming tonic" for Shek Yeung, who dutifully drank it. The thick ginger brew wriggled down her throat like a slimy, spiny animal. Like so many other objects in the midwife's home, the blue and white porcelain tea set cost more than most people could afford and looked at odds with the general disrepair of the one-bedroom dwelling. Fleshy oranges and loquats lolled in their beribboned baskets, carefully swaddled in cloth. How grateful all these families were to the midwife!

"How could you let this happen?" Tse Po-Po asked. "You're not some foolish young girl."

"There were reasons," Shek Yeung said.

"I have herbs. It may not be too late to end it."

"Will it be that bad?"

Tse Po-Po sighed again. "I suppose you've survived worse, but make sure you're on land this time. I can't help you if you're not here."

This hardly came as a surprise, but that didn't mean she was glad to hear her fears confirmed. She felt her nausea returning. But the old woman was right, Shek Yeung had survived worse. She'd made it through many things that she, by rights, shouldn't have.

She left Tse Po-Po's and wandered around town for a while. There was one more place she needed to go, but she couldn't muster the courage just yet. As she strolled, she noticed there were more beggars than usual, many of them either new to the area or new to begging. Another famine was probably underway. A middle-aged man begged for money to feed his family. A girl no older than thirteen begged for money to bury her parents.

Her suspicions about the famine were confirmed when she arrived at the marketplace and saw that the price of rice had shot up to five times what it had been the last time she was in town. One dau of rice, which lasted a small family at most a month, now cost the average fisherman at least seven months' wages. No wonder her fleet had grown. At last count, they'd crossed the mark for twenty thousand members.

A clamor on one of the side streets drew her attention. She edged closer, peering around the corner so she could see without being seen. Some townspeople had accosted a government official, a low- to mid-level bureaucrat judging by the plain gold finial on his red-fringed hat and the quail or duck on his mandarin square. The angry crowd barricaded the road and ripped aside the silk curtain to his palanquin. Why were famines happening more and more, they demanded to know, and what did the government intend to do about them?

"There have been a lot of typhoons," the bureaucrat said. "You can hardly blame me for that."

"Well, then why haven't you done anything to help the people whose crops were destroyed?" an old man cried. He was leaning against a young man to his right, maybe his son, who didn't look terribly healthy himself. They looked the way many of the people in her fleet did right before they joined.

"If you help one person, then you have to help everyone. The government doesn't have that kind of money."

"Didn't the governor just throw a feast for visitors from Peking last month?" someone else yelled.

At that point, additional guards arrived. Thrusting their spears, they dispersed the crowd. One of them knocked the old man down with a thwack of his spear shaft. The old man's son tried to help his father up, but neither could find any purchase, their feet slipping on the silty ground.

Shek Yeung resisted the urge to help. She worked hard to avoid scrutiny whenever she was alone on land, dressing in drab colors and eschewing accessories that signaled wealth. The last thing she needed was a visit to the magistrate for aiding "insurrectionists."

On her way out of the market, Shek Yeung almost fell onto a woman who was hunched on the ground. She'd stumbled over the woman's walking stick, which was lying a little bit off to the side. In front of the woman sat a dirty-looking tube filled with thin bamboo stalks: a fortune-teller. She might have been forty or sixty. The lines on her forehead were prominent, though perhaps only from going unwashed. Her rounded back could have been the result of advanced age or lifelong malnourishment.

At Shek Yeung's apology, the woman turned her head, but her eyes didn't focus on Shek Yeung—she was blind. "Read your fortune?" the woman asked the air to Shek Yeung's right.

"Not today," Shek Yeung said. Nevertheless she reached into her purse and pulled out a small copper coin, which she pressed into the woman's hand.

"I'm not a beggar," the woman said. "Take your coin back unless you care to hear what Heaven has in store for you."

Shek Yeung laughed. She liked this one. "All right, tell me my future."

"What do you wish to know? Whether your husband will take new wives? Whether your wealth will grow?"

"Tell me whatever you feel I need to know. You're the seer."

The woman smiled oddly. "If you're certain." She closed her eyes (this seemed to Shek Yeung a redundant affectation) and shook the canister in her hands. A single stalk fell out. She rubbed the pad of her thumb against the stalk to feel for whatever markings she'd made there and recited:

> The dark clouds arrive but do not cover the hills.
> White rain falls onto the boats while
> a wind suddenly blows across the land.
> Below me, the lake looks like the sky.

"A poem?" Shek Yeung said.

"Su Shi's poem," the fortune-teller said.

"Do you have one memorized for every one of those stalks?"

"It's no hardship."

"Impressive. So what does it have to do with me?"

"Isn't it obvious?" the fortune-teller said, sliding the stalk back into the tube and shaking it to mix everything up again. "Dark clouds signal rain, trouble. The wind disturbs the calm. In all the upheaval, you can't even tell the lake from the sky. Beware, because nothing is what it seems."

Shek Yeung considered the fortune. It wasn't what she would have liked to hear, but at the same time, she admired the older woman's candor. People like the Skymaster made their living telling people what they already believed or wanted to believe. Giving people bad news took courage.

Of course, being candid wasn't the same thing as being accurate.

"Thank you," Shek Yeung said. "May Heaven smile upon you."

"See you again," the fortune-teller said, which struck Shek Yeung as strange. Did this woman get a lot of repeat customers here on her little patch of dirt outside of the marketplace? Or was she just the traditional sort and used the more formal version of *goodbye* with everyone?

The kau-chim reading had had the unexpected side effect of distracting Shek Yeung from her uneasiness about her second destination. Before she realized it, she'd arrived at the sam-hop-yuen. She pushed on the front gate. It opened easily, now that there was no one left to bar it from the inside.

The kumquats had all rotted where they had fallen. Shek Yeung tiptoed around the courtyard to avoid stepping on their gray carcasses. Overhead, the longan trees were just starting to bloom, fuzzy little yellow flowers that gave the impression of mold. They wouldn't fruit for another few months.

It wasn't that she'd expected to find Wo-Yuet's body still there because the physician would have had it removed. Yet she turned every corner expecting to see something she would never be able to unsee—blood Wo-Yuet had sputtered up, maggots feasting on food she hadn't been able to keep down—and Shek Yeung had seen a lot in her life. She wanted to pretend that Wo-Yuet had died painlessly, that she'd left this world as softly as she'd walked upon it, like dew sinking into the earth or a bird's cry fading into the air. That she'd climbed a mountain utterly alone and ascended into Heaven. Not skin burning with fever, not a stomach distended in agony, not a chest unable to pull in breath.

Bodies were just bodies: they spilled, shattered, died. She knew this, but she couldn't bring herself to think of Wo-Yuet's body the same way.

Then again, every person she'd ever killed, she'd tossed into the sea immediately afterward. The bodies never stayed around long enough for her to have to witness their decay, the sea hiding her secrets, not to mention its own. She would probably feel differently if someone had kept the people she'd killed in view to remind her of her crimes. As for the times when she'd killed not out of her own volition but Cheng Yat's, she'd tried to convince herself that being tossed overboard did not ensure death. That the sea was, at times, kind.

Shek Yeung plopped down onto a chair in the main hall. Dust swarmed her face like gnats, and she sneezed. Offhandedly she observed that everything was exactly as her friend had left it. Despite the gate being unbarred, no one had looted the place. The sam-hop-yuen's more rural location probably had something to do with it, or perhaps the home had stayed safe by Ma-Zou's grace.

Someone would have to clean the place—sell whatever had value, dispose of whatever didn't. Then there was the matter of the property itself. It was a fine home, on a fine piece of land. There was no good reason to leave it deserted, yet she couldn't think of a single person she trusted to take care of it. Suddenly everyone in her life seemed unworthy. She had an image of her crew coming in, scratching up the camphor wood cabinets as they humped them about, knocking the calligraphy scrolls from the walls and then trampling them. All these base men with their base habits. Wo-Yuet hadn't been able to escape them in life. The least Shek Yeung could do was spare her friend indignity by their hands in death.

Sometimes she hated all of them. Sometimes she wanted to sink all her ships with everyone still on board.

Her gaze found the shrine of Ma-Zou in the corner. From underneath spiderwebs, the goddess was smiling that same little smile, or was it a smirk? She'd never considered that possibility before. Maybe the goddess was actually laughing at them all.

She felt it again, that empty yet teeming feeling, as if someone were setting fires inside her chest just to watch them die from lack of air. She could barely breathe. But even now the tears didn't come.

She dusted off the shrine and lit some incense, beseeching Ma-Zou on Wo-Yuet's behalf. She didn't want to imagine her friend as a ghost stalking a graveyard, pulling entrails from bodies, her mouth full of fetid blood. Perhaps that would be her own fate one day, but Wo-Yuet didn't deserve it. There were only a few truly kind people in the world. To have met one of them, to have been loved by her, and then to have lost her—Shek Yeung didn't know how to begin to think and feel about it.

There was a rustle behind her. She spun around, hand reaching for her cutlass, but found nothing. It seemed to her, though, that she whiffed jasmine perfume, just the tail end of it, like a warm conversation lulling into a drowsy silence.

She walked back through the courtyard and out the door, closing it behind her. No need to decide what to do about the house right now, she told herself. She would have time to figure everything out when the baby came. A month sitting around made for good contemplation time.

Tired and hungry, Shek Yeung set out for her usual tavern. Every muscle in her body ached after the walk to Wo-Yuet's, though normally she would have managed that distance fine. Her breasts felt tender from rubbing against the inside of her tunic. A part of her wanted to just lie down in the middle of the road. She gritted her teeth and hobbled on.

The owner welcomed her enthusiastically, showing her to her usual table in the back corner. From there she could see the whole of the sitting area, which was at the moment fairly empty, the lunch crowd having gone some time ago, the dinner crowd not having arrived yet. Without being asked, the owner's wife set down a small jug of white liquor. Shek Yeung reached for the jug, and then, thinking better of it, asked instead for some tea and braised duck. If the wife suspected something, then she hid her reaction well. She hooked her fingers around the jug handle again without so much as a pause and padded back to the kitchen.

The instant Shek Yeung saw the food, she realized there was no way she was going to be able to eat more than a few bites. Damn this child. After days on the water, she'd been so looking forward to eating something that wasn't fish. She tried breathing deeply to take the edge off the nausea, but that didn't work very well. For a long, panicked moment, she worried she was going to vomit right then and there, just double over in front of everyone. She didn't care what strangers thought of her, unless they thought she was vulnerable.

So she sat there miserably, picking at the skin of the duck with her chopsticks, placing on her tongue flakes of food so small she might as well have been eating air. "That's how you know it'll be a boy," the midwife had told her during her second pregnancy. "The bad nausea. Even in the womb, girls are considerate, obliging. Boys immediately proclaim what they want to eat and when."

About halfway through her tea, a clatter rang out from the front of the tavern. One of the patrons was berating a ragged middle-aged man who had apparently wandered in from the street to beg for money.

"Please," the poor man was saying. "It has been so long since my family and I ate. I have almost enough coins for a meal—here, look." At this he took out a small purse, which he jangled at the patron. "I only need a few more."

He had a slight accent, one she hadn't encountered very often since leaving her village. But his diction suggested a certain level of education, and her village hadn't exactly been known for producing scholars.

"Get away from me," the patron said.

"Have mercy, sir. My son is only three."

"Do you think I'm stupid? You'll just waste the money on liquor."

Shek Yeung looked at her own barely eaten duck. The nausea breached again before slowly, too slowly, disappearing beneath the deep waves of her breaths. "You," she called out to the poor man. "Come here."

He limped over—he had some kind of injury to his right leg. "Madam?"

"Take this duck to your family," she said.

His eyes widened. "I couldn't possibly—"

"It's fine, I won't be eating it. Here." She pushed the plate toward him. Maybe the owner could find this man a container for the duck.

Instead of leaving with the duck, the man sat down at the table next to hers. "You have my deepest gratitude, madam. My two children will be so happy. Do you have any children of your own?"

She hadn't planned on a conversation, had no energy left for one, but now that he was so close, goggling at her so appreciatively, she was finding it hard to shoo him away. "I also have two," she said.

"Ah, may Ma-Zou bless them. They're fortunate to have such a generous mother. Do you live around here?"

"Somewhat," she said, trying to be as vague as possible. "And you? That's not a local accent."

"You have a very good ear," he said. "I'm from slightly southwest of here."

So she was right that she'd detected a countryman. "But you studied elsewhere."

The man wagged a well-manicured finger at her. "You, madam, are very sharp. I did, in fact, take and pass the imperial exam. I even held a position as a civil servant until a higher-ranked official decided to make an example out of me. I was removed from my position, and now here I am."

"Why did he want to make an example out of you?"

"For criticizing the emperor, why else? A famine struck my hometown. When the emperor refused to send aid, I complained. This turned out to be unacceptable. Can you imagine? All these starving people, and no one to lift a hand. I'd never understood why people called bureaucrats 'pigs' until that point."

"They care only for their own interests," she said.

The man nodded vigorously. The long black wisps of his mustache juddered—he couldn't have been older than forty. "Indeed. I spent a lot of time in Peking. You have no idea the level of corruption there, the sheer blindness to what is happening not just in the country but in the world. Do you know, the emperor still does not see the Europeans as a threat, despite the improvements they've made to their ships? He still thinks of them as barbarians, which they admittedly are, but a powerful weapon in the hands of a barbarian is still a powerful weapon. The Portuguese and the English, especially, are problems. They eye our goods and seaways hungrily. If you ask me, it's only a matter of time before they make their move."

He leaned back in his chair, sighing. Shek Yeung felt a pang of sympathy. The two of them shared many of the same ways of thinking. In another life, they might have been friends.

"The emperor will fall," she said, trying to comfort the man. "Maybe not tomorrow, but eventually. He has too many enemies."

"What do you mean?"

"His very people are his enemy," Shek Yeung said. "And a ruler who doesn't have the support of his people can't be a ruler for long. Look at the rebellions that have been happening."

The man nodded. "You're right, there was that one a few years back. And, of course, there are the pirates."

"You think so?" she asked, trying to keep her tone light. "Aren't they just fishermen who sometimes turn to crime? Do you really think they're a danger to the emperor?"

"It's true, most of them are simply common folk who have had to make a terrible decision. I don't know that I would be able to refuse piracy if I were forced to choose between piracy and death. I've already been reduced to begging. I might have joined a fleet already if not for my family. As you may know, the punishment for piracy is death, no matter the reason. It's quite an unfair law. There are those who are pirates by choice, and those who are pirates out of desperation."

"I doubt the emperor sees it that way," Shek Yeung said.

"Not yet," the man said, "but that may change. When I was in Peking, there were a few high-ranking officials who were advocating for more leniency for pirates. Let them live, as long as they repent and pledge their allegiance to the emperor. The only pirates who deserve death are the unrepentant ones, the ones too fond of their own power, but as you might imagine, it's hard to tell between the two."

Shek Yeung smiled politely.

"Ah, but I apologize. You so kindly offered me and my family food, and all I've done is complain," the man said. From within the folds of his tunic, he produced a small, folded slip of paper. "I can't do so right now, but on my word, I will pay you back one day. If you ever need to find me, just ask for me by my name." He slid the paper toward her, grabbed the duck with one hand, and without another word, left the tavern.

Shek Yeung returned to her tea, chuckling, her mood lighter in spite of her physical discomfort. What a strange day it had been between the fortune-teller and this man, who was so accustomed to life as a bureau-crat that he went around leaving his name (on a prepared piece of paper!), as if his name alone would do her any good if she decided to seek him out again. In this world, the poor were nameless.

Still, she unfolded the paper. The first character was Cheung—she recognized it because it was the same surname as Cheung Po's. The second character was Pak, the word for "one hundred." The third char-acter she didn't know.

She called for the owner. "Maybe you read better than I do," she said to him when he came close. "What does this one say?"

He squinted at the slip. "Ling. You know, like 'years' or 'experience.'"

It took her a moment to understand: Pak Ling, as in the warning from Lam Yuk-Yiu and Choy Hin. As in the man who had put down the rebellion up north and was now tasked with dismantling the pirate alliance fleet by fleet.

She ran out of the tavern after him, her heart thudding, but of course he was already gone.

They'd sat only an arm's length apart from each other and carried on a friendly conversation, even though he could have attacked her or called in his men to do so, and she, hungry and tired, likely would have lost the fight. No doubt he had authority from the emperor to kill her on sight. If she'd been more naïve, she might have believed that the whole encounter had been happenstance, that he hadn't known her identity. Except, of course, he'd been dressed as a pauper. Clearly he'd tried to make himself appear less threatening. Perhaps he'd even done it to arouse sympathy.

Had he been following her since she disembarked this morning? What had been his purpose in seeking her out? To taunt her, extract information from her, or warn her?

She wanted to kick herself. Disguise or not, she should never have let down her guard. In this world, nothing was what it seemed.

Below me, the lake looks like sky.

What else had that woman said? Something about trouble, the wind disturbing the calm. White rain falling onto boats. The word for "one hundred" was a close homophone to the word for "white."

She hurried all the way back to the marketplace despite her body's protestations, hoping the fortune-teller hadn't already left for the day. She'd been to enough oracles to know when someone truly had a gift. Thankfully, the old woman was still in the same spot.

At the sound of Shek Yeung's footsteps, the fortune-teller looked up. "Read your fortune?" she asked.

"I was here earlier," Shek Yeung said.

"Mmm? Oh, yes. What do you need?"

"Your predictions," Shek Yeung said, taking another coin out of her purse and placing it in the other woman's hands. She needed to be sure. "Make another."

The fortune-teller shook her head. "Heaven reveals only so much. Its secrets are many and deep. I cannot tell you anything more today."

"Then tell me something that has already happened. Please."

"Fine," the woman said while shaking her head disapprovingly. Again she picked up the canister and shook the sticks until one fell out. Feeling the mark on there, she recited:

> Wordlessly, I climb the western tower. The moon is a sickle.
> A lonely tree grows in a deep courtyard in autumn.
> Though the parting is sorrowful and my mind runs wild, our ties
>   cannot be cut.
> I can taste the separation in my head and heart.

"You recently became separated from somebody," the fortune-teller said. "'Sickle' suggests death, though not necessarily. You feel sorrowful, but the bond between you and this person is so strong that even death cannot sever it." She put the canister down. "All right? Are you satisfied now?"

Shek Yeung made her decision then and there. They never did find someone new after their floating temple capsized with their "oracle" in it.

"Come with me," she said.

"Excuse me?"

"You have a new job," Shek Yeung said. "You'll make more than what you're making here, and you'll be respected by everyone around you. I give you my word."

"What are you talking about? I'm not going anywhere."

"Why would you insist on staying?" Shek Yeung said. "You most certainly don't have a family, by the looks of you, or am I wrong? If you do, I don't mind bringing them on board. They'll live better, too." She squatted so the old woman could hear her clearly. "Don't make me come back here with my men," she whispered. "It'll go a lot rougher that way, and if you do have family, it may not end well for them."

"You won't find me by the time you come back," the woman said.

"Would you like to test that? A blind seer who has probably read the fortunes of many people around here. How long do you think it'll take me to find you?"

The seer didn't respond. "Good," Shek Yeung said. She grasped the other woman's elbow to help her up, but the fortune-teller shook her off. She reached out a hand and found her walking stick easily. With it, she struggled to standing, muttering something under her breath.

"You can't just do this to others," the fortune-teller said to her as they made their way back to the ship. "Your will is not the only one that matters."

"This was done to me," Shek Yeung said. "All this world is, is people exacting their will on others. The sooner one understands that, the sooner one can move on. Otherwise you spend your whole life grieving." The words came out more bitter than intended. But why shouldn't she feel bitter? She'd been forced into a life in which she was violated every day. The old woman would only be forced to do what she was already doing anyway. And now she would be making a lot more money.

The fortune-teller stared at Shek Yeung with her unseeing eyes. "Human will is futile next to Heaven's will. The ones who don't understand this will incur Heaven's wrath, and that's when you will truly know the meaning of grief."

19

To explain the blind woman to Cheung Po, Shek Yeung had to first explain her encounter with Pak Ling. She woke him from his nap on some cargo in the middle of the deck. He could sleep almost anywhere, a talent of which she was deeply envious. In general, he comported himself with an air of languor, flopping eel-like from one place to another. The only exception was during battle, when he blew all his unspent energy.

At first Cheung Po only half-listened, clearly eager to get back to his nap, but when Pak Ling's name came up, he roused. Like her, he couldn't figure out why the emperor's prized hunting dog would have stalked so close only to leave without taking a bite. Suddenly, he leaned close and said, "Shit, do you think he followed you back to the ship?"

She shooed him to the side and sat on the cargo, her cold shoulder pressed against the pleasant warmth of his. "He already knows where we're docked, I promise. My guess is he told his men to look for us around town because he'd heard about the fleet's arrival. If they wanted to attack us, they would've done it already, though it's probably a good idea for us to disappear somewhere for a few months just in case."

"Then what was all of his work for?" Cheung Po asked. "To try to intimidate us?"

"I don't think so. I had the sense that he was . . . assessing me."

"You mean to figure out your weaknesses."

That didn't feel right either, but she said, "Sure."

Together with Binh and Old Wong, they discussed places where they could hide out for a while. Vietnam was the obvious choice, but the winds weren't great this time of year. More importantly, since the new imperial family's takeover of Vietnam, many Chinese pirates (in particular those like Cheng Yat, who'd supported the opposition) had lost their welcome. The punishment if caught? Trampling by elephant.

"What about Maynila?" Shek Yeung said. Pak Ling's mention of the English had reminded her of her little agreement with Buddhika. It was a good option: the direct trade route between Maynila and the Americas suggested the possibility of revenue, and the locals were probably more antagonistic toward the English than she was, the English troops having sacked the town some years ago. Informants wouldn't be hard to come by.

They decided to set out immediately. The situation wasn't ideal, but none of them wanted to wait around for Pak Ling to make a move. Ma-Zou willing, he would be preoccupied with some other matter, or better yet dead, by the time she returned to give birth.

Later that evening, as they lay in bed, Cheung Po asked, "Why didn't you eat your duck?"

"What?" She'd been on the brink of sleep.

"You said you gave Pak Ling the entire duck, and duck is your favorite. I once watched you eat one by yourself. Was there something wrong with it?"

There was no point in trying to hide what would become clear soon enough. "I'm pregnant," she said. "The midwife confirmed it this morning."

She felt him flip onto his side to look at her. For a while, he kept quiet, his breath warm against her shoulder, and then she felt his hand smoothing her hair. It was nice. "How long?" he asked.

"Enough to know for sure."

"We should return sooner, just to be safe."

"We return when it's safe to return, not a moment sooner. Besides, lots of things might happen between now and then."

"You shouldn't do any fighting from now on. We can make the squadron leaders handle the demanding stuff."

"Don't tell me what I can and can't do. And there are many things that might happen that aren't related to fighting."

"I guess." He lay back for all of a heartbeat before flipping onto his side again. This was surprising—usually he was asleep the instant his head hit the pillow. "Wait, does this mean Pak Ling knows you're pregnant? If he's been following you since you got off the ship?"

The thought hadn't occurred to her. "I don't know," she said. True, she had entered the home of a well-known midwife, but she could have been visiting for other reasons. Was that why Pak Ling had asked her about her children? In the hopes that she would, for some reason, reveal her pregnancy to a stranger? Or had he simply been trying to determine points of leverage? Thankfully, she hadn't visited Ying-Shek or Hung-Shek today. That would have been one more thing to worry about, if he'd learned the location of her sons.

"It'll be fine," Cheung Po said, but there was a hint of doubt in his normally cocksure voice that she didn't like.

. . .

Out of caution, Shek Yeung told only Yan-Yan and Ahmad about the pregnancy. Shek Yeung hadn't wanted to tell Ahmad, but Cheung Po nagged the whole way to Maynila, his reasoning being that they would need the boatswain's help with reassigning duties as the pregnancy progressed.

Did the fortune-teller know? It was hard to say. The older woman, whose name was Fan something or other, kept to herself on her little temple boat (newly acquired from a pigheaded merchant whose head no longer posed a problem), speaking with Shek Yeung and Cheung Po only when they sought her out. At first Cheung Po had been disbelieving of her powers, but a quick reading changed his mind. He wouldn't let Shek Yeung sit in on his session, though afterward he shared the poem:

I've traveled across many waters.
I've admired many flowers.
As I go up the river, there is a spring breeze.
Without realizing it, I've arrived at your home.

Who knew what the fortune-teller had told him it meant.

They sailed southeast from the Pearl River Delta, a longer open-sea crossing than they were accustomed to, but thankfully Old Wong knew exactly what he was doing. Shek Yeung would be troubled to find someone as gifted as the man when age or violence finally took him. Yan-Yan, once again, was overjoyed to be traveling to a new place. This time when the girl approached her with brush and paper, Shek Yeung rattled off a list of things to buy. Or rather, things to eat.

They dropped anchor some twenty lei south of Maynila to avoid the troops stationed there, who examined each ship coming in and levied taxes on the goods on board. Once on land, they made their way toward the city on foot. Cheung Po offered to hire her a phaeton, an offer she answered with a glare. The truth was she wanted nothing more, what with her fatigue, but then the crew would have been suspicious. At least the road to the city was beautiful. Everything seemed to grow here all the time. Tall palms shaded fields of tobacco and sugarcane. Giant cacao pods dangled cocoonlike from branches. Cinnamon trees, their slender legs denuded of bark, wafted their sharp, sweet perfume.

At length they arrived in Maynila. Despite having visited the place only twice before, Shek Yeung felt quite fond of it. It was early evening now, and the locals were out and about. The well-to-do women rode around in phaetons while the men assembled on the many bridges over the Pasig to chat, smoke, and watch the small boats gliding up and down the river. The women smoked, too, their fat cheroots girdled with colorful silks that matched their long skirts and their lacy, wide-sleeved shirts. Later they would all return to their homes, which perched atop tall posts, climb up the ladders to their front doors, and draw the ladders up behind them as though drawing up fishing nets weighted with irides-cent shells. From behind lattice windows would come snippets of conversation she didn't understand and the sound of music: the leaping sparks of rapidly plucked strings, the drizzle of small drums.

All this life in the world. All these people, just trying to make it to the next day and the next.

She and Cheung Po crossed the Pasig to the northern part of Maynila. The fleet had, since the days of Cheng Yat's forefathers, maintained a relationship with the taverns and shops in the Chinese-occupied neighborhood of Binondo. The then-emperor of China had decided to restrict foreign trade, and nothing so effectively solidified the influence of pirates and smugglers as lack of access to lucrative goods. The proprietor of Shek Yeung's favorite tavern in Maynila, Juan, was the descendant of one such pirate and a local woman. A reliable information broker, he spoke Tagalog, Spanish, and several Chinese dialects. His was the name she had given Buddhika.

In exchange for fifty gan of silk, ceramics, and medicinal herbs, Juan agreed to lodge her and Cheung Po in Binondo so she wouldn't have to trek to and from the ship every day. And what a strange place he acquired for them. Like many homes in Maynila, this one was elevated off the ground, with a thatched roof and windows pieced together from bits of seashell. But inside, lacquered Chinese furniture and European paintings warred for ascendancy. A golden cross like that she had seen in Lam Yuk-Yiu's quarters hung over the bed.

"Who lives here?" she asked Juan.

"Don't worry," he said. "They're dead."

"Not on my behalf, I hope."

"Oh no, they died many years ago. The English threw them in prison. Their nephew lost the house to me in a pai gow game."

"Ah." She really didn't understand Lam Yuk-Yiu's fondness for the English. "By the way, do you have any messages for me?"

"Are you expecting one? If you have a sense when it might come, it would help me."

She wasn't terribly surprised. Only a month or so had passed since she was in Taiwan, and in any case, Buddhika might have changed his mind in her absence. She just hoped he hadn't confessed their agreement to Lam Yuk-Yiu. "Never mind. What about stories? Heard any recently that I might like?"

"Maybe a couple," he said, scratching his chin, "but I need to go back to my shop now. Come by for a drink later, after the dinner patrons leave."

Thus she found herself alone with Cheung Po—no one else around, no crises to resolve. He was being uncharacteristically quiet, and she couldn't think of anything to say.

"I'm going for a walk," she announced.

He popped up from the bench he'd blanketed himself across as soon as they'd entered the house. "I'll come with you."

"Not necessary."

"I'll come with you," he repeated. For all the firmness of his words, his tone was unexpectedly soft.

They wandered back out onto the streets. The people here were friendlier than she was accustomed to back home. Many nodded politely, and several, concluding that she and Cheung Po were foreigners based on their clothing, greeted them in Cantonese. Every now and then, a particularly lovely young woman caught Cheung Po's attention. One with beesting cheeks even smiled at him as she came toward them. He twisted himself up so much to keep looking at her that he began to resemble a flag around a pole. Shek Yeung noticed herself reaching to twine her arm with his and stopped short.

"You can go talk to her if you want," she said, feeling awkward and maybe only the tiniest bit envious of the other woman's beauty. She had promised him that she wouldn't get in the way of his philandering.

"It's fine," he said.

"Why not?"

"No reason."

On the other side of the Pasig, they passed a Spanish hall of worship. The Spanish had built many of their temples here, each larger than the last, but this one caught their attention because of the large number of pregnant women and women with newborns who were entering and leaving. Cheung Po stopped walking and gestured at the entrance with his chin.

"We should go in," he said.

"Why?"

"Don't be so suspicious. Why not?"

"That's not a good reason."

"Just for a little."

He had a stupidly excited look on his face. She stopped herself from smiling. "Fine, but if they ask for money, we're leaving."

It was darker inside than expected. Now that the sun had set, the cavernous space was entirely candlelit, shadows flinching on the walls as if in vicarious pain with the bearded man in the barbed crown, whom she saw everywhere she turned. At the door, they watched the worshippers dip their fingers into some kind of water and then touch the water to themselves.

They followed the pregnant women toward the back of the building into a smaller room. Atop a center platform stood the statue of a goddess with long brown hair and brown skin, which caught the gleam from her golden dress and headpiece. In her arms she held an infant.

One by one, the pregnant women waddled up to the goddess, kneeling to kiss her feet. The new mothers did the same, but first they held their babies up to her. Before Shek Yeung realized it, she and Cheung Po had gotten jostled into a line with these women. She tried to find a way to leave without drawing attention to herself.

When they reached the front of the line, she moved to kneel as the others had. No harm in going through the motions, she supposed. No god or goddess anywhere ever punished a mortal's prostration. Cheung Po must have been thinking the same thing because he suddenly lunged forward and brought his lips to the statue's feet.

But when he turned around, he was wearing a silly smile. "Guess what," he said. "I felt a shock when I kissed her feet. And then like this warm feeling. I know she's a European goddess, but I think she's going to help us and this baby."

They were being herded out of the room now. Cheung Po was still talking. "I figured, since she seemed to be listening, why not ask her for more stuff? So I asked her to give us many sons." Past the myriad statues of winged, pupilless children, toward the side exit. "I also asked her to help us with this Pak Ling situation. I mean, maybe she has power only when it comes to babies, but you know, maybe not."

Out the side exit, into the night. Without making much of an effort to keep her voice down, Shek Yeung said, "What exactly do you think is going to happen?"

"Huh?"

"To us. You think we're going to have a bunch of sons and then retire somewhere with our money? Live to see our grandchildren and great-grandchildren?" She felt strangely angry all of a sudden. How dare he trust in the goodwill of the gods? Didn't he know Heaven hated the certainty of mortals? By being certain, he might have doomed them all to a terrible end.

Or maybe she felt angry because she wished she could believe in a future the way he did.

"I didn't say—" he began.

"No, really, I want to know. How do you think all this is going to end?"

He looked surprised, then confused, then annoyed. Even though she was the one who'd asked the question, she half-hoped he would just walk away so that they wouldn't have to continue this conversation. "If you must know," he said, "I want to go back to my village. Not right now, but when I have more money. It would really help my younger sister and her kids."

The revelation was so unexpected that she had to stop walking. For whatever reason, she'd assumed that he had no family left either. But not everyone lost everything to the pirates as she had. It never occurred to her that one could live this kind of life and still hold on to hope for another.

When she was a little girl, a fortune-teller passed through her village. She couldn't afford to pay for a reading, but she was terribly curious, so she shadowed the man for hours, hoping he would take pity on her. Finally, he said to her, "You want a free fortune? Fine, here it is: 'What isn't yours, isn't yours. There's no use crying about your fate.' Now go home."

She thought about that statement for a long time afterward, and eventually she came to a grudging acceptance of it. The fact was, sometimes nice people, like her mother, died early, whereas mean people, like the couple of aunties who were always yelling at her to be more ladylike, endured. But as she would learn the day the pirates came, what was hers wasn't even necessarily hers to keep.

"What do *you* think is going to happen?" Cheung Po asked.

"I don't," she said.

"But you pray. I know you do. What do you pray for, then?"

It was a tricky question to answer. She prayed for favorable winds, victorious battles. Sometimes she even felt certain, as she had when she was a child, that Ma-Zou was listening. Yet she never felt confident that Ma-Zou would grant any of her prayers.

"How much younger is your sister?" she asked, softening her tone.

"Four years. Last time I went home she already had three kids. She might have more now."

"You visit?"

"Not that much."

She had so many questions for him: Did his sister understand how he made his living? Did she know what he'd had to do to reach his current position? Every now and then, against her own better judgment, Shek Yeung found herself wondering if her father was still alive and what he would think if he learned of everything she'd done. Then she wondered what she would think if she learned he'd become like the very pirates who'd killed his son and raped his daughter.

Instead of asking any of those questions, she placed her hand on his shoulder and said, "If you care for her, hide your money well. Let her know where it is. In the end, that's all you can do."

Maybe that was why Cheung Po built so many temples, to coax Ma-Zou into granting his wishes. But if what wasn't his, wasn't his, then did any of his deeds matter? The concept of ming was something she never could wrap her mind around. If each person had a fate that was predetermined and irrevocable, then why did mortals pray to the gods?

"Well, I don't care what you think," Cheung Po said peevishly. "I think we're going to be fine."

She didn't have the heart to contradict him.

· · ·

They visited Juan's after he had closed for the night. The older man prepared some *sinangag*, which they wolfed down. As seemed to be the fashion for many men in Maynila, Juan went barefaced. Consequently, he looked at least a decade younger than his stated age of fifty-six, though of course that might also have been the result of his mixed ancestry, the darker skin obscuring any wrinkles, the wider facial bones resembling plump cheeks.

"Kwok Po-Tai has been seen around here," Juan said.

She and Cheung Po clinked down their chopsticks at the same time. "Oh," she said, while Cheung Po said, "Bastard."

"This was just two months ago. My people spotted him at a cock-fight. He lost."

"Good," Cheung Po said, while Shek Yeung said, "What business did he have in Maynila?"

"Really, all we have are rumors," Juan said, "but supposedly he's hiding from someone back in Canton."

This time they said the same thing: "Pak Ling."

"Who?" Juan asked.

"It doesn't matter," Shek Yeung said. "So he was in hiding?"

"Apparently he lost a sizable number of men and ships in some battle. He was here so he could regroup."

"How many ships?" Cheung Po asked.

"Not enough to end his fleet, but enough to scare him."

She watched Cheung Po out of the corner of her eye. He'd known Kwok Po-Tai for far longer than she. If he was concerned, then she needed to be, too. And indeed, Cheung Po looked a little queasy.

"You said you had other stories to tell us?" she said to Juan.

Juan leaned back in his chair and smiled unctuously. "Well, this one might not be as interesting to you."

"We're interested," Cheung Po said.

"I wouldn't want to bore you."

"How about another twenty gan of ceramics and silk?" she said.

"If you insist. Word is that if you have a lot of opium stockpiled, sell it now. The English are preparing to flood the market with it, and pretty soon what you have will be worth next to nothing. The Americans are also getting in the game with a different strain. It's of inferior quality but cheaper, or so I hear."

"The English have been smuggling opium into China for years now," Cheung Po said. "This isn't news."

"Look, my people tell me the English are going to ramp up their activities. Don't ask me why. Maybe they've finally had enough of your emperor's foreign policy. They're tired of losing money to Peking legally and to you pirates illegally."

They thanked Juan for dinner and retired to their new accommodations. Lying in bed, they discussed what they had learned. Cheung Po held her hand and was stroking the back of it with his thumb. The weather was really too warm for any kind of extended touch, but she couldn't be bothered to move. Besides, it wasn't all that bad. Cheung Po's hand was big, the pad of his thumb only the slightest bit calloused. She realized he'd been initiating casual contact more and more. When had it started? After Taiwan? She also realized she didn't always push him away.

Cheung Po thought they could hang on to their cache of opium for a little while longer because they would absolutely know if large shipments of the drug were suddenly crossing the border via the waterways they controlled. They could sell everything off then, if that day ever came.

"Willem was trying to warn me about this, too," Shek Yeung said. "I still don't understand why, and that worries me."

"So what if the English are trying to make more money?"

"It's not just the opium. They're also trying to turn us against the Dutch. It worked for Lam Yuk-Yiu, not that she needed much convincing. Maybe they're just hoping we and the Dutch will destroy each other and leave them to their smuggling. But Juan seems to think this has to do with the emperor's foreign policy. Willem also mentioned something to that effect."

"If anything, it sounds like the English and the Qing are going to destroy each other. Doesn't concern us."

"Why stir us up against the Dutch, then?"

"For fun?"

"I think they want us out of the way so they can do whatever it is they're going to do. Look, the part about the opium makes sense. Greed always makes sense. China has exports Europe wants, but Europe doesn't have any exports China wants, not even their black powder, so the current trading system is against Europe's favor. But if more people in China use opium, then Europe would finally have something to export because of all that opium they're cultivating in and around the subcontinent. What doesn't make sense to me is why they would want us out of the way. They must know that we're at odds with the emperor. The more we keep the emperor busy, the more opium they can smuggle. Wouldn't you want the enemy of your enemy to stay in the fight?"

"Maybe they don't know," he said.

"Impossible. If people in Maynila know that Pak Ling sent Kwok Po-Tai running, no way people back home don't. That's the other big unknown we're dealing with: Pak Ling. Maybe he's tricking the English somehow. Using them to help get rid of us."

Cheung Po let out a long sigh. "If Pak Ling is doing this, then we're in bigger trouble than we think. I don't like Kwok Po-Tai. You know this. But it takes a lot to scare him."

"I wonder how many ships he lost."

"We got out of Canton in time."

"But we can't stay here forever. Sooner or later, we'll have to take the offensive. Ideally, we find a way to assassinate him. You talk to your contacts, and I'll talk to mine."

"We can wait a few months," he said, his knuckles brushing the side of her belly. "One thing at a time."

Giving Pak Ling more time to strategize was a terrible idea, but she was too tired to argue. If only she weren't pregnant. Was it too late to end it? Even if it wasn't, she couldn't risk damaging the partnership she'd finally established with Cheung Po, who against all expectations had softened into the prospect of fatherhood. Perhaps she could pass it off as an accident, but who knew if he would believe her? He'd watched her give herbs to the female crew members more than once.

No wonder men trampled on women everywhere one looked—this inveterate vulnerability that lasted for nine months at a time, multiple times in a woman's life, followed by the achy, teary month of confinement afterward. At least for Cheng Yat's sons she'd had the privilege of a wet nurse.

She made a mental note to send a message to her contacts in Canton in the morning. Just because Cheung Po wanted to wait didn't mean she had to. She'd never have made it through her previous pregnancies alive if she'd allowed herself to succumb to the weakness of her sex. She had no intention of starting now.

20

Whatever she might have vowed to herself, Shek Yeung ended up relaxing into her pregnancy—not completely, but more than she knew she should have. She did in fact send a message to Canton the next day. But when she didn't hear back (perhaps the assassin had himself been assassinated), she forgot to reach out to her other contacts. So the months passed, and soon she resembled a peach right down to the dark cleftlike line that ran down the length of her belly.

This pregnancy was turning out to be quite different from her previous ones. Her age likely had something to do with it. Every morning she arose with a new ache in her body. Every night she collapsed into bed, only to awaken again because of a cramp or the need to urinate. But there was also the climate, which pressed close like a large, slobbery dog. There was the house, which was perpetually underlit. And then there was Cheung Po, whose suddenly detailed plans for upcoming campaigns left her with little to do. The result was that she wanted to sleep all the time. So for the first time in almost two decades, she granted herself this small kindness, sleeping past dawn, so deep in dreams that even a middling assassin could have taken her life.

For the first couple of months, Shek Yeung participated in the fleet's raids around Maynila Bay, though given her physical limitations, she mostly just shouted orders from the stern. She and Cheung Po made frequent visits to the fortune-teller on her little altar boat, who predicted again and again that their endeavors would meet with success. Poems about swallows and mountains prophesied narrow misses as well as resounding victories. Despite her obvious resentment, the older woman was cooperative, "reading" each stalk carefully, only stopping every so often to scoff or to scowl.

And meet with success they did. From the incoming Spanish galleons, they plundered silver, from the outgoing spices and textiles. Shek Yeung would have liked to participate in the raids until it was time for them to return to Canton, except at one point during one battle, she looked down to find a red thunderbolt across her belly. For a moment she couldn't tell if the blood had come from her or from someone else. This scared her more than she wanted to admit, so from that point forward, she stopped putting out to sea.

At first, she feared the raids would meet with failure without her direct involvement, but once again Cheung Po had everything in hand. He would have done anything, it seemed, to protect the baby. This included snatching up every amulet he could find, though he tried to keep them secret—understandable, she had to admit, given her outburst outside that European temple and her general thriftiness. She wouldn't even have found out about the amulets if she hadn't gone snooping through his belongings. Beneath a loose board in a cabinet sat twenty-some-odd charms made of brass, silver, and jade, purchased or otherwise. And there in the center, in a small cinnabar box, the kind in which one kept ceremonial seals, lay a delicately etched golden lock strung on a heavy neck chain. He must have commissioned the charm to "lock" the baby to life. The etching featured fish swimming under a sky simultaneously illuminated by the sun, moon, and stars.

She didn't bring up the issue with him. She didn't know how to verbalize her gratitude, frustration, and sadness. If he'd guessed that she would go looking and find everything, then he did not let on.

All in all, it was a good time. The crew members were excited to be in a new place, away from the emperor's dreaded hunting dog. They drank too much palm wine, ate too much *lechon,* and cozied up to the women in the brothels. For the most part, they stayed out of trouble per Shek Yeung's orders. She didn't want them to use up their welcome before she'd had a chance to resolve this Pak Ling matter.

Unfortunately, the extra downtime also created a few problems. Some of the men got seriously injured in fights while drunk, and one day while Shek Yeung was visiting the ship to discuss strategy with Ahmad, she saw Yan-Yan and the northern woman kissing.

Afterward, she pulled the girl aside. "You have strong feelings for her?" Shek Yeung asked.

Yan-Yan nodded.

"And she feels the same about you?"

Another nod.

Shek Yeung knew no good would come from her discouraging the relationship, but she also felt the need to say something. There was danger in people in this kind of life becoming deeply attached to each other. Out of the many sexual relationships that frothed up at sea—men with women, men with men—most were relationships of convenience. Once they reached port or returned home, the parties involved amicably parted ways. Relationships born out of true affection were more complicated to manage. The couple looked out for each other instead of the other crew members or the mission. They balked if she had to separate them by assigning them to different ships. Shek Yeung told the girl as much.

"You're in a relationship with Big Brother Cheung!" Yan-Yan retorted.

"That's different," Shek Yeung said.

"He likes you."

"Yes."

"You like him, too."

Shek Yeung supposed that was true. She liked him as a co-commander, when he wasn't being an idiot. She liked his loyalty to the fleet. But that wasn't the kind of "like" the girl meant.

In a way, she envied Yan-Yan and her ability to love in such a reckless way. She herself might have been capable of it once upon a time. How that must feel, all that freedom and vulnerability, like jumping off a ship in the middle of the sea. She'd tried to "like" Cheng Yat, really tried, telling herself that she might as well if she had no choice but to be with him. In the end, she'd achieved something very close to "like": confidence in him and in his commitment to keeping her alive. With a little more time, she could imagine feeling the same toward Cheung Po. It was the most she'd learned to hope for.

"Just don't become too—" Shek Yeung stopped herself. "A lot can happen, is what I'm trying to say. Heaven doesn't like certainty of mortals."

"I know," Yan-Yan said.

"Do you?"

The girl didn't answer. Shek Yeung decided to let it go. There would be other chances to convince Yan-Yan to see things her way.

. . .

About six months into the pregnancy, a message from Buddhika finally arrived. Juan stopped by the *bahay* unannounced one morning. Cheung Po was studying a map of the seaways in the dining room. Shek Yeung had just awoken from a particularly inauspicious dream. In it, she, wearing a red dress, received a pill from the goddess Kwun-Yam. She swallowed the pill, and her belly began to swell. Only then did she realize that it was swelling not with child but with blood, hence the redness of her dress.

"So Lam Yuk-Yiu's fleet is also in town," she said. Her stomach turned.

"No, no," Juan said. "Your informant sent a messenger. Not very smart, if you ask me. The more people who know what he's doing, the more dangerous it is for everyone."

"Dangerous" was an understatement. Lam Yuk-Yiu would cut off Buddhika's tongue and probably also his genitals if she learned he'd betrayed her. "And?"

"Well, the messenger was mumbly, and I had a little trouble understanding his Cantonese. But the gist is that the English and the Portuguese have formed an alliance."

"Alliance for what?"

"Flooding the market with opium?"

"The Portuguese never showed much of an interest in opium before," Shek Yeung said.

"The Portuguese are interested in money just like everyone else," Cheung Po said, looking up from his map. "Maybe we should sell off our stockpile after all."

They needed a long-term plan, and not just regarding the opium. Between Pak Ling and the Europeans' alliance, going from raid to raid was no longer an option.

After Juan left, she sat down with paper and a red ink set and made a list of the fleet's holdings. There was the Southern Cave that she had fought to keep out of Kwok Po-Tai's hands, as well as the cave with all the silver. There was the rice hidden under the Ma-Zou temple built by Cheung Po, though that cache would need to be replenished soon.

If the Europeans had indeed overcome their squabbles, pirating was about to become more difficult. She shuddered, imagining the Portuguese sailors who had killed Cheng Yat being backed by the English. Her fleet would have to make fewer sea raids, which would mean less food. She made a note to stockpile as much food as possible, but food was perishable. They might be able to lie low for a few months, but after that?

They would have to raid the villages that weren't loyal to the alliance more frequently. The Europeans didn't have a hold on the coastal towns, and Pak Ling would have a hard time splitting his attention between land and sea. The smaller towns were easy pickings. Even some of the larger, walled cities were vulnerable. The fleet had spies everywhere, and they would be able to tell her about weak points in the defenses.

Still, the idea bothered her. At sea, everyone was equal. You knew what you were risking when you set sail. Even as a fifteen-year-old, she'd understood this, and though she hadn't expected to have her life forever changed by pirates, she'd accepted the possibility of death by typhoon, by a sharp rock, or any other such thing. But to land, to penetrate and savage a village where people were simply living their lives—all those children running in courtyards, all those aunties gossiping while cracking sunflower seeds between their back teeth—well, it seemed wrong.

Not that she'd never done it before under Cheng Yat's direction. She just never liked it.

Shek Yeung took the map Cheung Po had been studying earlier and drew a wide, wavy line across the paper to mark the route, targeting the villages she believed Cheng Yat would have. She sat back and stared. It looked like a flying war banner, a trail of blood.

. . .

Seven months into the pregnancy, the unthinkable happened. In lieu of his priggish knuckle-rapping, this time Juan pounded frantically on the door. "It's gone," he said the moment Cheung Po opened the door. "The Green Banner Fleet. Pak Ling wiped them out."

Shek Yeung gripped the edge of a table to steady herself. "What?"

"There was a huge battle. Li is dead, along with most of his men. The remainder of the fleet has scattered."

"That can't be," Cheung Po said.

"When have you known me to be wrong?" Juan snapped.

Cheung Po didn't answer.

"He found their hideout somehow, Pak Ling. He must have had spies inside the fleet. He blockaded them and then didn't even engage. Just waited until they were desperate. Li tried to ram the navy, but there was no way, they had all those war junks."

"He did the same thing with the northern rebels," Cheung Po muttered.

"How many escaped?" she asked Juan.

"Not many? I'm not sure. A lot of people fought to the death instead of surrendering because they would have been executed anyway."

The Green Banner Fleet hadn't been the largest or strongest of the alliance, but nevertheless it had been important in maintaining order over the northeastern sector. Most important, Li had been a good commander: level-headed, fair, and wily, though apparently not wily enough. Not enough to identify the spy before it was too late.

Was Pak Ling's spy in her fleet even now? For a compromised fleet, they were certainly doing well. The spy had done nothing to help Qiu

Liang-Gong back in Taiwan, nor had he sabotaged any of the raids these past few months. In fact, the fleet was doing better than it had done with Cheng Yat at the helm.

Regardless, if the Green Banner Fleet had succumbed, then none of the remaining fleets were truly safe. This was likely Pak Ling's plan, to pick them off one by one, starting with the smaller fleets. The good news was that he wouldn't get to the Red Banner Fleet for a while. The bad news was that, by the time he got to the Red Banner Fleet, there would be no alliance left and the fleet would have to stand alone against the emperor's and the Europeans' forces. Would the odds be in their favor if this came to pass? She didn't want to have to find out.

After some discussion with Cheung Po, she asked Juan to send out a message. By the time the moon had finished a half-turn—pulling itself inside out like a shirt sleeve so that where was once dark was now light—all the parties in question had arrived.

With Cheung Po by her side, she entered the small back room of Juan's restaurant, her swollen belly leading the way. To Juan's young assistant, she handed the cutlass at her side, the dagger up her sleeve, and the flintlock behind her back. The boy gawped a little at all the weapons before hurrying off with them.

Cheung Po hadn't wanted Shek Yeung to attend the meeting. She hadn't wanted to herself. She'd worked hard to keep her pregnancy secret from most of her crew, and she trusted her crew far more than the people in this room. But the matter with Pak Ling took precedence over her cautiousness. One-fifth of the alliance, gone.

At the center of the room stretched a table of the long rectangular style favored by Europeans. Such a shape left no uncertainty about hierarchy. Lam Yuk-Yiu and Choy Hin had taken up the opposite ends of the table—the one to keep an eye on the door and the other to bar entry or escape. Kwok Po-Tai was alone, looking more haggard than Shek Yeung had ever seen him. Ba of the White Banner Fleet was missing. He probably died a long time ago, as Lam Yuk-Yiu had suggested.

She and Cheung Po sat in the only chairs left, opposite Kwok Po-Tai and flanked by the other couple. The positioning wasn't great because she and Cheung Po couldn't see each other without turning their heads.

They'd have arrived earlier if Shek Yeung hadn't needed to stop to urinate. She had the sense that Lam Yuk-Yiu or Kwok Po-Tai would lunge forward at any moment to skewer her with a hidden dagger.

In none of the stories about Ma-Zou was she pregnant. Yet everyone called her "Maternal Ancestor," because to be a mother was to fear for one's children, and of all the immortals, she was known to be the kindest.

"Pak Ling is too dangerous to let live," Shek Yeung said, skipping the niceties. "If we want to end him, we need to coordinate with one another. The Black Banner Fleet has already fought him, and I briefly talked to the man. Between us, we should be able to come up with a plan." She told them about the encounter in the tavern.

Kwok Po-Tai gasped. "Dark wispy mustache? Strange accent?" Shek Yeung nodded. "I believe I met him, too," he said. "Unfortunately, I did not pay much attention to our interaction. I assumed he was a drunkard or a madman and so ignored his rambling for the most part. He was complaining about the emperor, if I remember correctly."

"He didn't leave you his name?" Shek Yeung asked.

"No."

"I don't get it," Choy Hin said. "So he's going around meeting pirate commanders? Why? To see if we're loyal to the emperor? Of course we're not."

"He approached you, too?" Cheung Po asked.

"No," Choy Hin said, frowning, "but we've been in Taiwan. Maybe he hasn't crossed the strait yet."

"Did he ask you anything?" Shek Yeung said to Kwok Po-Tai, remembering the questions about her children.

"He asked about my family. I didn't answer, of course. And then, oddly, about the Tang dynasty poets. Now I wonder if he knew about my books and was trying to forge a connection."

"Who cares about any of this?" Cheung Po said. "We need a strategy."

"The strategy," Kwok Po-Tai said, "is gathering our forces and killing him without delay. My fleet might have suffered losses when we faced him, but we survived. If our fleets had been acting in concert, we would have been victorious."

Quickly, Shek Yeung counted the days: a month and a half until the child was due, another month after that to recover, by which point most of the seasonal crew would have returned home for the year. The fleet would be at half strength. "We can't attack yet," she said.

"Why not?" Kwok Po-Tai demanded.

How was she supposed to explain her reasoning without calling additional attention to the pregnancy? Men didn't plan around such things because they didn't have to. But if she brought it up, he would conclude that her motherhood was impairing her ability to lead. He might sow doubt among alliance members about her abilities. She'd worked so hard since marrying Cheng Yat to prove to everyone that she could do all the same work a man could do, all that work and more, really, because a woman was expected to be a man until the men around her needed a woman to step in to sweet-talk, to seduce.

Lam Yuk-Yiu, who had been quiet all this time, said, "It sounds to me like you want *us* to get involved in a bloody conflict because *you* lost face in battle."

"My face is not the issue, shrew. Pak Ling threatens all of us."

"Does he?" Lam Yuk-Yiu said. "Because as far as we can tell, he has no interest in Taiwan. The emperor has never particularly cared about what happens there, and Pak Ling, by all accounts, is doggedly loyal. It may be that as long as my fleet stays close to the island's coastline, he'll leave us alone."

"You can't stay close to the island forever," Kwok Po-Tai said.

"We can stay until Pak Ling dies, which will happen sooner or later. Time and fortune will take care of him for us."

Kwok Po-Tai sneered. "That is exactly the kind of cowardly thinking I would expect from a woman." He turned to Choy Hin. "And you? Will you allow your wife to make a mockery of the alliance like this? Or is she the true commander of the fleet and you just one of her male whores?"

Cheung Po tensed in his seat. His friendship with Choy Hin would prove to be a liability one day, Shek Yeung felt certain of it. She grabbed the hem of Cheung Po's shirt, silently warning him to stay still. "No one is saying that we leave Pak Ling alone forever," she said.

"I am," Lam Yuk-Yiu said.

"What is the point of the alliance if we do not combine forces when needed?" Kwok Po-Tai yelled. "I would never have to share my spoils. I would plunder whomever I wanted, regardless of whether they had an allegiance to one of the other fleets."

"You would be plundering a lot less if not for the alliance," Shek Yeung said, struggling to stay calm. She and Cheng Yat had laid out the same argument when they convinced Kwok Po-Tai to join, and it was exhausting to be having this conversation again. "Burnt-down villages can't pay tribute. You might be dead already by the hands of the navy, the Europeans, or one of the other pirate fleets."

"*If* you are around Canton," Lam Yuk-Yiu said. She was picking at one of her dirty, jagged fingernails with another. "The alliance is helpful if you do most of your work there. But the Blue Banner Fleet doesn't, at least not in recent years, which makes me wonder why we stay in this arrangement at all."

"You suddenly want to leave the alliance now that there is a task for you. How convenient," Kwok Po-Tai said.

Cheung Po turned to Choy Hin. "No one is leaving the alliance. Tell them, Big Brother." But Choy Hin just smiled dazedly. He'd probably floated away from the conversation on an opium cloud a while ago.

If Shek Yeung didn't do something now, all she'd accomplished was going to disappear. She could lie and hope that Lam Yuk-Yiu didn't see through the falsehood, or she could do as Cheng Yat had taught and interpret the truth in a way that benefited her. "The Dutch."

This got Lam Yuk-Yiu's attention. "What about them?" she said.

"I have heard," Shek Yeung said, "that the English and the Portuguese recently formed an alliance. If those two powers could look past their differences, then surely an alliance with the Dutch is already underway. Would your fleet really be able to fend off all three at the same time?"

"Where did you hear this?" Lam Yuk-Yiu asked suspiciously.

"My sources. As for Pak Ling, how certain are you that he will never cross the strait? Enough to stake your own life and the lives of your men? But let's say that Pak Ling keeps away from Taiwan. Wonderful.

What do you think will happen after he destroys the other fleets? There will be survivors—there are always survivors. Where do you think they will flee? Many of them will end up in your territory. Some of them may try to fight you for dominance. You don't need the extra trouble."

Out of the corner of her eye, she could see Cheung Po nodding. Kwok Po-Tai looked grudgingly receptive. She turned to face Lam Yuk-Yiu. "And even, even if you manage to subdue all the newcomers, absorb them into your fleet, ask yourself this: Is the maritime traffic around Taiwan able to sustain a fleet much bigger than the one you have now? Are those little fishing villages going to be able to provide supplies for all the extra men?"

Lam Yuk-Yiu glared at her.

"Some of your men can die now," Shek Yeung said, "or most of your men can die later. There's no way out of this without blood."

"I will confer with my own sources regarding this supposed alliance with the Dutch," Lam Yuk-Yiu said after thinking about it for a moment. "If there is any truth in this, then you will hear from me."

"Six months," Cheung Po said. "That should give you more than enough time to verify the rumors, Big Sister Lam. Then we reconvene."

They drank on it. Shek Yeung gave Cheung Po's forearm a quick squeeze. She knew he had proposed this to buy her some time. Coming from him, the appeal to wait seemed less like an admission of vulnerability and more like strategy.

But was there a way out of this without her blood and the blood of her crew? That was the question she had in mind a few days after the meeting. She and Cheung Po took a tender out to the fortune-teller's one-masted junk. Since their previous visit, the older woman had further embellished the shrine. Cheung Po had given her permission to decorate her boat however she wanted, trusting that an oracle would know best what would please Heaven, and she had committed to the task in the most extravagant ways, spending their money as a small act of revenge. In place of the old statue of Ma-Zou sat a larger one collared and cuffed with gold leaf, wearing a headdress fringed with jewels. (The old one had been a simple statuette with a black cloth that Shek Yeung had tied around her head.) Near the statue, the fortune-teller had arranged many gold sycee, most of them in the shape of boats. The fortune-teller had also bought herself new robes. At the moment, she was wearing a red silk piece embroidered with turquoise cranes. She'd put on some weight after a few months of eating the best food available to the fleet and, as a result, appeared much younger than before. Shek Yeung felt a swell of satisfaction: She'd done this. She'd improved this woman's life, even if the woman herself disagreed. After all, wasn't Shek Yeung's own life better as a result of Cheng Yat? Better even, maybe, than it would have been had she never left her little fishing village, where she likely would have been killed already by famine, pirates, or soldiers?

Wasn't it?

"You again, commander," the fortune-teller said upon Cheung Po's approach. It was hard to say how she knew, maybe something about his gait. Shek Yeung and Cheung Po were certainly not the only two people who sought her services. The fortune-teller waved in the general direction of a couple of stools. They dragged the stools closer and sat.

"A new problem has—" Shek Yeung said.

"Don't tell me," the older woman interrupted. "I pull the fortunes I pull and interpret them as I am moved to. You should know by now that Heaven rarely gives direct answers." She picked up the stalk that had slid from the canister.

> The flock of chickens calls loudly.
> They fight as the guests arrive.
> I chase the chickens up a tree.
> Now I can hear the knock on the gate.

"There's going to be a fight?" Cheung Po asked.

"Chickens are excitable, stupid animals," the fortune-teller said. "The new arrivals send them into a frenzy. But does the speaker try to calm them? No, that would be ridiculous. Instead, he chases them where they won't bother him. The newfound quiet is what allows him to hear the visitors knocking." She frowned. "This fortune could also be telling you to hide your assets and hide them well. In this case, the speaker might not have wanted his visitors to see his chickens."

"So . . . don't try to wrangle angry chickens," Cheung Po said.

It seemed clear to Shek Yeung that the chickens represented the many battles between Pak Ling and the pirates. There was no calming everyone, so best to gain some distance from the conflict. That was, after all, the reason they'd sailed off to Maynila. But if the fortune concerned the fleet's assets, then she would have to increase the security around their stockpiles. And given the inevitable expiration of their food stores, she would have to increase the frequency of raids, even with Pak Ling closing in.

As distasteful as she found the idea of land raids, the reality was that they needed to start immediately. There was no telling when Pak Ling would turn his attention to them. Her feelings about land raids shouldn't outweigh the security of the fleet—Cheng Yat wouldn't have let his own feelings interfere.

She told Cheung Po her plan to divide the fleet that evening: two-thirds of the ships would accompany him on the land raids, whereas the remainder would return with her to Canton before her due date. He was in a good mood, draped over a rocking chair in the *bahay,* picking the remnants of a particularly delicious meal out of his teeth. His good mood quickly disappeared.

"Pak Ling's people could be anywhere," he said. "How do you know he hasn't found out where we are?"

"Even if he knows, he has no authority here."

"Doesn't mean he can't hire an assassin. How are you going to protect yourself the way you are?"

"We have no choice. Without a good stockpile, we are at the whims of Heaven. One bad storm and it's over."

Cheung Po rocked himself up to standing and began to pace. "We can let some of the squadron leaders handle it."

She took his wrist gently. "I don't trust them. I trust you."

He glared at her, but he didn't look truly angry. "Don't flatter me."

"You know I'm not. Believe me, the biggest danger to me right now isn't Pak Ling. It's this child, and you can't do anything about that. What you can do is make sure that this child has plenty of food and money if the worst happens."

He shook his head in annoyance, but she knew she'd won.

Cheung Po left before dawn without waking her, though it seemed to her, as she lay half-dreaming, that she felt a warm hand on her head before she heard the door to the *bahay* gently open and close.

21

S aying goodbye to Maynila proved surprisingly difficult. In the city, Shek Yeung had become reacquainted with a kind of peace, as if crossing paths with a close childhood friend after many years: one got the sense, despite the stilted conversation and awkward pauses, that one was protected, maybe even cherished. She resisted the urge to look astern as the ship pulled away from shore. It was unlikely she would ever return to Maynila.

She asked Old Wong to chart a somewhat circuitous course for Canton that would avoid the areas where imperial ships were most often sighted. Running into Pak Ling or any of his underlings was a bad idea with only a third of the fleet. The long trip gave her time to think. She planned raids and drafted speeches to deliver to the other fleet commanders at their next meeting. But mostly she worried about where the delivery would take place.

That one at sea had been pure bad luck. Her second delivery had, for obvious reasons, occurred at the Cheng family estate. Now that Cheng Yat was dead and she had remarried, the estate wasn't off limits to her, not exactly, but his relatives had very much implied that she was not welcome outside the occasional visit with her sons. They hadn't opposed Cheng Yat's decision to marry her years ago, but they wouldn't have chosen someone like her had he consented to an arranged marriage.

"Your mother doesn't like me," she'd said to Cheng Yat after meeting his family for the first time.

"She doesn't like any woman who's not like her," he'd replied, by which he'd meant any woman from humble origins. The Cheng family might have made its fortune from piracy, but they, Cheng Yat's grandfather in particular, hadn't wanted to be remembered for piracy. So Cheng Yat's grandfather and father had both married patrician women, whose parents agreed to the arrangements with full knowledge of the Cheng family's reputation. After all, blood money looked and smelled and could be spent like regular money. But Shek Yeung's background wasn't the sole reason the Cheng family disliked her. There were some women who, having had no choice but to perform femininity for men all their lives, began to confuse their roles for reality. Such women loved to instruct other women on how to be a good mother, a good wife, a good daughter-in-law—a good woman. The Cheng women, with their molluscan bound feet and fainting fits, knew that Shek Yeung had little interest in—and worse yet, little need for—their instruction. This raised uncomfortable questions: Did any woman really need their instruction? If not, then why had they endured all they had endured?

So giving birth at the Cheng estate was out. The next logical option would have been the midwife's home. But Pak Ling might have already started surveilling the area, given that she'd been wandering around there that day. Would he ambush her while she was in labor? He seemed to be a principled man, his deception notwithstanding. If he did choose to attack her during her moment of weakness, would she be able to rely on her tears to save her? So many principled men, after all, felt an airy sympathy toward women, the kind of sympathy they might also direct toward an injured dog. Cheng Yat had been the exception. With him, there had been no sympathy, just expectation—she could either meet that expectation or die.

The only option left was Wo-Yuet's house. Out of habit, she'd made sure, when she went to the sam-hop-yuen, that she wasn't followed. Her best guess was that Pak Ling had paid various people in the town center to alert him if they'd spotted her, and that was how he found her in the tavern that day.

Anyone other than Shek Yeung would have found the idea laughable: to give birth in a place where a person had recently died, in a home that had never housed a family. "It's an invitation for envious ghosts," the aunties back in the village would have muttered while shaking their heads. But it made sense. Most people didn't know of Shek Yeung's association with Wo-Yuet, and the house was on the outskirts of town. Shek Yeung would reveal the location only to the people she trusted most: the midwife, Yan-Yan, and maybe also Ahmad, so he could stand guard on the road to the sam-hop-yuen.

Wo-Yuet's ghost would never hurt her. Shek Yeung couldn't say how she knew this, but she did. Wo-Yuet had protected Shek Yeung when she was at her most vulnerable, like taking the customers Shek Yeung feared and interceding when Shek Yeung got in trouble with Madame Ko, even when doing so meant raising Madame Ko's hackles. Shek Yeung simply could not imagine her friend being anything other than benevolent.

By the time the junk finally docked in Canton, Shek Yeung was so big she could barely move around. Many days of sleeplessness had left her feeling dizzy. Her vision occasionally fled, making her chase helplessly after it as if after a lost kite string. With help from Ahmad and Yan-Yan, she half-slid, half-rolled off the ship, and the three of them set off for the sam-hop-yuen.

The longans were beginning to decay, though a few still appeared to be edible. Yan-Yan plucked one from the branch and, digging her thumbnail into the skin, split it down the middle. She squeezed the flesh into her mouth, swirled it around for a bit, and stuck her tongue out at Shek Yeung to show a seed sitting there like a black pearl, laughing at Shek Yeung's beleaguered sigh. Meanwhile, the kumquat flowers were wilting, the leggy, light brown petals parting to reveal the fruit just beginning to crown.

The rooms were, unsurprisingly, even dustier than during her previous visit. She lay down on Wo-Yuet's bed, noting the little spots of dried blood on the blanket and pillow. Had her friend suffered right before she died? No, that was a ridiculous question—of course she had. The better question was, had she suffered much?

"I'll go fetch the midwife," Ahmad said.

Shek Yeung fell asleep almost immediately after he left. When she awoke, Yan-Yan wasn't in the room. Shek Yeung didn't call out to her, relishing the silence. At sea, one was surrounded by sound: people talking, or singing, or sharpening swords; the sails angrily puffing out their chests and then razzing out all the air; and always, always, the sound of waves.

The aunties said that the behavior that came most naturally to a baby was floating—*toss a baby into water and you'll see*—that it was the contact with and corruption by the earthly realm that robbed humans of this native ability. It followed, then, that humans returned to the water upon death. Maybe instead of sticking around to haunt the living, the dead simply went to this realm to rest, to float. That didn't seem so bad.

Eventually, Yan-Yan wandered back in, mouth stuffed with longan. "Want one?" the girl asked, the words leaking from between mashed bits of fruit.

"Any word from Ahmad yet?"

"No, but the midwife is far away, and you did tell him to be careful."

Shek Yeung patted her bedside. Yan-Yan plopped down on it. "I'm sorry to make you do this," she said.

The girl shrugged. "It's better than fighting with Big Brother Cheung."

Shek Yeung suddenly realized that Yan-Yan might have never actually killed anyone before. But that couldn't possibly be true. The girl joined the fleet years ago. Still, it wasn't as if anyone kept track of who killed whom during a battle. Shek Yeung had more than once suspected that some of her own crew members had been killed by fellow crew members with a grudge.

Most people found the first kill difficult. How quickly one grew accustomed to taking a life varied, but in most cases, by the fourth or fifth, one learned to swerve around the feelings as around dog turd. It was a fact that, before a person's first kill, that person was at a disadvantage in battle. But Shek Yeung didn't want to do to the girl what Cheng Yat had done to her. For many nights after her first killing, she'd awoken from nightmares in which she was conversing with the man she'd murdered. When she remembered halfway through the conversation that she'd murdered him, his throat opened into a wide red grin as if he'd pulled off the perfect practical joke.

A little after dusk, Ahmad returned with the midwife, a sack of rice, and a headless chicken. Tse Po-Po cooked up an unbearably bitter broth with the chicken and some fortifying herbs, slapping Yan-Yan's hand away whenever the girl reached for a taste. After dinner, the midwife performed Shek Yeung's first physical exam in months. "You're very big," Tse Po-Po said. "Bigger than last time."

"I feel bigger," Shek Yeung said.

"This baby, his size will be a problem."

"Are there any herbs for this kind of thing?"

Tse Po-Po made an equivocal noise. "Where's the father?"

"Somewhere else," Shek Yeung said.

"Close enough to get here quickly if necessary?"

"Why?"

The midwife shook her head and said, "No reason," and then added after a moment, "Well, he's a young man. He has time."

And though Shek Yeung liked to tell herself that she didn't care about Cheung Po, that she put up with him only for the good of the fleet, she found herself wondering how Cheung Po would react if she or the baby (or both) didn't make it. Would he mourn her? She hadn't mourned Cheng Yat, after all. There was no reason to believe that Cheung Po wouldn't immediately pick a new wife, someone young enough to bear him all those sons he wanted.

What does it matter how he would feel? she berated herself. *Dead is dead.* Except, for some reason, it did. She wanted to believe that all they'd been through together had made her not only a trusted co-commander to him but something more.

· · ·

Several days later, on a warm, clear morning, the contractions started. No storm at sea this time, no chatty servants clanging bowls and dishes. Shek Yeung awoke and simply knew it was time.

According to the aunties, one could sometimes tell when one's time was coming to an end. Old Chan, the town magistrate, awoke one day and asked his wife to prepare his favorite meal, congee with pork and leeks. The wife found the request a little strange (Old Chan wasn't in the habit of eating breakfast) but did as requested. After breakfast, Old Chan sat down in his favorite chair to watch the birds. When the wife went to fetch him for lunch later, he was dead.

Shek Yeung nudged Yan-Yan awake and had the girl call the midwife. As she waited, Shek Yeung placed a hand on her own belly. There wasn't pain yet so much as an uncomfortable stirring, like the key to a heavy lock slowly turning. "Here we are, little one," she said. "Where we go now is up to you."

Tse Po-Po arrived and helped her down onto the floor into a squatting position. It seemed to Shek Yeung that everything was happening faster than it had in the past. Soon the contractions were coming quickly. The pain made it difficult to think or, for that matter, see properly. Men believed that being a woman was easier than being a man because a man had to fight battles. As someone who'd endured both childbirth and battle wounds, Shek Yeung could say without hesitation that childbirth was worse.

"Well, at least the head is in the right place," Tse Po-Po said.

Yan-Yan sat wide-legged behind Shek Yeung, a warm rag in one hand and Shek Yeung's hand in the other. "Take deep breaths," the girl said, her voice steady. Shek Yeung glanced back at her and was surprised to find a calm expression on her face.

"Don't look at me, focus on breathing," Yan-Yan said. "I've done this enough times by now to know it goes much better for the mother when she breathes."

Life at sea changed you, usually for the worse, but sometimes for the better.

"Push harder," Tse Po-Po said. Shek Yeung bore down.

"Harder," Tse Po-Po repeated. "He hasn't even crowned."

One set of contractions gave way to another, and Shek Yeung lost track of time. At one point she became vaguely aware of Yan-Yan holding a cup of sour liquid up to her mouth and telling her to drink. She barely turned her head fast enough to throw it up, but Yan-Yan persisted, gripping her chin and tipping in more of the herbal concoction.

"Come on, get up, you need to walk," Tse Po-Po said, tugging on her arm.

"Are you joking?" Shek Yeung screamed.

The two other women yanked Shek Yeung up by the elbows and led her slowly around the room, once, twice. They stopped next to a post and leaned Shek Yeung against it. "Push again," Tse Po-Po said.

She pushed and felt the head crown. "Good, good," Tse Po-Po said.

For the briefest of moments, Shek Yeung had the audacity to believe the hard part was over, but then labor stalled again: the shoulders. This stupid child with stupid Cheung Po's stupidly wide shoulders.

"This is bad," Tse Po-Po said, fingers on the pulse point on the child's neck.

"How bad?" Yan-Yan asked.

"This needs to happen now," Tse Po-Po said to Shek Yeung. "Do you understand?"

The child didn't want to be here, Shek Yeung realized through the haze of pain. How could she explain it? She'd brought him here without his permission, abducted him from a place where he'd been at peace— just as the pirates had abducted her and she had abducted others. In vengeance, he was going to kill himself and her. And who could blame him? Look at this world.

"Cut him out of me!" Shek Yeung yelled.

"You'll die!" Tse Po-Po said.

"I don't care!"

"Not yet," Tse Po-Po said. "You're not dying yet."

I know you don't want to be here, Shek Yeung found herself thinking at the child. *But you're almost here anyway, so please, just try, and I promise I will do everything in my power to be a better mother to you than I ever was with Ying-Shek and Hung-Shek.*

And Big Sister, Shek Yeung found herself thinking at Wo-Yuet, *you've already done so much for me. I'm sorry to ask this one more thing.*

And Ma-Zou. Maternal Ancestor. You've said you owe me nothing, and I understand that, but tell me: What would you have me trade? My fleet? My life?

Using all the strength in her body, she gave a final push. Out of the corner of her eye, she saw a red light. In her gasped breath she whiffed the barest hint of jasmine. And she felt the shoulders slide free. *Thank you, thank you*, she thought. Growing up, Shek Yeung had never had a mother. But she'd had Ma-Zou and Wo-Yuet.

As she sagged to the floor and her vision faded, she wondered if the last things she ever saw would be Yan-Yan's mouth opening and closing, asking her a question she couldn't hear through the roar in her ears; Tse Po-Po's exhausted face; and behind the midwife, that red light burning brighter and brighter. If this was it, then so be it. People lived longer and shorter lives, better and worse. She knew better than to complain.

. . .

"Girl, why are you crying?"

"Ma-Zou, I don't want to die."

"Is it scarier to die than to live?"

"My big brother died, and I never saw him again. My father's probably dead, too."

"You didn't answer my question."

"I know all the ways that life is scary, but I don't know all the ways that death is scary because you never tell us. Heaven never tells any of us. Do we just reincarnate? Do we go to an underworld like the monks say, where we're tortured again and again for the bad things we did? Or do we become hungry ghosts like the aunties say, doomed to wander the world in misery forever?"

"You are upset."

"Of course I am! How are we supposed to live our lives if we don't know?"

"Some things are not for you to know."

"I thought you might say that."

"And now that I have said it?"

. . .

She didn't wake again until it was dark. From where she lay, the sky was a starless, moonless black, so devoid of even the slightest perturbation that she might have confused it for a flat, painted surface. But years at sea had taught her this: sometimes the most placid, featureless waters were the most dangerous because they ran the deepest.

She called for Yan-Yan and Tse Po-Po. The sounds barely scraped out of her parched throat.

A moment later Yan-Yan entered with the child. She looked incandescently happy with the bundle in her arms, as if she were the mother. "Do you want to see the baby?" the girl asked.

Shek Yeung held out her arms. Yan-Yan lowered the child into them.

Yes, there was that comically large head. There were those pouting lips and that pinched look of protest at having been brought into this world. *Yes, yes,* she said to the baby. *It's too cold and bright and dry here. I know.*

She began unwrapping the child of its many coverings. Ten fingers, ten toes. A strong heartbeat. She removed the diaper cloth, and fear flooded her all over again.

She was a girl.

PART IV

Red as the Sea

22

In one of the stories about Ma-Zou, she was an interloper.

The pregnant Madame Lam prayed to Kwun-Yam for another son who could assist his father and older brothers with fishing. Girls were useless on the sea—as the saying went, "A girl's virtue is having no talent." Before Madame Lam could finish the prayer, she was submerged by a lethargy so deep that she collapsed onto a nearby bench. Half-asleep, she sensed a gentle but powerful presence kneeling beside her. When asked about it later, she would describe the presence as one of infinite love and yet also infinite sadness, as alive and incandescent as it was cold and still.

In that moment, though, Madame Lam only lay there in her paralysis, feeling the presence lean close to her, lift her hand, and press into it what felt like a tiny pebble. "Will I meet you again?" she tried to ask when the presence pulled away. She was answered with the knowledge that this was merely the first of many encounters she would have with this being, though when and how she did not know.

When she awoke, she opened her hand to find a single pill there. She swallowed the pill, and from her belly burst a beam of red light so brilliant that later people several villages away would report having seen it. The Lam household bloomed with the scent of lotus, the delicate, sweet heart of it trailed by a long, hardy stem of green. When the red light had dimmed, Madame Lam found in its place not a son but a daughter. She understood then that Kwun-Yam had given her not the boy that she wanted but the girl that the world needed.

And, until the seas dried, the girl that the world would always need.

23

Shek Yeung stared at the child in her arms. The girl had cried— quite a bit, actually—before finally suckling a little and falling asleep, so no Heavenly child here. But she supposed not having a Heavenly child was for the best. For one, she couldn't imagine continuing to pirate with someone there constantly lecturing her on the sutras. For another, in her experience, stubbornness was a good quality to have in a girl. The girls who relented were the ones who never could hold on to anything. Sometimes when Shek Yeung recalled the story of Ma-Zou's birth, she wondered if the real reason the goddess didn't cry or speak in her first years of life was self-preservation. Ma-Zou's parents had hoped for a boy, and when one was unwanted, one quickly learned to fold away the parts of oneself that others deemed undesirable, drawing one's limbs in uncomfortably tight to prevent others from tripping over one's very existence. In women that meant opinions, dissatisfactions, and vulnerabilities.

Yan-Yan must have sensed Shek Yeung's uneasiness because the girl asked, "What?"

"Hmm?"

"Why do you look like you're going to a funeral? She's beautiful!"

"I just thought . . . the midwife said I would have a son. She was right the other times."

Yan-Yan pulled a face. "Why would you want another one? You've already got two."

And if it had been a different day—one in which she had not almost died—Shek Yeung would have stayed silent. Instead she told Yan-Yan about Cheung Po's deep longing for a son, about the deal she'd made with him to retain control over her half of the fleet. "I don't think I can do this again," Shek Yeung said. "I barely survived this time. What if he insists on a son? What if he uses my failure to uphold my end of the agreement as an excuse to take what's mine?"

"Do you really think he would do that?" Yan-Yan asked, sitting down and jiggling the child's foot free from the whorls of fabric. The next thing Shek Yeung knew, Yan-Yan had managed to fit the entire foot into her mouth. *Some women are meant to be mothers,* Shek Yeung thought. *Just not as many as people believe.*

Out popped the foot. "You agreed yourself that he cares for you," Yan-Yan continued. "You think he would start a war now? Son or not, she's his child."

"He still needs an heir."

"Then raise her to succeed the two of you. You do your job fine. It's not like she can't learn."

Now this was a strange idea: a girl raised to command the way Cheng Yat had been. Shek Yeung had been pushed into her role later in life. So had Lam Yuk-Yiu and the higher-ranking women of the various fleets. But what if she groomed this child for power from the start?

Yet for the life of her, she couldn't figure how it would work. Say you took a girl child and raised her like a boy, among boys her own age. Say the boys accepted her as one of their own, challenged her to footraces and wrestling matches. Say you could teach the boys around her to treat her no differently once she started to bleed.

No, this was impossible. Men were always going to perceive women as inferior because of women's lesser physical strength and because of the months at a time they got rendered helpless by pregnancy. Power was rarely presented on a platter to women. If a woman grew fat with power, she grew from scraps that had fallen off the table. Most important, a woman was always deemed unworthy of power until a powerful man proclaimed her otherwise. A truly clever woman, seeing such a proclamation coming, prepared well and early for the opportunity so that, when the day finally came, she could swiftly eliminate all opposition. For decades, the fabled Empress Wu hid behind a pearl screen at her husband's meetings, subtly shaping the course of the nation as she awaited the decrepit man's inevitable demise. When he died, she seized control with spectacular speed and cruelty, deposing her own son. She ruled into her eighties.

But most women, Shek Yeung included, were not as clever as Empress Wu. On top of all that, boys and girls learned different ways of being in the world, different strategies to meet their own desires and needs. Boys hurt and got hurt. If one boy stole another boy's toy, the second boy had little recourse but to fight if he wanted that toy back. Girls were expected to run to adults for help. Even still, they sometimes got punished for doing so because a good woman was supposed to be unselfish and share.

By sheer chance, Shek Yeung had sidestepped some of that dog shit. With a dead mother and a father who was often at sea, she and her brother had fought as though they were both boys. Yes, she usually lost, but she always left a big enough or deep enough mark that he regretted having picked on her in the first place. (Was war really any different? One couldn't win every battle, but one ideally left the opposing side wounded enough that they would think twice before charging into future battles.) In their final years together, she and her brother had been what one might call friends.

"She's asleep again," Yan-Yan said.

"Babies do that."

"Want me to take her?"

Shek Yeung tucked the child's foot back into the blanket. "It's okay. I want to tell her a story I once heard from a friend."

. . .

A long time ago, there was a girl who loved the sea. Not just loved, you understand—she fell in love with it. She decided to dive to the very bottom to find the dragon king who dwelled there, for only he could grant her the ability to live beneath the waves forever. Everyone in her village laughed at her. "You'll die for sure," they said. "You'll get swallowed by a whale before you reach the dragon king."

But what was love if not the promise of obliteration? The girl dove from a high promontory, piercing the skin of the water like a silver hairpin in the hands of a wronged woman. She swam past schools of fish more colorful than the flowers that maidens wove into their hair; wizened turtles that bore on their backs scars from the worlds they'd once carried; and groves of leafless trees that were hard as jade, each spiked branch bright red as if stained with the blood of those who'd swum past. She swam in spite of the pain spreading through her limbs and the doubt spreading through her heart. Finally, the palace came into view. It was more glorious than she could have ever imagined, guarded by gigantic octopuses with arms that wound around the palace and then clasped together. Shining shells tiled every surface. The seaweed in the garden stretched taller than any tree on land.

She begged the carp gatekeeper for an audience with the king and was led into a massive hall lit by incandescent fish. When she saw the dragon king, she shrank in fear. His countenance was red and scaly, and though he was dressed in a refined robe, his hair and beard were wild. Nevertheless, she approached the throne and stated her request.

"Why do you wish to live here?" the dragon king asked.

"The sea is a peaceful place," she answered. "I have spent many years gazing upon it, and even when it is perturbed, it is not perturbed for long. On land, we have war and hunger. My village was raided by bandits thirteen moons ago, and many people died. Others were taken away to be sold. I escaped only because I had hidden myself inside a stove pit, and the entire time that I hid, I feared they would light a fire and cook me alive. If I lived here, I would be at peace."

The dragon king thought about this. "Every creature who lives down here is my subject. If you wish to stay, then you must prove yourself useful and able to cooperate with the others."

Her first task was to show she could cooperate with the womenfolk by serving the king and his brothers at a banquet. The fishwomen held her fast, binding her feet with long strips of fabric, breaking her toes and folding them under. Then one of them grabbed the front of her foot while another grabbed her heel, and together they broke her arch. The girl heard the crack before she felt it, and the pain was so excruciating that she began to cry profusely. "Don't cry, no man likes the ugly face of a crying woman," one of the fishwomen said, scrubbing the tears from her face and then powdering over the tracks with rouge. Finally, the girl could fit into the tiny, finned shoes worn by all the servants, and she teetered into the banquet hall. There the dragon king and his brothers sat on tall-backed chairs that were once the carapaces of giant lobsters. On the table were gold platters piled high with gems and pearls. The men crunched handfuls of gems while the girl and the fishwomen poured wine. Every now and then she felt a sharp pain in her buttocks or thighs and looked down to find one of the nobles pinching her flesh.

Her second task was to prove she could cooperate with the peasants by harvesting seaweed with them. They toiled until they could barely stand, hacking away at the stalks. The stringy stalks resisted her efforts, lashing at her until her skin broke into thin red frowns that immediately washed away, leaving no evidence of her suffering. From a fronded chair at the other end of the field, an overseer shouted abuses at the peasants to work harder, faster.

Her third task was to prove she could cooperate with the warriors by training for battle alongside them. "But I thought everyone down here was your subject," she said to the dragon king. "Who are we being trained to fight?"

The dragon king huffed. "Silly girl," he said, "don't you know that one is king for only as long as one can defend one's kingdom?"

With the soldiers, the girl practiced sword forms until her bones ached and her joints creaked. During mock battles, the other soldiers, slighted by her presence—a human woman, of all the filthy things— thumped her with their clamshell mallets, piercing her with fishbone arrows. She might have died by their hands if she hadn't eventually picked up an arrow and stabbed a squadron leader through the eye.

Finally, the dragon king said, "You have successfully endured the trials." He opened his hand, and in his palm was a single, perfect pearl.

The girl knew she should be wary, given everything she had already experienced, but she was tired, hurting, and afraid of additional trials.

So she snatched the pearl from him. As soon as she gulped it, the trans-formation began. A cold colder than the deepest waters flooded her insides, seeping into her broken limbs. Her heart froze; her every muscle stiffened. From her skin grew scales hard enough to guard against even the sharpest blades; from the tips of her fingers and toes, claws sharp enough to shred any enemy; and from between her brows, that single, shining pearl. And she realized the error she'd made.

She had gained the ability to live underwater, but she had also lost the ability to die. Except the sea was not the joyful place she'd imag-ined. The girl understood now that the world was divided into the powerful and the powerless. To be powerless was to live and die by others' whims; to be powerful was to live in constant fear that others might one day take that power away. No part of the world was truly at peace. Peace could be found only in release from the cycle of death and rebirth, which would, as a result of her actions, forever be denied to her.

. . .

Shek Yeung didn't send a message to Cheung Po. She asked Yan-Yan and Ahmad to keep the child a secret until she figured out what to do. But the deception couldn't last forever. Cheung Po knew how to count, after all, and when a month had passed, he sent her a message. "When will I get to meet my son?" Cheung Po wrote.

In fairness to him, he wrote more than that. He recounted the fleet's recent exploits, the spoils they'd carried away from the home of one of the emperor's cousins before they burned it to the ground: the bolts of silk, the painted vases, the strands of pearls meant to dangle from officials' hats. "Don't worry, I saved a pin for you," he wrote.

"Tell Cheung Po," she said to Ahmad, "that the baby is alive but cannot have any visitors right now because of jaundice."

She passed the time with Yan-Yan. They gossiped about the other crew members, cooked inedible dishes from the half-spoiled longan they'd fermented, tried and failed to find ways to stop the baby's repeated fussing (singing didn't work, nor rocking, nor funny voices). When the child was quiet, Shek Yeung cradled her against her breast, enjoying the slightly salty and milky smell, and told her stories about not only Ma-Zou but also Wo-Yuet. The baby had big brown eyes ringed with black that seemed to blink faster whenever Shek Yeung got to the exciting part of a story, as if she understood what she was hearing.

Occasionally, Tse Po-Po dropped by with herbs, but the old woman thought both Shek Yeung and the child would be fine, so she quickly stopped visiting. "Like this is going to kill that shrew," she overheard Tse Po-Po saying to Yan-Yan. "She's going to outlive everyone, including you."

One night after Yan-Yan had put the baby to sleep, Shek Yeung asked the girl, "When do you think you'll have your own?"

Yan-Yan slid in next to Shek Yeung on the bed. Shek Yeung rearranged the blanket so that it would also cover the girl. "Dawa wants one soon."

"I asked about you, not that northern woman."

"I want one, too, just maybe not now."

"Why not?"

"We're busy, aren't we?"

"It doesn't hurt to start looking. I know how choosy you are when it comes to men."

Yan-Yan looked a little queasy. "Dawa can carry the baby. Also, I don't mind someone else's."

Shek Yeung snorted. "Based on what you've told me, she's even less interested in men than you are. At this rate, you'll never have one of your own." At least the girl didn't mind adopting. Children in the fleet got orphaned sometimes. And children in Canton lost their family all the time. Sometimes families sold their children, especially their daughters, for food.

When Yan-Yan didn't answer, Shek Yeung looked over and found her asleep—maybe. Yan-Yan's eyelids were fluttering lightly. The girl probably wanted to avoid another one of Shek Yeung's lectures. Shek Yeung burrowed under the blanket, careful to not steal it from Yan-Yan, and soon she was asleep, too.

. . .

At three months, Shek Yeung had an idea after watching the baby grab first at her own toes and then at a handkerchief in Shek Yeung's hand. She laid out a calligraphy brush, an abacus, a piece of fresh-steamed man-tau, a silver ingot, and her sheathed cutlass, then sat on the ground with the baby between her legs. It was too early, she knew—the ritual was usually performed when the child turned one—but she couldn't stifle her curiosity.

The child didn't move at all, just sucked loudly on her own fingers. "Come on," Shek Yeung said, gently nudging her. But apparently the nudge wasn't gentle enough because the child flopped onto her belly. Thankfully, she didn't cry. Shek Yeung would have had a hard time explaining to Yan-Yan why the baby was crying on the floor.

Shek Yeung had been about to give up on the exercise when suddenly the baby reached for the man-tau. "Oh," Shek Yeung said aloud.

What did reaching for food mean again? Calligraphy brush meant scholar, ingot meant merchant. Did food mean cook? A rich man's wife?

Later she asked Yan-Yan.

"Why didn't you tell me you were doing this!" Yan-Yan said, clearly annoyed at having missed the event. Then she said, "Maybe she was just hungry. We can repeat the ritual later."

"No, I'd fed her."

Yan-Yan huffed. "Then I don't know."

Maybe the child had indeed been hungry. Or maybe the results didn't count when the child was under a year old. And what if she had grabbed the cutlass? Hadn't Shek Yeung felt unspeakable dread when those tiny fingers grazed the cutlass, followed by profound relief when they continued on to the food?

After Yan-Yan calmed down, she sat down next to Shek Yeung. "I'm glad you're at least spending time with her," she said.

"There's not much else for me to do," Shek Yeung said.

"Oh, please."

"What?"

Yan-Yan looked like she was choosing her words. "You were . . . different with your sons."

"I had a wet nurse then. I don't have one anymore, last time I checked."

"I can tell when someone's doing something because they have to. Also, nobody *has* to give a baby the chau-chow ritual, certainly not months ahead of schedule during one of the few times their friend who has been tirelessly helping them take care of the baby was taking a nap."

"Will you let it go already?"

"I'm serious, though," Yan-Yan said. "I think the only way to get good at taking care of a baby is to do it. Being a woman doesn't automatically make you a good mother. So I'm glad you're spending time with her."

If Shek Yeung felt an upwelling of emotion hearing this—if she maybe even teared up just the tiniest bit—she quickly got herself under control. And if Yan-Yan noticed, well, the girl was too smart, and, in her own way, too kind, to point it out.

24

Cheung Po returned from his campaign a little after the child turned three months old. Ahmad had met him at a designated spot in town and given him directions to the sam-hop-yuen. Shortly before his arrival, Shek Yeung sent Yan-Yan to the market for the fattest chicken she could find and a jug of the finest wine. She laid out the feast in the main hall so that it would be the first thing Cheung Po saw. He would be tired and hungry from all the traveling. If she could get him drunk and fed first, he might be less reactive to the news.

Instead of sitting down to the meal, though, Cheung Po strode toward the inner quarters. "The wine can wait," he said. "I want to meet my son!"

At least she'd had the foresight to swaddle the child in too many layers of fabric. "Don't get too close," she said to him. "The child still has jaundice."

"I'll be careful," he said, picking up the child anyway. He plucked at a corner of the swaddling. "Does he need to wear so much? The weather's very warm."

"The midwife insisted. Don't undress him or he'll get sick."

That worked. He put the child back on the bed. "I didn't know jaundice lasted this long," he said.

"It does sometimes," she said. "Let's go have some food."

"No, no, I'm too tired. I'll eat after my nap." With that he plopped down on the nearest chair—so tired, apparently, that he couldn't even be bothered to walk to another room—and immediately fell asleep.

Shek Yeung noticed movement out of the corner of her eye: Yan-Yan was in the courtyard, gesturing at her to come outside. "What are you doing?" the girl whispered.

"I'm trying to find a good time," Shek Yeung said.

"And when will that be?"

"I'll know it when I see it."

"What if he catches you in the lie? How long do you think you can keep this from him?"

"I can lie until I'm dead," Shek Yeung said. "Now move. If he's not going to eat that chicken, I am."

Cheung Po slept through the night on that chair. By the time he awoke, Shek Yeung had already fed, cleaned, and reswaddled the baby. Over breakfast, he asked, "What should we name him?"

"What's the hurry?" she said.

He looked perplexed. "The sooner we have a name, the sooner we can register him as my heir."

"With Pak Ling's dogs sniffing for us?"

"I guess you're right," Cheung Po said. "That scoundrel, he's meddling with all our affairs." Most of the land raids had been successes, he explained, but their profit from the sea had dwindled in the last four months. Rather than directly confront the fleet, which would have resulted in massive casualties on both sides, Pak Ling had begun seizing merchant ships smuggling opium and other foreign goods. Without merchant ships, the fleet had no one to rob. "We can't keep raiding these little villages," Cheung Po said. "They don't have much. If we want to make up for what we're losing at sea, we need to target bigger towns, even the ones with fortresses."

Seeing her expression, he added, "I know, but I don't have a better idea." Cheung Po knew as well as she did that their people were at a disadvantage on land. Most of their strategies applied only to battles at sea: boarding, ramming, sinking. Their cannons weren't exactly portable.

True, they still had numbers on their side, but the thing with numbers was that they changed easily. As soon as the tide of a battle turned, a commander could go from having thousands of halfhearted men to only a handful of the most loyal (or the most foolish).

They passed another few days like this, with her feeding and changing the child only when he wasn't looking. The more time that went by, the more difficult it became to broach the topic with him. During meals, Yan-Yan side-eyed her as loudly as she clattered the chopsticks and bowls. Shek Yeung was starting to wonder if she could keep the child's sex a secret until she started to bleed. As for after that, well, who knew, Cheung Po might be dead by then.

Cheung Po was a reasonably doting father to his presumptive son, as Cheng Yat had been to his own children. This was a good thing as far as Shek Yeung was concerned. Hardness boded ill for the child's safety, whereas softness was a liability. Baby in arm, he debated targets of land raids with Shek Yeung. Tinpak, definitely. Hoiping, maybe, but they would have to find a way through those damn watchtowers the people over there kept building, their massive walls erected with pirates in mind. Yan-Yan chimed in occasionally with objections or concerns.

And then Cheung Po spilled hot tea on the baby.

Shek Yeung jumped up from her seat to grab a rag. By the time she returned he'd stripped the baby down.

"It's like this," she began.

"But the midwife said—"

"She was wrong."

He set the baby down on the table, not too firmly but also not quite gently, and left the room.

She started to chase after him but thought better of it, checking the child over instead, feeling relieved when it became clear that the tea had been absorbed by the swaddling. Then she returned to her quarters and, finding her slimmest dagger, slid it inside her sleeve. One never knew for sure. *Then* she chased after Cheung Po.

"What else are you lying about?" he demanded when he saw her.

"Don't be precious, I lie about everything I need to lie about," she said. "Only an idiot tells the truth regardless of circumstances."

"And you *needed* to lie about this?"

"You tell me."

He looked exasperated. "What did you think I was going to do?"

"You tell me."

"When were you going to let me know?"

"When I saw fit."

"Yan-Yan knew? Have you two been laughing at me this whole time?"

Shek Yeung pulled herself up to her full height. "Don't you dare do anything to her."

He slumped down into a chair. She felt herself relax a little. "So this is what you think of me," he said, sounding tired.

"This is what we think of each other," she said quietly. "Look at all the things we've done. We've given each other plenty of reasons."

She left him alone, afraid that the child would roll herself off the table if left unattended for too long. In the main hall, she wrapped the child up in clean fabric, leaving the spill to dry on its own.

Dinner passed in silence, but at least he showed up. After Yan-Yan carried away the bowls, he said, "My sister has a daughter. She's a smart girl."

Shek Yeung nodded.

"And girls can be very helpful, as long as you don't coddle them."

"You know I would never coddle any child of mine," she assured him.

"I'm not against having a daughter," he said. "I can't believe you thought I would be."

"I'm sorry."

"It's fine," he said. "In fact, this'll be a good thing. When she's old enough, we'll teach her how to do the bookkeeping. Yan-Yan could definitely use the help. And this way her brother will have a close ally on board once he's ready to command."

"Her brother?"

"Yeah, I mean, we're going to continue to . . ." He flapped his hand between them. "It'll happen at some point."

She didn't know how to explain it to him: the pain of childbirth, the aging body with its splintering frame, that moment during a difficult birth when a woman resigned herself to fate because there was nothing more she or anyone else could do. Young men rarely understood helplessness. All she said was, "No. It won't."

"You don't know that," he said.

"If you're so set on having a son," she said, "go have one with a whore. If you pay her enough, she'll do it."

"You don't mean that."

"You have my permission."

"And if I don't want to?" he said defiantly.

"Then go adopt a young boy, give him the fleet once we're dead," she snapped. "Why not? You were adopted."

"I was taken," he said, his voice hard.

"So was I, except nobody left me a fleet!" It was a cheap shot, she knew. Pain was pain: who was to say a piercing wound hurt more than a slash wound? One survived or didn't, and even if one survived, there was always a scar.

He stomped off. Sometime later she heard the main gate of the sam-hop-yuen open and close. She stayed awake well into the night to see if he would come back. When she could stay awake no longer, she brought the child, who usually slept in Yan-Yan's room, into her own. The thought had occurred to her that Cheung Po might return drunk and murderous.

He didn't return that night, nor did he return the following day. She considered sending Ahmad to look for him, but if he was actually taking her up on her suggestion of impregnating a prostitute, then she didn't want to interrupt what he was doing. If he was plotting the child's death, though, then she needed to drag him back as soon as possible before he could solidify his plans. Watching her pace, Yan-Yan said, "He's just gambling, Big Sis, I'm telling you."

She sent Ahmad after him on the third day. Cheung Po could be dead. It was unlikely, as the man was quite hard to kill (she'd considered the possibilities in the days after Cheng Yat's death): difficult to get truly drunk, quick on his feet, paranoid. But technically he could be dead, and if so, she needed to know.

When she awoke the following morning, she threw an arm over the spot where she'd laid her daughter. In place of soft fabric was something cold and hard, possibly metal. She shot up.

The child had something on (in?) her chest. Shek Yeung blinked frantically to clear the film from her eyes, scrabbling at the crust in the corners. Had Cheung Po returned? And how could she have slept so deeply that Cheung Po could have . . .

Even after her vision had returned, it took her a moment to realize what she was seeing. The metal wasn't the hilt of a dagger but the large golden lock that she'd seen back in Maynila, strung on a thick chain, which was now secured around the child's neck. On it, fish swam and leaped. The sun, moon, and stars shone.

25

The third lunar month in Canton: a fervent gust was sweeping from the hills down to the shore, wrapping around the frigid sea breeze to produce an offspring that was neither but also both. Awaiting the O Yam, Shek Yeung alternately sweated and shivered. Next to her, Yan-Yan bounced the baby. Shek Yeung held a rattle in her hand and shook it every so often to keep the child entertained. Each shake was greeted with a squeal of delight. In front of them, junks that had been docked since typhoon season unfurled their sails like flower-boat girls letting down their hair.

To work.

"Do you realize?" Yan-Yan was saying while Shek Yeung squinted at the belts and boots of the men around them in search of hidden weapons. "Six years now."

"Hmm?" Shek Yeung said, then, "Right. You were just a girl then. Hell, I was just a girl."

"But you still look so young! Anyway, the first time I saw the ship, I couldn't believe it. I grew up in a farming village, you know. I couldn't believe how big it was, but also, I couldn't believe that people could live on a ship for months at a time."

The first time Shek Yeung saw a three-masted junk, she'd just started working on the fishing boat. Peeping it from afar, she waved her arm wildly at her brother to join her port side. He sighed loudly. "The sea isn't for little babies," he said. "How are you gonna survive if you're gonna be this dumb?"

The first time Shek Yeung saw Cheng Yat's ship, her reaction had been more subdued. She'd lived on the flower boats for years, watching junks small and large glide out to sea. Still, it was an impressive vessel, and she'd allowed herself to fawn over it a bit, which was what Cheng Yat expected of her anyway.

What had Cheung Po's first impressions of the ship been? Being one of the "boat people," he must have encountered large ships long before meeting Cheng Yat. Then again, he might never have been *on* one until he was taken, and fear stretched things out in one's mind, leaving the memory misshapen and worn-through even after the threat had gone.

Almost two years had passed since Cheng Yat's death. It didn't feel like it. Everything she did for the fleet aligned so perfectly with Cheng Yat's will that it was as if the man were still here. She would never really be free of him.

"Men are no different from animals," he used to say. "Keeping them fed and occupied keeps them tame, but don't for a moment believe they won't revert to wildness the instant they feel hungry or restless."

Keeping them fed and occupied was exactly what she'd done. She knew that, without Cheng Yat's and then Cheung Po's commendation, many of them would have never tolerated her power over them. Animals turned against their owners slower than men turned against women in the face of the slightest dissatisfaction.

. . .

Among the first things Cheung Po insisted on when they returned to the fleet was consulting the fortune-teller. They laid the squiggling, burbling creature they'd taken to calling Siu Yuet—Shek Yeung didn't explain to Cheung Po why she'd chosen that name, and he didn't ask—in the older woman's arms. The fortune-teller ran her fingers over the child's face and handed Siu Yuet back.

"Well," she said, frowning, "I'll draw a stick in case I'm wrong. Face-reading is not my specialty."

She picked up the canister and shook it the way she usually did, but just as she tipped it over, a large junk sailed by, disturbing the small altar boat with its wake. Two sticks fell out.

"It doesn't count when more than one falls out, right?" Cheung Po asked.

The fortune-teller put the sticks back in the canister and repeated the process. The wind suddenly picked up, and again two sticks fell out. Shek Yeung had no idea if they were the same two. After a pause, the fortune-teller said, "It seems Heaven doesn't want to give you an answer at the moment."

"But it happened twice," Cheung Po said. "Shouldn't you at least read them?"

"That's not how this works."

"Just do it," Cheung Po said.

The fortune-teller read the first one:

> A spring breeze moves a spring heart
> My gaze flows to the mountain
> The trees there are strangely and beautifully colored
> A sunlit bird sings a clear tune

"That's good, right?" Cheung Po said. The fortune-teller read the second:

> New ghosts cry after the battle
> A lone old man frets and mourns
> Scattered clouds hang low at sunset
> Snow swirls frantically in the wind

"Like I told you," the fortune-teller said. "Heaven doesn't have an answer for you right now."

She refused to answer any of Cheung Po's follow-up questions. Eventually he gave up, and he and Shek Yeung returned to the O Yam with the baby. "What do you think happened back there?" he asked Shek Yeung in their cabin. He'd kept a hand on her almost the entire way back, more nervous about the fortune-teller's words than he would have admitted.

Shek Yeung shrugged. She hadn't missed the fortune-teller's frown as she'd dragged her fingers over Siu Yuet's features—how else could Shek Yeung have survived all those years on the flower boats, if not by attuning herself to every tiny expression from everyone? But exactly what the frown meant, only the fortune-teller knew. Illness? Death? Or just the simple unhappiness of so many women, that of being married off to a philandering or feckless or wrathful husband?

Alternatively, the fortune-teller might have simply been in a foul mood. Only days ago, Shek Yeung had denied her request for new clothes. She might have been frowning in protest.

Shek Yeung couldn't protect Siu Yuet from illness and death, but her money and power would protect the child from a torturous marriage. The alternative was unacceptable. Once a frightfully thin woman with a winding river of a spine begged Shek Yeung to let her join the fleet. This was at one of the smaller fishing villages west of Canton, maybe a year after Shek Yeung herself had joined. "Go home," Shek Yeung told her. "You don't know how to fight, you look like you can barely lift a sword. You'd be a liability."

"Then I'll kill myself right here," the woman said. "I'd rather kill myself than go back to my husband."

In a pitying mood, Shek Yeung relented. She invited the woman on board (to the raised eyebrows of the other crew members) and put her to work cleaning the ship. For days afterward, the woman thanked her profusely every time they crossed paths, to the point that Shek Yeung started to believe the praise the woman was heaping upon her, that she was a good person and a role model, that she saved more lives than she took.

What else could have happened to that woman except a prompt death? And now Shek Yeung couldn't even remember how she died, or for that matter, what her name had been, assuming she'd even bothered to ask.

. . .

For the most part, her crew reacted to her return just as she'd hoped they would: barely. They greeted her, offered customary comments about the baby's size or likeness, and then went about their day. It had apparently been business as usual while she was gone, and for that she was thankful.

They continued their raids along the southern coast, beaching and then quickly putting out to sea again like a serrated blade gashing the underbelly of China. Sometimes she and Cheung Po worked in concert, sometimes they divided their forces so they could target multiple villages at once. At first Shek Yeung stayed behind on the O Yam with the baby, but concerned that her men would mistake her absence for weakness, she soon rejoined them on the battlefield, leaving Siu Yuet with Yan-Yan. Not that Shek Yeung was in great fighting shape herself after months of nursing—she left the offense to the strongest of her crew, hanging back with the people who prepared projectiles and treated wounds. Besides, no one really kept track of who was standing where once the battle started.

By and large, the villages surrendered upon their arrival. Shek Yeung had spread the word that she would burn any village that resisted. But the people of Tinpak were either exceptionally brave or stupid because they'd set up a long barricade consisting of large bales of hay, pieces of furniture, and chunks of stone. It was nothing that Shek Yeung's men couldn't overcome, but of course complete obstruction wasn't the point. The hindrance allowed the village's fighters, few as they were, to hack at the pirates as they climbed over the barricade. At the very least it would discourage the pirates from carrying back to the fleet anything bigger than could fit in a sack, for example, another person.

Well, they hadn't come all this way for nothing. Shek Yeung gave the order, and her crew charged.

The agile ones scrambled effortlessly over the barricade, engaging with the villagers first. The strong ones threw their weight against the hay, knocking pieces off here and there to make the barricade easier to summit. Soon enough of them had made it over the obstacle that the villagers retreated up a narrow path toward the mountains, where the other villagers were probably hiding with the valuables.

Her crew gave chase, brimming with the energy that came with a fight almost won and the fury that came with having met with a fight in the first place. She knew from experience that a man who'd finally succeeded in subduing a resisting woman always found the energy to make it hurt more.

She trailed behind everyone, feeling strangely uneasy. For all the effort the villagers had put into building that barricade, they'd abandoned it rather quickly. But if they'd lacked faith in the barricade's ability to keep them safe, then they must have devised a contingency plan.

First came the screaming.

Then came the wounded, stumbling back down the path. She grabbed one of her men by the arm, and only when he winced did she notice the arrow in his shoulder, the fletching having broken off. "They were waiting!" the man cried.

She stopped a few more of the men trying to escape and pieced together the situation. They had chased the villagers up the path until they reached a clearing in the woods, where most of the villagers were hiding with bows and arrows and large rocks. Having gathered the pirates in one place, the villagers began firing and pelting from the surrounding trees. The narrowness of the path, along with the fact that people were still advancing up the mountain, meant that only a few men could escape at once, assuming they didn't get trampled first.

Shek Yeung turned and shouted to the people behind her, "Retreat! We need to clear the way!"

Down the mountain they ran. The wounded kept coming, and Shek Yeung almost fell a couple of times when someone jostled her too hard. She cursed when she saw the barricade ahead. She'd forgotten about that thing.

If climbing over the barricade had been hard before, climbing over the barricade injured was going to be harder. Some of the less injured tried to boost their more injured comrades over, while the selfish ones just hurdled the barricade on their own. The occasional scream sounded behind Shek Yeung. It seemed that the villagers had emerged from the trees and were now chasing them down the path, trying to shoot the pirates in the back.

She'd been about to climb over the barricade herself when she saw one of the villagers who'd fallen by the barricade move. His injury had prevented him from following the others up to the woods. She signaled to one of her stronger men. "Help me get him over the wall," she said.

The man looked back at the villagers in pursuit, then at her like she was crazy. "Now!" she said.

They managed to heave the villager over. Once on the other side, she ordered her man to drag the villager back to the ship.

Shoving off with the remaining crew, she finally saw in full the scene she'd left behind: the skein of bloody bodies by the barricade, villagers and pirates alike, and the long red thread unspooling up the mountain only to tangle again. If she'd led the charge as she'd always done before this pregnancy, she'd be among the dead.

Nearby, someone gurgled and then went silent. She heard a few grunts, followed by a splash. They needed to lighten their load if they wanted to get away before imperial ships arrived.

26

Shek Yeung threw the villager into the brig. At some point during the battle, she'd realized that the villagers had received help from Pak Ling, or at least one of his stooges. No way these simple fishermen had contrived this plan by themselves. They'd quite possibly also acquired weapons and training from Pak Ling—there had been too many arrows for a group of people who primarily made their living at sea.

The villager had a slash wound on his left thigh, just above the knee. It was hard to say if the wound had stopped him from retreating up the mountain or if he'd played dead to avoid continuing to fight. Interrogating a selfish man was one thing; interrogating a brave one was another. For both their sakes, she hoped he was selfish.

The area around the knee was already dying, the skin darkening, the smell of blood and pus a bladed putrescence. His wan face shone with sweat.

"Would you like some water?" she asked. Without waiting for an answer, she poured a cup and then left it just out of his grasp so that he would have to crawl on his injured leg to get it.

He didn't reach for the cup. Instead, he closed his eyes, as if to guard against temptation.

A brave man, then.

"You did well," she said, squatting so they were about level with each other. "We were truly surprised. You should be proud, outwitting us like that. My boatswain estimates a hundred dead, and more, even, after the injuries take their toll. But of course, you expected that." She pressed her thumb into the gash on his leg—that got his eyes open. A little bit of torture was sometimes necessary. "They were family men, you know, the ones you massacred. Fathers, sons. The women were wives and mothers. Not all that different from you, their paths just diverged from yours at some point, usually for no reason except misfortune. There are only so many options when one is hungry. Now I have to tell their families."

Something like sympathy or guilt passed over the man's expression. A brave man, but not a hard one. "And I don't know what to tell them," she continued. "That the people who took their father or son planned his death, that he didn't even have the chance to die fighting someone face-to-face?"

"We were defending ourselves," the man said. A good man, or one who believed himself to be good, protesting the maligning of his character. A man susceptible to talkativeness and therefore persuasion.

"You were," she said, "except the whole thing could have been bloodless."

"So we were just supposed to give you our food? Then my village would've gone hungry."

"I suppose that's true. There was probably no way for both your men and mine to be fed. Where did you get all those arrows, by the way?"

Like a brave man, he didn't respond. "I've been trying to figure out," she said, "how you knew we were coming and stockpiled all those weapons in time, how you came up with that little strategy. The only thing I can think is that someone in your village must be very clever. And that sounds like someone I need to either have in my employ or kill. I wonder if this person is clever enough to foresee me going back for them."

"We defeated you once. We can do it again."

"So soon, though? It must have taken this person months just to stockpile the arrows, and cleverness without resources only goes so far. If my fleet were to return now, nothing would stop me from going house to house, burning one after another with the people still inside, until someone hands this clever person over to me. I might start with the houses closest to the mountain. It'll prevent people from fleeing up the mountain and drive them toward the water, where my men will be waiting—"

"There's no one like that in my village," the man cried. "We just did what the official told us. He told us when you would come."

"How did he know?"

"I don't know, but he seemed sure. He said he was going to bring an end to pirating from here to the farthest reaches of China and invited us to join him in reclaiming the seas from your kind."

"I see." She pressed the cup of water into his hand. He drank. "An official came, gave you a plan and some weapons, and then left you on your own. You know, I can't help but think about your comment earlier, the one about whether your people should go hungry instead of mine. Except those aren't the only possibilities. The officials gave you weapons and used you to fight their battles, left you vulnerable to retaliation, when they could have just given you more food after we left."

After she left the prisoner, she found Ahmad and said, "Take the man in the brig and throw him overboard when no one is looking. I don't want him running his mouth about Pak Ling. It's bad for morale."

"He'll die from that wound anyway. You sure you don't want to try to get more information out of him while you can?"

"He's already confirmed what I suspected. A quick death will be a mercy."

"What did you suspect?"

Shek Yeung checked to make sure no one else could hear them. "That we have a spy in our midst."

27

To what extent could anyone be trusted? The promise of money or power was enough to sway most people. As for the rest, the threat of violence to themselves or their loved ones usually made short work of their principles. Pak Ling had plenty of money to promise the first group and plenty of power with which to threaten the second.

She recognized, of course, that she'd taken a risk in telling Ahmad about her suspicion that Pak Ling had installed spies in the fleet. Ahmad himself could be the spy, or one of the spies, but somehow she just couldn't imagine it. She'd invited him on board herself. Years ago an injury had left her recuperating in Canton, and during this period, she would take walks down by the docks every day. (She told Cheng Yat's family that she wanted to regain her strength, but in truth she was working, trying to catch the latest gossip about merchant cargo.) Over time she noticed one man who continued with his backbreaking labor even as supervisors' eyes were turned away. When she offered him a position within the fleet, she half-expected him to refuse, thinking that he was likely too honest for this line of work. To her surprise, he asked if he'd be able to practice his religion freely on board.

"What?" Shek Yeung had replied, confused. "I don't care what you do as long as you do your job."

Only much later did she realize that he'd probably been getting harassed on land. The Qing had forbidden even small gatherings of armed Muslims. In any case, she was glad he agreed to join because otherwise she might have had to abduct him.

Ahmad never shared with anyone why he'd left Malacca in the first place, though she'd gotten the impression that he couldn't go home even if he wanted to. This was more than fine by her. In many ways, the crew members with whom she felt the most kinship, the ones she trusted the most, were the ones who couldn't go home. One couldn't devote one's life to the fleet while longing for somewhere else. Even Yan-Yan, with all her ardor for the northern woman, had no plans to leave the fleet. Those two would quarrel eventually, given the northern woman's desire to settle down, but that was a problem for Shek Yeung to worry about another time.

Pak Ling had probably planted the spy, or spies, on the O Yam—a few months ago, perhaps, or long before that. That was what she would have done. It seemed unlikely to be Yan-Yan, whose life, should the fleet get destroyed, would be nothing but misery. Cheung Po would have to be an idiot or a madman to sink his own fleet. Who did that leave? Too many.

She told Cheung Po this when they met up again a few days later. His efforts slightly westward had met with success, suggesting that the spy was indeed on the flagship. "There's something else the captive said that's been troubling me," she added. "Pak Ling, or his representative, mentioned eliminating piracy from here to the farthest reaches of China. My guess is he has spies embedded in the other fleets, too. Remember what happened to the Green Banner Fleet."

"You think they'll believe us?"

"We still need to warn them. There's no point to the alliance if we're the only member."

They sent out messengers. The Black Banner Fleet, which happened to be nearby, quickly sent a message back. "Obliged," Kwok Po-Tai wrote in his overwrought calligraphy, each trailing stroke like a cut bleeding out.

They waited for word from the Blue Banner Fleet. And waited. After a month, they sent a second message. This time they heard back within a matter of days. The messenger handed Shek Yeung an exquisite mother-of-pearl tea chest that was too heavy to contain tea but too light to contain ingots or jewels. She shook it and heard a quiet thud.

The smell when she opened the chest made her eyes water. Buddhika was badly decomposed but still recognizable, scabs of rot all over, white fuzz bearding his once-youthful face—hard to say how long, depending on the conditions in which Lam Yuk-Yiu had kept the body. "Spy caught," the note read. "Or did you not think I would find out about the deal he made with you to betray me?"

Shek Yeung felt a pang of regret. She hardly believed herself to be a good person, but at least she never treated the ones she killed this way. She told herself this meant something.

"I don't understand," Cheung Po said, peering at the head.

She explained that she'd asked Buddhika to keep an eye on Lam Yuk-Yiu because of her increasingly erratic behavior. "It was for the good of the alliance," she said.

"Well done. Now we no longer have an alliance with them."

"Not necessarily. Choy Hin is still the fleet commander. The final decision is his."

"We have to go convince him in person. Lam Yuk-Yiu might try to intercept messages from us."

"We haven't even figured out who our spy is yet. There are more pressing problems here."

"So we keep this between us and essential crew members until right before we leave. How's the spy going to send a message from the middle of the sea? And even if the spy manages to get a message out after we arrive at Taiwan, by the time the message gets to Pak Ling, we'll be gone."

"What if Lam Yuk-Yiu opens fire on us?"

"She's not so erratic that she'd start a war with a larger fleet."

"I don't like it."

Cheung Po glanced around them. "Look, I didn't want to tell you this, but some of the men have been talking. About you, when they think you won't find out. They blame you for the bloodbath at Tinpak." He held up a hand when she opened her mouth to protest. "I know Pak Ling is tricky, and I probably wouldn't have seen it coming either.

But they think you should've. They think the new baby has affected your judgment."

"I have two other kids. *Now* my judgment's affected?"

"I'm not saying it makes sense. I'm saying it makes sense to them. And if we lose the Blue Banner Fleet . . ."

One bad raid was all it took. She'd never expected complete loyalty from these men, but she'd believed, foolishly, that after everything she'd done, she deserved some.

"Think of this as a favor to me," Cheung Po said. "Choy Hin has been a good friend. Let me pay back my debt to him by at least warning him about Pak Ling's spies."

"Give me a few days," she said. "I want to do some investigating first. In the meantime, tell Old Wong and Binh to get ready to sail. And give me a list of the men who've been talking about me."

. . .

Cheng Yat taught her a trick her first year on board. It went something like this: If you lock a man up and ask him about his suspected crimes, you end up with a silent man. If you lock a man up and tell him you've also locked up one of his accomplices, that you'll be lenient on the one who provides information first, you end up with a talkative man.

In the case of the spy or spies, Shek Yeung had no suspects in mind. But it occurred to her that perhaps Pak Ling was also trying to weaken the fleet by fomenting mutiny. (She would have done no different.) The ones questioning her judgment and the ones who'd informed Pak Ling about Tinpak might well be the same.

She seized the first man publicly and threw him into the brig. The truth was she didn't suspect him much. He was too hot-blooded to function as a spy—odds were he just got caught up in the moment when the others started complaining about her—but of course that was exactly why she'd seized him publicly. People didn't trust a man like that to keep his mouth shut.

The others she locked up individually in secret. Who else have you been talking to about this? she asked them. Who else on the ship? In the fleet? Outside of it?

Unsurprisingly, the dissatisfaction had spread to the other junks in the fleet. More than the O Yam had been involved in the raid, after all. She jotted down a list of names. Not a short list, but also not an unmanageable one. The only problem was that they all insisted they hadn't spoken to anyone outside the fleet.

It was true that such a tactic occasionally produced false accusations. Sometimes people spouted random names out of fear or confusion. A magistrate would have to spend a lot of time separating the innocent from the guilty. But she wasn't a magistrate. She was just angry and so, so tired.

She gathered the crew of her ship. The nineteen heads, blackened by their own blood and the blood of their compatriots, were cannonballs tumbling aft. Even if they hadn't been working with Pak Ling, they'd been fomenting unrest. One had to bring their complaining to a swift end, one simply had to. She shook out her arms. She didn't like ordering others to make kills that were her responsibility. It turned killing into an idea, and it was easy to get comfortable with ideas. "Tell the other ships what you saw today," she told the crew.

She returned to her cabin, where Yan-Yan was waiting with the child. "You should avoid going above deck with her for now," she told Yan-Yan.

"How many?"

"Nineteen."

"I'll change the books when I get a chance. Will there be more?"

"Who knows." She picked up Siu Yuet, who had no interest in sitting on her lap, squirming out of her hold to crawl around, circling back every so often to pull herself to standing. "Do you think it was too much?" Shek Yeung asked. She looked at the blood under her fingernails, ten little red crescent moons. A few had been right around the age her brother would've been had he lived. One the age her father would've been. Even if these men had actually been spies, there was no telling what Pak Ling had done to secure their cooperation, whom he'd threatened.

"It is if you're one of the nineteen. Or one of their family members."

"You know what I mean."

Yan-Yan threw up her hands. "When people are satisfied, nineteen doesn't seem like a lot, as long as it doesn't directly affect them. When people are dissatisfied, even one is too many. How many people die from famine every day? You don't hear the rich complaining to the emperor except maybe about the smell of the bodies outside their estates."

Siu-Yuet fell and started to cry. Shek Yeung shushed her, smoothing her cobwebby hair. When she had her face all scrunched up like that, her skin red and splotchy, she looked as Shek Yeung did whenever she was in a foul mood. That chin cleft, though, was definitely Cheung Po's fault.

The crying stopped. Every day she got a little better at motherhood, or at least that was what she told herself. Hung-Shek and Ying-Shek felt like Cheng Yat's children, were always meant to be. Siu Yuet felt like hers. When she first started suckling the girl, she'd found it painful— that small, scowly mouth struggling to latch properly, her frustration (and by extension, Shek Yeung's frustration) mounting. *No wonder the Cheng family relied on wet nurses,* she'd thought. And then there was that moment, the lips finding the right angle, the sequence of tiny clockwork movements, and suddenly she was not she but they, the pain gone away, flowing out, through.

"Is the crew satisfied?" Shek Yeung said. She was really asking herself, but Yan-Yan answered, "Some people are always going to be dissatisfied. The problem is when they're too good at spreading dissatisfaction. Then you need to do what you need to do."

Had Madame Ko needed to beat all those girls who tried to escape? Had Cheng Yat needed to behead all those crew members he'd caught stealing? Neither those girls nor those crew members had posed any real threat, and Shek Yeung might have made different decisions had they been her decisions to make. In her mind, something like stealing stemmed from petty disobedience, whereas fomenting unrest stemmed from malice. Yet Cheng Yat would have argued that acts of disobedience quickly led to unrest, which led to violence, which had to be met in kind. There was no stability without violence, nor was there peace in instability. Where was the line between stability and tyranny? She wondered if she was losing sight of it.

According to the Mandate of Heaven, if an emperor failed to meet the needs of his people, then natural disasters and rebellions followed. If a rebellion succeeded, it was because Heaven willed it, but if not, then the emperor had not yet lost the Mandate, which was a convenient argument because it allowed whomever was in power to claim that his power was righteous. Never mind that half of Canton was starving, never mind that the military might of the emperor made rebellion on land near impossible. Cheng Yat used to say, "The alliance is the only force in this nation remotely capable of rivaling the emperor. We may not be able to win against him, but we owe it to the people to at least balance the scale."

Before she realized it, she'd become empress of her own nation. She told herself that she would do better, that she would fulfill *her* part of the Mandate: keep people fed, distribute wealth fairly, and preserve life where possible. And she'd done that, she'd given this fleet everything. She told herself she executed dissenters only so that she could continue to fulfill her responsibilities to her nation, but maybe she was just another tyrant maintaining her grip on the Mandate by eliminating opposition as soon as it arose.

She would have liked to tell herself that this thought troubled her deeply. But the truth was, after everything she'd been through, she was finding it more and more difficult to care.

. . .

They burned some incense on the altar boat to bless the journey and set out once more for Taiwan. The winds were favorable this time of year, and they neared the island within days.

Ahmad was the first to notice something amiss. Lowering his spyglass, he said, "There are too few ships."

She took the spyglass from him. There were, indeed, too few ships patrolling the coast. Even if the fleet were out raiding, Choy Hin and Lam Yuk-Yiu would not have left their stronghold so sparsely defended.

Next they saw the smoke, the drawn and quartered remains of junks, the limbs of naked masts. The O Yam felt like it was moving both too fast and too slowly. From what sounded like a thousand lei away, she heard Binh shout, "Change course?"

She didn't answer. Binh shouted the question again.

"Stay the course," Cheung Po said.

They didn't prepare for battle. It was clear that whatever had happened had happened. Still, she checked the sword at her side and the flintlock behind her back. They beached, swerving around the larger pieces of flotsam. A few of Pak Ling's men had stayed behind to loot the Blue Banner Fleet's stores. At the approach of Shek Yeung's crew, they scattered. No one bothered to follow.

The main fortress door still swung on its hinges, the wood about as unscathed as anything hundreds of years old could be. Someone had unbarred it from the inside.

Inside, the smell was far worse. The last of the fleet had apparently barricaded themselves in here. The island's humidity and heat had made quick work of the bodies. A few days? A half-month? There were hundreds, at least. The other few thousand were probably in the sea.

She and Cheung Po made their way to the inner ring. Every room they passed had been looted clean, including the one that had contained the gold cross. Finally, they reached Choy Hin's room, where they found his body, torn through the chest by a single bullet, the flintlock still in his hand. Cheung Po knelt silently by the body for a long time. Then he pried his friend's mouth open and reached in with his fingers.

"Something we came up with when we were together," he explained. "Everybody looks inside pockets. Nobody looks inside the throat."

He pulled out a slip of paper and unfolded it. Shek Yeung tried to read it but found that she couldn't, not fully. It had been written in some kind of code, so she tried to read Cheung Po's expression. "It wasn't just Pak Ling," he said. "Someone named Qiu Liang-Gong led the charge into the fortress. Why does that name sound familiar?"

It took her a moment, but then everything became clear. "That government dog we ransomed. You remember, the pale one? Wouldn't talk to me directly?"

"Makes sense. He was held here for a while and had a chance to learn the ins and outs of the place."

"He did swear revenge."

"They all do."

"But they aren't all friends with the emperor."

"Anyway, we have a bigger problem," Cheung Po said. "Choy Hin thought he saw English and Portuguese sailors among them."

This surprised Shek Yeung. She'd known for a long time now that the English were planning something, but she hadn't imagined they would ally with the emperor, whose low opinion of foreigners was no secret. "Does the note say anything about Lam Yuk-Yiu?" she asked. They hadn't found her body yet.

"Died at sea. Was out with that all-woman crew she was putting together and crossed paths with some navy ships commanded by Wong Tak-Luk." At the confusion on her face, he added, "He's been active around these parts. Word is he's also originally from Taiwan. One of Lam Yuk-Yiu's countrymen."

Shek Yeung noticed she was holding her breath and exhaled. She couldn't describe this feeling that was something between relief and sadness. Lam Yuk-Yiu had been a difficult woman—cold, unstable, extraordinarily skilled. If she'd lived, she likely would have become a troublesome enemy. Still, Shek Yeung struggled to find joy in her death.

After they'd checked the rest of the fortress for survivors, they set out for the village she'd visited with Buddhika, hoping that the people there would be able to provide some additional information about the battle. She wasn't terribly surprised to find it destroyed. The villagers had regularly supplied the Blue Banner Fleet, after all, an offense punishable by death per the emperor, even though many of these people had never even set foot on the mainland and had possessed only the vaguest idea of this man who sat on his throne issuing proclamations.

She retraced her steps to the temple. Somebody had swung a mace at the belly of the stele recounting Ma-Zou's founding of this town, breaking it at the waist and leaving it kowtowing to its subjugators. The heavy and expensive-looking statue of Ma-Zou was gone.

Upon returning to the fortress, Cheung Po prepared Choy Hin's body while she searched for a large flat stone. Heaven had a sense of irony: Lam Yuk-Yiu, who'd felt deeply connected to this island, had died at sea, whereas Choy Hin, who'd spent years sailing up and down the mainland coast, had died on land.

She found a stone. Cheung Po finished cleaning, dressing, and wrapping the body. They placed the body on a small Blue Banner Fleet junk and, after burning some paper money, pushed the junk out as far as they could. He didn't try to hide his tearfulness, and she didn't comment on it. Then they buried some of Lam Yuk-Yiu's effects, including that European book of hers (which none of the looters had taken), in a silty patch of earth. On top of that earth they laid the stone.

At one point, on their way back to Canton, Shek Yeung found herself reaching for Cheung Po's hand. She didn't know if she was looking for reassurance or something else, but it didn't matter either way because Cheung Po gently shook her off. He didn't say anything to her for the rest of the journey.

28

She demanded a meeting with Kwok Po-Tai immediately upon returning to Canton. This time Cheung Po didn't complain. Even he recognized the need to reconsolidate the alliance, which at this point consisted of their two fleets. They needed a strategy, but more than that, they needed a pact to come to each other's aid at the first sign of trouble. That meant sharing information about the navy's movements and staying relatively close. No longer could they operate with their customary level of independence.

This much was clear: First, Pak Ling was working with foreign powers. Second, Pak Ling's spy or spies had also played a major role in the Blue Banner Fleet's destruction. That fortress door had been unbarred from the inside.

Without informing the rest of their fleets, they met at the Southern Cave, the location of which Cheng Yat had revealed to only a trusted few. Time was they would have met over drinks in the tavern at the center of town, but Pak Ling had essentially struck that tavern off their list of parley points when he approached Shek Yeung there disguised as a beggar. Together, she and Cheung Po moved aside the rocks they'd stacked in front of the entrance to prevent passersby from stumbling across their cache. Once inside, she took out her fire piston and, pumping the dowel within the narrow bamboo cylinder a few times, ignited the piece of cotton at the bottom of the cylinder. With the small fire she lit the lanterns on the ground.

Gradually the contents of the cave became visible. Cheung Po had done admirably to replenish their stores while she was pregnant. There in one corner, full sacks of rice sprawled belly up. In another corner, a sizable chest of silver sycee, half-hidden behind some rolled-up sails, caught the firelight and scattered it all over the cave as if burned. By her feet were bales and bales of opium that could be sold or bartered.

The fleet would be well fed for a while even if they needed to temporarily suspend operations. She allowed herself to feel a tiny bit of pride and relief at this.

Kwok Po-Tai arrived a little past the agreed-upon time with a man they didn't recognize.

"We told you," Cheung Po said. "Just the three of us."

"Yuen here is trustworthy. You have my word."

There was little point in arguing now that Yuen had already seen the place, so she gestured for Kwok Po-Tai to sit on a large container of rice. She and Cheung Po perched at an angle to him on a couple of tin chests.

"My apologies for the urgent summons," she said, "but I assume you've already heard?"

"I wish we were meeting under better circumstances."

"Indeed. Given these changes, I'm sure you agree that—"

"Is it true you arrived shortly after Choy Hin died?"

She was taken aback by his brusqueness. Usually one needed to ease Kwok Po-Tai into business with pleasantries.

"We'd have gotten there sooner, but we got delayed," Cheung Po said, glancing out of the corner of his eye at Shek Yeung.

"What a shame," Kwok Po-Tai said to Cheung Po. "You and Choy Hin were close, as I understand it."

"He was a reliable ally," Cheung Po said.

"Is that all?"

"Allies are important right now," Shek Yeung said, sensing an impending fight. "And that's the main reason I wanted us to talk today. Pak Ling has left us no choice but to partner more closely." She explained what they had found on Taiwan and relayed the contents of Choy Hin's note.

"You know, I trust, the legend of the zodiac," Kwok Po-Tai said. He stood, strutted over to the chest of silver, and picked up a piece to examine it.

"Who doesn't?" Shek Yeung said. "The Jade Emperor announced a race: whichever animal crossed the river first would become the first sign of the zodiac, whichever crossed second would become the second sign, and so forth."

Kwok Po-Tai seemed to be waiting to see if she inferred his meaning. She had a guess but kept her mouth shut. If he had something to say, he had better say it directly.

Finally, he said, "The mouse and the cat were friends. Both were bad swimmers, but both were also smart, so together they devised a plan to get across the river on the back of the ox. While on the ox, the rat pushed the cat into the river, causing it to drown. And that is why the cat is not in the zodiac, why cats continue to hunt rats to this day.

"There are different versions of this tale, of course. In some of them, the focus is on how the rat, after receiving a ride on the trusting ox, jumped onto the shore right as the ox neared it. That is why the ox is the second zodiac year and not the first." He pocketed the piece of silver without breaking eye contact with Shek Yeung, as if daring her to protest.

"I wouldn't have taken you for one to tell children's stories," Shek Yeung said sedately.

"True, I far prefer poetry. But children's tales sometimes relate the truth better than even the best poems by the best poets."

"Except there is no shore," she said.

"Pardon?"

"There is no shore anywhere in front of us. There is no first, only staying afloat. Even if Pak Ling dies, someone will eventually replace him. A rat would be stupid to not realize that."

"I've also seen a hungry rat eat so much that its stomach burst. It found itself in a granary and just couldn't stop."

Cheung Po sighed loudly. "We're not interested in taking over your damn fleet, all right? We have enough to manage on our own."

"Fine," Kwok Po-Tai said, "but I'll need some form of assurance, say, the location of Choy Hin's stockpile. I know it's somewhere on the Matsu islands."

"You stuffed pig—" Cheung Po began.

"Do you? Know the location?" she interrupted Cheung Po. If he did know, he never shared the information with her, and that was unacceptable. With Pak Ling nipping at their heels, the fleet needed all the resources it could possibly get.

Cheung Po's silence confirmed this. "Oh my," Kwok Po-Tai said, "have you two not discussed this?"

"It's Choy Hin's money," Cheung Po said. "He earned it. He has the right to bring it with him to the underworld."

"No dead man needs that much money," Shek Yeung said.

"He wouldn't even be dead if you hadn't insisted on first dealing with the spies!"

She took a slow breath. "If we hadn't dealt with the spies, we might've wound up as dead as Choy Hin. Also, it was your idea to capture Qiu Liang-Gong's war junk. If we hadn't, he wouldn't have sworn revenge."

"Did we even find the spies? You said that none of them admitted to working with anyone outside the fleet. Maybe the real spy saw that we were busy chopping people's heads off and told Pak Ling, who took the opportunity to attack Choy Hin."

"That would be a problem, wouldn't it?" Kwok Po-Tai said, looking smug. "For both of our fleets, if you haven't actually found your spy yet. If our fleets stay close, then a spy informing on one fleet's location is in essence informing on the other's."

"Like you've found yours already," Cheung Po spat.

"I have."

They had no way of telling if Kwok Po-Tai was lying, and he knew it. It was in his interest to cast the Red Banner Fleet as a liability—that was why he'd brought up Cheung Po's friendship with Choy Hin as soon as he arrived. And now Cheung Po had revealed their uncertainty regarding the spy's identity.

"Eighty-twenty," she said to Kwok Po-Tai. "You can have twenty percent of Choy Hin's stores." She pulled Cheung Po aside before he could protest. "You're the one who put us in this position. Money can be replenished. Lives can't. If we survive this, you can put money back in Choy Hin's hiding spot for all I care."

"Seventy to me," Kwok Po-Tai said. "I'm the one putting my fleet at risk."

"Sixty to us. If our fleet dies, yours does, too. It would be just a matter of time."

They settled on half each. After Kwok Po-Tai left, she and Cheung Po extinguished the lanterns, exited, and blocked off the mouth of the cave once more. On the rocks a little in the distance, they found Yuen's body: blow to the back of the head. Kwok Po-Tai had brought the man as a bodyguard and then disposed of him as soon as he was no longer needed. The poor man had posed no threat, but evidently that didn't matter to Kwok Po-Tai, who cared only about protecting the secret of Cheng Yat's fabled Southern Cave.

29

And what if Cheung Po was right? What if the spy was still on board, reporting every little secret to Pak Ling? What if, in taking the time to root out the dissenters, she'd indirectly caused the destruction of the Blue Banner Fleet? (No, she'd taken only a few extra days, no way Pak Ling could have mobilized an attack on Taiwan that quickly.)

What if Kwok Po-Tai was lying about having found his spy? What if by allying with him she was putting her own fleet further at risk? What if he'd lied simply to sow conflict between her and Cheung Po? (No, he was an opportunist, not an idiot, he knew well what would become of his fleet if hers were destroyed.)

What if Cheung Po was the spy?

She made every decision with the question of betrayal in her head. She answered every question about her decisions with a beheading. It was for the good of the fleet, she told herself, a few dozen dead was better than thousands. These men were potential mutineers. Finally, Cheung Po said to her, "You have to stop this. Terrified men do not make good fighters or loyal followers. Even Cheng Yat wouldn't have gone this far."

But how was she supposed to stop when there was so much to lose?

On the sixth sleepless night, she arose, slipped a thin waistcoat over her nightclothes, and boarded the altar boat.

The fortune-teller, abruptly awoken from sleep, wisely fetched her sticks without a word of complaint. Shek Yeung demanded the identity of the spy. "You've done this enough to know that's not how this works," the fortune-teller said, shaking the canister at her.

"Anything you can tell me is fine."

The fortune-teller produced a stick:

> I exhaust my tears for home as I travel
> Watching a lone sail at the edge of the sky
> Where does the ferry go, I wish I had asked
> The still sea darkens slowly

And then, unexpectedly, the older woman asked her, "What do *you* think it means?"

"Isn't that your job?" Shek Yeung said.

The fortune-teller just kept her eyes on her.

"Fine," Shek Yeung said. "There is only one sail, so that ship has to face whatever it'll face alone. No allies."

"And?"

"And there is a lot of uncertainty. The poet doesn't know where the ferry will go. Maybe no one knows where the ferry will go, including the crew."

"And?"

"The sea is darkening, which means the sky is darkening. That doesn't bode well."

"You've gotten good at this."

"That's it? I'm alone and uncertain, and bad news is coming? You can't tell me anything about the spy?"

"No, but if you really want more, I'll add this: The sea and the sky are both realms of the gods. If they darken, they do so at the gods' wishes. Also, the poet is longing for home. Maybe you are nearing the end of your journey, and instead of fighting the will of Heaven by trying to cling to this way of life, you should just stop. Go home. Let everyone else go home, too."

The fortune-teller stood and stowed the canister away. Shek Yeung realized her hands were trembling. What was it that Ma-Zou had said to her that day near the temple? *Go as fast as you can, until the wind will take you no farther.* Was this it, then? The changing of the wind.

Or was the fortune-teller lying as well? If Shek Yeung went home, then so did everyone she was holding captive. She didn't trust the older woman not to shape her divinations in a manner that benefited her. Maybe the "still sea" in the fortune portended smooth sailing. Maybe the "lone sail" meant that the Red Banner Fleet was strong enough to stand by itself against enemies. Come to think of it, she didn't even know if the poems the fortune-teller recited were the ones associated with the sticks she'd pulled. There was no compendium of poems and interpretations. There were only those little, nonsensical notches on the sticks that, for all Shek Yeung knew, had been gnawed by rats.

"Are you all right?" the fortune-teller asked, once again fixing her eyes on Shek Yeung in a way that felt all too seeing, too all-seeing, as if she already knew how everything would end.

· · ·

Two months later, a storm swept in with very little warning. Shek Yeung herself hadn't noticed the signs until it was almost too late: the hairs on her arms stood, and instinctively she took a deep breath, smelled the unmistakable, hollow smell of lightning, the air with its soul burned right out of it. In the space of only a few heartbeats, a dense column of clouds filled the sky. The sea sheeted toward them, as if a fine blade had slid under its flesh and were flaying it bit by bit.

Binh must have noticed the change around the time she did because the ship was already moving. They barely escaped. "Thank Ma-Zou," everybody was saying. Nobody wanted to offend Ma-Zou by being the first to point out that the storm had destroyed an entire squadron, the one that had been farthest out at sea.

Not much later they arrived at a village that had for years reliably paid its tribute only to find it empty. Most of the villagers, it seemed, had left a while ago to escape famine. A few corpses lay unburied, slumped on the ground or curled on their beds. So many hungry ghosts. The bodies, little more than bones by now, were paper cuttings punctured by air and light. *How full of nothing all humans are,* Shek Yeung thought absently, *just bits of substance drawn and held stubbornly together by will, animal habit, and the fear of what comes after.*

Ask yourself, girl: in which direction is the wind blowing?

Please, Ma-Zou, she prayed. *I'm not ready yet.*

But Ma-Zou must not have heard or cared because soon after that Cheung Po was beset by the Portuguese navy while doing reconnaissance with a small contingent near the Pearl River Delta. He survived, as did most of his men, but the damage to the ships was sizable. He returned with a dislocated shoulder for her to set. She made him lie face up on a cot and grabbed his arm, positioning it at right angles to his torso. Digging her heel into his waist, she tugged on the arm until she heard the telltale *crack-thunk.*

"Thanks," he said.

"It's fine."

"Sorry I blamed you for Choy Hin's—"

"It's fine."

"I just keep thinking, if I hadn't taken the ship from Qiu—"

"What's done is done," she said, sitting down next to him. He flipped over and buried his face in the blanket. "You made a decision. I made a decision. Maybe they were the wrong decisions, maybe not. But I am truly sorry for your loss. I know Choy Hin was important to you."

"I would've been fine just sailing up and down the coast with him," he mumbled. "I'm not saying I'm not happy commanding our fleet. I'm happy Cheng Yat left it to me. Or maybe I'm not. I'm not sure."

"You think he *should* have left it to you, but you didn't need it," Shek Yeung supplied.

"Right. When he sent me and fifty ships to help Choy Hin raid spice traders in the southeast, I didn't know what to expect from Choy Hin. He wasn't with Lam Yuk-Yiu then; his first wife had just died. I was seventeen, and the only kind of commander I could imagine was someone like Cheng Yat. But Choy Hin was different. He treated me like an equal."

She understood because she'd experienced something very similar with Cheng Yat. After years on the flower boats, she'd felt grateful to him for giving her any choice at all, even if he'd occasionally devised cruel stratagems to remind her that his word was final. Choy Hin had been this person for Cheung Po but better because he hadn't possessed Cheng Yat's cruelty. Cheung Po must have been fascinated. He might have even called it love.

Cheng Yat might have died more than two years ago, but he still haunted her and Cheung Po. Neither of them could make a single decision without considering what he would have done. It was a kind of possession, his spirit penetrating and animating them to remind them that he would always have the final word.

. . .

At least Cheung Po's reconnaissance trip had not been in vain. They now knew the emperor had indeed allied himself with the Portuguese and possibly also the English. The Portuguese were sending additional ships to meet with the Qing fleet in less than three months. Having dispatched most of the other fleets, Pak Ling was turning his full attention on the Red Banner Fleet, and, arrogant as he was, even he realized he needed help.

It was clear a successful meetup would bode ill for them. Still, they argued and fretted over it. Shek Yeung sought input from the crew, but they were also divided. Ahmad and Yan-Yan were of the opinion that they should return to Maynila for now, until they'd had the chance to replenish their numbers, whereas Old Wong recommended swift engagement on account of the winds this time of year, which favored junks over European-style brigs.

Cheung Po visited the fortune-teller. He'd asked Shek Yeung to accompany him, but she'd declined, still feeling uneasy about her last fortune. Yet the older woman apparently said nothing along the lines of what she'd told Shek Yeung because Cheung Po returned to their cabin looking as conflicted as before. "Heaven is undecided," he said. "Whatever happens, happens as a result of our own will."

"What *is* our will?" she asked.

He slumped into a chair. "Does it matter at this point?"

"We can hide," she said. "Go to Maynila for a while."

"This fight is going to happen sooner or later. I'd prefer sooner. It'll be rough, but you know I don't fight battles I can't win."

They began preparations. From the villages that had escaped the most recent famines, they extorted barbarous amounts of supplies. From the villages that had not, they recruited hundreds of members. The new crew happily ate the stolen food and pledged lifelong loyalty, a pact that might bind them for anywhere from another few decades to another few days.

"Welcome, friends!" she said, filling their cups and toasting them with her own, promising riches and glory, every other word out of her mouth a lie.

30

In one of the stories about Ma-Zou, she learned that even her powers had a limit.

The sixteen-year-old Ma-Zou was at home weaving while her father and brothers were at sea. Her parents had forbidden her from going out to sea, even though she was a stronger swimmer than her brothers and felt no particular affinity for weaving. She sat at the loom, feet tapping rhythmically on the treadles, body rocking from side to side as the shuttle glided from hand to hand like a boat across still water. The blue warp threads shimmered, giving the appearance of undulation, and suddenly the sea surrounded her. But this sea was angry, throwing itself against the little one-masted junk on which she stood. Blades of rain fell mercilessly. The wind roared its displeasure.

In the water, five men struggled to stay afloat—this was her father's ship, and her father and brothers were about to die. Ma-Zou called to them to grab her hand, but they couldn't seem to hear her; nor could she seem to move her limbs. She closed her eyes and focused on her heartbeat as she often did while meditating, slowing her blood until it was almost still, for the body is the universe and blood is the sea, and everything that will be, already is.

The next instant she was back at the loom. Madame Lam, finding her daughter in a trance, had shaken the girl awake out of fear. Ma-Zou keened, for she knew she'd failed.

The rest of the story Ma-Zou's father would tell upon returning home with only three of his sons. A storm had tossed everyone overboard, and while trying to keep his head above water, coughing up the seawater burning his lungs, he saw through the sting in his eyes his daughter amidships. She stood there in a red dress, untouched by the waves and the rain, which bent around her like diverted streams, as if out of deference, or fear. He resigned himself to death, thinking that his eyes were playing tricks as he neared his end. Then, impossibly, the sea changed, not only in quality but also in temperature. It became as a warm hand, scooping him out of the water and laying him gently on the deck. When he'd regained his senses, he saw that his three younger sons were back as well. They searched for his eldest, but the waves had already claimed him. Had Ma-Zou stayed in her trance for a moment longer, he might have been saved, but sometimes even the most powerful were powerless against chance.

31

They numbered six, each exceptionally well outfitted for war: five brigs and one frigate. The two-masted brigs carried, at Shek Yeung's best estimate, some six hundred men and one hundred large guns among them. The three-masted frigate alone bore along at a minimum hundred and fifty men and twenty-five large guns. All of them overflowed with superior European black powder.

In manpower, the Red Banner Fleet appeared to have the advantage—in ships, too. But Shek Yeung understood what the crew members who were prematurely celebrating with drink and opium did not. First, these Portuguese were soldiers, not hungry dock- and farmhands. Second, these were warships, not fishing junks with nets in place of armor.

And these Europeans abided no rules of engagement that she recognized. They almost certainly had them, but what were they and would they be extended to people like her? The imperial navy, for all its hostility against pirates, was at least somewhat predictable. Many of them were countrymen, and with the slightest divergence in fate, they might have ended up in Shek Yeung's employ instead of the emperor's.

To make everything worse, the meetup was happening during daytime. The Portuguese weren't stupid. There would be no fog cover, no surprise.

Half of the fleet, led by Cheung Po, already awaited in the estuary, forming a barrier between the Portuguese and the Qing upriver. The other half, led by Shek Yeung, would come in quickly behind the Portuguese to prevent escape. Any misstep from either front meant defeat.

She heard the Portuguese men-of-war's cannonade from approximately 150 lei away. By the time her half of the fleet approached the firing range, the battle was well underway. Through the smoke, she could barely make out Cheung Po's war junk, the one he'd captured from Qiu Liang-Gong, along with the smaller junks sinking around it, their burning red sails disappearing beneath the waves like so many little sunsets.

"Fire!" she yelled.

Her men hurled fire hawk pikes and thunderbolt balls. They fired their unreliable cannons as best as they could, only one out of maybe every twenty or thirty rounds flying far enough to actually reach the Portuguese men-of-war and then only to graze them slightly. The Portuguese, realizing that they were now flanked, maneuvered a couple of their ships so they could fire back more easily at Shek Yeung's.

Her ship shook but didn't sink. It was the largest of the fleet after all, Cheung Po's war junk notwithstanding, and the best armored. This stalwart craft was one of the few constants in her life. The double-masted junks did their best to stay in the fight. The ones with the most-skilled helmsmen, several of which had joined the fleet long before Shek Yeung, wove among the larger but less agile Portuguese ships to avoid direct hits. The single-masted ones never stood a chance.

Against well-armed ships, the best strategy was often to wait until they had exhausted their fire. And yet the Portuguese just kept firing. Had they traveled here with Europe's entire supply of rounds and black powder? So it was at some point during the third or fourth hour of engagement that the desertions started.

She should have expected this. Most battles at sea simply didn't last this long. The briefness of most engagements and the threat of death to aspiring deserters were usually enough to keep most people fighting until the end, but now her people were confused, tired, and as a result of her recent spy-hunting, probably more than a little resentful of her authority.

"Hold the line!" she said, but of course that accomplished nothing.

Suddenly somebody shouted from the port side, "They're boarding!"

Several of the Portuguese were already on board, whereas others were hacking through the ropes that bound the fishing nets and ox hides to the ship. It made no sense: if she'd had a ship as fortified as theirs, she would have simply kept firing or rammed the line. But there they were.

"Arms!" All the people who weren't currently operating large guns reached for their swords or pistols or spears. In the space of the maybe ten heartbeats she had before the Portuguese climbed aboard, she sprinted belowdecks, found Yan-Yan hiding in her cabin with the baby as Shek Yeung had ordered her to do, and said, "Barricade the door. Keep a weapon in your hand. And do *not* let anyone in except me, not even if it sounds like the fighting has stopped."

The Portuguese quickly swarmed the main deck, still outnumbered, yes, but better armed and better trained. Shek Yeung fought defensively, trying to conserve energy for what promised to be a long fight. She hovered a little off to the side of the younger, stronger crew members, waiting until they'd weakened an opponent enough so she could sneak in and deal the death stroke, freeing them to focus on someone new. When she noticed a Portuguese sailor using a pistol instead of a blade, she quickly closed the distance between them to nullify the advantage of his firearm, forcing him to draw his sword instead, which gave her enough time to run him through with hers. At some point, she found herself near the top of the stairs. That was when she glimpsed Yan-Yan.

Why had that ridiculous girl left the cabin? There she was, stubbornly blocking the door with a spear in her hands, the worst possible choice for the cramped conditions of the lower deck, but Shek Yeung never insisted that she learn to use anything else, did she? She'd thought she would be able to protect the girl from the worst of the fighting. A little off to Yan-Yan's side stood the northern woman, armed with two knives.

Another blast rocked the ship, a solid hit this time. It threw her to the deck and slid her several paces. Her elbows bore the brunt of the impact, and she felt skin scraping away from bone as she tried to stop her momentum with only her arms. What actually stopped her was the body of one of her best men. She pushed herself upright, hands slipping around on the bloody deck.

And that might have been the moment—or maybe the moment right after, when Shek Yeung noticed the new wave of Portuguese boarding—that she realized she might well lose everything today.

Death crept along the ship like poison vines, clambering onto one person, and then another, and then another, making blood blossom from chests and bellies and mouths. It sprouted shoots belowdecks. Out of the corner of her eye, Shek Yeung saw Yan-Yan lunge at a man with her spear and get knocked against the wall. The spear fell. Yan-Yan hadn't been able to make the kill, she realized. The girl had hesitated, and that was the opening the enemy needed. Shek Yeung elbowed her way closer, but the northern woman got there first, throwing herself at the man who towered over Yan-Yan. He stumbled, and his blade carved Yan-Yan's arm open.

The northern woman thrust a knife into the man's stomach and then, using both hands, pushed the blade down the center of his body, slicing him from sternum to groin.

"Get her inside!" Shek Yeung shouted at the northern woman, who nodded and dragged Yan-Yan back into the cabin. Not that that was going to do much good. The Portuguese would find them eventually, after they had killed everyone else.

Ma-Zou, I beg you.

The goddess, it was well established, went by two names: Ma-Zou, Maternal Ancestor, and Tin-Hau, Empress of Heaven. If one wanted something extravagant like riches or a household of sons, then one had to call upon the latter name. But if one needed urgent aid, then one had to call upon the former. Don't believe it? Pay attention the next time a child gets hurt and cries, "Mama!" See how fast the mother comes.

She'd no sooner whispered her prayer than someone called from the stern, "Help is here!" Shek Yeung ran back up to the main deck, and what she saw made her almost collapse in relief: a hundred black sails coming over the horizon, blotting out the sky.

32

A s Kwok Po-Tai's hundred-odd ships closed the distance, a large multicolored flag went up on the frigate. Immediately the same flag went up on each of the brigs, and the Portuguese aboard Shek Yeung's ship began to retreat, clambering back over shredded fishing nets and bodies. Her crew chased after them, trying to sneak in a few final thrusts of the spear or swings of the cutlass. Soon all six men-of-war had pulled away, abandoning the meetup, at least for now.

She told Binh, who was injured but still standing, to set a course for Canton, and then she bolted to her cabin. Yan-Yan was on the cot, bleeding through the layers and layers of bandage the northern woman continued to wind around her arm.

"We need more rags," Shek Yeung told Ahmad, who immediately left the cabin in search of some. To Yan-Yan she said, "Hang on, we're going to get you help."

Once back in the city, they could hire a palanquin to the physician, assuming that the girl didn't bleed out before then.

Ahmad returned with some rags. While the northern woman held Yan-Yan down, Shek Yeung unwrapped and rewrapped the wound, flinging the blackened cloth aside. "Dawa," Yan-Yan rasped, "it hurts."

Shek Yeung couldn't yell at Yan-Yan, so she yelled at Dawa instead. "What the hell was she doing outside of the cabin? I told her to hide."

"She did, but then she became convinced the barricade would never hold, so she hid the baby and came out. She thought that one body blocking the door was better than none."

"Of all the stupid . . ." Shek Yeung glanced at the corner of the cabin, where Siu Yuet was sleeping, unharmed.

When the palanquin finally pulled up in front of the physician's, Yan-Yan was no longer responsive. The man squinted at the wound and said, "I can stop the bleeding. After that, it's hard to say."

He shooed her away so he could work. *I already lost one best friend on your watch,* she wanted to say to him. *Don't make me lose the other.*

The fever started after the bleeding stopped, as they all knew it would. Shek Yeung bought the most potent herbs the physician stocked and made from them a bitter-smelling decoction, half of which she used to rinse and dress the sour-smelling wound. The other half she had to convince Yan-Yan to drink.

Or to be accurate, force Yan-Yan to drink. "No, no," Yan-Yan said each time, half-conscious, thrashing, face resolutely turned away from the cup. And each time, Dawa locked her in place from behind and gripped her chin while Shek Yeung pried open her mouth with one hand and tipped the liquid inside with the other. Both Shek Yeung and Dawa endured a few bites to the fingers this way. The violence of the process, of Yan-Yan's bodily rejection of them, made Shek Yeung feel as though they were brutalizing the girl. On a few occasions she had to remove herself from Yan-Yan's presence afterward just so she could calm her own nerves. The sight of a slack body that had given up the fight— she'd encountered it often enough on the flower boats.

In the end, all they could really do was wait and pray. After several days of fever—Shek Yeung was starting to wonder if she might not have used up all of Ma-Zou's favors with that final-hour rescue from the Black Banner Fleet—she went to the fortune-teller. "I don't care what you have to do," she said to the older woman. "You have a connection to the gods, you ask them to save Yan-Yan."

"I can draw a stick for your friend," the fortune-teller said.

"I don't want a fortune, I want help. What do you need? Expensive incense? Fruit?"

"My powers are what they are. Also, it is already fated how we all live and die."

"Your freedom, then. If you intercede and Yan-Yan survives, I'll let you go."

It seemed the older woman's eyes flicked to Shek Yeung's and then back to its usual spot off in space. "I can't guarantee anything."

"I'm not asking you to."

She sent Shek Yeung to buy supplies and hire musicians while she ritually prepared herself. Shek Yeung returned hours later with fine-grade incense, fresh flowers and fruit, paper money, sea creatures sculpted from agar, and two street musicians to whom she'd promised what must have sounded like suspicious amounts of money.

The fortune-teller had piled her own hair in the shape of a small boat atop her head, a red flower sticking out of it like a full sail. She'd also changed into a dark-blue short robe and a red skirt. The older woman set the altar with a sure hand, placing each offering on its own plate and then surrounding the plates with the flowers.

At the fortune-teller's signal, the yee-wu player began his bowing. The song was a touch melancholy if for no other reason than that it was slow, and all slow songs played on the yee-wu hinted at parting, each drawn-out note an outstretched hand. Then the gu-zang player joined in, each delicately plucked note a teardrop.

"Burn the incense," the fortune-teller said. Shek Yeung lit the joss sticks, bowing with them pointed first toward Heaven and then toward the Ma-Zou statue, three times each, before wriggling them into the sand in the brazier.

"Present the offerings." Shek Yeung set the paper money aflame.

"Kneel." Shek Yeung and the fortune-teller both kneeled.

"Kowtow." This they had to do nine times.

"Make your petition." Shek Yeung, still on her knees, fixed her eyes on the statue. "Ma-Zou," she said, "please spare Yan-Yan's life. I was the one who brought her into all this, and she got injured only because she was trying to protect my child." She closed her eyes and bowed deeply one more time. When she opened her eyes, she saw that one of the joss sticks in the brazier had gone out.

And then one by one, the remaining sticks went out.

"Oracle," she said. She described what had happened.

The fortune-teller frowned. Shakily, Shek Yeung relit the sticks—one didn't need to be an oracle to know this was a bad sign—but after a moment they extinguished themselves again.

"I think you have your answer," the fortune-teller said quietly.

"You light them."

"What's the use?"

"The gods like you more. You do it."

The older woman laughed. "Is that what you think? The blind woman who was practically starving before she got abducted by pirates is favored by the gods?"

"You'll notice you're no longer starving. In fact, you eat more than some of the men in the fleet."

"I hope your friend recovers, I do. But you don't fear for or mourn any other member of the fleet like this. You said to Ma-Zou that you brought your friend into this life as if you didn't bring most of the fleet into this life. Where's your concern for them? What about the ones you killed? Is your compassion reserved for so few?"

"I don't accept this," Shek Yeung said. She'd never heard her own voice so shrill.

"Heaven doesn't care what you accept and neither do I," the fortune-teller sneered, and suddenly Shek Yeung was filled with so much hatred for her that she couldn't contain it. So she raised her hand, ready to slap that look off the woman's face.

The woman flinched.

"You're not blind," Shek Yeung whispered.

It all made sense. Who else besides essential crew members knew about every raid ahead of time? Superstitious as he was, Cheung Po never embarked on a campaign without first seeking a reading. And when had she met the fortune-teller, if not on the day she met Pak Ling? For all she knew, Pak Ling had planted this woman in Shek Yeung's path that afternoon and asked her to deliver a fortune that would presage his appearance. Shek Yeung had invited his spy right into her fleet.

All the secrets she and Cheung Po had shared with this old woman, they were Pak Ling's now. All their hopes about their child, their fears and doubts about their future. Pak Ling had probably laughed at each one.

"How do you send messages to Pak Ling?" Shek Yeung demanded.

"What?" The fortune-teller shook her head. "Fine, I'm not blind. But people believe you more when they think you've been touched by the gods. And I was hungry. We were all hungry."

"Have any of your prophecies been real? No wonder you told me to retire. Was that Pak Ling's idea?"

She was still shaking her head. "I don't know what you're talking about, but my fortunes are as real as any reader's. You draw a stick, the stick is associated with a poem, and I interpret the poem the best I can in that moment. And sometimes certain images or words come to me. I can't control when or how."

Shek Yeung drew her knife.

The fortune-teller put up her hands. "I swear, I haven't lied to you about anything except the blindness. I'll prove it. Lately I've been hearing in my mind the words, 'Beware the tiger's mouth.' I'm not sure what it means, but I think you need to listen, I think the fleet's survival depends on you listening."

Shek Yeung slit her throat.

33

The fever broke on the ninth day. Yan-Yan asked for some water and then, later that afternoon, some food. Per the physician's instructions, Shek Yeung went to the market and bought three dau of ingredients for blood purification and fortification, and then she and Dawa made a broth that tasted as bad as it smelled. Yan-Yan was able to keep the whole thing down, was even able to poke fun at her cooking a little. It wasn't so long ago that their roles had been reversed: Shek Yeung, pregnant and nauseated, had gulped down every terrible thing that Yan-Yan had cooked so as to spare herself having to taste it. But what the dishes lacked in flavor, they apparently didn't lack in nourishment. She was alive, after all, as was Siu Yuet, who spent most of her time since the battle napping away in Shek Yeung's cabin as if nothing had happened.

When she noticed that Yan-Yan was using her left arm to feed herself, she asked, "Can you move the other arm?" Yan-Yan shook her head.

That wasn't surprising. Whatever the blade hadn't severed, the physician probably had. Yan-Yan didn't seem particularly saddened by the loss—whether she would later, after the relief of surviving such an ordeal had ebbed, Shek Yeung didn't know. Grief had the quality of a cast fishing line sometimes, in hand at the start, reaching the zenith only once it was in the distance, and not subsiding until even farther out, until it had traversed so much space as to have lost its force. Sometimes it never truly subsided.

What surprised her were the little slips of tongue and memory. One afternoon Yan-Yan asked for her. Shek Yeung hurried to the physician's, only to be met with confusion. Not only had Yan-Yan forgotten why she wanted to see her, she'd forgotten having sent a messenger in the first place. Another time, the two of them were chatting, and Yan-Yan said, "I want to see your . . ."

"You want to see what?"

A panicked look crossed Yan-Yan's face. "Your . . . that thing . . ." After a moment, she sighed and said, "Siu Yuet," and Shek Yeung realized the word she'd been looking for was "child" or "daughter."

Shek Yeung asked the physician about this.

"Well," he said, "fevers do that sometimes."

"Will she get better?" she asked.

He shrugged.

She had Cheung Po bring Siu Yuet over. When she placed the child in Yan-Yan's lap, Yan-Yan cried in a way that Shek Yeung had never seen from her before. Eventually she calmed down, and instead of talking about why she'd cried, she simply said, "These clothes are getting too tight on her. We'll have to find her bigger ones."

After a few more days, the physician decided Yan-Yan was well enough to be discharged, or as well as she was going to be. Shek Yeung had seen this coming and knew what she needed to do.

She hired a couple of palanquins to take Yan-Yan, Dawa, and herself to the sam-hop-yuen. Siu Yuet she carried in a sling across her chest. In the courtyard, the longan trees were bare, but the kumquat were starting to fruit again. Recent rains had thoroughly washed the stone tiles and gave the appearance of a well-kept home.

Yan-Yan settled into the main bedroom, where Siu Yuet had been born to a woman who'd borne her only as a bargaining tool. Shek Yeung had grown to care deeply for Siu Yuet over the past few months. There had even been moments she congratulated herself for successfully acclimating to motherhood, like whenever she stopped Siu Yuet from crying or made her smile. But once the battle started, all she'd been able to think about was the survival of the fleet. Meanwhile Yan-Yan had risked her own life to save Siu Yuet's.

"I know I said you could recuperate here for a while," Shek Yeung told Yan-Yan, "but I lied. I want you to stay here with Dawa and with the baby."

"Okay. How long do you want us to stay?" the girl asked, confused.

"This is your house now, Siu Yuet your daughter. And don't worry about money. I'll make sure everyone's seen to."

"Who's going to manage the fleet's finances?"

"Cheung Po and I will figure it out. You don't need to worry about it anymore."

"So you just decide that for me like my parents decided who I was going to marry?" Yan-Yan cried. "What if I don't want to leave the fleet?"

Shek Yeung's throat and chest were burning. "I don't care what you want."

Yan-Yan glared at her, and Shek Yeung felt the tiniest tinge of relief. Anger and hatred she knew what to do with. "You're of little help to me now anyway," she continued. "You don't think as fast as you used to. So just take the retirement. You were never really suited for piracy."

"Then why did you recruit me?"

Because you reminded me of the girl I'd been before everything. Because I knew you'd be safer in the fleet than out of it. Because I foolishly thought I could always keep you safe. She fixed her gaze on a spot behind Yan-Yan's head. "I make mistakes, too."

Yan-Yan turned her back on Shek Yeung. This was also preferable, made it easier for Shek Yeung to leave. On her way out, Shek Yeung added, "I think I've mentioned before my friend who lived here. If you ever need help, call on her spirit. I believe she will keep you safe. I believe this is what she would have wanted."

. . .

That night she told Cheung Po what she had done. He seemed disappointed but not particularly distraught—had Siu Yuet been a son, he probably would have reacted differently. "Well, it's not like we can't visit," he said. "Who's going to manage the money, though?"

"At the rate things are going," she said, "we might not have money left to manage. If this were a normal war of attrition, we'd have a chance. But we're not up against the emperor's fortune alone. Now we're also up against the Europeans'."

They talked and talked about it, but in the end, they didn't really have any other option. The Europeans were just going to send more ships. A rupture in the relationship between the emperor and the Europeans was possible, inevitable even, given enough time, but with Pak Ling arming every village along the coast and the growing number of European ships patrolling the waterways, the probability of surviving until the rupture was slim.

They sent word to Kwok Po-Tai to request his aid for the battle. They used up a sizable portion of their money to repair the ships that had been damaged by the Portuguese. They recruited more men, which proved not terribly difficult given the famine. To discourage desertion, they promised an increased cut to ship captains who braved the entire engagement while threatening those who were considering desertion with torture and death. They did this by hunting down the deserters from the previous battle and making an example of them. Taking a page from the emperor's book, she mounted the men's heads on pikes and then mounted a pike at the bow of each squadron leader's ship. Bloody pikes pierced bloodless cheeks, eyeless sockets, mouths open in soundless screams, two, three dozen heads stacked four apiece. This man had turned to pirating to pay the bride-price of the girl he wanted to marry. This man had celebrated the birth of Shek Yeung's first child with her and Cheng Yat. This woman had needed money to help her ailing father. Some of their names she knew; some she didn't.

"Let this be a reminder," she said to the crew of each ship.

She couldn't sleep the night before the battle, so she stayed out on the deck under the scythe moon. She wondered how Yan-Yan was healing, how Siu Yuet was eating. And if the edges of the scythe blurred at times, it was only because her yawns made her tear up. (Was the night bleeding onto the blade, or was the blade melting into the night?) At some point she heard a noise behind her and saw that Cheung Po had pulled up two stools. They sat there in silence for a long time. She took and held on to his hand.

The next evening, dressed in her black military tunic and pants, silver lamellar breastplate glistening from a fresh cleaning, she lined up the crew of her ship. Pacing from bow to stern, she aspersed each of them with garlic water from a silver jar, lingering on Ahmad (*may you see the shores of your homeland again someday*), Binh (*may your wits and hands remain quick into old age*), and Old Wong (*may you die in bed surrounded by family*). She handed each a piece of black fabric to wrap around the head.

The twelfth lunar month on the Pearl River Delta, with sails and spirits broken and then hastily, imperfectly mended, the Red Banner Fleet went back to war.

34

In one of the stories she told about herself, Shek Yeung was stolen away to the sea against her wishes. It was a beautiful story insofar as it was romantic and compelling, possessing all the easy truths that inspired sympathy. One day a powerful man fell in love with her and offered a choice: join him or die. Trembling, she accepted the cruel role he'd thrust upon her.

Except maybe she rejoiced a little, too. She ached all the time from her work on the flower boats and understood unequivocally that, in a few more years, even these men that she hated would abandon her for the younger, more beautiful girls, and she would be thrown out on the streets. After so long with so little, she wanted the life that had been denied her. She wanted money, respect, and the power to chart her own course.

Ma-Zou, you understand me better than anyone in the world. With you I've shared all my secrets. In you I've buried all my crimes.

In one of the stories she told about herself, Shek Yeung was molded by Cheng Yat into a criminal, a general, and a killer. "Your life depends on them knowing that you're in charge," he'd said, dragging to her feet one supposed traitor after another so she could demonstrate to the crew her readiness to mete out punishment, so she could learn to steady her hands. Her arms weren't strong enough in the beginning to sever the head on the first try, and she'd had to hack away, sweat and blood stinging her eyes.

Except there was also satisfaction, wasn't there, like that time she executed the man who'd raped a female captive despite her orders. How small he seemed cowering there, terrified for no other reason than that she'd made him so. *She* did, this once-young girl who couldn't even save her brother and father, who couldn't even . . . She knew she would probably never find the pirate who'd killed her family and sold her to the flower boats. For all she knew, he'd died in a battle immediately afterward. But she could pretend.

I feel remorse for some of the things I've done. I would do all of them again. What is remorse if not a privilege, the time to sit alone and cry for oneself?

In one of the stories she told about herself, Shek Yeung stayed with the fleet after Cheng Yat's death to protect the many lives that depended on the alliance's continued existence. Except Cheung Po likely would have managed on his own just fine. She just couldn't imagine, was too scared to imagine, the idea of the after. All that time to sit alone.

Ma-Zou, I've gone as fast and as far as the wind would take me. Now tell me how it ends.

35

The moment Shek Yeung saw one of the sails of the O Yam go aflame, she learned two important things about herself: First, she should've walked away from this life long ago, but she'd missed all the signs from Heaven that the winds of fate were changing. Second—

No, she was lying to herself again. She had seen the signs but interpreted them to suit herself. She hadn't wanted to give up her power, which at some point had become its own kind of tether, keeping her from the freedom she always said she wanted.

They were up against the same six Portuguese men-of-war as last time, in addition to a smattering of English brigs and Qing junks. This suggested that the Europeans had succeeded in meeting up with the Qing at some point after the last battle, though neither Shek Yeung nor Cheung Po had heard anything about it. Also, judging by how low the ships were riding in the water, the Europeans had replenished their black powder. One had to wonder what the Europeans were planning to do with such a stockpile in the South China Sea, or why the emperor and his advisers weren't more concerned about it.

Approaching at night, they'd set upon the European and Qing ships, which were anchored off a small island at the mouth of the Pearl River long used by Portuguese traders. For a while the battle had proceeded in their favor: with some clever maneuvering on the part of Binh and the helmsmen of several other junks, they'd succeeded in running one of the European ships aground. But then one of the other brigs had broken through the blockade formed by Shek Yeung's squadron and helped its compatriot refloat.

"Where is Kwok Po-Tai?" Shek Yeung said to Cheung Po, whose war junk had been too severely damaged by the Portuguese to repair.

"He'll come," Cheung Po said, looking unconvinced by his own words.

Overhead, the sail burned. Crew members rushed to put out the fire even as the European and Qing ships attempted to set new ones. Thankfully junks were rigged very differently from European ships, lacking the numerous stays and shrouds that would have helped the fire jump from one sail to another. Still, a sizable portion of the sail had already frizzled away, about the span of two battens. The junk's drive was now half of what it had been.

At the sight of the O Yam burning, the captains of the other junks lost their nerve. One by one they fled the battle, figuring that she couldn't hunt them down and kill them if she was dead. As for Kwok Po-Tai, he probably wasn't coming, either because he'd already been destroyed or because he'd also lost his nerve.

"Cowards!" Cheung Po yelled after the red sails disappearing over the horizon. "None of you deserve to fly this banner!"

With fewer ships around the O Yam to draw and block the Europeans' fire, the onslaught began, rocking the junk so furiously that she had to tie herself to the taffrail with a length of rope to avoid falling overboard. "We need to gather," she said to Cheung Po, "or they'll just pick us off individually."

With a torch, Cheung Po signaled the remaining junks. They formed a barrier between the O Yam and the European ships attacking it—it wasn't perfect by any means, but it bought the flagship a temporary reprieve, which bought Shek Yeung some time to think. If they could capture even one of the European vessels, then they could take hostages, assuming that those men weren't ready to fight to the death and that the men on the other vessels weren't ready to let any hostages die. Or perhaps they could retreat east. Those brigs were heavy and might not be able to catch up even if they decided to pursue.

The European and Qing ships moved into a ring formation around them. Cheung Po signaled the rest of the fleet to focus fire on the section of the ring that appeared most weakly fortified. This happened to also be the section of the ring that led upriver, where the European ships, with their deeper draft, couldn't follow. It was absolutely the right tactical decision, so she didn't countermand the order, yet there was something about the situation, what had that treacherous old woman said . . .

Beware the tiger's mouth. The entry point to the river was sometimes called the Tiger Gate.

"We can't go upriver," she told Cheung Po. But the ring was already broken, junks already escaping through the opening into some kind of trap.

"What? Why not?"

"I can't explain. Just, this reeks of Pak Ling."

"There's nowhere else for us to go! We don't have the firepower to make another opening."

"We'll crash through there," she said, pointing to a different section of the ring, one that was downwind and ever so slightly weaker than the others. "Gather the remaining ships. We go together."

"We have a burnt sail. We don't have the drive."

"I know." She placed her hands on his shoulders and looked him in the eyes. "Do you trust me?"

He laughed and sent up the signal.

With their sails let out athwartship, the remaining junks sped toward the point Shek Yeung had chosen. The initial impact of her ship against one of the Qing's knocked her to the deck. From her prostrate position, she could feel the hull splintering, hear the sails ripping.

So this is how it ends. Maybe I do deserve this, even if I never asked for any of it.

But the junk didn't sink. Pulling herself back up to her feet, she turned to face the spot they'd broken through, where two Qing vessels were listing after being repeatedly sideswiped by Shek Yeung's fleet. She grabbed the spyglass and pointed it toward the Tiger Gate. The European ships had blockaded the river mouth. All of the junks that had escaped upriver were trapped.

36

An attendant for Pak Ling's estate opened the main gate for Shek Yeung and Cheung Po and showed them into the entrance hall. "His Excellency will be with you shortly," the young man said before disappearing into one of the interior rooms.

The estate trumpeted a story of Pak Ling that drowned out the truth of him. If Shek Yeung hadn't known about his ruthless suppression of the northern rebellions, if she hadn't lost hundreds of her own men—thousands, depending on the outcome of this negotiation—to his wiles, she might have mistaken him for a scholar-bureaucrat, the kind of official more concerned with the codification of manners than with anything of import. The two-level building they were in had been built around a spacious central courtyard. Every carved window screen, every silk-paneled lantern, had that overly embellished quality that announced its owner as a person of means. High-relief figures glazed with celadon and oxblood told stories along the eaves: here, the story of how the monk Tang Sanzang subdued the powerful and rebellious Monkey King by tricking him into wearing a magical circlet that caused him tremendous pain whenever he disobeyed; and there, the story of the immortal Zhongli Quan who, in direct contrast to Ma-Zou and her four years of silence, cried for seven straight days after being born and then proceeded to speak in full proclamations, leading everyone around him to conclude that he was destined for greatness. (And what if Ma-Zou had done this? Would her family have thought her gifted or mad? Would they have simply abandoned her on a hillside after the fourth day of tears?) A large gilded plaque hung above the entrance to the main hall. Shek Yeung couldn't read all the characters, but they seemed to be from the Analects, something about how small men ruminate on money whereas great men ruminate on virtue and law.

How many people did one have to kill in the emperor's name to dwell in an estate like this? How many to be remembered as a great man?

"You didn't have to be here," she said to Cheung Po. She'd told him the same thing when they'd received the message from Pak Ling agreeing to the negotiation. There would be nothing stopping Pak Ling from trying to arrest them at this meeting, and if that came to pass, then it would be better for only one of them to be present. Cheung Po could instead take this opportunity to run, maybe back to his village, back to his sister and nephews.

Cheung Po smiled a little and said what he had then, too: "Well, we've come this far."

Pak Ling emerged from the room the attendant had entered earlier. "The honorable Mr. and Mrs. Cheung," he said, his expression perfectly placid. "This simple servant is delighted to welcome you to his humble home."

He presented very differently from how he had at the tavern. He still had a limp, though, and she thought she could still detect a hint of that rural accent, so maybe not all of it had been a lie. Yet even here Pak Ling sought to dissimulate: his black surcoat bore on its chest the square insignia of a crane, the symbol of a high-ranking scholar, as opposed to the lion insignia of a military official. On his head was a black velvet cap with fur trim, the dome of which was covered with red silk floss and topped with a red knob.

"Your Excellency," she said, parroting the attendant because she wasn't entirely fluent in the complicated system of court honorifics. She smoothed her long blue skirt and flowing tunic sleeves while he wasn't looking. She'd chosen to wear women's clothing instead of her usual military garb to this meeting. Pak Ling seemed to be the kind of person who cared about keeping the roles of men and women separate.

Nevertheless she'd wrought one tiny final act of defiance by wearing Han instead of Manchu women's clothing.

They sat down in the main hall, Cheung Po and Pak Ling opposite each other and Shek Yeung at right angles to them both. The attendant brought out a tea set. Pak Ling poured the hot water into the clay teapot and then emptied the teapot into a waste bowl. "One must first rinse the tea of impurities," he said, looking at Shek Yeung and Cheung Po, "or else dust will debase what is otherwise a strong and dignified oolong." He poured water into the teapot again and, after a quick steep, transferred the tea to a small pitcher, which he then used to serve, carefully keeping the spout pointed away from his guests. "You may think this tea ritual fussy, full of meaningless rules," Pak Ling continued, "but the rules are there for good reason. I serve the tea from a different pitcher and not from the pot itself to ensure each guest's tea has been steeped the same amount of time. I point the spout away as a precaution."

Shek Yeung and Cheung Po sipped the oolong with tight smiles. Only after they'd finished all the tea did Pak Ling speak again. "Do you know the major advantages the people of this great nation have over the barbarians of the West?"

It was a peculiar ingress to the negotiation. Shek Yeung had no choice but to play along. "Surely our hardiness is one of them."

"Our sovereignty over our boundaries and the stability of our government. For many generations now, we Chinese have prospered from an unbroken lineage of Qing monarchs, from the Kangxi Emperor to his son the Yongzheng Emperor, his grandson the Qianlong Emperor, and his great-grandson the Jiaqing Emperor. While the Europeans were fighting themselves, we were expanding our boundaries, from Taiwan-Fu in the east to Xinjiang in the west. We are like this Yixing clay"—here he gestured to the teapot—"which is renowned for its ability to absorb the flavor of the tea being brewed. Over time each pot develops a unique flavor from all the teas it has served that it then imparts to each subsequent serving. It absorbs, contains, and dispenses everything harmoniously.

"But for there to be true stability in governance, there must be cooperation. Stability through force is hard-won and short-lived. Stability through cooperation is long-lasting." Pak Ling wore an expression that managed to be both beneficent and insulting.

Cheung Po was staring blankly at the other man. "We would not have come if we had no interest in the possibility of cooperation," Shek Yeung said. "At the same time, cooperation is not subjugation."

Pak Ling laughed. "Of course not. It is no simple feat to subjugate someone the likes of you, as my men have discovered! Yet it seems to me you are in a quandary. After the battle at Tiger Gate, a good portion of your men are either gone or in my thrall. My informants tell me your ship sustained heavy damage. Cooperation, generally speaking, entails a sharing of resources, and right now, you don't have much to share. That is, except for—"

"Information," she said, completing his train of thought. "And expertise. You want our help hunting down all remaining pirates." Next to her, Cheung Po tensed.

"You did not earn your epithet as the Scourge of the South China Sea for nothing, Mrs. Cheung. Indeed, the endeavor of tracking down and bringing to justice the many pirates still out there is more time-consuming than I would like. Doable, but frustrating. I would sooner return to Peking and aid the emperor with more important tasks."

He signaled for his attendant, who brought out more tea for Pak Ling to waste through his elaborate rituals. What kind of tasks did a man like this consider "more important"? To Shek Yeung, this negotiation was a matter of life and death, not only for her but also for countless others. Was it possible that, to Pak Ling, this negotiation was already an afterthought, just another page in his long and continuing chronicle of victories?

"What's going to happen to the captured pirates?" Cheung Po asked quietly.

"Naturally, they will face justice."

"You mean death."

"I do not write the laws."

"But you're meeting with us, talking about cooperation, which means you can at least bend them."

"What he means," Shek Yeung said, "is that we are not comfortable with this proposal, though we remain hopeful that we can devise a proposal that will preserve face all around."

"I fail to see how. Men who fail to follow the rules must face punishment, lest they inspire others to transgress. As the Master says, 'When punishments are not properly awarded, the people do not know how to move hand or foot.'"

"Why should we follow your rules when your rules weren't made with us in mind?" Cheung Po said, his voice reverberating in the courtyard. "What did the emperor think was going to happen when he left his own people to starve?"

"The emperor is saddened by the plight of his people."

"Wonderful, we'll feast on his sadness."

She resisted the urge to intervene as she normally did whenever Cheung Po lost his temper. Besides, even if she could get him to calm down, their current negotiation strategy wasn't working. Men like Pak Ling valued the idea of law, regardless of whether said laws were equitable. The tea ritual alone had told her as much, the slavish devotion to form. The many quotes from Confucius and his ilk—men who'd tried to infer order from an inherently orderless world—were just confirmation.

She nudged Cheung Po with her foot. When Cheung Po glanced over, she indicated with what she hoped was an inconspicuous nod that he should continue with his show of rage. His expression didn't change, but he nudged her foot back. She hoped he understood her meaning.

"The solution I am offering is already far kinder than what any other in my position would," Pak Ling said to Cheung Po. "In exchange for cooperation, you and your wife are being pardoned for the countless atrocities you have committed. Do you realize the extent of cruelty you have shown?"

"No more than what you've shown," Cheung Po spat with, in Shek Yeung's mind, a touch more theatricality than usual.

"It is not cruelty but law and order. Without law and order, the people lose confidence in their rulers. As the Master says, confidence in the ruling state is more important than food. Death is the lot of man, but a state cannot stand without the confidence of its subjects."

"Without living, healthy subjects, a state is just an idea. Ideas can be replaced, but lives cannot." Cheung Po stood abruptly, clattering the tableware in the process, and said to Shek Yeung, "We're leaving. There's no negotiating with villains who believe themselves heroes."

This was her chance. She smiled apologetically at Pak Ling and called for more tea. Cheung Po sat. She took the clay pot from the attendant before Pak Ling could and then proceeded to replicate the ritual she'd observed. "Dignified conduct can be learned," she said, "if people are given the opportunity."

Pak Ling drank the tea, looking mildly impressed.

"I see your perspective, Your Excellency, but this quarrel between you and my husband puts me in a terribly difficult situation," she continued. "As you probably know, the fleet is half mine, half his. Even if I were to agree to your proposal, he would still be free to do with his half as he will. Not that I would leave him to face this alone. After all, I am his wife, and as disciples of Confucius would say"—she scoured her memory for something she could use—"the relationship between husband and wife should be as ruler and subject."

"You are familiar with the works of the Master and the Second Sage?" Pak Ling said, now looking genuinely surprised.

"I would not presume to use the word *familiar,* but I know wise words when I hear them, and I recognize a wise man when I see one. The fact is, the emperor has declared there would be no mercy for captured pirates, which means every pirate has a strong incentive to fight to the death. If my husband rejects your proposal, then we will have no choice but to go back to war. Our fleet, while weakened, is by no means tooth-less. Moreover, we will regain our numbers as soon as there is another famine, and there *will* be another soon, given how much of the land the emperor has reassigned for commercial crops.

"True, you may win in the end, but at what cost? Even if you survive it all, the emperor will consider you to have lost if you use up too much of his money dealing with his pirate problem. How certain are you that you can bring an end to this quickly? How certain are you that Ma-Zou favors you over me?

"There is no other way. We can both win today, or we can both lose." She sat back in her chair and folded her hands on the table.

Pak Ling sat there in thought for a long time. "So you are asking for . . ."

"A full pardon for everyone in my fleet."

"You are asking too much."

"I am not, and Your Excellency knows this. Most of my crew are not heartless criminals but family men. Without them, their families will starve, and in starving, many of them will turn to crime. Now imagine the praises they will sing of the emperor, of you, if you allow them to return to their families. Imagine all of their children growing up with respect for the Qing. By forgiving these men's crimes, you make it possible for the next generation to follow the rule of law."

"I cannot extend the pardon to those who were not in your fleet, nor to those who refuse to give up piracy," Pak Ling said.

"I would not expect you to."

This time Pak Ling signaled his attendant to bring over some liquor, and the three of them toasted to this agreement. "You know," Pak Ling said, sighing, "the Master offers insight about these very circumstances in the Analects. 'The man who is bold and dissatisfied with poverty will rebel.' He is right, of course. And who can be satisfied with poverty? With hunger? I was not wholly lying to you that day in the tavern, Mrs. Cheung. There are those of us in Peking who feel for these fishermen who turned to piracy to feed their families. Still, a crime is a crime."

"Will you be turning your attention to the remaining fleets after this?" Shek Yeung asked.

"Yours was the last for which I was responsible. Kwok Po-Tai surrendered to me a month ago."

So that was why the bastard had failed to appear. "I take it he is still alive?" Shek Yeung said.

"He is."

"What about his men?" Cheung Po asked.

"His men were not a part of the agreement he made with me," Pak Ling said, "though if he had made as convincing and impassioned an argument as your wife just made, their lives might have been spared. It is what one would expect from a mother."

After a couple more drinks, Shek Yeung signaled to Cheung Po that the two of them should leave. A sleeping tiger was still a tiger. On their way out of the estate, Shek Yeung decided to voice the concern that had been on her mind for months. "Now that we are allies, may I ask a question? The Europeans at the Tiger Gate, how did they come to partner with the Qing? Did you approach them?"

"Actually, they approached the court in Peking," Pak Ling said. "They were, as the emperor also was, deeply vexed by the successes of your fleet. You might be pleased to hear they deemed you to be the biggest threat to their enterprises in China. The emperor thought there would be no harm in forging a temporary partnership."

"And you?"

"Is there something you wish to say, Mrs. Cheung?"

She shook her head. "I mean no criticism. I simply wish to pass along a warning. There's a lot of talk in my network that these Europeans are growing increasingly restless, hungry. They want far more out of China. If you think that they'll be satisfied going back to the usual arrangement after the elimination of piracy, I'm afraid you're mistaken."

Pak Ling waved dismissively. "We are aware of the Europeans' designs. There is no need for you to concern yourself."

"With respect, I don't believe you know the full extent. You've seen their new ships, yes? Their stockpile of black powder? On whom do you think they'll be using that stockpile after the pirates are gone?"

"With respect," Pak Ling said, parroting her, "your fleet alone must have used up most of their stockpile."

"What about their smuggling of opium? Surely you've heard about their plan to flood China with opium."

"Opium is indeed a vice of many of our countrymen," Pak Ling said, sounding a bit irritated, "and unfortunately the Europeans seek to profit off this, but you can hardly call their scheme unexpected. Instead of attempting to control their behavior, we must control our people so that they do not succumb to this mind-numbing, body-weakening evil. Once we succeed, these foreigners will have no recourse."

If only people were as easy to control as Pak Ling seemed to believe. The Europeans' plan, or at least its general shape, slowly became clear to her. They wanted the pirate alliance destroyed because they perceived the pirates, not the emperor's forces, as their biggest barrier to dominance in the South China Sea. With the pirates out of the way, they could smuggle and control the price of opium with greater ease, perhaps use it to weaken the populace enough to somehow secure leverage over Peking. How exactly they intended to accomplish that last part, she didn't know, but if she understood anything about humanity, the method would be bloody.

"And what if you don't succeed in controlling our people?" Shek Yeung asked. "What will happen to them? What will these foreign powers do? The emperor needs to quickly realize that whatever cooperation they've promised him will reach only as far as the tethers of their patience."

Pak Ling just shook his head. "China's glory is forever."

She could have contradicted him then. She could have tried to convince him to see things her way. Yet a strange calm had settled over her. Her fight was finished. Whatever happened to the people of China in the future, happened on the head of the emperor and the heads of all the sycophants in his court who could not see beyond their own ambitions to the truth of the world.

She allowed herself to relax only after she and Cheung Po had put a good distance between themselves and Pak Ling's estate. Her instincts told her he would uphold his end of the agreement, but almost two decades of living among base men had woven into her a spider-silk sensitivity to ill will that also inadvertently shuddered at many other human foibles, those little petals of vanity or burs of pride. How well would this sensitivity serve her in civilian life?

"We should get back to the ship, tell everyone the news," Cheung Po said.

"You go ahead. I have business to handle."

"Do you need help?"

"It's personal."

"Oh."

"See you." Then as he turned to walk away, she touched his elbow and added, "Thank you." She could not have explained to him in even a thousand years the many feelings behind those simple words.

But maybe she didn't have to. He nodded in a way that suggested he knew.

What the future held for the two of them was anyone's guess. She hoped Cheung Po would one day get that large family he wanted, even though she probably wouldn't be the one to give it to him. He would leave her when he finally came to that realization. They'd come together to stay alive, which was different from staying together to live. Or maybe he truly cared for her and their marriage would weather this transition. She'd be okay either way, though, cutlass to her neck, she'd tell you that she would prefer it if he stayed.

She wanted so badly to talk to someone about all this that she soon found herself near the sam-hop-yuen. *You won't believe what has happened,* she thought she might start by saying, or *You can't understand the strain I was under,* or simply, *I'm sorry.* By the time she'd arrived in front of the gate, each option sounded more ridiculous than the last. Rather than banging on the door, she pressed her ear to it. It seemed to her, or maybe this was just what she wanted to believe, that she heard laughter coming from the courtyard, along with the patter of tiny feet and the clunk-swoosh of food-filled bowls being set on and then slid around a table.

What kind of stories about Shek Yeung would Yan-Yan tell her child? What kind of stories would she grow up to hear from others? That Shek Yeung was a villainess, drunk on power and greed, or that she was a witless whore who'd gone along with whatever Cheng Yat and Cheung Po had suggested? Alternatively, people might one day tell of her courage (because courage made for a more appealing heroine than desperation), this lone woman who stood against the corrupt Qing court. It was all fine. In the end, stories were not reality, could not be reality. The story-teller decided where to start the story and where to end it, which parts to sink into and which to skim over.

She set off toward the Ma-Zou temple but changed her mind about halfway there. Instead she walked along the shore until she found a relatively secluded spot. To her left a couple of old men were chatting with each other while waiting for fish to bite. To her right several children, no older than eight years old, were playing. Neither group paid her any mind.

This would do. The temple of Ma-Zou was as much at sea as in lacquered, lantern-haunted halls, perhaps even more so. Shek Yeung crouched, picked out a handful of the most beautiful seashells, and skittered them out toward the horizon.

"Ma-Zou, Ma-Zou," she said, "I brought a gift for you."

There was one poem Shek Yeung knew fairly well, by the poet Meng Haoran. She didn't know where she first heard it, and she definitely never tried to learn it, but somehow it found a way to nest in her memories:

> The provinces of Jing and Wu meet each other on the water.
> You depart in the spring when the river is wide.
> At sunset, where will this ship moor?
> Gazing at sky's end can rend your heart.

True enough, but one needed to gaze at the horizon to use a sextant and to quell seasickness. For poets, heartbreak was something to marvel at under a lens. For seafarers, heartbreak was something to ignore because once one stopped ignoring it, one could never not feel it again. How else could she have kept moving, how else could she have killed all those people, how else could she have kept all those people alive?

She didn't even realize she was crying at first. Loud sobs followed, and it was such an unfamiliar sensation—she hadn't cried like this since she was a child—that for a moment she worried she might die from this burning in her chest and throat, from her breath whooshing and whooshing from her body like an ebb tide.

Was this what Ma-Zou had intended for her all along? Was fate always driving her in this direction, or did she bumble her way here, surviving by her stubbornness, wits, and refusal to dwell too deeply on the cost of survival? By the belief that fate wanted more for her than the unnoticed death of a prostitute or the violent death of a criminal? Maybe Heaven had no will, just as the sea had no desires, and none of it, not the prophecies, not the prayers and offerings, had been real. Maybe all along she'd had only herself.

In one of the stories about Ma-Zou, she was just a mortal girl named Lam Mak-Neung who grew up in a small fishing village. She lived, she made the kinds of mistakes that all mortals did, and then she died. It was only after her death that people began to tell stories about her, writing her in their minds as girls were often written: delicately, bravely, profanely, sacredly.

If Ma-Zou had been just a girl, then she was long gone, like the girl Shek Yeung had been before all of this. That girl's ghost still came around now and then, flitting in and out of her dreams, asking Shek Yeung questions for which she lacked the answers, these particular questions as of late: *What now? Who will you be now that there is no need for you anymore? How will you reckon with everything you've done?*

ACKNOWLEDGMENTS

Thank you to Michelle Brower, who read the weird little stories I sent and for some reason thought it a good idea to take me on as a client anyway (and then for representing my even weirder pirate novel). There is a reason why your clients stick with you for years and years.

To Grace McNamee, who for some reason decided to buy the even weirder pirate novel. Thank you for being the most insightful and attentive editor out there—I could not have asked for a better experience.

To the Bloomsbury and Macmillan teams, past and present: Jon Lee, Callie Garnett, Valentina Rice, Rosie Mahorter, Marie Coolman, Lauren Moseley, Kenli Young, Phoebe Dyer, Nicole Jarvis, Akshaya Iyer, and everyone else who worked on the book. Thank you Yuko Shimizu for this astonishing cover.

To my NYU professors Sasha Hemon, Myla Goldberg, Hari Kunzru, and John Freeman for kicking my ass but, like, kindly. My writing improved tremendously under your guidance. I apologize for what you had to read from me at the beginning.

To Beth Parker for all your tireless work getting the word out.

To the entire Trellis team, in particular Danya Kukafka, Natalie Edwards, and Allison Malecha. I'm not sure how you find the time to do all that you do, as well as you do.

To the lovely people at the Rona Jaffe Foundation, the Martha Heasley Cox Center for Steinbeck Studies at San Jose State University, the Vermont Studio Center, the Community of Writers at Olympic Valley, the Writers Grotto, and the Bread Loaf Writers' Conference for your support while I wrote this book.

To Nyuol Lueth Tong, Claire Boyle, Bradford Morrow, Neil Clarke, Andrew Tonkovich, Paul Reyes, Karissa Chen, Rebecca Rubenstein,

Jesmyn Ward, Heidi Pitlor, Hannah Tinti, and Karen Friedman for choosing the short stories of a no-name writer.

To my NYU, VSC, Bread Loaf, and Writers Grotto friends for all your moral support through my failures, my successes, and my general neuroticism.

To Mazu and the ancestors, for showing me the way.

To my parents and the women of my family, who told me stories.

To Andrew, who listened to my stories from the very start.

A NOTE ON THE AUTHOR

RITA CHANG-EPPIG received her MFA from NYU. Her stories have appeared in *McSweeney's Quarterly Concern, Conjunctions, Clarkesworld, The Rumpus, Virginia Quarterly Review, The Best American Short Stories 2021,* and elsewhere. She has received support from the Rona Jaffe Foundation, the Vermont Studio Center, the Writers Grotto, the Bread Loaf Writers' Conference, and the Martha Heasley Cox Center for Steinbeck Studies at San Jose State University. She lives in California.